Michael Thomas has taught art history at Yale, has served on the curatorial staff of the Metropolitan Museum of Art, and has been a partner and executive officer of two major investment-banking firms, as well as a director of various business corporations. He is now a private financial consultant, and owns a small classical record shop in New York City. His previous novels are *Green Monday*, *Someone Else's Money* and *Hard Money*.

THE ROPESPINNER CONSPIRACY

Michael M. Thomas

CORGI BOOKS

THE ROPESPINNER CONSPIRACY

A CORGI BOOK 0 552 13270 5

Originally published in Great Britain by Bantam Press, a division of Transworld Publishers Limited

PRINTING HISTORY
Bantam Press edition published 1987
Corgi edition published 1987
Corgi edition reissued 1988

This book is set in 10/11pt Times

Corgi Books are published by Transworld Publishers Ltd., 61–63 Uxbridge Road, Ealing, London W5 5SA, in Australia by Transworld Publishers (Aust.) Pty. Ltd., 15–23 Helles Avenue, Moorebank, NSW 2170, and in New Zealand by Transworld Publishers (N.Z.) Ltd., Cnr. Moselle and Waipareira Avenues, Henderson, Auckland.

Made and printed in Great Britain by
Hazell Watson & Viney Limited
Member of BPCC plc
Aylesbury Bucks

*This book is for L.S.H., J.J.M.,
and those others whose friendship
has been steadfast no matter what.*

"By their various operations, immediate and remote, banks must affect, for good or evil, every individual in the country. Banking is not a local, temporary, or occasional cause. It is general and permanent. Like the atmosphere, it presses everywhere. Its effects are felt alike in the palace and the hovel."

—**William M. Gouge**,
A Short History of Paper Money and Banking in the United States, PHILADELPHIA, 1833

PROLOGUE

Good Friday

The place was perfectly situated for the evening's business. It stood almost exactly at the midpoint of the five-mile crescent of the bay; from the air, the sweeping shoreline resembled a crude sickle slicing into the water, marked by a pale, foamy smear where the easy wash of the bay tides met the dark rocks footing the bluffs.

The house sat close to the cliff. It was a loose, sprawling geometry of shingle and clapboard in the middle of what had once been a wide clearing in the surrounding pine forest — a glade, now covered with a roughly cared-for lawn. According to local legend, the Vikings had landed here and been slaughtered on the spot by local Indians, themselves now long since driven off, first by loggers and finally by the insistent encroachment of resort houses.

To sailors entering the bay on a misty day, the forest had an Arcadian, primeval appearance. The tree line formed a seamless viridian stripe along the bluff tops, interrupted briefly by the house and its lawn and then continuing northward again until, at its farther end, the lights of the cottages and the town signaled the indelible presence of civilization.

'I can never look at this without thinking of Locke,' said the elder of the two men standing on the porch. He was a spindly man in his middle seventies, somewhat bent by the years, his angular frame incongruously topped by a fleshy, childlike face.

'Locke?' said his companion. He was a stocky good-looking man, about twenty years younger. As he spoke, his hand rose to his breast pocket and instinctively rearranged a bright paisley handkerchief.

'Yes, Locke. He said, "In the beginning, *everything* was America." '

They were looking seaward from the wide veranda that was the older man's special pride. It was the only addition he'd made to the original plans when he rebuilt the house following the fire.

'Well,' said the younger man, 'the sun's going down. Shouldn't be too long now.' He looked at his watch. 'Wheels up at seven thirty, right? That's what they told you?'

'Yes, yes.' The older man sounded on edge, distracted. He scratched nervously at his tonsure of fluffy white hair.

Twilight was settling on the water. The white lines of the hull and rigging of the sailboat moored a hundred yards out were spectral in the fading light. There were no lights on the intervening bluffs. The other 'cottages' were unoccupied at this time of year and would stay that way until June.

'I just hope people won't notice,' said the older man.

'Notice what?'

'The aircraft. These helicopters make so much noise, you know.'

'Don't be ridiculous.' The younger man heard the impatience in his voice. He paused for an instant to let things settle. Then: 'Look, even if someone happened to pass by, the locals have seen choppers in and out of here for the last twenty years. They won't give it a thought. So don't you either.' He was obviously fond of his companion and prepared to be patient.

'Well, I hope so.' The older man sounded doubtful.

A light breeze off the water stirred the flags drooping from the cross staves of the flagpole.

'Goodness!' exclaimed the older man. 'I almost forgot to take the flags down. And it's after sunset!' He started for the steps.

'Leave it,' said the young man, laying a restraining hand on the other's arm. 'Why bother? It doesn't matter any more, don't you see? Come on, it's getting chilly. I think you ought to go inside. We need you at concert pitch for the next few hours. Are you all packed?'

It was as if he were getting an infirm old uncle ready to go off to the nursing home.

They went inside. At the door, the younger man paused and looked around. Tough country, this, he thought. Tough people. Tough old house. He smiled at his friend's back. And what a tough old guy you've been, he thought affectionately; all steel under those fine manners and intellectual bearing. At least until the last month or so. Well, getting old must be a bitch. The legs go first — and the nerves. Shit, he thought, I'm getting old myself. Almost fifty-seven. Well, not that old.

He took another look around. A hell of a lot had been hatched here, he thought: plans for triumph or tragedy, depending on how you looked at it. His inner eye was cold. There was little or no nostalgia in his own mental storehouse. To him, memory was a kind of inventory, a series of shelves to be checked now and then for goods as needed. Remembrance was just something a man riffled through until he found what he could use to get what he wanted now. The past could be a trap. Look back, and *wham!* — something blindsided you. A man couldn't get where he'd gotten, done what he'd done — what *they*'d done — if he let himself be tied in knots by the past.

'I just think I'll have another look round for that photograph of Grigoriy,' the old man said. 'I can't imagine where it's got to.' He sounded as if he were about to cry.

For Christ's sake, stop whining, thought the younger one. He was tired of hearing about that goddamn photo. He could understand what it meant; hadn't he been hearing 'Grigoriy this' and 'Grigoriy that' for fifteen years now? I know, I know, he thought. Just take it easy. Humor the old fellow.

'You probably left it in Boston.'

'Cambridge.' The old man smiled. 'You never do get it right, do you? No, I'm certain it was here.'

'OK, chief, I yield to your point of order: Cambridge. Go have another look.' He snapped a mock salute. It'll give you something to do, he thought. 'I hope the rest of your stuff is all buckled and zipped. When these guys get here, they're not going to want to stick around for high tea.'

His own luggage — four suitcases, two suit bags, a shoe-case, and two briefcases — was stacked neatly by the front door.

13

It was a lot — in spy novels, defectors traveled lighter — but where they were headed was known to be a lousy place for clothes. He was vain about his appearance, so he'd packed enough suits to last the second lifetime to which he was now going.

Ropespinner was over. Complete. Finished. Only the next forty-eight hours remained.

Ropespinner. That was the name — like Cosa Nostra or the Company — that the old man and his Russian pal, Grigoriy Menchikov, had dreamed up, their private code name for what the old man also sometimes called 'our great enterprise of the last thirty years.' The name came from something Lenin had once said: 'Capitalism will sell us the rope with which we hang it.'

Ropespinner: a grand plan to subvert Western capitalism finally and forever. From within: by debauching the banking system that was supposed to be the stable, steady heart of free enterprise.

And they'd done it, by God!

They'd induced the condemned man to plait his own noose. All that was left now was to spring the trap, and that was what they were going to Moscow to do.

His mind jumped ahead to Monday, to the press conference when they'd announce to the world just exactly what they'd done and how they'd done it.

He supposed he'd have to wear the goddamn medal the old man had brought him from Moscow; the damn thing could pull a first-class job of tailoring right out of shape. He'd already planned his getup: the new Holland and Sherry nine-ounce blue-gray pinhead worsted, one of the new shirts from Sulka, and — to add insult to injury — an official bank tie. He'd tried on one of the new suits. The fit was perfect, even if the material was heavier than he usually ordered. Well, winter there was known to be a bitch and, besides, the heavier goods might last longer, maybe the rest of his life.

He looked at his watch — 6:53. He was itching to be off. That was his style. If you come to a decision, then damn it, act on it! Get up and go. No shilly shally!

14

Goddamn, he found himself thinking, we've really done it! We've broken the goddamn bank! The banks. The entire goddamn Western banking system. The entire goddamn West! And just two guys! Well, three, if you counted Menchikov. Himself out on the front line; the old man working the room; the Russian behind the curtain pulling strings.

Who could have thought it possible? He hadn't — that was for damn sure, and he'd been cut in after it was well under way. Would he have played it differently if he'd been in on the scam from the beginning? He doubted it.

No: he never would have thought it possible, not even now when he looked back and saw for himself exactly what the old Russian had seen way back — when? — '45, '46? How could people, guys who were supposed to be so goddamn smart, be so dumb? What the hell did they think they were doing; where the hell could they think this was taking them, other than right down the toilet? Them and their banks and their countries. The Western governments had cooperated right along, too: Washington and London and Berne. One by one the old barriers had come down, one regulation after another, all toppled in the name of efficiency and competition.

When he looked back on it, it was as if he and the old man had spent thirty years systematically sabotaging a great edifice, like one of those French cathedrals. Planting a charge, sawing a joist halfway through, weakening a buttress. Now all that was left was to push the plunger and detonate the whole mess.

Their Moscow press conference would be the detonator. The goddamnedest show-and-tell the world has ever seen.

He liked the timing. Well, he thought, I would — since it was my idea.

Nine A.M. Moscow time the Monday after Easter. Which meant the big markets in the Far East, Hong Kong and Tokyo, would still be open. Most of Europe would just be waking up; the United States would still be sleeping off the last of its long holiday weekend.

But the financial circuits of the world never slept. This crisis would race along those wires like flame along a fuse, setting off one explosion after another until it all blended into a single

15

great fireball and the circuits melted and the sun went out.

How would it go exactly? he wondered.

He had his own idea. The bank's computers had spat out a menu of 'downside scenarios,' as the think tankers in Research and Futuristics languidly called this category of statistical game. To these thirty-year-old rocket scientists it was all hypothesis verging on fantasy: never-never land, 'can't happen here,' strictly 1929 fairy-tale stuff.

The Japs would kick the first domino, he was pretty sure of that. They knew they were in a dollar trap and they didn't like it. He suspected — hell, the tape *said*! — that they were already trying to phase out, in orderly retreat, their $75 billion commitment in the US bond market. This would kick off the panic rush for the door. First the Tokyo and Hong Kong bond traders would wipe the floor with the Asiadollar and Eurodollar markets and then get after Wall Street, which would still be rubbing the sleep out of its eyes when the phones started to ring and the telexes went crazy.

The options and futures markets would split like a melon — so much for hedging — and then after that it would be a cascade of default, drowning Wall Street and Threadneedle Street and Hong Kong like Atlantis, until finally all the securities markets shut down and night descended on Western capitalism.

Meanwhile the bank wires would also be brought to the melting point by hot money — Arab, Filipino, Mafia, Cayman Island — trying to head for the exits. Trillions, literally *trillions* of dollars fighting to get out through a shrinking pinhole. Just the way it had happened at Continental Illinois a couple of years back. Well, just multiply Continental Illinois by infinity, he thought, and you'd have some idea of how it was going to be.

The Fed would be pushed to the wall. Not to mention the other big central banks, England, France, and Japan, the Deutsche Bank. Lenders of last resort. The gospel was: In a financial crisis, keep the lending window open, but now this would be impossible. The printing presses would burn out trying to keep up with the demand for money.

All just as they'd planned and worked for. The system had put itself in a vise. On the one hand, the big depositors would

16

run for the exits. On the other, borrowers — everyone from Brazil to secretaries a couple of hundred bucks in the hole on their VISA cards — would have the perfect excuse to take a walk now that it was revealed that their plunge into debt was part of a sinister Soviet conspiracy. To do otherwise would be un-American, undemocratic, anticapitalistic.

The pot of chaos would bubble even more frantically when he gave out the names in his suitcase, from the weekly printout he'd ordered up from Overseas Private Banking — names and sums and the identifying numbers of accounts representing what the papers called 'flight capital.' Big numbers: $90 billion from Mexico, $50 – $60 billion from Brazil and Argentina, and so on. That would have them out in the streets of Mexico City and São Paulo and Lagos, howling for blood, looking for heads to decorate the tips of pikestaffs.

What they would announce from Moscow would just be pulling the trigger. The cartridge was in the chamber, primed, begging to be exploded. Even if he and the old man just sat still, the whole thing would probably blow up of its own accord. You could feel it in the air. People were starting to get edgy. It didn't make sense, the stock market going through the roof and the economy doing nothing. Sure, the Dow had closed Thursday night well over 1800, but it had given up 80 points during the holiday-shortened week; gold had made an ominous little spike at the last London morning fixing. On the credit front, the bank's own postings showed credit delinquencies starting to accelerate on the high end. It all added up: the smart money was getting edgy. Something it didn't like was making its nostrils twitch.

But, on Wall Street, it was still wine and roses. It was too tough to go cold turkey on easy money, so the prevailing theory was that if you could push your problems off until tomorrow, you didn't have any problems. Postponement was the same as cure.

So just tune in, friends, to 'Good Morning, Moscow,' and watch our Easter Special.

Easter Monday. The day after the great feast of Christian renewal and regeneration. He liked that bit. Loaded with irony.

17

The old man was very big on irony. That's what Ropespinner was, he liked to say: a gigantic exercise in irony.

Which would not be lost on the President, who might still be on his ranch when the news broke. Talk about Judas! Why, only three days ago, he'd been the President's fair-haired boy, standing next to the nation's Chief Executive in the East Room of the White House, sharing — stealing — the spotlight, bantering with the press corps.

When this news broke over Santa Barbara, or the White House or wherever, the President'd probably let go in his pajamas. Designer pajamas, probably — forced on him by the First Lady. Funny thing about the President's wife. Tuesday, at the White House, amid all the hallelujahs and praise-be-to-free-enterprise bullshit, he'd looked over while the President was going on, and there was the First Lady giving him the regular fish eye. Well, knowing her, she hated the idea of anyone taking the limelight off her husband.

Well, if she hated that, boy — was she ever going to hate this! Right out the window would go those fond dreams of hers about history putting this President right up there on the same pedestal with Washington and Lincoln! This President was going to be one with Andrew Johnson and Harding and Hoover — just as the old boy fussing around upstairs had always predicted.

His thoughts wandered momentarily to his own estranged family. He hadn't seen or spoken to his wife in ten years. He never saw his son either. Poor kid, after this, he'd probably have to change his name. The name would be like a scar, a brand. He'd have to take flight, too, just to get away from the reporters wanting to know about his dad's motives.

What the hell did motives matter? he thought. You got where you got however you got there, period. It all came down to the bottom line, and his was blind to motive, uncomplicated by ideology. Not like the old man. The old boy was a believer, who could go on and on about how America was a filthy, wasteful, uncaring country, all mouth and no brain and no heart, which deserved what Ropespinner had done to it.

The sheer thrill of pulling it off was where he got his kicks.

Watching it work out like a giant board game or puppet show. Except this was for real; this was played with real money and real people. That was its excitement for him: the size, the sums, the reverberations, watching the marionettes twitch on the strings he manipulated.

Upstairs he could hear the old man bumping around. All this fuss over a lousy photograph. Those goddamn silver-framed mementos. Funny how some people went in for them, as if getting your picture taken with Kissinger or some Arab king meant you were worth a damn. If that was all it took, he thought, chuckling, Chase Manhattan would have been Number One all the way. As for himself, he'd left his own souvenirs back in the office. Come Monday, let Wall Street eat silver frames for breakfast!

He wondered how the press would handle the story. What Ropespinner had done and caused and why and how. How drastic the situation had become. There could be no more hiding from facts. All that held things together now was a kind of communal willingness to ignore reality; it was as if a form of laughing gas had originated in the White House and spread through Wall Street and Europe and Hong Kong and everywhere life was reduced to money.

Then there was his own big story. From Number One here to Number One there. From the corner office of CertCo Center to the Chief Executive's office in the Soviet Ministry of Finance. Executive mobility.

That was why he could be exultant. For him, it was a new beginning. The biggest job a financial type had ever been offered.

It would have been easier, of course, if Menchikov hadn't suddenly shuffled off four months ago. Nicer for the old man to have his chum around. Well, that's how life went. And there was still plenty of compensation. As the old man put it, 'My Nobel Prize makes me famous, but Ropespinner will make me immortal.' Immortality enough, he thought, for a dozen men — more than enough for everyone.

He went to the window and looked out. It was dark now. His watch said 7:04.

The old man came back into the room. 'I just can't find it,' he said. 'Not anywhere. I can't imagine—'

The younger man cut him short. 'I told you not to worry. You probably stuffed it in some drawer. Christ, you told me it's been a dozen years since you looked at it last.'

'I know; it's just that it was taken a long time ago,' the old man said sulkily. 'A long time ago. When Grigoriy and I were young and in—' The old man suddenly broke off the sentence. After a moment, he said, 'It just means a lot, don't you see?'

'I see.' The younger man grinned. 'Go back and have another look.'

He returned to peering out the window into the night. Outside, the wind had built to a dull moan. He strained his ears to hear over it.

'I still wonder . . .'

The old man's garrulity interfered with concentration. Was there something out there? Yes! The younger man held up a hand.

'Wait! I think I hear them.' His ears had picked up a faint popping noise. He squinted his eyes. To the south, he now made out a blinking light, which grew larger as the noise grew louder.

'They're here.'

The old man looked at his watch. 'They're early. I don't like that.'

'For Christ's sake, we're not trying to rendezvous with Halley's comet.'

Goddamn it, he thought, get hold of yourself. You're supposed to be Mr Smooth, Mr Cool and Collected. Lay off the old guy. Everybody's nerves are ragged.

'I'm sorry,' he said. 'I'm jumpy too. Look. But it's almost over now. In five minutes, we're gone. We'll be eating caviar for Easter breakfast.'

They stood together watching as the helicopter emerged from the darkness, its floodlight swinging along the surface of the water. The machine racketed overhead; the pitch of its engine changed as it prepared to land on the front lawn.

'Well,' said the younger man, 'show time!'

He led the way into the hall and picked up one of the suitcases. It felt heavy, a reminder that he wasn't too young himself any more. The old man took their briefcases.

The idling helicopter on the lawn whacked at the night with an awful roar; its searchlight flooded the leaded-glass oculus above the front door with brilliance. The world seemed to burst with noise and light.

The younger man felt reborn.

'You first,' said the older man, opening the door.

Outside, it seemed as if the sun had come to earth. Just as it ought to be, he thought. As he went toward the light and the noise, he said to himself, This must be what it feels like to enter heaven.

He had that way, saw the trail and picked up one of the .... loose by the girl, realising that he must carry her himself any up ... ... He did that took their ... salad.

The silent billion man on the large window at the night was in hard part. Its something thought he looked ... plus corner above the long drawer with ... distance. He was leaning against a hard ... with some subjects ... .

"That bigger ... too reborn ...?"

He first ... All his ridden sun, moved it his seat outside. It was not as light his had gone toward what it it ... it was close, he thought. And he was ... behind the light on the parthad as light ... Old gran had done it next like to their ...

THE PAST

1935–1955

Uncle Waldo

CHAPTER ONE

In June 1935, at the graduation exercises at Columbia University, Waldo Emerson Chamberlain — a twenty-two-year-old prodigy from Worcester, Massachusetts — simultaneously collected a bachelor's degree in Economics *summa cum laude*, a master's degree in Business Administration, and the degree of Doctor of Philosophy in Economics. The next day he left for England to study with John Maynard Keynes.

He couldn't wait to get away from America. Though his academic feats had been widely and rapturously reported in the Boston and New York papers, and his picture had been in both the *New York Times* and the *Boston Transcript*, within the bosom of his own family Waldo's accomplishments invariably were accorded second place, by a wide margin. The very week before Waldo's graduation, it had been announced that his brother, Preston, seven years the elder, had been admitted to membership — the youngest partner ever — in the most prestigious and influential law firm on Wall Street. At the Chamberlain dinner table, it was made clear to Waldo that Preston's partnership was a *real* accomplishment, achieved in the real world of men and matters, and that it utterly eclipsed Waldo's triumphs: his flimsy bits of engraved vellum, even his splendid valedictory oration, which had so impressed Columbia's President Butler that he reprinted it in the alumni bulletin. As usual, Waldo had played his strongest card only to have Preston trump it.

It was in the nature of the times and his highly conventional parents that Waldo developed a genius for economics instead of poetry. Money was a paramount consideration in the

25

Chamberlain household and about the only subject of serious discussion. Not that the Chamberlain family had money worries. His father was a moderately important officer in a marginally solvent New England steel fabricating company with a small legacy on the side, his mother a well-regarded Worcester clubwoman and do-gooder with a modest annuity provided by a couple of textile factories on the banks of the Merrimack. Eager strivers for social position, neither parent was equipped by temperament to understand the aloof, intellectual child whom his mother publicly called 'my sour little cherub.' Waldo understood them, however, simply by seeking to understand the force that he knew ruled their minds: money.

Waldo's feelings about his brother, Preston, were exacerbated by his parents. They made it painfully clear at the dinner table that what few glittering prizes the world offered went only to men of their older son's bluff and thrusting style. So by the time he went off to Columbia, Waldo well and truly hated his older brother and would continue to do so right up to the day of Preston's death forty years later. Hated him, despised him, loathed him, viewed him with contempt. Time seemed only to uncover new layers and forms of animosity, to provide the basis for an entire geology of ill will. Indeed, Waldo often felt grateful for these malignant feelings, which supplied him with incentive and motivation. Often, through the years, he reflected it had been his feelings toward Preston, as much as anything, that had impelled him to push ahead with the great secret business of Ropespinner. It was revenge on a world which, to Waldo, seemed infused with Preston's personality and values.

He was careful, however, never to put his feelings about his brother on public display; he was certain that Preston himself, tucked up in his carapace of ambition and certitude, was unaware that his younger brother's attitude was anything other than devoted and supportive, putting his own genius in Preston's service. Thus, the world would come to perceive Preston Chamberlain as the man of action, of fire, flair, and presence, and Waldo as the intellect scheming behind the curtain, whispering in the king's ear.

26

Preston helped this perception along. He deferred to no one in his vocal public appreciation of his younger brother's formidable intelligence, the younger man's uncanny intuition about the tectonic forces that ground and hissed beneath the surface of commerce and capitalism. Preston always found a place for Waldo on his team, included him in his deals, opened doors and opportunities to him, made him money. They collaborated, right up to Preston's tragic death, in a great 'joint career' — as *Fortune* put it — that enhanced the reputations, influence, and personal fortunes of both men. In American life, the Chamberlains were a brother act as potent and lustrous as the Dulleses and Kennedys. Knit by blood, complementary of intellect and disposition, intensely useful to each other, the Chamberlain brothers were the cynosure of that world in which the big decisions and the big money were made.

Although they often appeared to share the spotlight, it was Preston, the doer, for whom commercial America reserved that extra whistle of admiration. Waldo was under no illusions about this. He might have his professional laurels, his consultancies, eventually even his Nobel Prize, but it was Preston who had created CertBank and CertCo, Preston who had taken the reins of a middling, stuffy New York trust company and built it up to the greatest single financial institution in the world. Waldo might be consulted by presidents and premiers, but it was to Preston they turned when there was man's work to be done. It was Preston who had helped Wild Bill Donovan start the OSS and helped Allen Dulles reorganize the CIA; Preston who had accompanied FDR to Yalta, Truman to Potsdam, Ike to Pyongyang, Kennedy to Berlin; Preston who had been a moving force in Nixon's 1968 comeback. Over time Waldo too would keep similar company and would also travel to significant meetings with great men, but it was as if his entire life was branded with a footnote: he was Preston Chamberlain's brother, and that — said the world — was the largest single reason he had gotten where he was.

That asterisk on his record burned in Waldo's mind like a brand and fed his hatred. In time, this hatred grew to include the entire American business polity. In Waldo's eyes, Preston

27

was America. For three decades and a bit, Protestant Executive America looked into its mirror and was pleased to find Preston Chamberlain looking back: churchly upright, square-jawed and thin-lipped, radiating a buttoned-up rectitude and optimism that gave the lesser and the wavering, whether American or heathen, a healthy uplifting dose of Yankee pride and courage.

Waldo, however, saw his brother plain. This was, to tell the truth, unusual for him. He was better at figures than men, at concepts than souls. His mind operated with a remarkable reductive clarity, but it was a clarity that penetrated institutional structures better than personalities. It could — like Glendower — summon up the great determining forces that underlay economies and markets, yet it blurred when it came to understanding another man. Indeed, Waldo would have admitted that he only really understood three men in his life. One was Preston.

The better he knew his brother, the more he disliked him. Fate gave him plenty of opportunity to practise the emotion. He hated Preston's luck, he hated his persuasiveness, he hated his looks. All these could be put down to envy, but there were other, more transcendent objects of dislike. He hated Preston's hypocrisy above all, and he hated America for letting Preston get away with it. Only an indefensibly worthless culture could permit someone like Preston to scale its heights, thought Waldo. He knew his brother for a man who sat in select Manhattan and Washington clubs and spoke easily with intimates of 'kikes' and 'niggers.' He knew him for a man who emoted publicly on social justice and Christian charity but in truth believed none of it, who secretly opined that America would be better off with the armed forces in control and the darkies back on the plantation. He knew him for a man who spoke in certain dark corners of 'Franklin D. Rosenfelt, the head Yid,' although FDR could fairly have been considered one of Preston's more important patrons. Public opinion and the press might hold that Preston Chamberlain epitomized the best of America, the fine, fair, classic essence of the American character, but to his younger brother he incarnated the worst.

In other circumstances, with another vocation, Waldo might

have become an expatriate, a Jamesian stipendary with a useful allowance from a rich and powerful brother, turning out fragrant essays in the London Library or on the terrace of a Tuscan villa. Indeed, Waldo did often visualize himself as one of the last Concord patricians, one of a shrinking number who would oppose the brusque new breed that gloried in the American Century. Men like Preston's friends Henry Luce and John Foster Dulles had all the answers. Men of Preston's kidney, men of the moment, strode briskly ahead while scholars like Waldo lagged behind, tottering under the burden of history.

Not that Waldo cast so narrow a shadow. By the time he retired from the Harvard Business School faculty, American finance and commerce were to a great degree dominated by men and women whose minds had been deeply affected by the insights gained in his universally famous course, 'Money Markets and Business Strategy,' or — as it was known to anyone who'd ever heard of the Harvard Business School — 'Money One.' He taught the course, built on the belief that finance was the sovereign business art, from 1937 to his retirement in 1982, beginning as a young instructor and ending as Certified Guaranty National Bank Distinguished Professor of Finance. In addition, he served as Mission Chemical Research Visiting Professor at the Sloan School at MIT. The work he did there on the correlation of population growth and economic demand led to the formulation of the 'Chamberlain Effect,' for which he would win the Nobel Prize.

In retirement, he remained active, his influence lively, his advice sought after. He was an advisory or emeritus director of a half-dozen corporations, a valued adviser to two federal agencies, and a consultant to corporations and commissions. Even when he was well over seventy, his income approached half a million dollars a year.

Over the years, he had come to terms with most aspects of his life. Homosexual urges that had briefly raged in him as a young man abated early. He aged prematurely. By the time he reached forty, in 1952, he was already known on his two campuses as 'Uncle Waldo,' a bachelor in the old New

England sense, a neutered, spindly figure, gloomily precise in dress and manner, a touch distant, known to be parsimonious; all in all, a bit otherworldly; standoffish at first introduction but capable of being gently humorous, reflective, and attentive. There seemed nothing mean or eruptive about him, which stood his career in good stead. America preferred its intellectual geniuses to be on the mild side: better an Einstein than a Beethoven.

In fact his animosities were his passion, his mistresses, his nourishment. He served and craved them as if lovestruck, committing his mind and soul to them. Yet, as it had from his birth, his intellect set its own course; it steamed majestically on, oblivious of the sea, while the frailer craft of his feelings made heavy going in its wake.

He would gain his fortune, his fame, his Nobel Prize. The Chamberlain Effect would be engraved on the tablets of economic theory. But there was no doubt in Waldo Chamberlain's mind that Ropespinner was the greatest work of his life, and very possibly of any man's. Even as it approached 'publication,' as the moment neared when, after thirty years of secret work, the experiment could be revealed to the world and its latent consequences unleashed, Waldo still thrilled to the very grandeur of the conception.

For Waldo, the operations of pure intellect transcended issues of morality. It scarcely occurred to him that his own impetus to a special form of satisfaction, his own need for certitude about the nature of things, was every bit as aggressive and driven as his brother's. It never occurred to him, for instance, to reflect whether Ropespinner might be treasonous. What was treason anyway? To betray; that was one thing. But simply to stimulate, so as to hasten the process of another's self-betrayal; could that be treason?

Waldo knew, when Ropespinner was eventually revealed and economic chaos ensued, that voices from the heart of the whirlwind would probably scream 'Traitor!' at him even as they sank into the perdition they deserved, the ruin they had themselves invited. Well, was it treason? How could it be? No secrets had been sold. No polity betrayed, except by that polity's own base nature, which Ropespinner merely exploited. He was no Fuchs, no Philby, no Blunt. There were many things one might call Ropespinner: a giant hoax, a great experiment, a test of a theory, a conspiracy. But treason? Well, hardly, thought Waldo. Who indeed were the guilty? Surely those who followed were as much at fault as those who led. No one had been forced to heed or follow Ropespinner. The destructive armies had been conscripted by their own greed.

Ropespinner had simply been a hypothesis tested in a laboratory. It was like any other biological experiment: breed the virus, acculturate it, see what happens. Ropespinner had simply been a question of finding the right man, putting him in the right place, and letting economic forces and human nature interact. Just as Grigoriy had foreseen, if the culture was already fermenting in the test tube, it was just a matter of finding the right virus to activate it.

Of course, Waldo had to admit, it hadn't all gone as smoothly as it might have. There had been bumps to flatten, barriers to be brought down. There had even been a few deaths, but — as Menchikov pointed out — there would always be casualties in a war. Indeed, thanks to Waldo, at least one innocent life had been spared. Memories of what it had been necessary to do only rarely flitted mothlike across Waldo's awareness. After all, they spent thirty years actively working on Ropespinner; it would be almost forty years since that gray afternoon in London when the Russian had first proposed the idea.

Waldo and Grigoriy Menchikov first met in 1935 when Waldo arrived in England at Keynes's invitation. When the great economist came to Columbia in 1934 to receive an honorary degree, it was logical that Waldo, the child wonder of the Economics Department, should be put on display. Keynes was impressed with the young man. An invitation to cross the Atlantic soon followed.

Those two years were the happiest of Waldo's life. In Keynes he found an exemplar and lifetime idol. In Grigoriy Menchikov he discovered a soulmate.

He was set to work helping to revise and correct the proofs of *The General Theory of Employment, Interest, and Money*, which would be published the following year. Keynes only taught on weekends; during the week he remained in London, where he led an active business and social life and was a mainstay of the Bloomsbury Group. Waldo was housed in rooms not far from King's College, with a pleasant view of the Cam; he was also now and then invited to stay with the Keyneses in London. It was there, at 46 Gordon Square, during a dinner party on a hot evening in July 1935, that he met Grigoriy Menchikov.

Menchikov was a large, shambling man a dozen years older than Waldo. He declared himself to be a poet and was ready at the merest hint to declaim a sample of florid, overcharged verse in thickly, often grotesquely accented English, but he was also strikingly conversant with politics and economics. No one seemed quite sure how he had come to attach himself to the Keynes household — some said he was a distant cousin of Keynes's Russian wife, Lydia Lopokova. In any case, he was amusing, helpful company, he could be almost handsome when he combed his hair and sponged his suit, and his wandering curiosity suited Keynes's own wide range of interests.

If anyone in the Keynes set was surprised when Waldo and Menchikov succumbed to each other, no one said anything. After all, there were rumors about Keynes himself and the painter Duncan Grant.

There was no doubt in Waldo's mind — then or ever after — that he and Menchikov fell in love during that long summer. It would be the only time Waldo would ever feel that way. Menchikov seduced him completely, bewitched him body, mind, and heart. He took immediate possession of Waldo and set the young man's cold, small soul afire. The physical possibilities they explored were finite, but their embrace of intellects knew no limitations. Throughout life afterward, Waldo would know exactly what women meant when they spoke to him of the erotic power of intellectual brilliance. He knew firsthand how it felt to be coupled in the searing embrace of a powerful mind. So strong was the effect, it seemed to him that he and Grigoriy practically hallucinated first principles; that the underlying order of things came to them as a matter of instinctual right. To Waldo, Menchikov seemed to possess a divining rod that led him by the shortest way to the mysterious heart of great matters.

It was a violent squall-like furor of heart, mind, and libido that Waldo experienced. He was normally unassertive, yet he felt like shouting the affair from the spires. But Menchikov, usually vociferous to the point of grossness, insisted on absolute discretion.

During the year they met when they could — but only in London, never in Cambridge. Waldo adored Cambridge. It was a dazzling company that passed through Keynes's rooms in King's College, quite as impressive as the brilliant levees in Gordon Square. The great economist was a pillar of the secret Cambridge society known as the Apostles. Waldo was taken with them and fancied speaking to Keynes about becoming an Apostle himself. Indeed, to a young man, especially a young American, the Apostles and their set cut bewitching figures: especially Guy Burgess, frantically gay and witty, and the effete, mysterious Anthony Blunt, thin and chilly as an inquisitor.

When Waldo spoke of them, Menchikov warned him off. 'Don't get involved with those silly buggers, Waldya,' he said. 'Drunken fools and queers.' The way Menchikov said it, the things that he and Waldo did with each other seemed raised to an entirely different, higher plane.

Their affair lasted through the next summer. The *General Theory* was published in April 1936, and in July, Waldo accepted Keynes's invitation to accompany him on a trip to Russia. His motive was personal. Menchikov had returned to the motherland in June, and the weeks since had been an aching time for Waldo. How his heart leapt when the Keynes party detrained in Leningrad, and there was Grigoriy!

He bore Waldo away forthwith. The fortnight that followed was the emotional and sexual apex of Waldo's life. Never again, even when the world's honors and acclaim seemed his, would he believe himself to soar as high; never again would he burn with a passion in which were subsumed the noblest, most exquisite, most intense feelings a human being could ever hope to experience.

Menchikov took him to a place by the Black Sea, a secret colony of young men, serious bright young men of similar inclinations and great plans: engineers, scientists, technicians, thinkers. The days burned them brown; they swam naked and roasted themselves dry on the beach and plunged again into the water for coolness; at night Waldo lay in his lover's strong embrace. Their euphoria stretched their minds; there was no problem so abstruse, no line of inquiry so darkly thicketed, that did not seem at least to yield a hint of its inner secrets. They remained there for two weeks, the two wisest young men there had ever been, in the grip of the finest passion ever known. Waldo was reading Shakespeare. With much giggling, it was proposed that the group put on *The Tempest*. Menchikov took the part of Prospero; Waldo played Gonzalo. The evening was a huge success. Afterward, the cast signed Waldo's copy of Shakespeare. All agreed that this was Paradise. With such as us in control, they said as one, who could doubt that the world could be put right?

Finally, though his heart tried to deny the fact like a recalcitrant puppy setting his nails in the ground, Waldo knew this golden time was over and that he must now return to America. Two days after leaving Moscow, Waldo bade the Keyneses goodbye in Stockholm and sailed on the *Gripsholm* for New York. It would be eight years before he would see Menchikov again, or hear a word from or about him.

CHAPTER TWO

Waldo returned to a warm welcome in America. Enthusiastic word about his work with Keynes had traveled between Cambridge, England, and Cambridge, Mass.; hardly had his feet touched Pier 84 when he was offered two positions at Harvard, given a choice between the Economics Department and the Harvard Business School. The invitation to teach economics was intellectually tempting, not least because Joseph Schumpeter, the Austrian economist whom Waldo greatly admired, had recently joined the Harvard faculty. But he elected instead to teach at the Business School. He wanted to be involved in the real world, Preston's world. Keynes insisted that a man's feet should remain rooted in actuality. Keynes taught that the job of the man of intellect was to exercise his mind upon the real problems of life. America remained gripped by depression. Wall Street was 'in irons,' as the Quiddy Bay sailors said, its once powerful sails luffing impotently; across the nation, the once mighty industrial machine coughed by fits and starts. A new generation of private-sector men of drive would be needed to lift the country from its doldrums; the divine mission of the Business School was to identify those young men and equip them with the tools and the values, in particular the can-do spirit, that would enable them to relieve America's commercial and financial misery. The presumption was that the men who instructed those leaders would be as Socrates to Alcibiades, scarcely less powerful or less esteemed than their pupils.

Preston approved Waldo's decision. Indeed, when Waldo was asked in 1939 to go to Washington to work for the New Deal, his brother was forthright.

'You stay in Boston, Wally,' Preston insisted. 'This New Deal's just hogwash. What ails this economy can only be fixed by rearming. War's what the world needs, and war's what the world's going to get. Look at the Germans! Ten years ago they were flat on their fannies. That Hitler's a real get-up-and-go chap, the type of man we need. Not like that Jew-lover in the White House.'

Preston talked that way all the time now. It disgusted Waldo. He knew Preston had acquired the habit in the course of currying favor with his clients and clubland cronies. That it appeared to have worked for Preston seemed to Waldo to confirm his awful suspicions about the true character of America.

Of Preston's success there was no longer the slightest doubt. In the two years Waldo was overseas, Preston had taken control of the management committee of his law firm. He had been put on a couple of appropriately grand corporate boards. He was mentioned as a future Overseer of Harvard. His ace in the hole, however, was the effective control of Guaranty Manhattan Trust Company, to which he had succeeded by trusteeship when a senior partner of the firm died. As sole voting fiduciary for a group of family trusts that controlled roughly 40 percent of the bank's stock, Preston promptly caused himself to be elected Chairman of the bank's board and its Executive Committee.

As New York banks went, Guaranty Manhattan Trust was by no means the largest or most openly powerful, not remotely in a league with J. P. Morgan & Co. or the Corn Exchange Bank. But its reputation was unblemished, at a time when a number of the city's largest banks were still reeling from scandal and the wake of the crash, and it was where some of New York's oldest, most prominent, and still most intact private fortunes entrusted their investments. Clearly, if the country ever reawoke economically, an institution like Guaranty Manhattan was ideally situated.

By the standards of his world, Preston had everything. His two children — a girl and a boy — were designed to specification: small, blond, clear-eyed little Episcopal gentry. The son, Peter, was his father's favorite. His Uncle Waldo liked him well enough too, although he found him a little flip and tricky.

An ideal family then, the envy of the eyes that followed them down the aisle each Sunday at the fashionable East Side Church of All Angels and All Souls, where Preston was chief warden. Preston's first wife, a pillar of clubs and charities, died of a stroke in 1944, rolling bandages for the Red Cross in the basement of the Colony Club. A year later, he remarried: the widow of an old friend. About Preston there was no breath of scandal, no mistress hidden away downtown, no financial speculations, no heavy drinking. He was securely ensconced on the topmost floor of American commercial life.

Waldo's own star was rising. When war broke out in 1941, he had become a full professor at the Business School. Money One was a popular, talked-about course; he was very much a man to watch.

Privately, his heart was sick. He thought often of Menchikov, grieved for his friend and lover with a desperate foreboding. He was certain that Menchikov had perished in Stalin's purges. He pored over the few souvenirs he'd kept from their magical summer fortnight together: a photograph, some notes, the copy of *The Tempest*. The memories remained strong for him, but as time passed, his physical longings disappeared. It was their intellectual mating that Waldo missed. He knew somehow that if he should live to be a hundred, a hateful thought, there would never again be a time like those weeks with Grigoriy.

His teaching really didn't engage the full reach of his mind. He found himself spending more time with Schumpeter and with some young economists at MIT. He began to look more closely at capitalism, to probe its drives, personality, and character, as if he were interrogating another human being. The litany of accusation and confession that had followed the stock market crash fascinated him. How vulnerable the great system seemed to the small impulses of individuals! No one was willing to admit that the system itself might be thereby fatally flawed, that the central flaw was human nature. To Waldo, the market system's impelling drives were greed and ego, base emotions; hence, base outcomes were inevitable.

37

Human nature was implacable, unalterable. This was the demon with which his friend Schumpeter was wrestling. How long, after all, could the lid of self-restraint be kept on in an economic system that celebrated egoism and evangelized greed?

He pondered these questions in the place he loved best in the world, an old house on the Maine coast that he'd wheedled his mother's spinster cousin into bequeathing him. Getting that house had been his one clear material triumph over Preston.

The big rambling 'cottage' overlooking Quiddy Bay had been built just after World War I by Cousin Martha's late father, a Boston eccentric. Preston and Waldo visited there for a fortnight every childhood summer, and the brothers loved and coveted the place each in his own way: Waldo for the forest walks and for the long afternoons reading on the wide seaward lawn; Preston for the active, competitive life, the sailing and swimming races and the tennis matches at the Quiddy Point Yacht Club. Cousin Martha's house was more their home than the Victorian mansion in Worcester.

In early 1941, it was apparent that Cousin Martha was desperately ill. Waldo went to Maine to see her; Preston couldn't — the bank was taking much of his time and he was deeply involved in positioning himself in Washington for maximum personal military advantage when war came.

Cousin Martha was grateful for Waldo's visit. She was the sort of woman whose heart instinctively goes to life's underdogs; she was pleased to see that the young man's studiousness had paid off. Although she knew Preston was more likely to have the means to keep the place up, and did have a family to enjoy it, something impelled her to decide that the house would be Waldo's when she died.

'You do so remind me of Father, Waldy,' she said. 'He liked his hours alone too. Come with me. I want to show you something.'

She led Waldo upstairs to the bookshelf-lined hall that had been his childhood treasure house. She took down six inches' worth of books from the end of a shelf, reached in, and twisted a knob. When she next pushed against the shelf, it revolved, revealing a tiny office, just large enough to accommodate a desk and an easy chair and a small table on which was stacked a moldering jumble of radio and telegraph equipment.

'Toward the end of his life, Father imagined he was a British secret agent. He used to come here and hide. It was his bolt-hole in case the Kaiser's men came after him.'

Six weeks later, Cousin Martha was dead and Waldo inherited her house.

Preston took this small defeat with reasonable grace. On the way back to Boston from her funeral, he offered Waldo $75,000 for the house, a very considerable sum at the time. The offer was rejected, and that was the end of it. In November, Waldo Chamberlain hosted the first 'Thanksgiving at Quiddy with Uncle Waldo.' It would become a regular family tradition, continuing in war and peacetime, for thirty years, until − in 1970 − a tragic fire destroyed the house, the tradition, and nearly all the family.

Less than a fortnight after the first Quiddy Point Thanksgiving, the Japanese bombed Pearl Harbor. As usual, Preston had done his homework. Within twenty-four hours after the *Arizona* went to the bottom, he had secured a commission as a first lieutenant in Army Intelligence; he would end the war a chicken colonel reporting directly to the Secretary of War, an old acquaintance from New York lawyering.

Waldo's war didn't go badly, either. A senior colleague from the Business School drafted him to Washington to work as liaison with an economic group the British had set up in Washington. Some were men he knew from his Cambridge days, and Keynes's spirit presided over their sessions, so he was entirely comfortable. Later, Preston got him involved in advising the OSS on economic warfare. It was interesting work, he felt he was playing a vital role in a cause in which he believed, and as Preston pointed out, he was making connections that could only prove useful when the war ended.

By the turn of 1944, it was clear that Germany would be defeated. No less than any other man, Waldo admired the valor at arms of the Allies, the bravery and gallantry and doggedness that had carried the cause on the battlefield. But he saw, too, that the Allied victory was in large measure the result of

America's economic and geographic advantages. Indeed, secure behind its oceans, the country was rich again. Men he knew on Wall Street, who'd stayed behind while their partners and colleagues went off to war, were remaking fortunes on a scale the investors of the twenties would have envied. For all its trumpeted privations, ration stamps and the rest, the country was prospering, growing fat and rich again while half of London lay destroyed and private Pentagon conversations spoke of ten million Russian dead, perhaps more. Along Embassy Row one heard ghastly rumors of what was happening to the Jews.

This all left Waldo deeply troubled. America would emerge from the war rich, even allowing for the losses to be sustained in the expected eventual invasion of Europe and the Japanese homeland. The postwar world would see great economic imbalances. Peace was going to be difficult, he thought. Keynes believed that peace was harder to manage than wartime; in war any politico-economic system functioned well, but in peacetime? Look at what had happened after World War I.

In June 1944, the Allies landed in Normandy. The war was obviously in its final phase. A few months earlier, the idea of planning for peace and its problems had finally been given teeth. An international conference on postwar reconstruction and finance was agreed upon, to be held that coming July at a New Hampshire resort called Bretton Woods. Waldo was invited by the Undersecretary of the Treasury, Harry Dexter White, to join the American delegation.

Waldo was thrilled with the appointment. For one thing, Keynes would be coming! It had been almost exactly eight years since they parted in Stockholm after the trip to Russia, but they had kept in touch. Keynes had written Waldo a number of approving, even flattering letters and had taken note of Waldo's work in a number of published papers. *Continue in this vein*, Keynes had written on one occasion, *and the rest of us will slip into your shadow*. Heady praise for a young man just thirty-two the day the Bretton Woods Conference opened.

Waldo found Harry Dexter White interesting. The man's forecasts for Bretton Woods seemed prescient. On the eve of the conference, he told Waldo that the Russians would be particularly difficult with respect to the US–British proposal for the establishment of a world bank and an international reconstruction fund.

And so they proved. Again and again during the conference, it seemed as if White knew exactly what was in the Russian delegation's instructions.

But Waldo's thoughts about White – indeed, even his excitement at seeing Keynes again – were unexpectedly blown away the night before Bretton Woods got down to business. It was the closest Waldo would ever come to fainting from sheer emotional turbulence.

The conference's first evening formally opened with a solemn, tendentious speech by Henry Morgenthau, the US Treasury Secretary. Afterward, Waldo hastened to the room where Keynes was giving a private dinner. He greeted Keynes, moved on, and had begun to chat with Dean Acheson when, out of nowhere, he felt an emotional rush that he later confessed 'seized me like a whirlwind.' He looked across the room, and there, smiling like a cat who had swallowed the world's last canary, was Grigoriy Menchikov!

It was all Waldo could do not to dash across the room; he excused himself from Acheson and walked as steadily as he could over to where Menchikov stood, feeling as if at any instant his emotions might send him flying through the air into the Russian's arms. He felt dizzy. His heart drummed.

Menchikov spread his arms. 'Waldya,' he said, 'Waldya, Waldya. My friend, my friend!' A theatrical tear ran down the Russian's smiling face. Waldo felt his own eyes fill.

They fell on each other with the forlorn exultation of soldiers who have survived a murderous battle. No one seemed to take notice of their embrace; the amity between the United States and its noble ally the Soviet Union was then at its richest and deepest.

Keynes had separated them at dinner, but afterward they rejoined each other and went outside. It was a warm, moonless night. Neither said much for a time; each was busy sorting out his feelings. Waldo waited for his friend's lead, for some indication of what their relationship was, what it would be, if indeed there was to be a relationship. Even face to face, he felt no physical pull. What his soul had been telling him for eight long years was confirmed. Theirs was a love affair of the intellect, truly, purely Platonic. At that moment, Waldo felt immensely proud, rare, unique.

Finally, Menchikov began to reminisce. Not about Cambridge and tea and strawberries beside the Cam, or Bloomsbury and the agreeable evenings at Gordon Square, but of the years just past, since he had last seen his dear beloved Waldya. His voice intoned great sadness; his whole person seemed wrinkled and aged by sorrow and mourning; unmistakably, it said, we — all humans — have crossed some kind of gulf, seen things that have marked us forever. Our illusions are gone. The bridge to the happy, hopeful past is destroyed and can never be rebuilt as it was. The possibilities we once saw are unrecapturable, left behind on the far side of the chasm.

'All dead,' he said at length. 'All of them.'

All of them? thought Waldo. All the young men of that summer on the Black Sea beaches? Is it possible? Grishin, with a face like a soapstone Buddha, who played Ariel? Potrovy, who drank too much and was so wild as Caliban? A dozen names came to him, all flowers of the blossoming Russia that was to be.

All dead, repeated Menchikov; some in the war by the Germans, but most executed by Stalin or dead in the gulags.

'Stalin must be mad!' Waldo exclaimed.

Perhaps, Menchikov replied evenly. Certainly the Generalissimo was paranoid, and yet with reason, wouldn't Waldya have to say? What good was the word of the West? The Germans were the West, weren't they? Weren't the Krupps good capitalists, wasn't Ribbentrop a champagne salesman? Didn't all good capitalists drink champagne? Even Keynes?

Waldo didn't demur. He wasn't a political man. History taught that nations routinely disavowed their word. Among sovereign nations, contracts could only be enforced by war.

'And how were you spared, Grigoriy?' he asked, wanting to change the subject.

Sheer luck; there was a man in Moscow, someone close to Stalin, who stood up for him. Besides, said Menchikov, he knew the West.

'For my rotten poetry, I might have been shot,' he told Waldo, laughing. 'Vishinsky, he likes all poets shot or in Siberia. But I'm telling them I know Keynes. That I understand how you think in the West. Stalin needs that. For him the war is not over when Germany is done. Is just beginning. America? For him it's just Germany all over, but bigger, luckier. You sent troops in 1917 to the White Russians, don't forget. Stalin hasn't. To him capitalism is all the same. Evil!'

'And do you think that too, Grigoriy?'

Menchikov shrugged his shoulders. 'I don't really know, Waldya. Some days, yes; some days not so much. It's difficult in wartime. War is no time to judge people or nations. Either they behave the best or the worst, but practically never just as themselves.'

He began to talk gloomily of the future. It was going to be very difficult. What could men like himself and Waldo do about it? Use their minds, he supposed. Be creative; find new solutions. Bridge the chasms of mistrust, the enormous disparities of ideology and advantage. It was very unpromising. Twenty million Russian dead and nothing to show for it except a beautiful country blackened by fire and slaughter, and the rest of Central Europe the same, even Italy. What about Monte Cassino? By now, what did it matter whose bombs they were? People wouldn't forget.

Waldo felt shamed. He hadn't missed a good meal the entire war. He went where he pleased when he pleased; all he had to do was flash his pass. He thought of Preston with his textile company shares and his wheeling and dealing, of an industrious, secure civilian population busying itself in preparation for the fruits of victory and peacetime. Twenty million dead! Could that be right? How did you pull yourself together after that, after Stalingrad, after Leningrad? Beyond the oceans, ally and foe alike would spend perhaps a generation putting themselves back together again — if they could. Not America: America would simply move overnight from bombs to iceboxes, from

43

walkie-talkies to radios or perhaps even this thing called television, from tanks to motorcars.

Menchikov must have seen the shadow on Waldo's face. His boisterous humor returned.

'Ah, but Waldya, not to worry, not to worry! Intelligent men like ourselves, we always find ways to amuse us. Do you know this Schumpeter? There's a brilliant man! Do you know how fortunate you are, Waldya? In the evening, you can go to your study and read and write: books, magazines, journals. It's different for us. In the evening, we kill Nazis and they kill us!' Menchikov slapped his thighs with both hands. 'Anyhow, Waldya, I'm hoping we'll be doing something together sometime, you and I.'

The conference ended full of hope, even though the Russians had been difficult, full of suspicion, grabbing for every edge, exercising every scintilla of leverage. Waldo hoped Menchikov might join him afterward in Maine, but Menchikov said no, the Red Army would soon be at the Elbe; his place was with his comrades.

In the year that followed their meeting, guilty feelings within Waldo intensified to the point where he began to worry that he was going mad. Then came Hiroshima and Nagasaki. Preston, who made a specialty of letting people know how close to the heart of things he was, had let slip over July Fourth that something big, something huge, was up in the Pacific Theater. The self-approval in his brother's voice put Waldo on his guard to expect the worst, but this was simply beyond imagining. When the first casualty estimates came in, his first thought was, Grigoriy is right, we are no different from the Nazis.

Preston was of course exultant.

'Roasted a couple hundred thousand of the little yellow beggars,' he crowed. 'The war'll be over in days, Wally! Then we can deal with the Reds. Point the bomb at Uncle Joe and get back what Irving D. Rosenfelt gave away at Yalta, for openers — although if you ask me we ought to let him keep the damn Polacks!'

Later, as the details came in, as the world learned that there was more to the atomic bomb than an exponentially giant explosion, as some of his physicist acquaintances at MIT explained the long-range consequences of radiation, Waldo Chamberlain began to feel that being an American was to be an accomplice to a vile and wicked act. A nation that could do this did not deserve the blessings God had showered upon it. He saw his students in a new light, and with a rage he had not felt before; he saw them as budding Prestons rushing to get a jump on what promised to be a long stretch of fat years. He began to despise himself for his work, for helping to create the agents who would consolidate the American Century.

And yet something kept him at Harvard. For the moment, he decided the thing to do was to put all thoughts of good and evil to one side, to purge such considerations from his mind, to retreat into pristine intellection, to pure theory, to a view of the world that reduced economic life to a giant statistical game. Yet he could no longer deny that there was a dark moral underside to capitalism. He took his clue from a young scientist at MIT who'd worked at Los Alamos under Oppenheimer. Building the bomb, said the young physicist, had been 'a real lark' — as if the destruction of a hundred thousand people was some kind of parlor trick. Once again Waldo found himself confronted with the soul of America and loathed what he saw.

CHAPTER THREE

On Easter Sunday, April 21, 1946, Lord Keynes died at his country house in Sussex. Waldo traveled to the memorial service in London.

It was not an easy trip to arrange, and an alternative service was to be held the same day in the National Cathedral in Washington, but Waldo felt he owed Keynes this last gesture of respect. Keynes had shaped him intellectually and spiritually; he had imparted to Waldo the conviction that the intellectual — as much as the so-called 'man of action' — should have a go at the real world.

How right Keynes was! How neutering the classroom could be! Take a man like Schumpeter, of great intuitive genius, but whose influence scarcely extended beyond the lecture hall. Or the statistical maggots at the University of Chicago who believed themselves to be accumulating a critical mass of data from which monetarist truth must emerge. Smart men, the lot of them, but not a patch on Keynes, whose shadow stretched into both Whitehall and the White House.

England was a country he barely recognized. The physical ruin wrought by the Blitz and the V-2s was the least of it. Victory seemed to have brought more despair than exultation. London was grim, soot-choked, despondent. Whatever there had been to draw hope from seemed to have vanished with the need to fight and defend.

Attlee was Prime Minister now; Churchill had been defeated in the general election the year before: voted out, it was said, by the very fighting men he had inspired to victory, common soldiers who — with victory in hand — had reverted to type and voted against the class system incarnated in their officers. This, at least, was the interpretation retailed by Waldo's acquaintances in the Athenaeum and the Reform Club. Whatever the cause, a brave self-sacrificing war had yielded a gloomy, starved peace.

Waldo put up in a small hotel on a bomb-scarred street in South Kensington. The accommodation was minimal; the amenities none. On the morning of the memorial service, he rose early and made his way along the Thames embankment toward Westminster Abbey. He looked about him and mentally contrasted what he saw in London with what he had left at home. Here, he thought, an entire *people* has borne the brunt. To be sure, there were thousands of households in America wreathed in mourning, but in America the only price paid by a vast civilian population had been in the coin of inconvenience. Protectively cradled by two oceans, America had emerged not merely victorious but rich.

It made him feel guilty, a fit object for scorn and derision, as if every London eye turned on him, on his new shoes and fresh shirt, on his lanky, unmistakable 'Americanness'; turned on him and secretly hated him. He was glad to reach the Abbey, to blend with the crowd and lose himself in the protective etiquette of the cortege.

Then all such feelings were blown away when he looked up the aisle of the church and saw Menchikov!

It was not until after the service, while the crowd dispersed amid murmurs of the great loss England and the world had suffered, that Waldo could seek his old friend out. But when he started toward Menchikov, he was drawn up short. Grigoriy looked right at him — and right through him. The look he gave Waldo was bleak and empty. Waldo's heart sank. Confused, he raised his right hand to wave feebly, imploringly, but Menchikov abruptly turned and walked away. Rooted to the spot by indecision, Waldo watched the Russian make his way through the crowd and climb into a chauffeured Austin sedan parked in Victoria Street. At that instant, he felt a slight tap on his hip and something slithered into his overcoat pocket: a piece of paper. He looked around but recognized no one.

He paid his respects to Lady Keynes and Keynes's parents. They were fond of Waldo and pleased he had come; he had been a favorite pupil of the late lord, and his work on the *General Theory* had been helpful. Keynes had held great hopes for him; he must not disappoint those expectations. Men like him were urgently needed.

He was so nervous he could barely get out the pat formulas of condolence. Nor could he concentrate on the words and inquiries pressed on him suddenly by men he'd known from Cambridge, from Bloomsbury, from Washington during the war, from Bretton Woods. All he could think of was the slip of paper in his pocket. He daren't take it out!

By the time he finally disengaged himself, his nerves were singing like wires in a storm. He was committed to a late lunch in Cheyne Walk, so he made his way back beside the Thames, trying to puzzle out what could be meant by Menchikov's distant behavior.

He knew that things had gone from bad to worse with the Russians. Only the month before, Churchill, speaking in Missouri, had warned of an iron curtain that had descended to shut off East from West. In Central Europe, the crushing heel of conquest and repression had simply changed from Nazi to Russian. He knew from Preston that the new Central Intelligence Agency, which had replaced Donovan's OSS, had targeted the Soviet Union as 'the enemy.' He could only suppose it was the same with the other side. Could this explain Grigoriy's coldness?

He leaned against the embankment wall and pretended to stare down at the sluggish gray-brown water. No one seemed to be taking particular notice of him, so — as casually as he could manage — he reached into his pocket and took out the folded paper.

It was a note in Menchikov's handwriting.

Waldya. Better we not be seen together just now. Please meet me 16:00 Russian Church Emperors Gate. Off Gloucester Road.

48

After lunch, he walked until he found an empty taxi cruising in the sparse afternoon traffic. He had gotten a rough idea of where he was going from a London street atlas, and the driver knew exactly. They drove along past buildings pitted with the scars of wartime. The driver chatted on about how much they missed the Americans; his voice seemed to plead for a resumption of the war, anything instead of this grim, gray way of life. It was clear that, with peace, something had ebbed out of the British spirit. What had been won faded away; what had been lost remained. Waldo suspected it might be the same across Europe. But not in America.

Emperors Gate proved to be a cul-de-sac just north of the intersection of the Cromwell and Gloucester roads, off an un-distinguished, battered square identified as Grenville Place. The church itself was an ordinary stone building. A low iron fence fronted a small, dark forecourt; three pointed arches sheltered the short flight of steps that led to three doors. Overhead, a carved inscription in the stonework declared the church to have been built in 1873 as a Presbyterian house of worship.

The place seemed deserted. On the stoop rested two milk bottles. On the middle door, which was locked, a sign — clumsily lettered in English and Russian — identified the place as THE RUSSIAN CHURCH IN EXILE and listed the times of services.

Waldo tried the door on the left. Also locked. The door on the right gave way to his shove, however, and he entered a dim interior, the air pungent with candle smoke. Menchikov was sitting in the pew nearest the door, his feet stretched into the aisle. There was no one else inside.

They embraced and for a long moment said nothing. Then Menchikov guided Waldo to a pew, where they sat down.

'I'm so sorry, dear Waldya, but these days it's not so good between your country and mine. Not with the English, either.'

They talked for a while of cabbages and kings. About Waldo's work, and about how it was in Russia now, and about the ongoing Nuremberg trials and the United Nations. They talked about Attlee's nationalization of the Bank of England, and about Yalta and Potsdam.

49

'I am meeting your brother in Yalta,' Menchikov said. 'Did he tell you?'

'No, but he wouldn't know we are friends unless you said something to him.'

'I'm not, of course. It would only be trouble for you. I think he is not so nice a man, your brother. He brags and intrigues. I think he makes it very difficult for Harriman and Stettinius, and now Marshall too. Your brother is liking war. He likes it so much, I think he has never seen it except in books or in the cinema. I think I understand why you're not liking him so much. Oh, Waldya, my dear friend, this is my despair of your country. So many Preston Chamberlains, and only one Waldya.'

They talked then of Keynes, of his greatness, of his capacious, compassionate spirit.

'I think it's a good thing Maynard's dying just now,' said Menchikov finally.

Waldo was taken aback. 'I don't follow that, Grigoriy. What in the world do you mean?'

'Waldya, you knew Maynard. A man with a mission. You remember he's saying what that mission was? You remember — that night the Woolfs got so crazy mad with each other.'

Waldo's mind went back to that night. How sad it can be to recall the times we were happy and hopeful, he thought. 'Of course I do, Grigoriy. He said his mission — his, ours, all of us — was to save capitalism from itself.'

Menchikov beamed. 'And that's why I'm saying it's good he's dying now. A man should be able to die with at least one illusion intact. That was Keynes's fond illusion. He loved capitalism; it's why he's hating Marx and Lenin so much. But ten years from now — fifteen, maybe, unless I am wrong — I think maybe then he won't be thinking such good things about it.'

Waldo was tempted to let this pass. It sounded like *apparatchik* pap. So entirely unlike Grigoriy, he thought. 'I don't know how you can say that.'

'Waldya,' said Menchikov, as if patiently explaining to a child, 'do you see how much the world has changed? How is like a new geologic era, this?'

'I suppose you're talking about the bomb,' Waldo replied. He sounded petulant. He didn't want to talk about such matters.

Menchikov shrugged. 'A little bit,' he said. 'The bomb is a big thing, sure. The biggest trouble man has ever made for himself. America has it now only, but unless you're dropping it on us soon, we will have ours also. Then war will be impossible, because — *boom!* — everybody is blown up, and the point of war is someone wins and someone loses; not everybody, not no one. So the bomb is now just there, like sunrise. And so it will be until maybe comes a day when there is no sunrise.' He shrugged again. 'The bomb? It's a big thing, so big we can't do much about it. Maybe it's good you have it first. If Stalin had it, he would drop it tomorrow. On New York, Washington, Chicago. *Poof!* But America won't, even though there are people like your brother who think you should. Because right now, you think America is good, is God's country, must be, because you won the war. You won it because you were on the side of the angels, that's what people like your brother think, and you know, Waldya, he's right about those angels. Twenty million dead Russian angels! Anyway, that's another subject. You know what is ENIAC, Waldya?'

'Yes, of course. The Army's computing machine at the University of Pennsylvania.' Where was this conversation going?

'Waldya, such machines are unbelievable, what they can do. But ENIAC is just the first, like the Neanderthal, like the Cro-Magnon. It will have children and grandchildren and great-great-great-great-grandchildren who will make calculations like millions per second. Beside such machines, the bomb is nothing. These machines will change the way we think and what we can do — including shooting bombs at each other like arrows.'

Waldo nodded. His colleagues had told him about ENIAC. It was incredible. There was not a science, perhaps not an art, that wouldn't be revolutionized. The amount of data that could be handled was comparable to damming the Mississippi. He was looking forward to the day when he himself could make use of this power.

Menchikov continued. It was the potential increase in the mass and velocity of transactions and information that intrigued him about the computing machines. In time they would have to grow so large and efficient that the amount of information they could handle, and the rate of speed at which they could process it, would overwhelm the ability of human beings to cope with it, and so, he declared, judgement would be overwhelmed by efficiency.

'If Maynard had seen such machines,' Menchikov concluded, 'he would know his mission is doomed. You know Maynard said to me once that judgement is to capitalism what the secret police are to a totalitarian state. Without judgement, you will have financial anarchy or worse. These machines are not having judgement, Waldya. That makes them very dangerous. Twenty years from now, you give me these machines as they will be and one smart man to use them, and I am making capitalism destroy itself without revolution!'

He sounded so positive, Waldo chuckled. This was the old Grigoriy of late-night 1930s London, champagne exuberant, bellowing, outrageous.

'I really think that's a little far-fetched,' he said.

Menchikov didn't appear to hear him. But then the Russian looked up sharply. 'You think so? You, a genius like you? I am shocked. Think, Waldya, think what I am saying. You know America. Every country has a soul, and every soul has a weak point. *Un point d'appui*. You know who was W. M. Gouge?'

'Of course. *Paper Money*. Published in 1833.'

'You know what he said about banks then? They are the weak point of economics. Weakest because everybody thinks the strongest, that's the funny part. Do you think there was any difference in 1833 from 1933 or there will be in 1983, say? It's always the same. Greedy people, stupid money, always the same mess! The big lie of laissez-faire! And everybody thinking all the time that because the banks are big and built from marble that they will stand strong and firm when all else is falling like jackstraws.'

Waldo laughed. 'Grigoriy, you surprise me! I thought you

52

were a poet and a warrior and a diplomat. What's all this talk of banks?'

'I *was* a poet. Now, twenty million dead later, I have to live in another life. But the poet never dies; the poet peers into man. It's the proper study. That's what Pope is saying. You know Pope?'

'A bit.'

'You remember what Lenin is saying, that capitalism will sell communism the rope with which we hang you? Personally, I think Lenin's getting it wrong. I think in the end you will hang yourselves. I think you will sell yourselves the rope.'

Which was, Waldo reflected, more or less what Keynes feared and Schumpeter foretold. It was not an idea he himself found utterly far-fetched or — in his darker moments — uncongenial.

'I'm telling you, Waldya,' Menchikov said. 'With just one man, the right man in the right place, and I'll wreck your US capitalism.'

Ridiculous, thought Waldo. For all its faults, capitalism was still a remarkable, resilient way of reconciling social man with his economic alter ego. Its economic excesses might seem suicidal, but they had never proved politically terminal, although who could say how the Depression might have turned out if the war hadn't come along?

'One man? That's idiotic,' he exclaimed. 'Absolutely idiotic!'

The Russian grinned. 'Waldya, don't be so quick. Think what the Germans did with Lenin. They sent him to Russia in a sealed railway car just so he could make mischief. The czars were ruling Russia for a thousand years and one man is finishing them off. The German General Staff knew what they were doing. They were transporting a virus, one tiny virus that would be making a plague and destroy the Romanoffs. And they were right. They saw what the right man in the right place at the right time could be doing. You think American business is different?'

'Well . . .'

'Think of a virus, Waldya. Think. There are poisons today, one drop will poison entire lakes and reservoirs. There are

53

men like that: in the right place at the right time with the right power. Lenin was one. Napoleon too. Leaders. Men who make other men into fools or fanatics.'

Waldo nodded. There was no point in fighting history. But the conditions had to be just exactly right.

'Think of what I'm saying as like what is happening in the fourteenth century, when the plague came off a boat in Venice as a germ probably no bigger than a pinhead in the blood of a rat. That rat found another rat to bite, or a person. And so it went. Within ten years, a third of Europe *kaput*!'

'I still say it's far-fetched. What are you talking about, some giant swindle?'

Menchikov roared. 'Oh, Waldya, not at all, not at all! Swindles are criminal; swindles are to make money. This is not some Ponzi or Jay Gould trick. This is the biggest financial adventure ever!'

Despite his doubts, Waldo found himself intrigued. His mind went off on its own, as if Menchikov had pressed a starter button, and began to assemble the bare elements of a case like those he assigned his Money One sections. Maybe this was not all that ridiculous, he thought.

'Go on,' he said. 'What sort of man would you look for? Where would you find him?'

Again Menchikov laughed. 'Where else, Waldya, but your Harvard Business School? Don't look so shocked. The kind of man we want is the same as the Business School wants. Ambitious. Maybe arrogant. We nurture him. We implant him among the elite. This is what the Harvard Business School is about. This man must know finance, because what I'm thinking must be done with finance and money, not with steel mills and grocery stores. Finance is your specialty, Waldya. You're teaching that business is ninety-nine percent finance. I'm not agreeing, but I suppose it's easier that way. What I'm saying is, simply: If I want a malaria mosquito, I go to a swamp. If I want a man to turn capitalism inside out, there is only one place to look, and that is the Business School of the great Harvard University.'

'Well, I can tell you there are no Marxists at the Business School.'

'Waldya, don't be simple; it's not becoming. I'm not talking about Marxism. Marxism is nothing to you or me. This is an economic experiment, Waldya. Advanced Applied Economics, I'm calling it. Just something you and I are making to test a theory. Something we take off the paper and give life to.'

Menchikov went on. It was just like proving an equation, a laboratory formula. The right elements would be combined in the proper sequence and relationship. First the Business School, the nurturing culture, petri dish, rat's bloodstream. That was where the man would be found. Next the culture in which he would be implanted.

Menchikov grinned. 'Let's play a little question game now. In your opinion, who's the biggest American businessman ever? I'm giving you a hint, too: this was not some inventor but someone who was a true business king of finance.'

Waldo thought. By definition, Menchikov had excluded the Fords and Edisons; the production and corporate dynasts: Rockefeller, du Pont, Carnegie; the Harrimans and other railroad moguls. A financier, he decided, and the answer was obvious. 'Morgan.'

Menchikov grinned. 'Ah, good, Waldya. Just so. In Russia it is said that America went to war against the Kaiser to protect the overseas loans of the House of Morgan. Can there be greater power than that? Now, tell me, Waldya, what was Morgan?'

'A banker, of course. But a kind of banker that doesn't exist any longer. He couldn't. Those were different days, Grigoriy. Much of what Morgan did would be illegal today.'

'Waldya, today is not tomorrow, nor is 1907 or 1929. I am thinking of fifteen, twenty years from now, maybe more. The war is just now over. America is just now rich again. The Depression soon will fade from collective memory. Then also the war, and what it was asking of people. You think in 1929 speculators remembered the Somme? Don't be foolish. Our virus must be a banker, of course. On a scale like Morgan. And banking will change, because the thirst for money never slakes. And banks are special. They are where the money is. They know their customers' secrets, Waldya. They are the heart of the system. What better rat to carry our virus than a bank?'

Menchikov paused. He reached into his overcoat pocket and produced a battered paperbound book, a much-read Tauchnitz traveler's edition. He thumbed until he found the page he wanted.

'Are you remembering your Bagehot, Waldya? His *Lombard Street*? A great book about finance. Listen: "Actual crime will always be rare; but . . . sometimes we must expect to see it: the magnitude of the temptation will occasionally prevail over the feebleness of human nature. But error is far more formidable than fraud: the mistakes of a sanguine manager are far more to be dreaded than the theft of a dishonest manager. Easy misconception is far more common than long-sighted deceit. And the losses to which an adventurous and plausible manager, in complete good faith, would readily commit a bank, are beyond comparison greater than any which a fraudulent manager would be able to conceal, even with the utmost ingenuity. If the losses by mistake in banking and the losses by fraud were put side by side, those by mistake would. be incomparably the greater." Are you beginning to see what I'm seeing, Waldya?'

'I think so.'

'Of course you do. You're a brilliant man. Just imagine. In America as I'm seeing it, you will think that to imitate is to compete. Is easier to imitate; cheaper, too. You will compete not by making better, or safer, or easier, but just cheaper. The quicker the profit it promises, the better you will like each new idea. You Americans confuse success with truth. Our little virus will incubate new ideas about banking and infect other banks with them. Will put bombs under your Federal Reserve. Our little virus will come to be seen as a great genius. He will have many ideas, by what Bagehot says, "adventurous and plausible." Innovative ideas, Waldya. New ways of doing banking. Each idea will bring a big, fat, immediate profit so each will be widely copied, usually by lesser men who don't see the consequences. And each will have a long-term cost, so much that when all those costs are added up at the end, the American system cannot bear it. It's so simple, don't you see? This is Lenin's rope.'

Waldo did see. It was diabolically simple. And it would probably work. Waldo thought back to the Crash, to the trading companies, to Krueger and Toll, to the South American loans of 1927 and 1928, to the folly of the banks then. Of Charles E. Mitchell of the National City Bank: in March 1929 a hero; a short time later, a fool, perhaps a felon. How could one distinguish between a leader and a Pied Piper, know whether one was being led to the summit or over the cliff?

'And, Waldya,' Menchikov said, 'we have a bank, don't we?'

Indeed they did: Preston's bank. Now what they needed was the man.

Whether Waldo was 'recruited' that afternoon in the dank and cheerless church soon ceased to be a consideration. As he saw it, there were neither politics nor ideology to Menchikov's scheme, which they code-named 'Ropespinner.' Waldo was swept up by its intellectual allure; it became an obsession. He never thought to ask himself whether Menchikov had taken advantage of him, had traded on a spectrum of feelings ranging from guilt to intellectual conceit to draw him into a sinister scheme to promote the interests of the Soviet Union. To Waldo, intellection itself was motive enough, especially in the absence within him of any gripping emotional or political loyalties.

At the end of their meeting, he and Menchikov embraced and took their leave of each other for (as always seemed to be the case) possibly the last time. As he turned into the Gloucester Road, searching the gloaming for the light of an empty taxi, Waldo's mind was already preoccupied with setting up a personality matrix in his mind so that, should a likely candidate appear in Money One, he would be sure to recognize him.

CHAPTER FOUR

By January 1953, when Waldo sat with Preston on the VIP stand and watched Eisenhower sworn in, he was totally committed to the idea of Ropespinner. Already America was turning out in a way that promoted his ultimate alienation from the very society in which, paradoxically, he would grow rich, influential, and famous.

Waldo was now a dominant figure at the Business School. MIT repeatedly pressed him to join its economics faculty, and in many ways — indeed, in most ways — he found the atmosphere a mile down the Charles to be more congenial. But he was looking for a man now, and he was certain — just as Menchikov had foretold — that if the man he sought was to turn up at all, it would be at the Business School, with its special distillate of arrogance and ambition, that essence of superiority which so reminded him of the Cambridge Apostles of twenty years earlier.

He was as committed, then, as any kid-gloved English Oxbridger recruited in the thirties for the long march through the institutions of Western capitalism. Yet it did not reek of espionage or betrayal. He was backed up by no clandestine apparatus; all he had was a rotating list of *noms de poste* and addresses where he could write Menchikov.

He had also been given a special telephone number, to be used for situations of extreme emergency; what these might be Waldo could scarcely imagine.

Thus he would have rejected any suggestion that he had crossed the line into treason. The years just past, 1951 and 1952, had seen the conviction of the Rosenbergs, the appearance on the national scene of McCarthy, the flight of Burgess and Maclean.

People who sold secrets, who conducted their dark business through ciphers and diagrams and hollowed-out pumpkins. People who betrayed comrades and countries, brought death or disgrace to people who trusted them. There was no way he could consider himself, or be considered, as of their company or party.

His brother cheered the conviction of 'those sheenie traitors,' the Rosenbergs; he would exult in their execution two years later. Preston had backed MacArthur against Truman. He had been one of the first to support Senator Taft, and − as soon as he saw how strong the tide was running − one of the first to desert him for Eisenhower. He liked the look of a red-baiting California congressman and had helped persuade the General to put Nixon on the 1952 ticket.

Preston now stood very close to the absolute top of American power. His entrée to the smokiest rooms was assured. His boards were the best, as were his clubs, his church, his addresses.

Preston was virtually out of the law now, although he remained on the letterhead of his old firm as 'of counsel' and was paid handsomely for directing business its way. He enjoyed the exercise of influence, but he had no desire whatsoever to convert it into public position. He declined ambassadorships and sub-Cabinet positions. A monthly round of golf with the President was all that Preston Chamberlain needed to put his personal and commercial interests across, and a round a month he was granted.

The bank was Preston's life now. He was immersed, to the point of monomania, in building it into the most powerful financial institution in America. By the dawn of the Eisenhower era, it was no longer the staid old Guaranty Manhattan Trust Company. In 1950, Preston had merged the Guaranty with Certified National Bank, a huge but sleepy outfit with a vast, fallow corporate business that nicely complemented Guaranty Manhattan's patrician connections.

The merger had been Waldo's idea. Banking was still basically a matter of taking in deposits and investing them in triple-A loans or high-grade treasury and municipal bonds. Essentially all that differentiated one bank from another was size. But that was enough for now. If and when the right man appeared, the bigger the rostrum prepared for his coming the better.

Preston installed Waldo on the board of the merged bank and engaged him as a consultant at the then-munificent sum of $10,000 annually. Waldo's formal connection with 'the Cert,' as the merged bank came to be known, opened up other lucrative avenues. Within a short time, Waldo was being paid as much as $200 a day to consult with a number of the Cert's corporate customers, including several Wall Street firms. These led to other relationships for Waldo, and he in turn used whatever influence he acquired to see that the bank gained a number of remunerative new accounts.

He enjoyed all this immensely. He began to dabble in the stock market, following the example of his master, Keynes. He lacked, he knew, the gusto for speculation that had made Keynes so successful an investor, but he enjoyed his little fliers; not only did they turn him a decent profit — by 1953 he was well on his way to being a millionaire — but they helped him understand how Wall Street worked, and that was further grist for Ropespinner's mill.

The Cert prospered. In the two years following the merger, the bank's deposit and asset base had grown to the point where the Cert stood in fourth place among New York banks and sixth in the nation. With each increment, Preston's ambition grew; he had taken dead aim at the top of the list. Someday, he confided to Waldo, the bank was going to be larger even than Giannini's Bank of America in San Francisco. The key was to overwhelm the competition with matériel and manpower, 'just as the US overwhelmed the Krauts,' and so Preston had begun to staff the bank with smart young business school graduates; gone were the days when a new Cert vice president could boast that he was the first senior officer of the bank not to have been a member of the Ivy Club of Princeton. Preston depended heavily on Waldo to identify the best men in the Business School and do his damnedest to see that they ended up at the bank's headquarters at 41 Wall Street.

Waldo waited and watched. His fortieth birthday came and went. His days were busy, his influence and investment accounts growing by the hour. He seemed born for the part he played in public: lanky yet cherubic, affable company at the boardroom table and in the private dining room and useful at board meetings and planning conferences, giving no hint of the inner fires that burned so fiercely.

In 1952, he published *The Economics of Collectivism*. It was a success — 'absolutely alters the conventional view of the economic possibilities of Marxism-Leninism,' wrote the *Atlantic Monthly* — but hardly the *magnum opus* on money flows that the Charles-side academic community expected of its brilliant Professor Chamberlain. Six months after the book's publication, however, respect changed to dumbfounded admiration. In two substantial appendices, Waldo's book had postulated certain outcomes for the Soviet economy that even his admirers dismissed as far-fetched in their pessimism. The dubious words were hardly out of their mouths when the revered French journal *Cahiers Economiques* somehow obtained top-secret internal Soviet statistics that confirmed Waldo's predictions practically to the decimal point.

Overnight, Waldo became known as a seer. The demand for his consulting services doubled, and he was awarded the gold medal of the American Economic Association.

This triumph was mostly Menchikov's doing. *Just for practice*, he wrote to Waldo on the letterhead of the Bayerische Wirtschaftsschule, one of his dozen-odd correspondence covers. In his letter, Menchikov referred to their 'little joke' as 'disinformation.'

When Waldo was awarded the AEA medal, Menchikov wrote — on the elaborately crested notepaper of the Grampian Club:

I am delighted for your gold medal, although under the circumstances it must seem to you not unlike the Piltdown Man being honored by the Royal Society, or your own Mr Ponzi by the Investment Company Institute.

Delighted as he was to have Menchikov's amused con-gratulations, and pleased as he was to have completed so successful a test — a first firing, as it were, of their intended victim's capacity for suicidal self-deception — Waldo had still not found the right man.

61

He had been looking for almost seven years now. There had been one or two possibilities along the way, men who seemed to possess the requisite qualities of mind and psyche, but who on close inspection lacked the spiritual and financial disinterest that he and Menchikov deemed essential. Either those men turned out to have excessively strong political or social convictions, or they turned out to be too keen about money.

Waldo screened candidates, cultivated and got to know them, and discarded them. Few survived sufficient scrutiny to be mentioned in his letters to Menchikov. Yet his enthusiasm for the project never flagged.

The world, he felt, was certainly moving as Menchikov had foreseen. The feelings of community and interdependence engendered by the war were slipping away; in their place now began to march narcissism, solipsism, paranoia, and self-indulgence. He could sense a new spirit even as early as Korea. It might be that America, the birthplace of 'all or nothing,' was simply too vast a nation to fight small wars with conviction. Whatever it was, Waldo sensed that public opinion was turning in the direction of 'every man for himself.' Patriotism was all well and good, but especially for the other fellow. To die for one's country was hardly the best way to put a second car in the garage. The country was awash in goods and the love of them; its ravening appetite was stimulated to frenzy by a new factor, television, which pushed the possibility of material luxury into the humblest, most hopeless shack. The more he saw and heard, the more convinced Waldo became that America was a nation that didn't deserve its luck.

What he saw abroad reinforced his conviction that the world was changing. He traveled extensively, often as a member of quasi-official trade and academic delegations sent to parade the American gospel. The rest of the world was rising from the ashes, yet America didn't seem to grasp that fact.

Such considerations were very much in his mind when Waldo returned from a trip to Japan to begin the 1953-1954 academic year. Then, within six months, he was able to write Menchikov that he thought he had at last found Ropespinner.

CHAPTER FIVE

Every now and then a figure arises from the mists of time and circumstance who forever epitomizes a particular period in the history of an institution, who so consummately represents its spirit and style and values that he is forever it and it is forever him. Say 'Princeton' and one thinks of Scott Fitzgerald. Say 'Virginia' and one thinks of Thomas Jefferson.

From 1953 on, Manning Mallory became such an embodiment for the Harvard Business School. Within the compass of his career, he would come to epitomize everything the Business School admired about itself and everything the school represented to its adulators and critics both. Later, of course, he would come to incarnate everything that was — according to one's light — marvelous or despicable about modern banking.

By the 1953 Thanksgiving break, the entire Business School had become aware of a presence in its midst. It was impossible for Waldo to ignore a rising tide of faculty enthusiasm for this first-year student named Manning Mallory. At first, Waldo was inclined to dismiss the boy as just another Faculty Club nine days' wonder. His interest in Mallory quickened, however, when he learned that the young genius's true love was finance and that his ambition, his calling, was Wall Street.

Finance and Wall Street! When he heard that, Waldo's curiosity quickened.

In those days, the best men from the Business School went into production and marketing. The employers of choice were the great corporations that had driven the postwar boom: General Motors, Bethlehem Steel, International Harvester.

Finance was still a stepchild of industry, a distant if no longer poor cousin; it was a backwater suited to small men with the souls of accountants. As for Wall Street, which had spawned and nourished those builders of paper pyramids in the late twenties, disgrace had fostered somnolence. The Street was back to being a demure locus for bond financing and small brokerage dealings, a place where idle sons bought seats on the Stock Exchange and traded odd lots of blue-chip stocks. As for banking — well, banking was work in which a rich aunt was more useful than an MBA degree.

Waldo was out to change this. He was the acknowledged leader of the forces of finance within the Business School, chief apostle of a discipline that was trying to push to the fore a new religion, which, he believed, would transform American business as thoroughly as Christianity had changed the Roman empire. In time, the perspectives he preached in Money One would cause a revolution, but in 1953 that revolution was barely under way.

Through the autumn, Mallory consolidated his leadership of the first-year class. He led his section to the touch-football championship. He organized an investment club. He set the style and the pace.

Waldo scrutinized Mallory's history. He came from northern Wisconsin, where his late father had been a country banker. He had gone to school at Madison, served in the army for two years, arrived in Korea too late for the fighting, mustered out, and come to the Business School on a scholarship established by the Mesabi Trust.

In the second term, Mallory came under Waldo's direct surveillance. He was, by miles, the best student Waldo had ever taught in Money One. Beyond his flair for personal leadership lay an intuitive grasp of financial concepts that Waldo found astonishing. He began to sense that he had found the man he needed.

So Waldo began to cultivate Mallory, to learn about him at first hand. Why Wall Street? Waldo asked him. Why not banking, which was in Mallory's blood?

Well, said Mallory, banking was boring; his father had been a bore.

Waldo began to wean Mallory away from Wall Street. Wall Street, he argued, was for mere commission men, men without principal. Banks were where the money was, and — in the end — money was power. He talked and Mallory listened.

The more time he spent with Mallory, the more convinced he became that Mallory was his man. As his colleague who taught Marketing put it, 'Waldo, in all my years here, I've never had a student with such an instinctive gift for selling an idea.'

The head of a major New York advertising agency who held a colloquium in which Mallory participated put it even more strongly. 'You know that kid with the yellow tie? The snappy dresser? Well, I can tell you, unless my forty years in this business are wrong, and I've known 'em all since Albert Lasker, that kid's a natural marketing genuis. Got an instinctive sense — I could tell — of how selling works. Sees how the pieces fit, kind of sees it from the inside out. I could just smell it. Too bad that kind of talent's gonna be wasted on Wall Street. Wall Street doesn't sell, it just peddles.'

Waldo took these observations to heart. 'You know,' he counseled Mallory, 'if you allied your gift for selling with the economic power of a big bank, you could revolutionize banking and, through banking, all of finance. Banking doesn't have to be a bore. It can be just as exciting, as action-filled, as any line of work on earth.'

Of course, Waldo thought, banking wasn't *supposed* to be exciting. That was the point. Whenever banking turned exciting there was trouble, as in the 1920s.

In no time, Mallory and Waldo had become inseparable. Gradually, the visions Waldo spun took hold of the young man. By the end of the academic year, Waldo was absolutely certain that Mallory was the man for Ropespinner. And he had swayed Mallory on the subject of banking.

'You know,' Mallory finally admitted one evening as they walked beside the Charles, 'I think you're right. I sort of like the idea of churning up that business. My old man was an all-time stuffed shirt. Primmer than the Lutheran parson, as if banking were a religion. That's why I never wanted to be a banker; I didn't want to be like him, period. My old man had two suits: one blue and the other blue. Maybe that's why I like clothes. I'll say one thing about my old man; he could make people jump and tip their hats.'

'Was it him, do you think,' Waldo asked, 'or the bank he represented?'

'Oh, hell, the bank,' said Mallory. 'Back home, you walk down Third Street and there are these three banks, lined up like churches. A man just has to know that's where it's at.'

'Where *what* was at?'

'The power in town. The influence. The center of the web. The place to be if you're worth a damn.'

'Besides the influence, what about the money?'

'Well, that too, I suppose. But just making money doesn't interest me much. It's too easy.'

What Mallory liked, Waldo knew by now, was to manipulate, to persuade people to see and do things his way. And he could do it. He dominated his section utterly. He seldom shouted down, seldom strong-armed or bullied. The essence of his leadership was the admiration he induced in nearly every place he went, admiration to serve as advance man for his silver tongue.

And yet Waldo was certain that, under his smooth and charming plausibility, Mallory harbored a considerable contempt for the classmates who deferred to him, took their cue from him, all but did his bidding.

Not that he didn't have his quirks. Waldo was fastidious, but Mallory's concern with his own appearance struck even him as obsessive. The little Mallory earned from his bursary job went right to J. August for suits and neckties. Nothing flashy; Mallory had a natural sense of elegance that was itself an asset; he communicated it to the class, which dressed after his example with a dogged devotion that would have gladdened Beau Brummel. Immoderate it may have been, but Waldo simply wrote it off as the sort of peccadillo permitted in exceptional men, exceptional enough to justify Mallory's amazing self-confidence.

Waldo communicated all his musings and analyses, the

66

'Mallory equation' he had constructed, to Menchikov, along with the young man's particulars.

Tutor him, make him out to be something special, and let him and the world know about it, he was instructed in return. *And keep him aware*, said the letter, from one 'Jules Philippe Bufort, Agrégé of the University of Lyon,' *that although he is a very extraordinary young man, he is from a very ordinary social background, which — in the skies where he intends to soar, dear Waldya — can prove more disabling than stupidity. Meanwhile we will do some looking of our own into Mr Mallory.*

Thus was born the partnership between Manning Mallory and Waldo Chamberlain that would in its time become as famous in the world of banking as that of Price and Waterhouse in accounting or Goldman and Sachs in investment banking or Procter and Gamble in consumer goods. Men who were at the Business School in 1953—55 would speak of those days in tones appropriate to having been present at Creation. In time, it would be a mark of distinction to be able to claim to have been 'at the B School with Manning Mallory.'

Mallory became Waldo's protégé. He relished the older man's sponsorship; he wasn't afraid to admit the advantage of patronage and connections. Many saw the relationship as almost paternal, as if Waldo was intent on replicating himself in Mallory, even though Waldo himself was still a young man, scarcely past forty.

There was not a breath of suspicion of anything untoward between them. Mallory was no Casanova — and thank God for that, wrote Waldo to 'Fred R. Groves, care of American Express, 11 rue Scribe, Paris' — nor was he celibate, not a stick in the mud who held himself reproachfully above the pleasure of Boys' Night Out at the Old Howard and afterward. Indeed, the consensus viewed the relationship as a sort of cousinhood, since Waldo's baby face greatly diminished, if it did not quite cancel out, their difference in years.

It surprised no one when Mallory chose to intern the summer after his first year at Preston Chamberlain's Certified Guaranty National Bank. After all, Waldo was openly scouting talent for his brother's bank. What was not generally known was that Preston himself was looking for a young man he could groom to succeed him someday. Mallory could be that man, Waldo told his brother, so that the seed was already planted on that morning in June 1954 when Manning Mallory walked through the heavy bronze doors of 41 Wall Street as a Cert summer intern.

Mallory graduated a year later with honors — Baker Scholar, *Business Review* board, and the rest — but it was his relationship with Waldo that was the laurel most others envied. He had not been modest about it, or circumspect, and as degrees were handed out, more than one classmate murmured how interesting it would be to see how teacher's pet did now that he was out in the big world on his own.

Waldo had caused Mallory to be taken into the wider circles of the Chamberlain family, where he was generally liked and admired — except, naturally, by Preston's son, Peter, who was a year younger than Mallory and himself a business school star at Wharton.

Peter's feelings about a prospective rival at his father's bank were understandable. He had expected — indeed, dreamed his entire life — of working at the Cert, of succeeding his father.

It turned out that he didn't know his father's mind, perhaps never had. In 1955, Preston — displaying his famous unbending New England probity — decreed that there would be no nepotism at Certified Guaranty National Bank as long as he ran the place. So it was arranged for Peter to go to the Chase, where Jack McCloy was only too happy to have him, and where it was agreed that Peter would stand out like the Koh-i-noor diamond in a field of agates.

Peter wasn't satisfied with this; his personal qualities notwithstanding, he recognized that the Rockefellers owned the largest block of Chase stock and they didn't share his father's views on nepotism, which gave David Rockefeller the inside track.

But Preston's decision was set in concrete, so Mallory arrived at the Cert a predestined favorite at court.

There remained but one more preliminary step for Waldo to take, one last clearance to be obtained. In the summer of

1955, Waldo took Mallory to Europe for a three-week vacation, a graduation present with ostensible cultural overtones. They followed the conventional itinerary: London, Paris, Venice, Florence, Rome. Mallory took in the culture without comment or enthusiasm. It didn't bother Waldo, who was himself uninterested in paintings and architecture. Lunch at I Tatti with Berenson left them both unimpressed; they preferred the tea Waldo had arranged at the Helbert Wagg Bank in London and enjoyed meeting Jacques Rueff in Paris, whose ideas, both agreed, made so much sense that it was unlikely they would ever be taken seriously. What Mallory enjoyed most of all was shopping for clothes, on Savile Row, at Charvet, and along the Via Condotti. He had saved most of his earnings from his summer job, and he spent them carefully. He was close with a dollar, Waldo observed, and looked down on people who got into debt. Waldo put this assertion down to bad memories of his boyhood.

In Rome they made the chance acquaintance of an émigré Polish economist who happened to be occupying the table next to theirs at Doney's on the Via Veneto. He commented on the colorful passing parade, and they struck up a conversation.

It was Menchikov. Mallory had the tin ear for languages of the typical Midwesterner, and to his hearing Menchikov's heavy accent might just as well have been Swahili as Russian. The three of them spent the better part of five days together in the Holy City, taking in the sights with a vacant eye, eating and drinking in voluptuary quantities which Mallory found unbelievable, but on which the gourmandizing 'Dr Pojarski' insisted.

At the end of the Roman sojourn, on the eve of Mallory and Waldo's departure for Naples to embark on the *Independence* for New York, Waldo and Menchikov conferred.

'He is our man — no doubt,' Menchikov declared. 'Waldya, I esteem you for finding him, for your patience. Our people have examined his history. Everything is as it seems. There is no troubles, no women, no scrapes or things we should be knowing that we don't. He is perfect, because, as you say, he is above all genius for selling. For numbers I'm not thinking he's Einstein. Numbers is nothing, though. It's how he knows words! Put him on a soapbox in Hyde Park, and I'm telling you in ten minutes they would be following him anywhere. In my mind: no question. He is our man.'

'But do you think I can persuade him when he learns what we're up to?'

Menchikov nodded and leaned closer. 'You know what I'm thinking, Waldya?' he said confidentially. 'I'm thinking, Why must this young man be knowing just now? A boy just getting started, why should we trouble him with such things? Just now, what we will be wanting him to do can be as good done just for ambition as from any other motive, no? So for the time being, and maybe always, it's just you and me who are knowing about Ropespinner.'

And so it came to pass, on a sticky September night in 1955, that Waldo Chamberlain came to Mallory's small Manhattan apartment and proposed a Faustian bargain.

He refused Mallory's offer of a gin and tonic, took a chair, and said, without preamble, in the even voice he had rehearsed all the way down from Boston on the train, 'Manning, I have been doing a great deal of thinking about your career. As you know, I think you are precisely the sort of man who can make a great difference to this country. So does Preston. You have come to share my belief that banking is the huge opportunity of our era, even though few people have the vision to see that now. The old fogies still haven't gotten over the Crash, but I see in you the force and ability that can erase those memories and transform banking into something both grand and exciting, into the dominant economic power in the world.'

As he spoke, he watched Mallory carefully. He was pleased to see that his words made the young man glow like the radium dial of a watch.

'But to change the face of banking, to — well, bring about the sort of revolution that will equip American banking to meet the demands of this century and lead into the next, requires not only ability, which you have in abundance, and not only an institutional foothold, which I believe Preston's bank can be for you; certainly you're off to a splendid start there from what I hear. But it requires something else.'

'You're going to say "luck," aren't you?'

'I am.'

Waldo smiled. Let Mallory think he'd anticipated the turn in the path to which Waldo had carefully led him. Confidence always helped.

'Manning, luck is so important. Look at Preston, how he stumbled on control of the Cert — not that he hasn't done wonders with it. But he had to have it first. That's the problem. One can be a genius; one can be articulate and charming — indeed, you have those qualities in full measure. You have been the most satisfactory student I have ever had. I would like to see you where you belong: at the very summit of American business. Your career would be the justification for my own, don't you see? I want you to be my monument as well as your own.

'I'm proposing therefore to become a silent partner in your career. I have connections; I have some influence with Preston; I have, I think, a certain native ingenuity. Like any scholar, I would like to see my ideas have some influence in the real world. Through you, I believe they can. For your part, I think our collaboration can overcome nearly every obstacle with which life is likely to confront you. Barring extreme misfortune or miscalculation, I see no reason why you cannot someday stand at the very pinnacle of American private influence — and, very possibly, public as well, politics being what it is in this country.

'But you must not expect to bring it off entirely on your own. Together, however, I believe we can do it. We can at least swing the odds in our favor. Two hands are always better than one.'

Mallory thought it over. 'Two hands.' He grinned. 'Like Adam Smith, eh?'

'In what sense?'

'You know. You can be my "invisible hand." '

'Indeed so,' said Waldo.

But as he nodded in agreement, his mind fastened on the irony of the young banker's reference. For Adam Smith had written, '[Man is] led by an invisible hand *to promote an end which was no part of his intention.*'

THE PRESENT

November

CHAPTER SIX

PARIS
Monday, November 18th

From his station opposite the reception desk, the chief concierge of the Hotel François Premier, Wladimir Alphonse-Marie Coutet, known as 'Alphonse' to most of the hotel regulars, watched the elderly Russian make his way unsteadily through the front door. He stumbled; the young footman manning the door caught his elbow, steadied him, and then stepped aside adroitly. Alphonse nodded approvingly. Well done, he thought. An agile, discreet response to its clientele's peculiarities and infirmities was the hallmark of a great hotel. For an instant, his mind went back to the time when he, too, had been a boy keeping the door.

The Commissar's showing his age, Alphonse thought. Not surprising — he must be well over eighty. Still, it was sad to see him this way, old and alone at the end of an evening. But then, thought Alphonse, nothing is as it was. Having dealt with that monumentally discouraging fact, he fixed a welcoming smile on his face as the old man approached the desk. At the same time, he slid from sight the newly purchased microcassette recorder with which he had been fiddling. It was a wonderful new toy, this tiny machine, and he just about had its intricacies mastered. The latest technology, absolutely, the salesman had said, which was why it was so very expensive; even as he paid for it, Alphonse had silently sworn to conquer his addiction to gadgetry; another telephoto lens, another camera, another video this or audio that, he thought, and those Iranians in the rue Lepique will own my soul!

'*Bon soir, mon Ministre.*' He spoke in French to the old man. 'I trust your evening was pleasant?'

'*Ah, oui, mon cher Wlady,*' the old man rumbled. It was evident that a great deal of Beaujolais had been drunk at Chez l'Ami Louis, and very likely several rounds of Armagnac. 'But now, Wlady, here I am! Alone. All alone!' He tapped his chest lightly. 'A pitiful thing, eh, for a man in the fullness of life to be alone of an evening in Paris.' The old man's French was heavily accented and often improvisatory, but he was fluent and comfortable in the language. 'The fact is,' he continued, 'I'm never alone. Never, never. Always with me now are my soldiers, my ideological *copains*.' He grinned hugely and cocked a thick thumb back over his shoulder at two men standing just inside the revolving door, boorish types in bad suits and awkward shoes; right out of the American cinema, Alphonse thought, stock company KGB. The assumption backstairs was that they were on hand to keep the old Commissar from getting out of control, from making a fool of himself with drink or a girl. The Russian was a minister after all, if only of low rank and in cultural exchange. 'A minor dignitary trafficking in painting exhibitions and ballet' was how he described himself. Alphonse wasn't so sure. His own notion — which he kept to himself — was that there was more to Menchikov than there appeared. Thirty years in a great hotel gave one a nose for the subtle aromas of position and privilege. For instance, Russian officials of higher rank were obliged to stay across the river in the dreary Russian Embassy in the rue de Grenelle, but not Menchikov.

Alphonse reached behind him and took a key from the mail slot, handing it over with a small smile that dispensed carefully weighed measures of familiarity, discretion, and indulgence.

'*Et les jeunes filles,*' he asked in a low voice, 'they gave satisfaction? They looked charming?' The girls were the best he could do, a couple of Dior house models who liked the idea of getting a good dinner and a few thousand francs in return for little more than a smile.

'*Ah, oui.* They were charming indeed.' The Russian sighed. 'Such pretty girls, Wlady. But I could not do them justice. I'm a bit done in this evening. It's been a long day. Too many grave responsibilities of state.' He winked at Alphonse. 'You understand. It leaves no time to pursue the joys and follies of youth.' He winked again.

Alphonse nodded with deep sympathy. In the old days, he thought, there would have been a girl from Madame Claude on each arm and caviar and iced vodka and champagne waiting upstairs. In the old days, there would have been wee-hour complaints from other guests about the noise, and belowstairs, over a dawn cup of coffee, there would be a chorus of admiration for the Commissar's capacity and gusto. When he made love, the floor waiters averred, the Commissar roared like a bull, and the sound could be heard all the way to the Trocadero. No longer. These days the girls were handed thick packets of worn banknotes and sent home intact.

To keep up the pretense that such past glories were not just distant memories now, Alphonse had ordered two magnums of Pol Roger to be sent upstairs to the suite. He asked if the minister required anything else.

'*Ah, non, Wlady.*' The old man shook his head, absent-mindedly fingering the rosette of the Légion d'Honneur in his buttonhole. Then he pursed his lips. 'Only if it's possible to give me back thirty years.' He shook his head slowly.

We'd all like to have the last thirty years over, thought Alphonse. If only le bon Dieu would just give us back the last fifteen years, return things to the way they were before the Arabs changed the old ways forever, that would suffice. That had been a different world with different courtesies, different rules. Then came the Arabs and their bankers and brokers and other commission whores, and next the Japanese, and now — just as if it were VE Day all over again — the Americans, brandishing their high-priced dollars like broadswords.

In 1945, Alphonse often thought, we owed them something. They liberated our country for us; they deserved something for that. But 1945 was forty years in the past. How long could one be expected to go on paying? Now they badgered him for tables at Taillevent and then canceled equally abruptly — without so much as a hundred francs' worth of apology.

Alphonse felt his world was being despoiled. The François Premier was his home, his Eden. One star ('*gratin de queues d'écrevisses; timbale de rouget; pâtés aux truffes*') and four forks, as well as three turrets ('quiet situation, agreeable comfort') in the latest Michelin. The hotel's fifty rooms and suites were booked years in advance, often by clients who had been coming here since the days of the ocean liners.

The Commissar was a very old client, who had first appeared around 1950. He had promptly ferreted out that Alphonse was Russian by descent. He claimed to have seen Alphonse's Russian soul in the young man's eyes. Russia was like a birthmark on a man, he said; you could never truly hide it.

It was true. 'Coutet' had originally been 'Kutitsky.' Alphonse's parents were not fancy White Russian émigré nobility of the kind that novels were written about. They were small Moscow bourgeoisie, but in Paris — where Alphonse was born — no better than peasants. Russian was spoken at home; three times a week he had been dragged across Paris to the church of St Wladimir in the rue des Saints-Pères, where the air was choked with candle smoke and regret. Especially he hated the mood at home, the incantatory sadness, the recollection of old shrouded people expressing a yearning thick enough to cut for a cold distant country of scant interest to a budding Paris cosmopolite like himself. Well, at least he'd forgotten most of his Russian; he retained just enough to deal with the Commissar and the vestiges of the White Russian community who now and then came to the hotel for tea.

'Ah, well, Wlady,' said Menchikov. 'Soon it must end. You know what Shakespeare says, "As you from crimes would pardoned be, by your indulgence set me free." Do you know Shakespeare, Wlady? *The Tempest? La Tempête?* I'm even playing Prospero once, Wlady. But so long ago!'

The old man straightened up. He reached into his pocket for a five-franc piece and gave it to Alphonse.

'If you ever go to St Wladimir's, light a candle for me, for all of us,' he said.

He turned away.

'*Bonne nuit, mon vieux ami.*' As he headed for the ancient birdcage elevator, he waved to the pretty night cashier. '*Et bonne nuit à toi, ma petite.*'

Alphonse smiled to watch him go, upright as a dragoon, flamboyant as a Zouave. One of the last Cossacks, Alphonse thought; there will be no more like that one.

Then, halfway to the elevator, Menchikov seemed to stumble. He gasped loudly, straightened himself for another pace, and another, then gave a violent, ripping cough and collapsed on the floor in a puddle of clothing and limbs. The room key fell from his hand and clanged on the marble. Alphonse heard a thud as his head struck the hard floor.

Instinctively, Alphonse grabbed his little tape recorder. The movement was second nature to him. On weekends and his hours off he prowled Paris, festooned with cameras and recording equipment, fancying himself a crack photo-journalist from *Match* or Tele-2, or perhaps a counter-espionage ace from the DGSE, on the spot, equipped not to miss an electronic trick.

He rushed around from behind his desk, shouting as he went for the night cashier to ring up to Suite 30−31, which was occupied by an American doctor.

The two bodyguards beat him to the old man's side but seemed as unable to help as he.

From the floor the old man looked up. He tried to say something. He was trying to call to Alphonse: 'Wlady, Wlady . . .' As he watched, the old man's face began to change color; its robust ruddiness began to dull. The Russian's eyes cast about in desperation, seeking hope and help; his chest heaved, and yet he seemed paralyzed, in the grip of some terrible final force. For a moment, his eyes lit on Alphonse's anxious face, and then the old man began to cry out, as if trying to tell something to someone, to Alphonse, to anyone. Automatically, Alphonse flicked on his recorder. The Iranian who sold it to him had sworn it would pick up a whisper at twenty meters.

Menchikov was fighting to get the words out between great gasps, expelling them as if each breath were a breeches buoy to life. It was not a language Alphonse knew, although it sounded like Russian. A dialect, perhaps. Alphonse thought he heard him now say 'Waldya, Waldya.' Was that his name in this strange dialect? Then there was more he couldn't translate.

'Let me in here!'

It was the American doctor. Alphonse was pleased that he had immediately thought of him. Other concierges in other hotels wouldn't have responded so quickly, he thought.

The American squeezed in between the two KGB types. 'You've got to give us some room.' He glared and turned to Alphonse, whom he recognized. 'Support his head, will you?'

It was one of those situations in which the man with knowledge controls absolutely. The Russians drew off to one side. Alphonse put down his recorder, knelt, and cradled the old man's head as gently as he could. He thought he could feel him slipping away; he wanted to squeeze the head, as if that would stanch the invisible outflow of life; he felt utterly helpless.

The doctor placed both his hands on the old man's breastbone and pressed violently. It was doing no good; anyone could see that. A small group had gathered at a polite distance. Looking around, Alphonse saw thankfully that they were mostly fellow members of the staff. Thank you, Lord, for your discretion, he murmured to himself. The doctor continued to push sharply against the Russian's chest. No good, thought Alphonse, no good at all. He's going.

The old man's head turned slowly, as if driven by some lugubrious rotary wheel; his gaze fixed on Alphonse, but it was obvious that he was looking right through the concierge, past and through him into another world, perhaps past, perhaps future. Again he began to speak. The words were a jumble now: rambling, incomprehensible. Alphonse looked down at the tiny blinking red eye of his recorder, instinctively making certain that it was functioning. He tried to hold the old man's head as gently as he could.

He felt something against his leg and looked down. The old man's hand was pushing against him, spasmodic, involuntary, opening and closing, seeking a grip. Alphonse placed his own hand in the Russian's. He felt something in his palm, then the old man's hand relaxed.

'Gone, I'm afraid,' said the American doctor. Alphonse lowered the old man's head to the floor as gently as he could. He opened his own hand and looked in the palm: another five-franc piece. His eyes began to moisten, but he suppressed the tears. It would not do to weep here in the foyer. A *chef d'équipe* must set an example for the staff.

'What was he talking about?' asked the doctor.

'I don't know,' Alphonse replied. 'It was not a language I know.'

He suddenly felt very apprehensive. He looked down. Beside the old man's head, the tiny red lamp on the recorder seemed now to blaze like a torch, drawing attention to itself. He put a hand over it, and — as discreetly as he could manage — he slipped it into the pocket of his befrogged tailcoat. He made himself look directly at the bodyguards.

'It was a dialect. I don't know it,' he replied in clumsy Russian, without thinking. As he spoke, he feared he sounded apologetic, like a child who had eavesdropped on forbidden matters and was now trying to fib his way out of a dreadful punishment. Trying to put a better face on things, he repeated his denial in French and English.

The doctor stood up and pulled his bathrobe around him. 'What's the drill now?' he asked.

'I have to call the police,' Alphonse said. 'These gentlemen will undoubtedly wish to make arrangements with their embassy.' He was trying to be helpful, as if his solicitude would somehow cancel their awareness of him. The tape recorder in his pocket felt as large and obtrusive as a steamer trunk.

'Well, come on,' said the American doctor. 'Let's make that call. Jesus, I hope there won't be any formalities. I've got a reservation at the Tour d'Argent tomorrow. If I don't make it, my wife'll kill me. It took us a hundred bucks in overseas phone calls to get a booking. Who was this guy, anyway?'

'A Russian diplomat,' said Alphonse. 'In the arts. Ballet, you know. He stayed here often. He was called Menchikov. Grigoriy Menchikov.'

The doctor extended a helping hand to Alphonse and assisted him to his feet. The Russians had moved over to the corpse; one of them had covered the face with his raincoat. The other was looking right at Alphonse. His eyes were like gun barrels.

CHAPTER SEVEN

PARIS
Thursday, November 28th

The ache in her shinbone told Elizabeth Bennett that it would probably rain during the day, which added an extra measure of sourness to her waking mood. She was still tired; Heathrow had been fogged in until nearly ten o'clock, and by the time things were sorted out at the Paris end and she made it to her apartment on the Île Saint-Louis, it was almost two in the morning. To make it worse, her day in London had been a virtual bust. She'd walked into Christie's prepared to bid up to five million dollars on the Van Eyck drawing of 'St Josephine' from Corcoran Abbey and found herself in the midst of a pissing match between the Getty Foundation and the British Rail Pension Fund. The drawing had finally gone to the Malibu museum for five million *pounds*! The damn Getty's out of control, she said to herself as she flexed and stretched under the covers. The whole market's out of control. Ten days earlier she'd sat in Sotheby's New York auction room and watched an album of Redouté flower watercolors — the sorts of things that ten years earlier had been agreeable stuff to hang in a guest room — sell for $5 million. Maybe Concorde *ought* to be a seller in here. When she got to the office, she'd talk to Tony about lightening up. They had a number of things in the Treasure portfolio that were ideally matched to the mood of this market.

She rubbed her lower leg, flexing the knee. How could something still hurt after all this time? My God, it had been fifteen years since the fire! Weren't broken bones supposed to heal and never be heard from again? She did a little more internal accounting. The leg was bad enough; worse still was the fact that fifteen years ago she'd been twenty. Well, just. Now she was thirty-five. Well, just.

Her ankle ached as she walked gingerly across the cold floor to inspect the day. It would work itself out after a few minutes, she knew.

The weather wasn't anything to talk about. The sky had that familiar grainy pewter look, but at least it didn't feel like rain. On the far bank, the trees on the quai des Célestins had surrendered their last leaves. Winter is here, said the air and the sky. I just have to get away this year, thought Elizabeth. Maybe I'll try the Club Med. I'm old enough, and by February, I'm sure I'll be desperate enough.

After her bath, she examined herself in the mirror: not bad at all. She wasn't conventionally pretty. Her nose was too long and her customary expression too knowing and skeptical. And why not, after fifteen years on my own in the big world? she thought. She ran a hand through her hair. Nice and thick and dark, the latter admittedly with a little help from Alexandre. Should she wear it up? No. Down and long made her look younger.

She examined her body: A-1 condition. My legs could be shapelier, but there's nothing wrong with the rest. Especially my breasts. God, she thought, they've been the same size since I was sixteen. And I've still never really grown into them. She remembered how her stepfather Peter used to stare. By now, of course, they'd lost their virginity, but still they drew glances. She supposed that was some kind of advantage.

She looked over the rest of herself. All as it should be. Thighs and butt to scale, and firm; the hair at her crotch shiny and thick; veins tight, back of hands unspotted. All in all, every indication of making forty in fighting trim. Physically, that was. Whether her mind and soul could see her through to the horrors of forty and beyond was another question.

Dressed, she took another last look in the mirror. She had bought the dress at Kenzo's shop across the square from her office. It made her look like a sophisticated Frenchwoman. She went to great lengths not to look like the pert, mannishly dressed ladies from New York or Chicago or London who trooped through the office peddling stocks and bonds and syndications.

Am I un-American for wanting not to appear American? she asked herself as the elevator rattled its way down. She thought not. Especially in Paris. Be honest: there wasn't anything left for her in America except memories, and bad memories at that. No family — unless, by some reach of the imagination, she counted Uncle Waldo. But even he hardly entered her mind now. He was just another name on her Christmas card list. He never called or wrote her, but she didn't begrudge him that. At least Uncle Waldo had been there when it counted.

For an instant she found herself wondering how he was getting along, but then she stopped the thought right there, before the mnemonic tenpins started toppling as they frequently seemed to in her sleep — crashing in the middle of a dream, waking her — and there she would be again: staring at the ceiling and asking herself what the hell the dream had meant.

At the kiosk at the corner she bought the latest issue of *Paris Match* and the *International Herald-Tribune*. She walked briskly across the Louis-Philippe bridge. The Seine was taking on its chilly winter coloring, more gray than brown. Much as she liked living on the Île Saint-Louis, the apartment was becoming a touch confining, especially now that Luc often insisted on spending the night. She preferred to go to bed with Luc at his place off the rue Jacob; that way she knew that after a decent interval she could get up, dress, and go home. She preferred to wake up in her own bed: alone. But he was sweet. Perhaps, Elizabeth thought absently, I should go for something grander, something in the Marais, maybe even in the Place des Vosges. Luc would like that.

Lord knows I can afford it, she thought. She was making a lot of money now. Concorde Advisors did well enough for its investment clients to pay its own people extremely well. While Elizabeth wasn't quite in the same compensation league with the people who ran the bulk of the portfolios, especially the traders who'd arrived in the last three years, she certainly had no cause for complaint. Paris might be expensive, but it wasn't totally out of control, not by comparison with the horror stories that friends brought back from Manhattan or Tokyo. Between what she made and what she'd inherited, she could afford to live pretty well as she chose, to dress as she liked, to have a housekeeper, to get her hair done at Alexandre, and to keep the wall of her privacy in good repair.

She cut behind the Louvre, dashed across the rue de Rivoli and took the passage through the rue des Petits-Champs, where there was a coffee bar she liked to stop at in the mornings and get her mind organized before the rodomontade of the office.

She ordered coffee and a roll and did a rapid mental stock-taking of the business at hand. In London she'd had lunch with the Sotheby's jewelry people; they were planning a big sale in St Moritz in February. That would be a good place for her to slot the big maharajah-quality Cartier pieces now reposing in the gem vault in Zurich. She'd bought them as a single lot for $2 million from a Singapore jeweler who claimed to have picked them up from a despot on the lam. At the height of the ski season, they could bring as much as $7 or $8 million. Better now than later, she thought. The market looked softer. Ideally she should have sold them the winter before. Now, as she told Tony, 'the fat cats look all new-wived out.'

Well, in this business it wasn't all gravy; you made mistakes. She was still long a fair amount of eighteenth-century English furniture in a Bath warehouse, and the 'English country look' was losing momentum among the rich ladies of New York. Perhaps she could lay off what she had left by selling it to some new hotel in Atlanta or San Francisco, where chintz and English were still hot and the hotel market wasn't saturated. Right now, Irish Georgian was the rage, but if she had to make a bet, based on her sources among the fashionable New York and Paris decorators, French gilt was the coming, or coming-back, thing. She made a mental note to check up on a Greek who was said to be in tough shape financially and whom she recalled as bulling the market in Louis Quinze right after OPEC II. It might also be worth taking another look at Biedermeier.

Still, the portfolio wasn't exactly hurting. Concorde owned

85

the big Renoir 'Ball on a Terrace,' now on anonymous loan to the Boston show; the exhibition alone was worth a 20 percent rise in the Renoir market. Then there was the big Van Gogh. If the Gould picture was worth $10 million, then a really good Arles picture like hers had to be worth $20 million minimum. And there was the stuff she was a silent partner in: a great Claude with Clyde Newhouse, the Newport furniture from Birchwood, the Matisse sketchbooks, and so much more. She currently had around $50 million in partnership with art dealers on four continents. All in all, she was as fully committed as she cared to be just now, and she liked the look of her portfolio.

Elizabeth Bennett was Associate Managing Director in charge of Rare Art Investments for Concorde Advisors SA, a firm that managed money for a select individual and institutional clientele. As investment managers went, Concorde was in the middle range. About twenty in staff oversaw around $3 billion in investments. In markets like today's, Elizabeth knew, Concorde's small size and agility were incalculable advantages. The firm's traders had a sixth sense for the mood of the herd, for knowing when a barely perceptible lowing and shifting among the institutions signaled the imminence of a stampede. Concorde was a firm that thought in global terms, routinely investing in a dozen markets around the world. It was a polyglot organization made up of worldly people who feared provincialism and trendiness as much as cancer.

The organization chart in Concorde's elegant brochures divided the firm's investment activities into three segments. One group managed stock and bond investments and attendant options and futures. Within the firm, they were known as 'the Paper Pushers.' Another group, 'the Dirt Diggers,' was responsible for real estate, oil, gas, and other minerals, and gold and silver. The third, 'the Seekers After Lost Treasure,' watched over a portfolio of paintings, drawings, and sculpture, antique furniture and antiquities, objets d'art, gemstones and jewelry, rare postage stamps, coins, and the like. Tony Thynne, the firm's founder and Executive Managing Director, liked to keep around 5 percent of the clients' assets in various types of Treasure, stored around the world against what he felt was the certain coming of the revolution.

As chief of the 'Seekers After Lost Treasure,' it was Elizabeth's responsibility to sell Chippendale and buy Boulle, to switch out of sapphires and into diamonds, to determine that Fragonard had peaked and Gainsborough was undervalued, to beat the Getty Museum to the punch on an Ingres drawing and then turn around and sell it to Malibu six months later at a good markup.

It meant keeping her ear to the ground and her nose to the wind. She traveled a lot — too much for her taste, although in the beginning she'd found it exciting. Ten days every two months were spent in New York; three days a month in Switzerland; a day every fortnight, on average, in London, often more. New York was where the noise and most of the money was, but in her world at least, the brains and expertise were still in London. It was a schedule that didn't leave much chance for romance, let alone love.

Next to the traveling, the clients were the toughest part. Not just the ones who tried to get her in bed; a number were very attractive, and — face it — that kind of money could have an allure of its own, so in a way it surprised her that she'd only slipped twice: once in Madrid and once in Rome. Her end of Concorde seemed to excite the firm's clients into an unusually keen interest in their investments. The Paper Pushers didn't have that problem. They could inform a client in Detroit or Dubai that Concorde had taken a $100 million position in IBM or Chrysler common stock, and the client would just stare out the window. But let Elizabeth display a picture of a Queen Anne table in which a client now had a tiny undivided interest, and the client would invariably want to fly to wherever the object was, to see it, and then would usually ask to borrow it to dress up a mansion or chalet.

This was out of the question, of course. Concorde's treasures were locked away in high security warehouses in a dozen countries, or in safe hands as anonymous loans to a flock of great museums. It helped to keep them on public view, since public awareness was a significant stimulant to desirability.

87

Three of the firm's corporate clients now insisted that Elizabeth work with them on company art-acquisition programs. Tony told her to go ahead; the client, after all, was king. 'Just make sure you get paid for it,' he told her. 'And keep the dough. Preferably under your mattress.'

That was the way Tony was. Loose and skeptical. They worked so well together, and she was so immersed in her job, that it was hard now for her even to believe that they'd been lovers once. She'd met him at a party about a year after she'd come to Paris for Sotheby's. There had been the usual sparks and glances; the affair had ripened, become impassioned and declarative. He was working days and nights building up his new firm. It was going like gangbusters, but he needed someone who knew about art and stuff like that — he had an idea the art market was going to go through the roof. So, one morning three weeks into their affair, she got up out of his bed, showered with him, dressed with him, and accompanied him to his office and started work at Concorde, telephoning Sotheby's at lunchtime to tell them she would now be a client instead of an employee.

A couple of months later, not entirely to her surprise, his whole heart drifted back to his once, future, and always mistress, his work, but it made no difference to her prospects at Concorde. He didn't avoid her or make her otherwise uncomfortable. They were as good together at work, he told her, as they had been in bed, and the firm was really going to go places and she with it. She was grateful. Not for the job, but because he left her feeling neither like a pensioner, a scorned woman, nor a lovestruck cow, and so she stayed and prospered.

The sharp taste of her coffee brought her back to the present. She ran a quick eye over the papers. Nothing new — all the usual unlovely tidings. Another meeting in Washington on the Mexican debt crisis. Another strike at Renault. Soccer violence in Turin and Sheffield. An earthquake in Chile. Famine in the Sudan. She turned to *Match*, sipping her coffee.

She skipped through a summary of the recent doings of the princesses of Monaco and a gory recapitulation of an accident involving a lorry and a high-speed train. She read the first few paragraphs of an article on millionaires, flipped through a half-dozen pages on the home life of French television and soccer personalities, and a stiffly posed portrait of the presidents of France and Italy on the steps of the Élysée Palace. There was a two-page spread headed MORT D'UN GRAND AMI DE L'ART FRANÇAIS. She skimmed over text and photos — it seemed a Russian arts minister had fallen over dead in a chic hotel — and continued on, wanting to find a piece on a famous but seldom-seen château that the magazine's cover had promised.

Then something tickled in her memory and made her turn back to the article on the deceased Russian. She went over it again. The man had died in the Hotel François Premier. She knew the place; Luc liked to go there for a drink. The dead minister's name was Menchikov. Grigoriy S. Menchikov. The name itself meant nothing to her, stirred no whisper of recognition. She looked again at the photographs. It was the usual assortment of black-and-white and colored pictures, memorabilia of a long life and career. Here was the man in the fullness of age posing with Giscard on the steps of the Petit Palais. Another of him — much younger — standing beside the de Gaulles and the Khrushchevs in a box at the Bolshoi. None of this rang a bell.

Then, at the bottom of the page, something made her mind stir.

It was a very old photograph, taken during the war — outside Stalingrad, the caption reported — showing Menchikov, in uniform, with Marshal Zhukov. Both men were smiling confidently.

There was something there she seemed to recognize, as if she knew that face, but from where? She drummed her fingers irritably on the table. She was fiercely proud of her prehensile visual memory. It was a natural talent bordering — so her admirers told her — on genius. It was true that once she saw a painting or piece of furniture, she seldom forgot it, seldom lost track of its name, its provenance, and where and under what circumstances she had first laid eyes on it. She looked at the photograph again. Menchikov. No, the name meant nothing; it was the face. She felt as if a screen had been inter-posed between herself and the exact memory she was searching for. She could sense it out there, but it was imprecise, too vague and shadowy to quite make out. She pressed her eyes shut, wanting to squeeze forth the specific recollection like water from a sponge. Nothing came.

She finished her coffee. It happened very rarely, to be sure, but this wasn't the first time her powers of recollection had come up dry. The thing to do was to go easy, give memory its head; if it wished, it would tell her what she sought. And if it didn't, the memory probably wasn't that important.

At the office, the usual uproar prevailed. Tony, talking loudly over the speakerphone to what she gathered was Salomon Brothers' London office, waved her to his desk.

'OK, Sheldon, we'll take twenty million of the issue, but you tell Gutfreund this's the last of his dogs we're gonna walk! Give my love to Nancy!'

He hung up.

'Well, you look pissed off. Another Frog done you wrong?'

'Hardly likely, not after the short course in men I got from you. It's just that I'm having trouble remembering where I saw something. You know how I hate it when that happens. Anyway, it'll come to me. Want to hear about London?'

'I do. Be brief, however. I'm having a crisis of confidence and I've decided to act rashly.'

'Which means what?'

'Tell me about London first.'

'Briefly, London was a bust. I got whipsawed by the Getty and the Brits. The prices are insane. In my despondency, I did wander into Piccadilly and spent a little of our clients' money with Eskenazi.'

'Just like a woman to go shopping when she's down. Tell me all.'

'I spent a half million of our clients' money on two Chinese jars.'

'The kind that "move perpetually in their stillness," as I think the poet said? Half a million? Dollars?'

'Pounds. They're very beautiful late Ming. The Victoria and

90

Albert vetted them for me. No one there had seen this particular glaze before. Needless to say, the V and A wants these pots so badly they can taste them, but they've got no money. I've left them there on loan for the time being. It won't hurt to have the museum looking at them every day. It concentrates a curator's salivary glands most wonderfully.'

'Provided the Limeys ever get back in the chips.'

'They always seem to manage, don't they? What's this about you having a crisis of confidence?'

Tony shook his head, as if he didn't really quite believe what he was about to say. 'Well, last night, like St John, or, as some of our clients might prefer, like Abu ben Adhem, I had a dream, call it a revelation.'

'Pale horse, pale rider?' Elizabeth knew about apocalyptic dreams. Her own nights were filled with them.

'Pale junk bond, bright red default. And when I awoke, I was converted. The noise you hear from our fixed-income gang across the way is the orderly liquidation of our three-hundred-and-thirty-million-dollar position in so-called junk bonds while a grateful America sleeps. Thank God for the twenty-four-hour market! I figured we'd better cut and run while Drexel Burnham's still got a line of credit to buy this garbage back with.'

'Why so precipitate a departure, my liege lord? I thought you just loved these junk bonds?'

'Call it instinct. Shit, no, call it nerves! I'm suddenly scared shitless about Mexico. And about Brazil, Argentina, Nigeria, Egypt, Poland. About Iowa farmland and Marina del Rey condominiums and a million new square feet of office space on Columbus Circle. I think the Dow's about to take off, so why not switch? The rules of this game say that garbage should be the last in and first out, so I am politely but hastily taking my leave of US Bullshit Triple-C zero coupons, and No Name floating-rate variable supplemental subordinated debentures, and National Garbage redeemable exchangeable pass-through certificates, and if Drexel calls, even if it's Milken himself, tell him I'm out to lunch until 1990 — or later!'

'Mexico?' Elizabeth said. 'I thought Mexico was all ironed

out. Didn't I read that even as we speak the great men are meeting in Washington to put it to bed for once and for all — for the umpteenth time?'

'My sphincter's telling me that umpteen may be one time too many. I want to sleep o' nights. The shit's too deep. This time I don't think Mallory's gonna bring it off.' He reached for the phone.

Mallory. Funny that name should come up just now, thought Elizabeth. First she'd thought about Uncle Waldo, and now Tony mentioned Manning Mallory, another name from the past. Mallory had been Uncle Waldo's protégé. Peter hadn't liked him, nor, according to Peter, had Peter's father. And yet look how famous and important he'd become! She even remembered being taken to Mallory's office one time. By Uncle Waldo. After the fire.

The fire divided her life and memory, although she hardly remembered the event itself. The period of recuperation was clearer in her mind. It had taken a while to get back on civil terms with life after the fire. Thank God for Uncle Waldo. She and he had been friends from the minute they met. She really should write him, or do something. After all, it had been Uncle Waldo who'd perceived that she needed a whole new life in a place far, far away. He'd pulled one of his infinite supply of strings and arranged for her to enroll in Sotheby's Fine Arts Course. Got her off to London and established her there. London cooled her down and consoled her. A year at Sotheby's, then — thanks to a second helping of Uncle Waldo's influence — she'd gone up to Cambridge to finish her degree, and after that she was on her own and on her way. Sotheby's had hired her immediately; they'd moved her to Paris after three years, and there she'd met Tony. Just in time, she thought. Sotheby's was rumbling about sending her back to New York, which meant she would have had to quit anyway. She hadn't yet been ready to face America.

But now I can, she thought. Even though I hate it, I can face it if I have to. I have faced life and fought it at least to no worse than a draw. The trick was to see life as it was: an unending series of impending crises, one on top of the next, to be fled from if at all possible. If not, to be punished by and by each punishment to be shriven, to gain an extra dollop of toughness, to seal up another pore of vulnerability. Little by little by little. Each time the tears were fewer and slower to come. Eventually a state of grace would be attained: when life finally let you alone.

For now, however, Elizabeth felt herself merely to be moving between finely graduated circles of emotional purgatory. That's why someone like Luc was at least useful. He was good at what she needed him for, and because he was so bound up in himself, he never saw that she was using him.

As if in response to her drift, the phone rang. It was Luc.

He grilled her on London and she answered the usual questions about whom she'd seen, which restaurants were of the mode and moment, what the right people were enthusing over. The be-all and end-all of Luc's existence was to be '*branché*,' the French equivalent of plugged-in.

'You're such a yuppie, darling, to want to know these things,' she told him at the end of her recital. 'Don't always be so concerned with being BCBG' — *bon chic, bon genre*.

'I am not in the least BCBG. That is yesterday's phrase, anyway,' he said, in mock resentment. 'And it is to my professional interest to be *branché*.' She really couldn't quarrel with him there. Luc was director of advertising for the Paris equivalent of *Business Week*; he was generally deemed to have made a great success and to have an even greater future, thanks to an uncanny, un-French ability to make the hard sell.

He was three years younger than Elizabeth, which allowed her, she claimed, to pull rank on him — or tease him, as she pleased — with impunity.

He really was sweet, darling Luc. Sweet, passionate, intelligent, generous, good-natured, cultivated, lighthearted, ambitious. Foolish when she needed him that way. Everything that a woman could expect of a Frenchman.

But he wasn't 'it' for her, nor was she 'it' for him. Their emotional cultures were too different. Nevertheless, their mutual awareness and acceptance of the inevitable dead end of their relationship made it possible for them to sustain what

93

they had as long as it caused neither of them any difficulty or real pain. Someday, she knew, Luc would marry the chic young *fille de bonne famille* of his aspirations. There would be photos of the wedding in the snob magazine *Point de Vue Images*, and the right connections in Deauville and the shooting country, and so on. And Elizabeth would probably wander on into the next circle.

'Listen, my heart,' he said. 'I can't see you tonight. A big client's in town from Los Angeles. You'd hate him. He's insisting on the Crazy Horse. And then I have to find some girls. But this weekend, that's something else. I've got a real treat for you. Can you be ready at six tomorrow?'

Can tomorrow be Friday? she thought. Is it Thursday already? She looked at the calendar on her desk. The date was printed in red. My God, she thought, it's Thanksgiving Day. In Paris, it was just another Thursday.

'I suppose I can,' she said. 'What's the plan?'

'A little tour round Alsace. We're meeting someone. An old friend of mine from Wall Street. He's called Francis Mather. You'll love him. He's very interesting. Even by your impossible standards. Indeed, he's most unusual.'

'But is he suitably *branché*?'

Luc's tone was exaggeratedly arch and self-satisfied. 'I think you'll find he's about as *branché* as you can get.'

Elizabeth refused to bite by asking a follow-up question; instead she let him fill her in on the details of the excursion. Mather was probably a big Wall Street investment banker, undoubtedly from one of the top houses. Luc worshipped investment bankers. They were his gods. On the whole, Elizabeth found them limited.

It was going to be a festive weekend, Luc declared. Without, he warned, too much culture, although his friend insisted on seeing the famous Grünewald altarpiece at Colmar. The food was the thing. The plan was to travel to Strasbourg on the 'Nouvelle Première,' the high-speed train. At Strasbourg they would pick up a rental car. The attraction of the train was its menu; it was supervised by the chef owner of Jamin, the fashionable restaurant. Tables had been booked at Illhaeusern, the Armes de France at Ammerschwihr, and at Schillinger's in Colmar. A total of six Michelin stars, Luc observed with gusto.

'It is the only time of year for Alsace,' he asserted.

Of course it is, my sweet, thought Elizabeth. Another small space of days decreed by the BCBG crowd to be 'the only time' for Alsace, for Brittany, for Normandy, for Venice, for Megève. She promised to be at the Gare de l'Est no later than six on Friday.

Hanging up, she felt a sudden chill. It was Thanksgiving at home, and it had been at Thanksgiving that the fire had occurred.

She had little enough memory of that horror. The sheer frightfulness of the episode had undoubtedly caused her subconscious to bury it irretrievably deep. All she remembered was going to bed at Uncle Waldo's and nothing after that until the firemen were lifting her onto a stretcher from the lawn where she'd hurled herself from an upstairs window.

She shivered again and collected herself. Time to get to work. She took up a folder that contained recent submissions from gem dealers. It might be a good time to buy gemstones. Things were coming unglued in South America, and the market seemed to be flooded with world-class emeralds priced for quick sale.

Her elbow brushed the copy of *Match* she'd bought that morning and knocked it to the floor. Leaning to pick the magazine up, she looked once again at the photograph in which Menchikov was shown staring down the advancing panzers. She examined the picture closely. Once more she felt the faintest throb of recognition, but nothing she could put a finger on.

With a little snort of vexation, she dumped the magazine into the wastebasket. She felt discombobulated by the day, by the failure of memory, by a face she couldn't place.

The morning's *Figaro* was on her desk. She skimmed it hastily, almost angrily, unable to concentrate, and flung it too into the wastebasket. In her distraction she missed a brief item reporting that the badly beaten body of a man had been discovered near Billancourt; the remains had been identified as those of Wladimir Alphonse-Marie Coutet, 62, *célibataire*, of a street near the rue de Bretagne and chief concierge of the Hotel Francois Premier, rue Bayard.

CHAPTER EIGHT

WASHINGTON
Saturday, November 30th

As the Reuters correspondent announced loudly to everyone within hearing, there couldn't be a Jack or Jill in the room who honestly believed that this would really be the end of it, that a satisfactory final solution to the Mexican debt problem had indeed been devised and agreed upon. But the bell had rung, and like Pavlov's dogs they'd jumped, and so here they all were yet again, crowded into the small auditorium in the Treasury Building, grumbling about working on a weekend, while they waited for the great man of world finance to come onstage and lie to them one more time.

The briefing began right on schedule. At just after ten o'clock, Manning Mallory led in the by-now-familiar cast: representatives of the sovereign fiscal powers making up the so-called 'Committee of Nine,' the Mexican finance minister, and the usual supernumeraries and observers from various Washington and international financial megaliths. The principals took their seats at a long table that had been placed under portraits of Hamilton and Mellon and the incumbent Treasury Secretary, a normally twinkling man whom the press crowd liked, but whose face today bore unmistakable signs of chagrin.

Center stage was reserved for Manning Mallory, Chairman and Chief Executive of CertCo and its principal subsidiary, CertBank, the old Certified Guaranty National Bank, 'the Cert.' Mallory was de facto chief negotiator and principal spokesman for the Committee of Nine. On his right was placed the 'guest of honor,' the Finance Minister of the Republic of Mexico. The remaining seats were occupied by the other members of the Committee: the President of the International

Monetary Fund, the Governor of the Bank of England, the chief executives of the Bundesbank and Credit Suisse, ranking officials of the central banks of Japan and Saudi Arabia, the finance minister of Italy, representing the EEC, and the chairman of the Hong Kong and Shanghai Bank, representing the Asiadollar market.

Mallory waited a moment to let the press settle down. At the table onstage, papers were shuffled; the Mexican fidgeted with a gold pencil. Finally, Mallory stood up.

'Well, ladies and gentlemen,' he said in the flat tenor with which the world financial press was familiar, 'I'm pleased to tell you we have an agreement on this little problem of ours.'

He grinned. He was still a good-looking man, surprisingly youthful, considering he was over fifty-five. The sandy hair had thinned and grayed a bit, and there were a few more lines around the clever mouth and the optimistic, calculating eyes, but otherwise he showed few of the scars and twitches that usually came with the territory. As always, he was flawlessly turned out. Mallory's faultless tailoring was his public trademark. Ten times on the Best-Dressed List; a Fashion Hall-of-Famer. More than one observer had commented that his elegant suits had such commanding style that they appeared perfectly capable on their own of bringing the trickiest negotiations to a triumphant conclusion.

Mallory had presence, no doubt about it. He could make every individual in a roomful of people feel singled out and fortunate to be in his company. And why not? He was the banker of bankers: the most quoted, admired, imitated, idolized man of finance in the world.

He beamed down at the Mexican finance minister, who smiled back wanly.

'No blindfold, please,' cracked the reporter from the *Financial Times*.

'We uncorked the champagne a few minutes ago,' said Mallory. 'At ten thirty-four precisely, for you sticklers for detail.' He grinned as his audience scribbled. 'It didn't make for a very festive Thanksgiving, may I say, not with over a thousand banks to sign up, plus the Federal Reserve.'

In the audience, the man from the London *Times* turned to his compatriot from the *Observer*. 'What did I tell you? You're going to owe me that tenner,' he whispered. He shot his hand in the air and signaled vigorously for attention.

'Harry, let's just hold the questions until I run through this,' Mallory said. The hand came down. Mallory ticked off the terms of the new Mexican credit agreement. The revised agreed debt balance was $120 billion, including accrued interest. The creditors had agreed to reschedule as follows: half of principal repayments would be deferred for ten years, as would be some portion of interest, which would now run at the lesser of 12 percent or two points over LIBOR, the London Interbank Offered Rate, the linchpin for pricing international dollar transactions. The IMF would make an additional loan of $5 billion, half of which would be paid against accrued interest, half of which would be held in escrow against future interest payments.

The Republic of Mexico had agreed to certain concessions, Mallory stated. These were: nationwide ceiling on wages; immediate cessation of agricultural subsidies; the unrestricted opening of the Mexican economy to imports and foreign investment; a three-year moratorium on land reform and related social programs; a trust fund in which the revenues of the Mexican national oil companies would be sequestered and applied to debt repayments.

'Jesus Christ!' said the reporter from the *Newark Star-Ledger*. 'You know what this is? This is New York City and "Big MAC" all over again! He's turned the fucking Mexican government into another Municipal Assistance Corporation.'

'This surprises you?' asked the woman next to him, who watched Washington for *L'Exprès*. 'He's very versatile, your Monsieur Mallory. He has also helped your Mr Pickens turn the Unocal and Phillips balance sheets into maps of Mexico.'

Onstage the Mexican minister appeared to be examining his fingernails.

Or his stigmata, thought the *New Republic*'s man.

There were a couple of other points, Mallory said, that represented interesting innovative departures from what had been done before with Mexico and other debtor countries.

The Times man nudged his *Observer* colleague. 'Here it comes. Get that ten dollars ready.'

'For one thing,' said Mallory, 'the Mexican Government has agreed to submit its future budgets to this Committee, which has been granted line-item veto powers.'

The crowd stirred at this. This was like Uncle Sam allowing the Bank of England to sign off on the US budget. Mallory hastened on.

'The other is that, for the first time, the Federal Reserve Board, appreciating the gravity of the situation, has become a party to the agreement.'

Mallory paused for effect.

'I'm pleased to say the Chairman has agreed to supply additional reserves to the participating banks.'

'I'll just take that tenner now, if you please,' muttered the man from the London *Times* to his neighbor. He called out, 'Doesn't that mean, sir, that the Federal Reserve is, in effect, guaranteeing Mexico's obligations under this agreement? Isn't this the equivalent on the international front of the FDIC's action in the Continental Illinois situation when it bailed out the holding company's bondholders? Is this what the Federal Reserve is supposed to be doing? Is this legal?'

Mallory smiled indulgently. 'To take your questions in order, Harry: first, the Fed's participation is not, quote, "in effect," end quote, but completely unconditional. Which in a way answers your second and third. Let me just say that the Chairman of the Federal Reserve Bank appreciates that this is a tough situation. No time or place for cowards now, or little legal niceties.'

'Well, they got Volcker at last,' whispered the reporter from the *Dallas Morning News* to his neighbor.

Other questions followed quickly. Some were censorious. Wasn't this a recipe for social and political upheaval in Mexico? Was the Fed's action constitutional? Where was the Chairman of the Fed, anyway?

Mallory parried them all in his elegant, easy way, domesticating the petulant tone of the interrogation. A placid mood settled on the audience as he infected them with his own beaming confidence. Within twenty minutes, he had most of them purring.

Finally, a man stood up at the back of the room, a thin pockmarked fellow wearing thick glasses, and with his hair combed up from just above his right ear in a transparent effort to hide the onset of baldness. When he spoke, there were audible groans from around the room.

'Mr Mallory,' he asked, 'I think you've just described to us about as vivid an example as I can imagine of adjusted supply-side market economics at work. And a very considerable feat of fiscal engineering, if I may say so. I'd just like to ask, sir, how you would personally rate this alongside some of the other feats of financial entrepreneurship in which you've been involved? Such as "petrodollar recycling," for example?'

The journalist addressing Mallory was Bernard Grogan, the syndicated columnist and Director of Editorial Policy for the *Wall Street Journal*. He was not a favorite with many in the room; indeed, among them he was usually referred to as 'Manning Mallory's puppy dog.' Grogan claimed his detractors spoke out of envy of his influence on and access to the great banker.

There was some basis for their envy. A former liberal who, as one colleague reported, 'had discovered around 1975 that the rich served better claret,' Bernard Grogan was an arch defender of free-market — some said 'free fall' — economics and of a politics of finance that had been described as 'jackboot capitalism.'

The beguiling economic ideology for which Grogan fronted had been made particularly alluring by Manning Mallory, to whom Grogan had attached himself like a remora to a shark. The relationship was symbiotic. Mallory took good care of Grogan and vice versa. Grogan's *Journal* column was a forum for sanctimonious deprecations of any regulatory trespass on the money markets — usually by men who mere hours before had committed the fiscal equivalent of thuggery.

There was no doubt in anyone's mind, however, that Mallory deserved the label of banking genius with which

Grogan automatically prefaced any mention of him. The man had a gift for innovation, and who could deny that the financial crises and opportunities of the day required innovation after innovation? The problem was, as Mallory's critics complained to ears stopped up with profit, that the genius banker himself had innovated many of the crises for which he was subsequently called upon to innovate the solution.

These naysayers were disparaged by the Grogans as men out of tune with truth and the age. After all, wrote Grogan, if Henry Kaufmann and his ilk were so smart, why hadn't interest rates obeyed their gloomy prophecies? Where was the predicted Apocalypse? Why hadn't the deficit and the debt crisis buried the world? Because of the genius of men such as Mallory, wrote Grogan, and the good sense of those who followed him and committed their institutions to the Cert's line of march.

This weekend's Mexican coup would be just one more in a series of inventive triumphs that stretched back through Manning Mallory's career at the Cert like a giant string of pearls. There was hardly a single great innovation, hardly one giant step forward on the path that had taken American and world banking from the green-eyeshade days into the heady, enterprising world of the present, that hadn't been dreamed up and put into practice by Mallory and the cadres of bright, glib, aggressive young men and women he sent out across the world to colonize in the name of the Cert. He'd cut the Peruvians out of the market when they'd tried to repudiate, hadn't he? He had the President's ear, and he could sweep all before him with the sheer brilliance of his inventiveness and the enthralling force of his powers of persuasion. Reporters with considerable time in the outfit had spent years watching Mallory alter himself to suit the needs of the moment. One moment all sheer charm; the next, cold and aggressive. Bullying, if need be, or wheedling; intense or offhanded: he could do every turn as needed.

There was no question that he and CertBank had been the pathfinders. Man and institution had combined to transform the face and nature of banking, and with it the face and nature of whole economies, of nations. Mallory and CertBank had perceived markets and opportunities where others had not; Mallory and CertBank had grasped how the business of banking might be wholly redirected and redefined, its nature irrevocably, irresistibly altered. 'He came to banking and found lead,' Bernard Grogan would write that very evening, 'and he turned it into gold.'

Obviously no revolution could be so pervasive and upending without the odd misstep along the way. Lesser men could not replicate every atom of genius, and so there had been moments of crisis, usually precipitated by modest talents aligned with oversized ambitions who sought to outdo the master, who took themselves and their institutions too close to the edge of peril and even occasionally over the brink. But not Mallory. The earth opened and swallowed huge banks in Chicago and Seattle and New York, banks that had aped the Cert's gutsiness and flair and aggressiveness, but CertBank stood like a rock.

Now he had pulled off another one. On Monday, there would be the usual criticisms from the Nervous Nellies and Doubting Thomases. They would wail that the Cert, which they invariably described as the 'Pied Piper of finance,' had taken world banking, and now even the Fed, too far out on a fragile limb, too far down the road to disaster. There would be complaints that a slower, more reflective approach was needed, that the system now moved much too fast for mere men to manage, that it was about to spin out of control. There would be the usual nattering from the accountancy professors that the banks were technically under water, and from deadbeats and numbskulls like the farmers and the oil industry that they had been buried in debt they'd never really wanted. So what, said the Grogans, look at the bottom line. Let the market render judgment. The truth is in the clearing price.

And now another unassailable victory had been added to history's ledger. Now it could be reported on this crackling fall morning that the world could sleep easier yet another night because Manning Mallory had somehow pulled its fiscal chestnuts out of the fire. Sure, the man sometimes acted like he was God in a $2,000 suit, but look at the results. The point was to enjoy the omelet, and to avoid being one of the eggs.

All these sentiments could be found somewhere or other in the press corps as they watched and listened to Mallory field the questions coming at him from all quadrants. He wore them down, seduced them, turned the odd arrow aside; he used facts; he used philosophy; he was homey; he was professorial, slangy, and eloquent. In the end, there was nothing left to ask.

Seeing they were finished with him, he moved closer to the front of the stage.

'We've all been through a lot,' he said, sounding deeply serious. 'Not just on this Mexican business, but for some of you going back a long, long way. A long way. Some of it's been pretty tiring and tiresome. But most of it's been a hell of a lot of fun.' He brightened.

'So I guess if anyone does, it's you old comrades in the trenches who deserve to get the news first.'

He paused, pursed his lips, obviously concentrating on getting the words and the effect just right. Finally he shrugged, smiled wistfully, and said quietly, 'The bottom line, friends, is that I've decided to retire from the Cert.' He held up a hand and stilled the buzz of disbelief and curiosity that erupted from his listeners. 'The bank will be issuing a statement Monday.'

He looked at the floor, then out at his audience again, and added, 'Perhaps "retirement" isn't the right word. I'm going to stick around until next Thanksgiving. That's almost a year. There's some unfinished business I want to deal with. I want to help the President get the Banking Deregulation and Fiscal Competitiveness bill out of Congress. The total repeal of Glass-Steagall would be the best monument a commercial banker could ask for. The securities business is too vital to the nation's interests to be left to investment bankers. The President has a couple of other things he wants me to look into. I'll stay on a few corporate boards to keep my hand in. It's just that I've done this long enough. I want to go sailing while I'm still young enough to man the tiller.'

A dozen questions burst from the audience. Mallory took them neatly, amplifying on his plans, speaking of the joy his years of service at the Cert had brought him. Then he held up both hands, bringing matters to a close, and walked briskly offstage, leaving a stageful of the most influential financiers in the world to figure out what to do with themselves.

THE PAST

1955 – 1970

Manning Mallory

CHAPTER NINE

Long before Mallory would announce his surprising early retirement, banking historians stamped the decades of his ascendancy as the 'Age of Mallory,' a golden era in which a staid and bloodless business was alchemically transformed into an adventurous, entrepreneurial vocation, rich in celebrity and influence. The example of the New Banking's charismatic, exhortatory leader drew to the profession a generation of dashing, buccaneering types who once, like Mallory himself, would have scorned the very name of banker.

The growth of the Cert was chronicled in Bernard Grogan's authorized history of the bank, *From Spuyten Duyvil to Satellites: CertCo and CertBank 1830–19??* commissioned to mark the 150th anniversary of the establishment of the bank's Jacksonian progenitor. The four chapters devoted to the Mallory years were titled 'A Step into the Future, 1955–62'; 'New Frontiers, 1963–70'; 'The 1970s: A World of Challenge'; and 'Into the 1980s: Triumph and Opportunity.'

Mallory's progress from a 1955 cashier trainee at Certified Guaranty National Bank to Chairman and Chief Executive of CertCo, the multi-limbed jet-age financial services company into which the bank had been metamorphosed, was mirrored in the bank's statistical profile. When Mallory came to work at 41 Wall Street in 1955, the Cert's total assets were slightly over a billion dollars. When, some thirty years later, he announced his impending retirement, the bank's 'footings' in every category that mattered — total assets, book value, deposits, investment and trust accounts, branches, employee and depositor count, market share — had grown a hundredfold.

Indeed, in the year Mallory would announce his intention to retire, CertCo's consolidated *profits* just about equaled the amount of its total assets three decades earlier.

The stock market supplied its own hosannas, marking up the total value of CertCo's outstanding stock, the price rising as Mallory himself rose in the bank and the banking community.

No matter, Waldo would reflect, that the bank's assets increasingly included technically impaired loans totaling several times its capital, or that its unstated 'off balance sheet' obligations and commitments raised its contingent risks exponentially. Indeed, if a run on CertBank had obliged it to liquidate its assets to meet its liabilities, or if its commitments should be called in, the bank would be insolvent, beyond the help of the complaisant regulators, accountants, and attorneys whose blindly self-serving collaboration had been as vital to Ropespinner's ultimate triumph as the banking system itself.

Mallory's career was the central element in Waldo's agenda for Ropespinner, which he described to Menchikov as 'a calculus of debasement and destabilization.'

Waldo believed that economic behavior was virtually reducible to equations of the same sort that govern other forces of nature. Like a physicist, he sought to describe economic phenomena and predict economic outcomes by shorthanding his observations into formulas. It was simply a matter of taking observed conditions — in banking and finance, for instance, the market and regulatory climate, the way business was done — and factoring in certain constants: notably those aspects of human nature that drove capitalism. A plus B plus C times D equals X. No more complex than high school algebra.

Menchikov preferred his metaphor drawn from physics: analyze the nuclear core, bombard it with high-energy particles long enough to produce instability, and either fission or fusion will result. Either would do nicely.

The object — he wrote Waldo — was to determine which 'particles' were most highly charged and potent.

Consider Mallory himself as such a particle, he advised. If he could be sufficiently accelerated through the force field

108

of American competitiveness, it seemed likely that a host of other red-hot neutrons could be sparked in his wake. God alone knew, thought Waldo, thinking this over, how much damage they could do to a banking system that prided itself on its low profile, low-key stability and circumspection.

Waldo was clear in his own mind that he had identified and targeted the elements that needed to be destabilized, the vital organs targeted for fatal infection. There were the regulatory institutions — the Federal Reserve and the FDIC — and the law: the Glass-Steagall Act, a body of federal and state banking legislation governing everything from the establishment of branches to the level of interest rates on deposits.

Legislated regulation didn't especially concern Waldo. Laws were just so many words on paper, subject to circumvention by artful attorneys or cancelation by corrupted or purblind lawmakers. Existing regulation embodied the cautious spirit of an age burned by crash and default. Time alone would probably take care of that.

Time alone might also wear away the much more formidable forces for restraint that came not from Washington but from the vivid memories of bankers themselves, memories that expressed themselves in caution and a sense of community, a faith in experience and character; it added up to a precautionary wisdom, a wisdom of older men.

In 1955, banks were steeped in this wisdom. As Mallory himself said, banks were looked upon as churches, the moral and ethical centerpieces of their communities, rooted in local service and interest, cautious with their depositors' money, conducting a careful business based on slogans like 'Know your customer.' To ambitious young men it was sleepy, boring.

Mallory found it so.

'I should have gone to Lehman Brothers after all,' he complained to Waldo after he'd been at the Cert for just eight months. 'You led me down the goddamn garden path. Christ, Waldo, all we do is take deposits and buy municipals and pocket the tax spread. If a guy comes in and wants to borrow money for more than fifteen minutes, unless he's GE or GM or was in Skull and Bones with someone on the board, we look at him like he was Oliver Twist asking for a second helping and kick his goddamn tires until his car falls apart!'

Waldo placated him. 'Be patient,' he counseled. 'Your time will come. Don't listen to all that talk from your friends at Lehman and Goldman, Sachs about what they're doing. They're nothing but glorified stockbrokers, Manning, jumped-up customers' men. Banks — as Mr Sutton has observed — are where the money is.'

He made certain, however, that Mallory stayed very much aware of Wall Street. Even then, it was Waldo's intention to remarry banking and Wall Street. Mallory could be the broker in that union.

Waldo had thought long and hard about the shape and dynamics of American financial history. The more he looked at it, the more he became convinced that the boom — bust cycles characterizing the national financial chronicle derived from the uneasy dynamic between Industrial America on one hand and Financial America on the other, or — as Waldo thought of them — between Main Street and Wall Street.

They functioned in the nation's business life almost as the two hemispheres of the brain operated in the life of the mind, dividing up activity while striving for ascendancy.

Main Street was a world of work, of factories, labor, shops. Making and selling things. Main Street was lined with giant entities, like Standard Oil and AT&T, and with corner restaurants and gas stations and dry goods stores. Main Street made and sold everything from bread to bonnets.

Wall Street was solely of, by, and about pieces of paper. Wall Street was psychologically remote from the factory floor and the hand-soiling realities of production and marketing for which its pieces of paper stood. Yet Wall Street was where the ownership of Main Street was lodged. In that fact alone, Waldo felt, lay a tremendous opportunity for Ropespinner.

The object must be to return the upper hand to Wall Street, just as had been the case in 1888, in 1907, in 1929. Panics started on the floors of exchanges, not factories; in gold rooms, not gold mines. Time and time again, said Waldo's reading

110

of history, it was when the Wall Street crowd took over the controls that the economic locomotive ran off the track.

In the middle stood the banks, mediating between Wall Street and Main Street, yet, being financial institutions, always leaning toward the Wall Street side of their nature. Bankers' genes were Wall Street genes, especially in the big cities. If the banks were conservative just now, it was because bankers still awoke in the middle of the night, trembling and sweaty with thoughts of the Crash. But in time a new generation would take over: ambitious, overcompetitive young men to whom 1929 would be merely a date on a page; such men would sever the roots of memory as if with an ax, not realizing that those tendrils were also the rudder cables.

When he laid his insights before Menchikov in a series of letters, the Russian responded with enthusiasm. He did not, however, remind Waldo that much of this had been postulated by Marx. He knew that Waldo had never paid more than fleeting attention to Marxian theory, believing it to be wholly ideological and thus a priori untrue, and that the dismal performance of the Russian economy confirmed his prejudice. It would have been unseemly for Menchikov to observe that Russia and Marx came together almost by happenstance; that the Marxian experiment was intended for a capitalistic-industrial economy of precisely the sort at which Ropespinner was aimed.

In those early days, pulling the agenda together was like juggling. A dozen issues engaged Waldo's attention and clamored for inspiration: how legally to find a way around the Federal Reserve's iron grip: how to 'dehabituate' (Menchikov's word) the relationship between banks and their depositors; how to engineer a massive increase in the money supply (almost impossible to have a financial cataclysm otherwise); how to destabilize exchange rates, perhaps eliminate the gold standard or at least the heritage of Bretton Woods; how to ignite a commodity-driven inflation. Each was so rich in possibility.

In the meantime, Waldo fixed his main attention on the furtherance of Manning Mallory's career at the Cert.

He operated very circumspectly. Within the bank, when he came for board or committee meetings, he kept his distance from Mallory.

He preferred to work through his influence on Preston. Thus in 1959, when Preston was thinking of putting Mallory into the bank's Retail Division — for which Waldo knew Mallory to be temperamentally unsuited — he prevailed on his brother to transfer the young man to the Wall Street Group, where he flourished like an otter in a stream.

It didn't take long for the world to see that Mallory was a born leader, a natural influencer and manipulator of other men. He wrapped their admiration about himself like a magic cloak, just as he had at the Business School.

And then there was Menchikov, available when needed, to convert every obstacle into opportunity.

'Someone up there's watching out for young Mallory,' Preston observed one day to Waldo. 'I can understand the other lads tying themselves into knots trying to keep up with him; they end up choking to death on his dust. But by God, the boy's lucky! I like that in a man.'

Mallory's luck was Menchikov. All Waldo needed to do was write, and plausible misfortune would fell another rival. This young man got drunk in the wrong place at the wrong time, another was publicly disgraced in a squalid hotel, this one was reported to have said something which cost the bank a customer, and so on. From administrative speculations to badger games to messy little foreign exchange scandals, Menchikov seemed capable of engineering anything. Thus close to a dozen careers fell apart at crucial junctures.

'Sometimes I think God is telling me he wants your Mister Mallory to run this bank,' said Preston, laughing.

And so Mallory grew within the Cert, grew in reputation, in power within the bank, and in influence outside. His connections burgeoned; he developed alliances, coteries, nexuses of support.

Such was his self-confidence that he took it all as his due. That he should prevail was as much a matter of right as accomplishment.

Not that he was vain with Waldo. He acknowledged his mentor's contributions and told Waldo it was thanks to him that the Mallory career was generally acknowledged to be rumbling irresistibly along a straight track to the leather armchair and mahogany partners desk from which Preston Chamberlain ruled the Cert and its fiefdoms.

As Mallory and Waldo got used to each other, their collaboration came to operate almost as if by rote. Waldo would suggest a direction and Mallory would devise a new instrument or specific strategy; together they would meditate on it, refine it, dress it up with the glossy verbal patination Wall Street fancied. Mallory would then set the Cert's shoulder firmly to the shiny new wheel and proclaim and propagate the new gospel from the podium of the bank's eminence. Other banks would follow the Cert's lead, frequently hastily, since reflection and competitiveness were ill-matched bedfellows, and within weeks the new gimmick would be as accepted and widespread in American banking as if it had been proven over the course of years and certified from heaven by Morgan himself.

Preston marveled. 'The lad's the best talker of claptrap I ever heard, better than FDR!'

And if there was a problem or unexpected obstacle — well, Menchikov saw to that.

And all the time Mallory remained innocent of the powerful forces working in his behalf.

Would it go better if Mallory knew about Ropespinner? The question recurred to Waldo during the early years and then faded as success fell upon success. Mallory was rising like a comet; to Waldo it seemed unlikely that Ropespinner's progress could be improved or accelerated by bringing Mallory 'into the loop,' as Preston would have put it.

Moreover, Waldo admitted to himself — and to Menchikov — the fact that he really couldn't make a reliable forecast of Mallory's reaction should he be told. Better to let it run as it was; let Ropespinner gain in size, complexity, immediacy, consequence; let Mallory's career bloom and flourish, advised Menchikov, writing as 'D. Herbert Oxblood,' of the 'D. Herbert Oxblood Institute of Applied Economics, Visalia,

California.' He advised Waldo, *Soonest is seldom best. As the old Irish song says, 'It may be for years, or it may be forever.'*

Comforting advice. And so Mallory flourished, and the bank flourished, and in time they coalesced, Mallory and the Cert, their identities blurred and blended, one and indivisible, world without end.

CHAPTER TEN

What Waldo would look back on as the first truly giant step toward the eventual destabilization of the banking system was the invention in 1962 of the negotiable certificate of deposit. Ironically, it was a step first taken elsewhere, although the earliest seedling was nurtured at the Cert.

Late in 1961 Mallory had been promoted to Vice-President and Assistant Chief Cashier, second in command of the department of the bank responsible for funding the bank's lending operations. It was a considerable advancement, but Mallory didn't see it that way. He longed to become involved in the mighty corporate connections he had glimpsed during a training stint in the Cert's National Division.

He expressed his dissatisfaction to Waldo with his usual impatience. The 'liability side' of banking was a bore, hustling for deposits, kissing the asses of low ranking corporate assistant treasurers, performing a thousand sycophantic tasks designed to translate customer goodwill into balances.

'It's important to learn the *whole* business of banking,' Waldo advised. 'Create an administrative constituency for yourself. No one ever really talks to these back-office people. Everybody knows you're the fair-haired boy around here, Manning. If you make the people backstage believe that you think what they're doing's important, they'll go to the barricades for you. In addition, let's you and I try to do some ingenious innovating on the funding side.'

Mallory took Waldo's advice, although he chafed. Even he admitted he had come quite far extremely fast: Vice-President after only six years.

Now, Waldo felt, was the time to make haste slowly. Preston had taken him aside to complain about Mallory's drive. 'The lad's a genius, but I do wish he'd slow down a bit. No one likes to come in second, mind you, but there's a time and a place for everything. I like to think we can compete as hard as the next fellow and still be gentlemen about it. I don't mind telling you I had a call from George Moore at First City about Mallory's aggressive behavior during the Climax Molybdenum negotiations. Not that I'm unhappy that we won out as the company's agent bank, but it's understandable why George is miffed.'

'Mr Moore is not exactly uncompetitive himself,' said Waldo. 'Citibank is hardly a little gray lady.'

'Quite so. I gather that the Climax negotiations turned into a *mano a mano* and Manning ran rings around this young fellow Wriston they're all so high on over there. Still, it really won't do to have our junior people speaking up to George. Manning seems to respect you, Wally. Have a chat with him. For his own sake — and my peace of mind. Coming from me, it would be too much of an executive rebuke.'

Waldo promised to speak to Mallory, and so he did. At the conclusion of their little chat, he left Mallory with the germ of an idea he had been ruminating over for several weeks.

'You know, Manning, if commercial banking's going to grow to meet the economy and not concede the high ground to the investment banks, there's going to have to be a way for you to compete for market funds. I'd say it's now or never, what with the treasury bill rate as low as it is. Have you ever looked into the possibility of making your certificates of deposit as freely tradable as treasury bills or prime commercial paper? Compete in terms both of price and liquidity? It might not hurt to have a little chat with some of your friends in the treasury market to see what could be done.'

As it happened, the negotiable certificate of deposit was an idea whose time had come. Like the airplane, the bold new instrument seemed to have been invented simultaneously in several places. Citibank in fact beat the Cert to market with its CDs, and banking chroniclers subsequently credited a

Citibank team headed by Wriston and Exter with inventing the new paper, a fact that rankled Mallory. Indeed, from that time forward, Mallory seemed to target Citibank as 'the enemy' — a Satan to be outmaneuvered or outdone at every possible turn.

The negotiable CD was an instant success on every count. It freed banks from traditional constraints on size and lending practice. When it came to lending funds, a bank simply didn't apply the same microscopic scrutiny and rigid credit standards to putting out money it had 'bought' in the open market as it did to cash entrusted to it by depositors.

Wall Street was always looking for new products to peddle and trade, and it loved the idea of marketing a freely tradable ninety-day promissory note of First National City or Cert Bank or First of Chicago or Bank of America. A new type of security meant new markets to be opened up, new purses to reach into.

Within six months, a half-dozen Wall Street houses were making active liquid markets on the certificates of deposit of the dozen largest US banks; within a year the number of acceptable names had swollen to the hundred largest banks. Once again, thought Waldo, Say's Law — that supply creates its own demand — had been proven.

More important, Ropespinner now had in hand a potent particle with which to bombard the stable nucleus. On the surface, the negotiable CD seemed a useful, even salutary tool for promoting economic growth by enlarging the resources of the banking system. It permitted the best banking names to go into the open market and offer investors a new and desirable short-term investment which, even if it was subject to stringent interest-rate ceilings, offered the incomparable attraction of decent liquidity.

That was the way it seemed to the world at large. To Waldo, however, the negotiable certificate of deposit was the first step in a financial chain reaction. The faster the market grew, he judged, the more dependent the banks would become on this form of financing to meet the demand for credit. Already bank analysts and strategists were using words like *permanentize* in reference to the role of the CDs in bank financing. The logic was: if a short-term obligation could successfully be renewed time after time, rolled over and over and over continuously, as certain and rhythmic as the waves of the ocean, should it not be viewed as truly long-term capital and as a legitimate source for funding longer-term loans?

Waldo listened to these arguments, and nodded sagely, and smiled inwardly. If ever there was a surefire recipe for banking disaster, it was to borrow short and lend long.

He could see other benefits for Ropespinner. Unlike most other nations, America was instinctively habituated to borrowing. Americans weren't parsimonious, didn't keep their mites tucked away in their mattresses, and they were used to getting what they wanted — right away! The costs of credit were therefore, by Waldo's lights, a more significant factor in the general level of prices in the United States than elsewhere. These costs were restrained by an elaborate fabric of interest rate ceilings. The negotiable CD represented the first tiny rip in this fabric. CDs competed in the financial markets with other types of 'deposit' security, from treasury bills to savings-and-loan certificates. The more important CDs became to the banks as sources of loan capital, the more vulnerable the banks became to short-term interest rates. If these should move above the levels the banks could legally pay on their CDs, the banks would be squeezed. Something would have to give to avoid a crisis; it could only be the New Deal ceilings on interest rates, and another nail would be driven into the coffin planked with those once-lively memories of 1929.

String this out logically, thought Waldo, and over time the banks, those marble bastions of financial solidity, could be transformed into paper palaces, houses of cards.

Mallory assumed the role of prophet of the new financing. Preston, rankled at having been beaten out on the CD by Citibank, reassigned Mallory to the Wall Street Division, to make sure the Cert got the lion's share of the business. In the circular world of high finance, the Cert sold its paper in the primary market — to corporations awash in surplus cash — and frequently reloaned the proceeds to the Wall Street houses who made the secondary market and financed their inventories of CertBank CDs with call loans.

His stint on Wall Street was Mallory's time in Eden. Here were men and markets uniquely attuned to his skills; they rhapsodized over his capacity to seize upon a business or financing concept, locate and extract its nugget of salability, and cut, polish, and set that nugget like a jeweler. Mallory exuded a dash and fire people weren't used to seeing in a banker. His drive and energy were infectious; Wall Street had rumbled back from the Kennedy–US Steel crisis and the President's assassination. Confidence was on a roll. The nation's financial system was the ornament of its commerce. The exchanges were steaming.

If Mallory liked Wall Street, Wall Street loved Mallory.

He epitomized what *Fortune* hailed as 'a new breed of banker, risk-oriented, visionary, unshackled.' *Forbes* praised him as 'a paradigm of the new market economy banking' and pictured him on its cover along with Wriston and a promising young Texan named Ben Love. The 1964 issue of the *Bawl Street Journal*, the parody souvenir published in conjunction with the annual outing of the Bond Club of New York, featured a caricature depicting Mallory as a Roman gladiator, foot on a pile of bodies variously labeled CHASE, CITI, B OF A. The cartoon was labeled 'The Banker Who Takes No Prisoners.' More to the point was the rubric inscribed on the cartoon Mallory's shield: COMPETE OR CAPITULATE!

Waldo was delighted with it. A new Age of Personality was dawning in American business. The Depression had driven businessmen underground as far as personal publicity was concerned. But by 1964, with the Dow afire and the man in the street throbbing with stock market fever, visibility was beginning to be back in vogue. And Mallory's picture and pronouncements were beginning to appear with regularity. He was becoming a public figure, sought after for his ability to open the rhetorical window on vistas of astonishing breadth and profitability.

'Someday,' he declared to a convention of Midwestern bankers, 'I wouldn't be surprised if a billion-dollar CD sold in the open market.'

'So it may,' Waldo admonished Mallory, 'but I think that's rather beside the point. If you were really clever, you'd set your mind to figuring out how to market and process a hundred-dollar denomination. It's hardly fair for you to pay Standard Oil four percent for the use of its money simply because they can buy a hundred-thousand-dollar minimum, which the small depositor can't. You can hardly say, Manning, that as things stand today, the little guy gets a square deal.'

The 'little guy' was the backbone of the deposit base. Patient and loyal: to his employer, his bank, the management of the companies whose shares he might own. If only . . . thought Waldo. If only Mallory's 'little guy' could be set to chasing overnight interest rates with the same avidity that oil company treasurers were starting to do.

If only . . .

In mid-1964, Preston bowed to pressure from all sides and promoted Mallory to Senior Vice-President and placed him in charge of his great love, the Cert's Wall Street Division.

It was what the Street wanted, and it repaid Preston by marking up Cert shares by 10 percent. Bank stocks were the rage now.

There had been a time not so long ago, Waldo remembered, when banks had been considered about as exciting investment vehicles as the local gasworks: utilities that provided money instead of electricity. Predictable, reliable, solid. And boring, boring, boring; the sort of thing one bought for widows and orphans.

Mallory and his generation were changing that. Banking was glamorous now; banking was a growth industry. Preston had yielded to the times and let Mallory publicly announce the Cert's intention of 'managing' its business to obtain a sustainable annual growth rate of 15 percent in the bank's earnings per share. Privately, Mallory intimated to favored analysts in the investment community that 20 percent was more like what top management had in mind. When word of this got around, what could other banks do but declare similar goals? Where one led, all must follow — or lose 'market share,' words never before uttered in connection with banking.

Never, Waldo thought approvingly, discount loss of face as a motivator. In Wall Street, 'face' could amount to hard cash. Boasts made — and lived up to — translated into a rising stock price. Boasts unmet — notably failure to hit proclaimed or anticipated earnings targets — sent stocks reeling, cost jobs and perquisites, and meant a loss of esteem and respect that could lead to a place below the salt at the tables of captains and kings.

Bank shares had come to be monitored by a dozen specialist research houses. Banks were prized investment banking prospects, eagerly courted by all the top Wall Street names. It was all coming together very nicely, thought Waldo. It might take years for the full, explosive effects to be felt, but if he was right, any wait would be worthwhile. If he was right, investor capitalism would be stood on its head, turned inside out — and all in its own name!

Historically, the Cert's predecessors had served as fiduciaries or money managers for nine out of ten of New York's richest families; at one time, they had represented the largest combined single pool of investment capital in the United States.

By 1965, the bank had been overtaken by J. P. Morgan & Co. as a manager of other people's money. The word was that the Morgan bank was more forward-looking. There were plenty of smart people at the Cert, but they needed their feet held to the fire, needed to get with it, get in step with new wave money managers like those Houston fellows, Fayez Sarofim and Coe Scruggs, needed to be more adventurous.

Here was something worth pondering, thought Waldo. Within weeks, he had a plan.

Until the early 1960s, the equity ownership of the US economy had been vested in a large, discrete, and (above all!) patient group of individuals. But by 1965 it seemed to Waldo that this was changing in a way that could only harbor exciting long-term possibilities for Ropespinner.

The postwar boom had been for the most part industrial: steel, automobiles, petroleum and chemicals, aircraft. The chosen instrument of the US economy had been the highly structured, unionized public corporation. Employee and executive benefit and pension plans had been created that began to be flooded with funds clamoring for investment. These were managed, by and large, by conservative men in bank trust departments, men whose sense of risk was mirrored in their quiet gray suits and sturdy brogans.

Now, however, stockbrokers and their institutional clients were fomenting new approaches to large-scale investing. Waldo read about it; he heard it in his classroom, from his colleagues who sat on fiduciary boards, from the corporations he counseled. As he thought about it, he came to see exactly how it might play into Ropespinner's hands.

Preston proved every bit as receptive as expected to Waldo's urging that he install Mallory − in the interest of keeping the Cert competitive in the field − at the head of the bank's Trust and Investment Division. Mallory was a man in touch with the age, argued Waldo. No crust over his eyes. He was just the breath of fresh air and insight needed to bring the Cert's investment activities into the twentieth century, to seize back the leadership of the institutional investment community from Morgan and Bankers Trust.

'I don't know why I didn't think of it myself, Wally,' Preston said when he'd thought it over. 'Why, just the other day at the hospital meeting it came up how badly we'd done compared to Morgan. I can tell you, I didn't like it one bit to have to sit there watching Hinton of the Morgan grin as if he'd swallowed the proverbial canary. And then the other evening at the Gorse Club . . .'

And so Mallory was placed in charge of the bank's investment area. It was widely expected that he would apply the same flair to the deployment of $6 billion in investment funds that he'd brought to every other area of the Cert's operations. What was not expected was that he would lead the way to an eventual revolution in the way corporate America would be allowed to conduct its business.

Mallory made his inaugural speech as head of the Trust and Investment Division to the annual convention of the Investment Banking Association in Boca Raton. It was a sultry night, even for south Florida in November, but the distant thunder that hung in the air was drowned out by the seductiveness of Mallory's remarks. His words were calculated to reverberate through Wall Street and the City of London, in every exchange and bourse in the world, in any place where investment decisions were urged and made.

The tantalizing vision he proclaimed that night, of CertBank's 'total commitment to total return,' was of a tree growing to the sky with fruit for everyone. He chided his colleagues in the investment institutions for past caution, for what he called 'our nitpicking insistence on investment "balance," between bonds and stocks, between income and appreciation, an insistence which has only cost everyone money!' America was on the verge of a decade of exploding growth. It was time to get on board, to go into the equity market with both hands and two shovels, the way the Cert was going to do. If the Cert liked a stock, there was going to be no limit to how much it would buy. Why, if the bank could accumulate 40 percent of great companies like IBM and Standard Oil, it would!

His speech was interrupted a dozen times by applause. This was a savvy audience, capable of instant recognition of its own best interests. This could be Golconda, El Dorado, the passage to the Indies. If institutional investors around the world followed the Cert's lead — and why shouldn't they? — an institutional stock-buying frenzy could be launched that would enrich Wall Street to the end of time. Here was a license for the Street to wholesale stocks at retail prices.

Waldo had foreseen all of this. Still, even he was astonished at how easily and thoroughly it went. Mallory's speech had been timed to catch the Friday papers; it made the front page of the *Times*, was an AP, UPI, and Reuters lead, and earned the young banker his first feature story in *Business Week* and, together with Preston, his first appearance on the cover of *Time*.

And so the great decade-long institutionalization of the stock markets was launched. It was — as Waldo had foreseen — a stampede, a feeding frenzy. Fattened by corporate contributions to their benefit plans and by a massive convergence of savings from around the world, the appetite of the institutions for stocks seemed insatiable. Ironically, thought Waldo, the management of corporate America hastened to facilitate a process which, over the long term, could only put itself at risk. Institutional analysts came to be courted, wined and dined, fed tidbits of confidential information along with Chateaubriand. The institutional share of daily trading activity grew from roughly 20 percent to over 50 percent. In time it would reach 80 percent.

Larger and larger percentages of major corporations came to be owned by fewer and fewer, but larger, investment institutions. Sooner or later, Waldo guessed, this sort of concentration could convert what was now a market in shares into a no-less-active market in companies.

As the action quickened, the investment community's view of itself and its work changed. Gray suits were shucked in favor of gaudy finery and body jewelry. Discreet toiling in the vineyard yielded to champagne at the Ritz; personality cults formed around the more dashing money managers. They called themselves 'gunslingers' and used a tough-guy vocabulary. One day, Waldo thought, these people will enjoy seeing corporate managements jump. He watched as a highly profitable apparatus of publicity sprouted. Glossy fan magazines appeared.

No one seemed to grasp the implications of what was happening. Old communities of interests were being dissolved. The passivity of the individual investor had been a priceless asset for corporate America. His patience had underwritten the cost of research and development and experimentation; it had given industry the time it often took to do its job properly and management the freedom to indulge itself.

'You know,' Mallory observed, returning from a weekend on an oil company's shooting preserve, 'I begin to wonder if a few of our larger corporate clients aren't being run principally for the entertainment of their managements.'

Well, thought Waldo, if they were, then they were fools to support what was going on. The interests of institutions were not those of individuals and thus not necessarily those of managements or employees. The sympathies of the fund managers began and ended with their own fees and the ticker tape.

This wholesale transformation of equity ownership, which Waldo would later regard as perhaps Ropespinner's most fore-sighted initiative, would lead inevitably to a frenetic competition for accounts. This would in turn create a manic emphasis on short-term investment performance as a selling point. Accounts meant management fees. Money managers' first loyalties were to their own compensation, masked by platitudinous talk of 'acting in the best interests of our fiduciaries.'

The institutionalization of the ownership of corporate America absolutely restored Wall Street to the ascendant. The herdlike rush of so much concentrated buying power into equities produced a raging market that overwhelmed other forms of business. Finance and speculation eclipsed all other forms of business activity in the public awareness. The nightly news programs implied that the true measure of the nation's economic health was the Dow-Jones stock average.

Other men might have paused to savor such progress. Not Waldo Chamberlain. He had little patience for work in process. By 1967, he had his gaze fixed overseas, where new frontiers beckoned.

Before 1966, Waldo had assumed the Cert's foreign business to be about the same as it always had been: richly furnished offices of convenience in Paris and London, manly paneled premises in the rue Cambon and Berkeley Square where unctuous managers attended to the needs of the bank's wealthy customers, changing dollars into crisp new pounds and francs, arranging lines of casino credit, dispatching discreet monthly payments to mis-tresses and catamites, and giving the visiting offspring of impor-tant clients a cup of tea or a glass of sherry or, in extremely important cases, lunch at Lucas-Carton or the Mirabelle.

When he went abroad with his brother for a look, he was amazed at the extent to which opportunity, the pace of change, and aggressive management had irrevocably altered American overseas banking. The Cert's Mayfair townhouse and the Paris *maison particulière* had been supplemented by ten floors in Bishopsgate and an ugly office block just off the Étoile. The vapid young Yale men who for fifty years had carried parcels

125

from Charvet to the Crillon had been displaced by crisp hard-edged MBAs who specialized in trade finance and foreign exchange. CertBank had added offices in Zurich and Geneva, Monte Carlo, Düsseldorf, Beirut, Hong Kong, São Paulo, and twenty other cities. There were CertBank pigeonholes in Liechtenstein and the Netherlands Antilles. Each month the large world map that covered an entire room of the bank's boardroom seemed to blink with more little lights, like newly discovered stars, red for a branch, yellow for a representative office, blue for 'an agent on the ground' — these most notably across the Middle East — and white for 'targets of opportunity.'

Waldo and Preston crisscrossed the Cert's overseas domains, accompanied by a Cert officer named Frank Laurence, a man about Mallory's age and — like Mallory — a newly minted Executive Vice President. Laurence was a certified banking prodigy in his own right. He ruled CertBank's overseas dominions from the bank's London headquarters.

As he watched Laurence with Preston, Waldo marked him down as a threat to Mallory. Preston was obviously taken with the young man; he was more Preston's sort: Princeton; Harvard LLB; three years at Sullivan and Cromwell before switching to banking; member of the Racquet Club and the Gorse. Laurence's father was president of a major West Coast bank and a chum of Preston's from the Bohemian Grove. The young man was to the executive suite born and bred.

From Sydney, Waldo addressed a letter to 'Prof. Dr Nels Fjelstrup' at an address in Oslo, outlining Frank Laurence's particulars and his own concerns relative to Mallory's future. This was a problem Grigoriy would have to deal with. The best Waldo could do would be to intrigue against Laurence with Preston — and that tactic could turn against Ropespinner's interest. He left the matter in Menchikov's hands and turned his mind to working out the possibilities inherent in a financial phenomenon that had burst upon his awareness with the force of a bomb.

Eurodollars.

Eurodollars. Asiadollars. Dollar balances maintained beyond the borders of the United States and thus beyond the control and reserve requirements imposed by the Treasury and the

126

Federal Reserve Board. Dollars belonging to foreigners, spent in France by tourists, in Germany for machine tools, in Saudi Arabia for petroleum. Dollars belonging to expatriate Americans, to individuals or multinational corporations, left overseas as a matter of convenience, or out of fear of US taxes, or to take advantage of relatively high overseas interest rates. The reasons for keeping dollars overseas varied from depositor to depositor, but there was no shortage of motives, and so there was a vast quantity of such currency in circulation or in banks. Hundreds of millions, perhaps billions. Indeed, during the Cairo–Johannesburg leg of their trip, Preston boasted – odd boast for a banker, national guardian of the currency – that no one could tell within $200 million – $200 million! – how many such 'foreign' dollars were outstanding. Years later, when the Eurodollar pool approached a *trillion* dollars, Waldo would remember Preston's boast and smile and shake his head. How small and ordinary seem those brave new worlds on whose verge we have all stood incredulously.

Better yet, without the Fed to inhibit the process by imposing reserve requirements, there was no limit to the number of Eurodollars that could be 'printed' overseas. A dollar held by a CertBank customer in Frankfurt could be loaned on the bank wire to a borrower who placed it on deposit with Dresdner Bank in Cologne. Now each bank would reflect that dollar in its deposit accounts, and so one had become two. The possibilities for further multiplication and subdivision seemed inexhaustible to Waldo, limited only by the demands of world trade to finance itself. As matters stood, although the sums under discussion were substantial, Waldo could see that they fell far short of the amounts needed to create utter havoc with the world economy and with the monetary system established at Bretton Woods.

Once again he found himself thinking, If only . . .

If only something could be devised to precipitate an overnight artificial explosion in the value of world trade, in the price of some world commodity, this could – properly managed – bring about a massive expansion of the worldwide supply of dollars, which the Federal Reserve would be helpless to limit or control.

If only . . .

127

CHAPTER ELEVEN

By the summer of 1970, all the problems appeared to have been worked out and everything seemed to have dropped neatly into place for Manning Mallory. On July Fourth, Waldo sat alone on the wide porch of his Quiddy house, reviewed the progress of Ropespinner's timetable and agenda, and dashed off a letter to Menchikov.

They had every reason to be satisfied. Mallory's path was cleared of all rivals. It could only be a year or two now at most until he would become Chief Executive of the bank. Preston would soon turn sixty-five. While he hadn't said as much, it was obvious that the succession at CertBank was a closed matter.

Menchikov had wrought his sorcery, and now Mallory stood alone on the step beneath the throne occupied by Preston Chamberlain. Frank Laurence had been eliminated as a serious rival the year before. CertBank International had been racked without warning in mid-1969 by a foreign exchange scandal in its Hong Kong branch. The money involved wasn't large, but the scandal was noisome, and the financial press made the most of it.

Preston, at a loss to explain how or why such a thing could have happened, took it personally. Heads rolled, beginning with Laurence's. CertBank International was gutted and the division added to Mallory's line of command. In line with his new responsibilities, he was named Senior Executive Vice-President and Chief Operating Officer of CertBank, and Executive Vice-President and a member of the Executive Committee of CertCo, the bank's holding company. At forty, the bank's future was his.

Mallory had come a long way. Waldo felt pleased and proud with the way the young man had grown into his role. Sublimating the normal instincts of young men to rely exclusively either on feel or book learning, Mallory had struck a balance within himself that made him seem mature beyond his years. If he seized opportunity aggressively, he did so with a panache that even his harshest competitors found irresistible. His private life was impeccable. His marriage and home life, such as they were, essentially consisted of sporadic visits to a Westchester suburb, where he kept his wife and son — of whom he seldom spoke. Nor did Waldo ask after them; he saw them as Mallory did: necessary accouterments to a splendid career.

His true bride, family, and very existence was the Cert; his true offspring the schemes he hatched that kept the Cert a step or two ahead of its competitors and yet never — for all their daring — got the bank into trouble or disgrace; his true home the gray limestone tower at 41 Wall Street. He was a loner, whose remoteness made him intriguing.

On business matters, he was the most accessible to the press of the world's ranking bankers. But the journalists were scarcely more enthusiastic in their praise than Preston Chamberlain.

'Wally, he pulled that Norsk Hydro syndication out from under Deutsche Bank as neat as mom's apple pie.'

'Manny Hanny thought they had us outflanked with Overseas Coastal, but after Manning got through with them, I had to call Gabe Hauge and ask him if he preferred mustard or ketchup with his crow.'

'I can tell you, Wally, if we get the GMAC lead, it'll be ninety percent Mallory.'

Wherever one turned, it was Manning Mallory this, Manning Mallory that. *American Banker*'s 'Bank Executive of 1969,' *Institutional Investor*'s 'Banker of the Year,' *Fortune*'s 'Man of the Year.'

Mallory lapped it up. As he confided to Waldo, 'Eat my dust, Walter Wriston.'

We can almost draw a circle around Manning's career, Waldo wrote 'Prof. Tze-Chung Chen,' *and mark it complete*.

Across the bay came the muffled boom of a starting cannon. The annual Independence Day Regatta was under way.

He sealed the letter. So much had been done. So much was in place. Ropespinner had indeed come a long way. What a genius Menchikov was to have foreseen it so clearly! How acute had his perceptions been! It went far beyond what Grigoriy modestly claimed: that his instincts about America came from reading and rereading Tocqueville.

What did Tocqueville know of computers, for instance? Look at the new technology of banking, in which CertBank, thanks to Mallory's personal involvement and enthusiasm, was the acknowledged leader. Just as Menchikov had foretold, ENIAC's progeny had matured into a formidable brood. The latest generation of computers could already produce and process data and transactions at a faster clip than human judgement — which the machines did not supply — could deal with.

The counting house had been replaced by the impersonal, somehow unreal computer screen. Banks and corporations were now able to move their free cash balances in Pavlovian fashion, reacting instinctively to the possibility of earning a fraction of a farthing more in Singapore than in Berne. In a way, thought Waldo approvingly, it made a game out of the system. What possible difference could it make to a billion-dollar corporation like Exxon to earn an extra .0005 percent on $20 million of overnight money? What possible difference could $100 make to Exxon?

But that, he knew, was no longer the point. It was the game that counted. The computer had made it unreal, and the generations of machines to come would only be faster and larger; judgement and reality would be left farther in the lurch by the speed of the process, by the thrill of it all.

The institutionalization of the stock market was far advanced. Look at CertCo. In 1955, when Mallory had come to the bank, two insurance companies, two mutual funds, and a handful of bank-managed trusts had between them owned perhaps 75,000 of its shares, less than 2 percent of the total. As Waldo sat on his porch, watching the colorful twinkle of bright sails on the bay, over 22 million shares, nearly 45 percent of the total outstanding, were in the hands of 127 investment institutions, many of which had not existed in 1955.

In 1955, Preston had been able to control the Cert with 150,000 shares in trusts he dominated, thanks to the complaisance of passive stockholders content with regular increases in the quarterly dividends. In 1970, though he would have been loath to admit it, Preston governed the bank at the sufferance of a coterie of institutions, most of them (unlike individuals) tax-exempt and thus with little compulsion to invest for the long term; many of them managed by fast-trigger types who rather liked blowing in and out of a big stock and watching the executive suite shake in the wind.

There had been one or two systematic accidents along the way, which Waldo saw as gratifying evidence that the system was becoming unstable. The Cert had by and large been barely grazed. It had not been too badly burned in the 1966 credit squeeze; it had pulled back just before Penn Central collapsed scarcely a month earlier.

All in all, the domestic banking situation was filled with promise for Ropespinner. Lending was ceasing to be a matter of evaluating collateral and character; increasingly, banks bought money in the open market for X percent and sold it at Y percent, often not bothering to match maturities.

'The risks in this business are grossly overestimated,' Mallory told a breakfast meeting of Boston financial journalists. 'I think we have established that the market is there for us when we need it, and that therefore any talk of a liquidity crisis is sheer kerfuffle.'

His remarks were repeated, in a burnished form, by Bernard Grogan in the next morning's *Wall Street Journal*, and stock market confidence ratcheted up a notch or two in the face of pretty discouraging economic news. Once again Waldo observed to his mirror his mild surprise at the truth of Mallory's privately expressed dictum: 'Put in enough of a commission for the goat and you'd be surprised how easy it is to sell goat's milk as cream.'

The Euromarket continued to burgeon. By 1970, no one

knew how many dollars were in the pool, and as long as there seemed to be a supply sufficient to meet any demand, no one really seemed to care — at least in the private sector. By now the banks had followed CertBank's lead in using the Eurodollar market to mint loanable dollars at will, without so much as a by-your-leave for the Federal Reserve. Mallory had also pushed the Cert heavily into foreign exchange trading. Daily clearances in the exchange market were pushing against what Waldo believed to be the existing system's limits of tolerance. Sooner or later this slosh of homeless dollars must overwhelm the probity of exchange rates.

On the home front, too, the Fed's iron grip seemed to be loosening. The invention of the one-bank holding company, an innovation to which CertCo beat out Citicorp by a matter of days, allowed banks to circumvent the Federal Reserve as they pleased when it came to raising money. With the complicity of Wall Street, the one-bank holding companies — CertCo, Citicorp, Chase Manhattan — could buy funds in the open market at rates that banks proper were forbidden by law to pay. The holding company format permitted them to operate with license and equanimity wherever the money flows were to be located. CertCo was as comfortable in Bangkok as in the Bronx; it was easier for Mallory to pull a billion dollars out of Bogotá than Boston.

Mallory was exultant. 'If we can do this overseas, how the hell are they going to keep us from going interstate? There's something un-American about letting a bank like ours do as it pleases in London but not in Los Angeles!'

Other barriers were crumbling. The old connections of habit and mutual interest that tied depositors to their local banks suddenly seemed out of date, now that banks were bidding openly for funds and the increasing categories of deposits were free to chase the highest available rate. The Penn Central crisis had obliged the Fed to remove the ceilings on large-denomination certificates of deposit. Thus another of Mallory's competitive camels had got his nose under the tent. If everything worked out logically, Waldo expected that another decade or so would see a wholesale dismantling of interest

132

rate ceilings. The possibilities implicit in that were almost too numerous to list.

In all these ideological struggles against the confines of regulation, Mallory was to be found at the forefront. His gift for knowing what would fly led him instinctively to a political vocabulary. He was gaining recognition as a spokesman, *the* spokesman for an open economic society.

Untrammeled by regulation: 'If our society can be liberated from the arcane and archaic rules which frightened bureaucrats imposed in panic nearly forty years ago, a new Golden Age...' (Mallory to the National Association of Homebuilders).

Untrammeled by government interference of any kind: 'The Federal jawbone is as lethal to the aspirations of free enterprise as that with which Cain slew Abel' (Mallory on the Op-Ed page of the *New York Times*).

Untrammeled by any constraint other than that imposed by the All-Sovereign Market: 'I'd have to say, Mr Spivak, that risk is the best arbitrator of sound banking practice, and we bankers are the best judges of risk' (Mallory on *Meet the Press*).

To the investor on the street, the Wall Street player, the great bankers who stroked each other in clubs, a splendid New Order was incarnated in Manning Mallory. The decade and a half of his ascendancy was the most progressive and positive era that banking had ever known, an era of liberation, in which the banks were beginning to be able to play the game they had enviously watched their Wall Street cousins playing on the other side of the fence. Best of all, thought Waldo on his porch, everyone seems to think this is a wonderful thing.

Now there was talk of bringing Mallory into politics. As Waldo knew, politics held no allure for Mallory, who dismissed politicians as small-timers and their power as phony. Mallory liked pitting himself against the big hitters, his competitors in the other banks and whoever happened to be Chairman of the Federal Reserve Board, to those who occupied what Mallory referred to collectively as 'the grownups' table.'

All in all, it was a most satisfactory state of affairs, thought Waldo: many credits, few debits, and much work still to be done.

Waldo had few complaints about the way things had worked out for himself. He had become an idol of the business community in his own right. His second book, *Money, Banking, and Corporate Policy*, had established itself on publication as the standard text in its field. He sat on the boards of a dozen corporations. His consulting fees had risen to $1,000 a day; his lecture and seminar fees were several times that. He could have filled his calendar thrice over, fifty weeks a year, with professional engagements. He had just turned fifty-eight, and middle age had given him a truly avuncular appearance: spindly and painstaking, his childish features seamed with the cares of the world. His was a shoulder on which even the toughest executive could lean for comfort and counsel. He felt no guilt about what he was doing. It had worked out just as Grigoriy had said: as an experiment in a laboratory.

The forces of free finance had arranged themselves in response to certain stimuli as obediently as molecules proving a theorem. It was almost beautiful, thought Waldo, for whom the true elegance was the dance of numbers across a page.

I concede you the palm, he had written only a month earlier, to 'Dom Alois Flugl, OB,' at an accommodation address near Augsburg.

> *You have seen what I imagine Schumpeter saw as well, but could scarcely bring himself to write. Perhaps it is what Marx also sensed, although I have never been able to get through Marx. As an empiricist, a measurer of observed phenomena, I would put it this way: Capitalism is potentially the best of all economic systems, but like all systems of enterprise, and perhaps all systems period, it depends for its thrust and perpetuation upon the basest, most ignoble human drives, most notably greed and egoism. That is its fatal, its suicidal paradox.*

Far out on the bay, Waldo could just make out the tiny multicolored sails of the QPYC Rainbow Fleet. He felt himself content and drowsy. In its way Ropespinner *was* noble work. No society deserved to endure that so compulsively dissipated its resources out of self-indulgence. The thought pleased him, as did the prospect of a warm, calm summer on the water.

He sat rocking. Soon it would be time to get going. He could mail the letter to Menchikov on his way over to the Yacht Club where, as he had each year since the war, he would lead the singing of 'America the Beautiful' at the annual Independence Day clambake. His conscience was clear, his mind busy.

So much to be done. Lectures to write, the new book to polish — wait until the economics profession got a look at the new theory he was proposing — Ropespinner's future to plan, and fresh corn and the gifts of the sea and long afternoons on the water. The outlook was blissful.

Then, out of the blue, the sky fell in.

CHAPTER TWELVE

Shortly after Columbus Day, 1970, Waldo received a call in Cambridge from Preston asking him to come to New York for a special meeting of CertCo's Executive Committee.

'Nothing to get the wind up about, Wally,' Preston assured him. 'Housekeeping, mostly. I've had an idea and I'd like to get the committee's thinking on it. Do a little brainstorming.'

That made Waldo suspicious. Preston wasn't a brainstormer. Preston's meetings were carefully prepared, agenda at each place, the participants given at least a week beforehand to review the materials under discussion. Meetings were built around audiovisual presentations that would have done an advertising agency proud. It also surprised Waldo that the meeting was to be at Preston's Fifth Avenue apartment, and not at 41 Wall.

When he arrived, two of the five outside members of CertCo's Executive Committee were drinking coffee with Preston in the handsome Regency library. Waldo sensed that some discussion had already taken place. Three committee members were absent: the two other 'outsiders,' in Europe, and Manning Mallory in Hong Kong.

Something is definitely up, thought Waldo. After the usual pleasantries, Preston posed himself against the mantel, under his prized Copley portrait of a Chamberlain ancestor, a picture that Waldo found dreary and pretentious.

'Well, fellows,' Preston said, using what Mallory called his Frank Merriwell voice, bluff and familiar, 'I guess you're wondering why I asked you to come here today. The fact is, I've got a bee in my bonnet.'

He paused for effect.

'Fellows, I've done a lot of thinking about the bank these last few months. I can tell you it started out at the Grove last summer. I had a chance to chew the fat with Art Burns . . .'

Well, that's accurately put, thought Waldo. The present Chairman of the Federal Reserve had got the banks through the Penn Central crisis by opening the money window. Once open, never again closed tight, thought Waldo. 'Bank liquidity crisis': the scariest words in Washington's lexicon. Like 'Fire!' in a crowded theater.

'Banking's changed a lot,' Preston continued, 'and I'm not getting any younger, you know. We have an obligation to think about the bank's future. I know I've been doing that. Took a lot of long walks at Fishers Island in August. Then, last week I saw Art — and Bill Martin, who if you ask me was the best damn chairman they ever had at the Fed — at the Greenbrier and we spent some time together, and that pretty much made my mind up for me.'

Waldo relaxed. He wondered why he didn't feel more exultant. The great moment was obviously at last at hand. Preston was going to step down, to make way for Mallory. Ropespinner was through to the top.

'To hear Art and Bill talk,' said Preston, 'the next few years might be pretty rough. The dollar's in tough shape overseas, and the feeling I got was, Don't look to Washington to fix it. Nixon doesn't seem to be very interested in exchange rates; that Kraut professor he's got whispering in his ear couldn't care damnall about economics, although I'm told he likes the caviar as much as the next chap. And, frankly, none of us are confident that this fellow Connally at Treasury's the real McCoy.'

No news there, thought Waldo. This regime in Washington was the most second-rate in his memory. The way the country was going, there was probably worse to come. In retrospect, Truman was looking pretty sound and FDR positively godlike.

'I can also tell you fellows — strictly on the QT, of course; Art wouldn't like this to get out for attribution — that the Fed's pretty concerned about the banking system. Penn Central knocked 'em for a loop. The CD market's blown up out of

137

all proportion. They don't like what's going on. This business about the Chase getting into the real estate business has them hot and bothered. I can see why. David's a prince of a fellow, but he doesn't know his ass from an arquebus about real estate.'

A heavy chuckle ran around the room.

'So the bottom line is they want us banks to throttle back. Take a harder look at our lending policies. What it adds up to is two steps backward before we take the next big one forward. I can tell you that Art's less than enthusiastic about these acquisition loans we've all been making. Matter of fact, I've made a note to speak to Manning when he gets back about putting a little more distance between the bank and this fellow Ling. Never liked the idea of some Johnny-come-lately from Houston or wherever buying a steel company in Ohio. Jones and Laughlin can't make money as it is; it's not likely to do better if it's got to factor in the cost of being bought with its own assets. How'll our interest get paid? Anyway, the bottom line is: Washington's asking us, politely, to step on the brakes for the time being.'

'And will you?' asked Waldo.

'You bet I will!' said his brother. 'I'm old enough to remember what it was like around here in the thirties. But frankly, I'm too old to fight this kind of a war alone, Wally. The horse is too rank for this old jockey to handle all by myself. We need a new man in the saddle.'

Waldo couldn't help himself. 'Which means you're turning the bank over to Manning? Finally, Pres! Well, I have to say I don't think you could put the place in better hands!'

But as he said the words, he felt a tremor of unease in the room. Preston paused, looked at the carpet for a moment, and then jutted a smile at Waldo.

'Well' — he paused again — 'not exactly, Wally. I don't exactly know how to put this, but it just seems to me that under the circumstances, Mallory — bright as he is, mind you — isn't the fellow I want to take over the wheel of this particular ship in these particular seas.'

Waldo's world glazed over crimson. His brother's explanation seemed to be coming from a great, great distance —

barely audible above the roaring in his ears. He started to say something.

'Now, Wally,' he heard Preston saying, with that patient condescension Waldo had hated all his life, 'I knew you'd take this hard. Believe me I did. Damn it, I've stayed awake nights trying to figure out how to cushion the shock. But it just beats me how to do it. We all know Manning's your protégé. People around here aren't as blind or stupid as you sometimes seem to think we are. We all know you've been behind a lot of the stuff Manning's gotten the credit for, but as long as it was good for the bank, I let it go by. Besides, Manning's about the brightest fellow around. Almost too clever, too bright, too go-go for an old fuddyduddy like me. I'm extremely fond of him myself, but, damn it, Wally, at the end of the day I have to do what I believe, as a fiduciary for our stockholders and depositors, is in the best long-term interests of the bank!'

While Waldo gathered his thoughts, his mind now working coolly, calculatedly behind his mask of shock, one of the other outside directors spoke up.

'I have to say I'm surprised myself. For the last couple of years I suppose I've taken it as a given that in the due course of events Manning would take over for you. The man's a genius. When it comes to banking. This is the greatest bank in the world, Pres, the one all others look up to, and next to you, he built it!'

Preston turned on him. 'A lot of people helped build CertCo to where it is, Johnny. A lot.' The other man looked at his hands.

Waldo cast around for help from his fellow directors. Silence. It was clearly Preston's show.

'Wally,' said Preston, 'no one argues that Manning's not a star. Hell, compared to the rest of us, he's Gable and Tracy and John Wayne rolled up into one! He'd have been one even without your coaching, brother dear. Nevertheless, the fact is that my short hairs are telling me that what makes for stardom these days isn't necessarily what makes for sound banking. I think things are moving a little too fast around here, not to mention the damn foolishness I keep seeing our

139

competition getting themselves into. The way it is, half the time I don't really know what's going on. We're starting to behave too much like our little friends on the Stock Exchange, and that's what got us into trouble in 1929. I don't suppose any of you have tried to track what our foreign exchange people are up to. Like that Hong Kong business last year. How the hell did that happen? I'd've bet dollars to doughnuts that if anyone around here had a handle on his operations it was Frank Laurence, and yet look what happened! It's these damn computers. They make everything happen so fast. Too damn fast, if you ask me! No one has time to think. And I don't mind telling you I don't like the way certain people like getting their picture in the papers.'

'Are you saying that Manning's so-called "high visibility" has been bad for this bank's business?' asked Waldo. 'Because if you are—'

Preston raised a placatory hand. 'Wally, take it easy,' he said firmly. 'Of course it's been good for business. But now it's time to slow down. We can afford it. My problem is, I doubt Manning's capable of slowing down. Or hiding his light. I never in my life saw a fellow who liked the limelight more. Must take him an hour to get dressed; never see the fellow in the same necktie twice. I suppose you don't think I've noticed how he plays up to this fellow Grogan at the *Journal*?'

'Preston, this is the way banking is nowadays,' Waldo shot back. 'Manning's one of the people who've shucked off the green eyeshade and brought us into the twentieth century.' He tried to sound reasonable. Behind the screen his mind was organizing a damage control party to save Ropespinner.

'That's precisely my point,' Preston responded. 'And now it's time to take stock. Mallory's sort of personality was ideal while we were building the bank, but now that it's built, I think we ought to consolidate. Let our competition do the pioneering, test the footing at the edge of the abyss. Let the Citi and Manny Hanny and Continental Illinois be the ones to get their rear ends in a sling.'

'Is it appropriate to ask if you've got anyone in mind?' asked one of the other directors, as if reading from a script. 'Frankly, looking around the bank, I can't say any names come to mind.'

Oh, my God, thought Waldo as he saw Preston start to nod. Of course! As it usually did, his mind took off reflexively, shipping ahead to conclusions others would struggle to reach. He knew the answer.

'I have,' said Preston. He took a deep breath, as if he knew that what he was about to say was shocking, presumptuous. 'The fact is, I've decided to bring Pete back from the Chase.'

For a moment there was silence as the others digested this information. Waldo could see that his colleagues were surprised; Preston's strictures against nepotism were legendary.

But there was no capital Waldo could make of that. Not any longer. Peter Chamberlain had established himself as a known quantity. He had proven to be a first-class banker, had risen to Senior Executive Vice-President, a member of the office of the Chief Executive at the Chase, and a director of the bank and its holding company. Higher things were rumored to be in store for him. The Chase was a well-known administrative snake pit. Manning had told Waldo he had heard that now Herbert Patterson had edged John Place, Place would leave, Peter would be promoted, and within a year or so Patterson would be edged sideways or out and Peter would take over as David Rockefeller's sole heir, with this fellow Butcher backing him up.

Unlike Mallory, Peter Chamberlain was not widely known outside banking circles. The ration of publicity at the Chase was reserved exclusively for its chairman, who had an entire apparatus within the bank, led by a sort of administrative valet, an Osric in gray flannel, who beat the publicity drum for D.R. At the time the Cert had been chosen by the government to review the Ginnie Mae financing, Mallory had made the cover of *Forbes* for a second time and been the subject of a three-page article in *Newsweek*. Peter Chamberlain's picture had been published twice in *American Banking*. Nevertheless, Waldo knew, among bankers Peter Chamberlain's stock stood very high.

What shocked Waldo was that Preston's near-Calvinist probity should have countenanced Peter's scandalous private life. Or that David Rockefeller, himself not a little blue in the stocking department, should have turned the other cheek when, just five years earlier, Peter had run off with the wife of a man in the Chase's Chicago office.

Waldo didn't like the new Mrs Peter Chamberlain. She struck him as pushy and flashy. She came already equipped with a child, a daughter, and she and Peter had promptly produced a little boy of their own, an accomplishment Waldo considered unseemly for people past the age of thirty-five. Nevertheless, blood counted, so Waldo flew the family flag, and Peter and his new family were invited to Quiddy every Thanksgiving.

Actually, Waldo had to admit he had grown genuinely fond of Peter's stepdaughter. She was twenty now, a sophomore studying art history at Radcliffe, and Waldo made a point of having her to dinner in his Cambridge apartment at least once a month. She was said to have a bright future. Indeed, Waldo's friend Sydney Freedberg, the Norton professor and a true connoisseur of budding art historians, characterized Elizabeth Bennett as one of his most promising students and proposed to take her on as a summer research assistant in her senior year. Elizabeth was quiet and self-assured, so entirely different from her mother that Waldo could only assume she took after her father. In any case, Elizabeth made the crowded Quiddy Thanksgivings bearable for Waldo. He looked forward to seeing her there in a few weeks' time, provided he could get this problem settled.

Preston was still talking. Waldo's mind, which had briefly slipped away, as if into executive session with itself, returned to the present. A germ of an idea was pushing toward the front of his consciousness, an idea that made him grow cold and yet offered the only way out. In the background, he heard one of the others asking Preston if he'd spoken to David Rockefeller about Peter. The great banks of the world observed a cautious intermural diplomacy when it came to stealing one another's people.

'Not yet,' said Preston. 'He and that circus troupe of his are off gallivanting around the Middle East until the beginning of the month and then it's Manning's and my turn to kiss hands in Teheran. I've made a date to see him right after Thanksgiving. As a matter of fact, the Monday we get back from Quiddy, Wally.'

Waldo's mind was on automatic pilot, going through the checklist. What had happened in this room was a dead issue, beyond alteration. But there were certain things he needed to know.

'What about Peter?' asked Waldo. 'What have you said to him?' He prayed that Preston was still a stickler for form in some things. He got the answer he wanted.

'Not a word. Can't, either; not until I've had a chat with David. That's why I'll have to ask you gentlemen to keep what's been said here in this room until after Thanksgiving. May I have your word on that?'

The other two nodded. They were old-fashioned souls, Waldo knew, and thank heavens for that, because they would keep their word, and he needed time.

We have roughly five weeks, he thought. He knew what he must do, but before then he would have to talk to Mallory, who wasn't due back for another fortnight.

He knew what to do, yes; but now events had moved onto another plane, and to carry on he knew that he would also first have to inform Mallory about Ropespinner.

He supposed it wasn't strictly necessary to tell Mallory everything. It might not even be necessary to tell him anything. After all, Waldo knew exactly what needed to be done, and he had decided that it should be done, notwithstanding that the thought of his own loss — well, his massive but temporary inconvenience — aggravated him.

Nevertheless, after much dithering, he decided that he must tell Mallory. The only solution he could find involved a psychological burden that he simply could not bear alone.

The delay before he could see Mallory seemed interminable, and even then he was able only to catch the banker on the fly, between a change of suitcases en route from Tacoma to Asunción.

They met in a Manhattan apartment maintained by one of Waldo's consulting clients. Mallory seemed impatient, out of sorts. He wanted to know why they couldn't have met at his place or in the CertCo suite in the Waldorf Towers. Waldo assured him that he would understand when he heard what his mentor had to say.

'OK,' said Mallory, 'I'm ready when you are. Don't let me put you off, Waldo. I'm pissed, frankly. I suppose you've heard that Washington's jawboned your brother out of making what they call "nonproductive" loans? Merger financing. Fat rates plus nice loan fees going in. I've got a dozen we can commit on tomorrow, but it's no go. That's a lot of money out the window, Waldo. This is very profitable business. Anyway, what's up?'

Waldo hesitated and bought time by assuring Mallory that acquisition lending was an idea whose time had not yet come. It would, although possibly not for a while yet; the memory of the collapsed financial pools and pyramids — Shenandoah and Blue Ridge and the Insull empire — of the twenties was still too fresh in the minds of too many men. Let it incubate.

It was the resentment in Mallory's voice that determined Waldo's order of battle. He had debated long and inconclusively with himself about the sequence in which he would say his piece. Finally, he had decided to let his sense of the moment make up his mind for him.

He began by telling Mallory about the meeting in Preston's apartment. He recited what had occurred. When he had finished, he crossed his hands over his stomach and watched the impact of his narrative sink in.

Mallory said nothing for almost a minute. Then he shook his head, whistled through his teeth, and got up quickly, as if propelled by an adrenal rush he couldn't subdue. He left the room.

When Mallory came back, he was pale. 'Sorry,' he said. 'Thought I was going to blow my lunch. Couldn't.' He sat down heavily. 'Those dirty sons of bitches,' he muttered. He shook his head again. 'Those dirty fucking sons of bitches!'

Waldo watched him, waiting for Mallory to say something

144

more, but nothing was said. The wheels were turning, but spinning as if in snow or sand. Mallory had no answer.

After a minute, Waldo added an additional dash of spice to the stew. 'I suppose,' he offered mildly, 'it would be possible for you to work with Peter?'

Mallory examined him as if he had said the world was flat. 'Don't be disingenuous, Waldo. You know the answer to that. Even if I said yes, the fact is that when Peter takes over, the first thing he's going to do is cut my nuts off. I've got fifteen years down there. The place is full of my people. People who owe me for their careers! Customers who want to deal with me! Peter's no dope. He knows that. He can't function with me and my private army around. So he'll neutralize me first. Put in his own board. Consolidate from the top. Shit, I'd do the same thing. Peter's not so stupid he'd try to superimpose a lot of jerks from the Chase. He'll make it so I have to get out. Find somewhere else to go.'

'Well, what about another bank?'

'Waldo, think! The Cert is *my* bank! It's where it's at for me! Yesterday I was Numero Uno in the whole world. Six weeks from now I'll be just another Number Two! Maybe I'd find something at Citi or Chase, something ornamental, Vice-Chairman in charge of kissing ass. I'd rather be fucking dead! You think I want to go through the rest of my life knowing every jerk in town's saying, "Capable chap, but not quite capable enough"?'

Mallory shook his head. His mouth tightened almost convulsively, as if he was about to break down with anger and frustration. Then he got hold of himself. 'Those fucking sons of bitches,' he muttered again. 'Fifteen fucking years.' He sounded as if he was about to cry.

Waldo went for Mallory's mood like a striking snake. 'Well, Manning,' he said, 'there is one thing.' And he told him about Ropespinner. Told him everything. Told him about the smoky hours after Keynes's funeral, and Menchikov setting forth his great idea. Told him how he had been discovered, cultivated, and used. Told him about the subtle 'contributions' Menchikov had made to Mallory's great career. Told him what it was all about, what its objectives were, even what it was called.

He knew he could be taking a great risk, and yet somehow he really didn't think he was. Mallory's whole being had been pushed to the edge by Preston: his life, career, pride, ambition, ego, the whole ball of wax. Now it was Mallory peering down into the abyss.

When he finished, Mallory looked at him incredulously. For a moment time seemed to hang in the balance. Then Mallory began to laugh, and Waldo knew he had won.

'Well, I'll be a son of a bitch,' Mallory said. 'This is turning out to be a hell of an evening for me, Waldo. First you tell me I've been backstabbed and everything I've worked for and wanted is about to be snatched away, flushed right down the toilet!

'Then you calmly inform me that for the last fifteen years, all the time I've thought I was becoming the greatest banker in the world, a man of vision, a hero of capitalism, I've really been an unknowing pawn of the International Communist Conspiracy! That all the time I've been making the world safe for banking I've really been conniving at the destruction of the American way of life!'

He started to laugh, then shook his head. 'Jesus Christ, Waldo, is this for real? Or am I dreaming?'

'It's absolutely for real, Manning. But think of it as an experiment. Did you have a chemistry set as a boy? Think of yourself as the vital ingredient.'

He watched as Mallory got up and went across the room to make himself a drink.

When he came back, it was clear he'd thought deeper through the implications of what Waldo had told him. He made Waldo go through it again, step by step. When Waldo finished, he laughed again, obviously at some inner joke. He knocked back his drink, put down the glass, and said, 'OK, you've told me A and you've told me B. What's the C? There's got to be one. You want me to guess? I will. The sixty-four-dollar question is: Do I go along, or do I go to the FBI?'

'And what would you tell the FBI, Manning?'

Mallory shaped his right hand into an imaginary revolver

and flicked it at Waldo, clicking his tongue. He obviously had no answer.

'Now, Manning, there *is* an alternative. It involves some — well, *sacrifices*. I needn't go into those. It's the course events take from tonight that we need to agree upon. I've taken a risk in telling you everything, but there's no other way. We can go forward or stop right now. Do you want to think it over? There's not a great deal of time, but I'm sure a day or so wouldn't matter.'

'It sort of plays itself, doesn't it?' said Mallory. He was calm. He might have been thinking his way around a loan restriction. 'A: I say no to the Red Brigade and ride off into the sunset, and in six weeks the phone'll start ringing with headhunters asking if I'd consider becoming Vice-Chairman of E. F. Hutton. Big fucking deal! B: I throw in with you and the Red Menace and the game goes on, right?'

'That is more or less correct,' said Waldo.

'The question I've been asking myself is: Does this really change the game?'

'I think that's something I can't answer for you, Manning. I have my own opinion, however.'

'And what is that?'

'I think it doesn't change it. I think it all *is* a game, you see. I think, if anything, this makes it even more fun — adds a new dimension, if you will.'

Mallory thought for a moment, then leaned forward conspiratorially. 'I kind of agree with you. You're right about it's being a game. It was a game back at the B School, and it's a game at the bank. After you get to a certain level, it's not even about money. It's the competition, the thrill of the hunt; it's beating out the other guy. It's anything that takes you higher, faster, farther. It's not making anything except making something bigger. With banks, big is what counts. And being first to the wire. Winning. And that's what I like about it: the game part. I like competition. I like winning. I like the feeling I get watching these jerks out there tying themselves in knots trying to trump our ace. Maybe that's what they call "power." I don't give a shit about the money. I don't even give a shit about getting my picture in the paper, or being famous, except that it helps us against the other banks. And I sure as hell don't give a shit about the future, because I'm not going to be there to see it!

'Waldo, the bank's the only game I know. It's the big table. Only grownups get to play. I've got fifteen years tied up here. I'm fucked if I'm going to start off all over again in East Podunk or Seattle. But suppose I say OK. What's the bottom line?'

'The bottom line?'

'Where does it end? It has to end someday, doesn't it? When?'

Waldo hesitated. Be honest, he told himself. 'Manning, I'm not sure I know. Well, I suppose I do, actually. I suppose there will come a day when we would have to take wing.'

'Do a Philby, huh?'

'In a manner of speaking.'

For a while both men were silent — Mallory thinking, Waldo watching.

Finally Mallory said, 'You understand I don't give a merry screw about the politics?'

'I do understand; indeed, as far as the politics of this go, I consider myself an agnostic. I will say that I find America rapacious, wasteful, inhumane, and I think it deserves whatever it brings on its own head. Basically, however, I consider myself as participating in an interesting scientific experiment. In mass psychology, if you will. Or physics. Or virology.'

He told Mallory about Menchikov's metaphors.

'And I'm the germ that poisoned Lake Superior.' Mallory laughed. 'I'm flattered!' He paused, but only for a second. 'Count me in!'

Waldo said nothing.

Mallory got up and stretched. He went to the window and looked down at the street through the blinds. When he turned back, he said, 'Christ, I've been a spy for five minutes, and already I'm acting like Secret Agent X-Nine. Technically, what am I, Waldo? A financial mole? What would they call me in Dzerzhinsky Square?'

'I don't know.'

Mallory sat back down. Suddenly it seemed as if there was nothing left to say. Then he brightened.

'You know, this puts a whole new glow on things. It sort of gives a point to the whole thing. Gives it a kind of shape. Before, it was just a business of running faster and faster without knowing where the finish line was, unless it was death or retirement.'

He got up.

'Well, I'm off to South America in the morning. Hey, this is going to be fun. I'm going to turn that fucking Wriston inside out trying to keep up with me. You know, Waldo, you've taken an enormous load off my shoulders. A couple of times I've pulled up short. Been worried about taking the bank too close to the edge. Now I find the bank didn't give a shit about me!'

They shook hands. At the door, Mallory turned and grinned at Waldo.

'You know the funny thing?'

'No, what?'

'The funny thing is: I was just thinking that between working for the greater glory of capitalism and the shareholders on one hand, or working for Moscow to turn the whole fucking system upside down on the other, I can't think of one goddamn thing I'd have done differently!'

Waldo gave Mallory the benefit of an extra day in which to change his mind. He expected to hear nothing and he heard nothing. The next morning, when he called the bank, in a way hoping (he later supposed, mulling the whole business over) for a reprieve from having to take the next step, he was informed that Mr Mallory had left the night before for South America. Waldo had his answer.

That evening, for the first time since he had been given it, Waldo dialed the emergency number with which he was regularly supplied. He would have preferred to exchange letters with Menchikov, but there was not enough time.

He was called back within an hour. He outlined the problem.

The next afternoon, he was called in Cambridge and given instructions and a cover story.

He assumed that Menchikov had at least been put in the picture. He hoped so. It would mean that Menchikov would have endorsed Waldo's one tiny concession to conscience and emotion, his unspoken admission that, great as it was, Ropespinner was not worth every last single flickering candle on earth.

The Thanksgiving fire at the Chamberlain house was not the worst disaster in the history of Hancock County.

Strictly speaking, the *worst* disaster had been the loss of a fishing boat during the '38 hurricane. Twelve people had been lost then; here the dead count was only five, and at least one person had gotten out. Two, if you counted Waldo Chamberlain's not being there.

The fire chief guessed the fire had started in some old wiring. Then the old insulation had burned; the poison smoke had probably got 'em before the flames did. The way the house was set back in the woods, it was darn near halfway burned down before a late-night fishing boat had spotted it while making its way back to Quiddy. By the time the volunteer fire department got there, all that was left to do was wet down the embers.

Such a terrible tragedy, mourned the locals: Mr Waldo's brother killed, and his wife, and their son, and *his* wife, almost a bride too, and their little boy. All the Thanksgiving party except Mr Waldo, who was away, and the young lady, who had been in the back bedroom, away from where the fire started; that had surely saved her, even though it was still a miracle she got out. The way she'd come through that upstairs window, why, it was like she'd been shot or throwed through it. Well, fear did that to a body. Anyway, she wasn't burned too bad, although she was in shock. The ambulance had taken her to Portland.

A good thing too, probably, the way these reporters from as far away as Boston had suddenly materialized. Of course, Mr Waldo was famous, and his brother too, but these fellows were acting like his brother's death was on a par with the Kennedy killings or that colored fellow who got himself shot

150

down in Memphis a few years back. Everybody in Quiddy knew Mr Chamberlain's brother was a big banker down in New York, but up here he had always acted kind of stiff and stuck-up. 'Course he only came up Thanksgivings and maybe a few other times.

From the sheriff's point of view, the worst part was having to tell Mr Waldo, especially this way. Here it was, a lovely clear morning despite the house smoking and the corpses in those bags they'd borrowed from the Bangor Police laid out on the lawn waiting for the coroner, and suddenly — *whuckety-whuck!* — here came Mr Waldo in a helicopter, back from some meeting or something he'd been called away to. Lucky thing, that, for him, but what he must have thought, swinging in over the trees that way and seeing his house just a pile of wet ashes and all, and the body bags on the grass, and such. It was a mercy he hadn't had a heart attack, even though he wasn't all that old a man. Not even sixty, Mary Arthurs said, and she should know.

He just seemed stunned when the sheriff told him what had happened. Didn't seem to understand, which wasn't surprising. Asked about the girl and was happy — the sheriff guessed — when he found out she was all right, even if she was in shock and couldn't seem to remember anything. After that he'd just kept mumbling about rebuilding the house, which the sheriff thought was pretty gritty, just like it was gritty of him to give some time to those reporters and all, especially since all they wanted to write about was who Mr Preston and Peter — at least *he* used to come here regular — had been, how important and that sort of thing.

Anyway, it was a mercy to the sheriff when Mr Waldo asked the pilot who'd brung him if he'd mind flying him down to Portland where the girl was, and maybe after that to Boston. The pilot was a regular fellow and, besides, what could he do under the circumstances, and so everyone breathed just a bit easier when the helicopter finally lifted off, bearing away its cargo of trouble and sorrow, and they could get back to living, which was what a body had to do, no matter what.

THE PRESENT

December

CHAPTER THIRTEEN

PARIS
Thursday, December 12th

Elizabeth sat at her desk, idly watching a sparse rain dribble out of the smoky-gray sky into the place des Victoires, and wondered if it was conceivable that she could be truly falling in love.

No, no, no, she thought, it's simply impossible. The scheduling alone put it out of the question. He in New York, as committed to his work as much as she was to hers; he rooted by vocation to one place while she spent half her life trooping around the world. If it was going to work out, something would have to give, and — damn it! — there wasn't another job like hers anywhere else on earth, but there was also no way she could see for him to rearrange his affairs to suit hers.

It was obviously impossible. And yet, and yet . . .

Well, she'd just have to see how it went. The scheduling could be arranged; things like that always could. It was the feeling that couldn't be arranged around, and the feeling was distinctly there. She was going to London toward the end of the month; she'd call Heywood Hill to get her the right books to bone up on. The bookshop's proprietor, an old friend, would want to know why these books; he'd guess something was up. Perhaps he could also recommend something; and not — as he usually did — eight hundred pages by George Eliot.

Why do I always do this to myself? she thought. At her age, life and love ought to go together easier; romance should be little more than a matter of sifting through the stock on hand, to turn up an agreeable, attractive man from Christie's or one of the ministries or even a bank. No one from Wall Street; the kind that talks about deals all the time. Although Francis had talked about money — but not in a way she would have expected.

Nothing about him was what she ever would have expected.

Damn Luc! She shook her head and tried to study the folder before her. Julien Agnew had an exclusive on a 'superb' Guido Reni in a private Scottish collection, a 'Joshua' which was probably a pair to the striking 'David' in the Louvre. The transparency looked terrific, and Guido Reni was coming into his own after a century of being dismissed as merely an assembly-line source of sappily sentimental Madonnas. Agnew's asserted there'd be no trouble about an export license. Elizabeth wasn't so certain. The new director of the National Gallery of Scotland was very aggressive. Anyway, if she wanted, she could see the picture in January in New York, where it was being cleaned at the Met by John Brealey preparatory to going to Detroit for an exhibition.

Now the prospect of New York in January was positively appealing. She called Julian Agnew and made a date to meet him in New York the first week of the New Year.

Her phone rang. London again, this time the head of the furniture department at Sotheby's. The week before he'd accompanied her through the Clichy warehouse where Concorde stored its French furniture. He'd been impressed. He hadn't realized that Concorde had bought many of the pieces she showed him. Now, over the phone, he importuned her to put the Riesener *bureau plat* and the Louis XV *secrétaire* in the big sale Sotheby's was scheduling for May in Monte Carlo. He knew exactly who'd go after them, he said: a woman from New Jersey, another from Los Angeles, a man from Nashville, an Arab from London, possibly the Getty. They would bring at least seven figures each. Pounds.

Listening to his pitch, Elizabeth smiled at his choice of words; the art world still spoke of three genders of big spender: men, women, and Arabs. When he had finished, she teased him for a moment by fibbing that Christie's also wanted the pieces and had offered to waive the seller's commission. She didn't mind lying to the auction houses; they lied to everyone themselves. She extracted a satisfactory deal: no commission to be paid by Concorde, the two pieces to be fully illustrated in the catalog in color — with details — and a kill fee equal to 20 percent of Sotheby's recommended reserve if the pieces didn't sell. This was her own innovation. It kept the auction houses honest and saved her the trouble of reintroducing into the market objects tarnished by going unsold against an over-optimistic reserve. Unlike dealers, Elizabeth never put objects in auctions simply to establish a floor price. Tony's motto was: When you want to sell, sell!

She said she'd think it over; she knew she'd probably con-sign the stuff to Sotheby's. Compared to its rivals, Sotheby's might seem a shade vulgar and promotional, but for this sort of thing they would put on the dog. Just now, Christie's seemed a little out of phase with the times.

Nevertheless, she was damned if she was going to make this young man's day right off the bat, let him trot off to Jermyn Street thinking he'd earned the price of a champagne lunch at Wilton's. Anyway, she'd want to talk to Herve Aaron and to Rossi at Aveline; they might have some private clients for the big pieces.

Hanging up, she found that her mind had again turned, for per-haps the hundredth time since the weekend, to Francis Mather.

She and Luc had arrived in Colmar late Friday night; Mather hadn't shown up until Saturday lunch. He met them at the Haeberlins' restaurant in Illhaeusern, having driven up from Basel, where he had been giving a seminar. Probably on Eurobonds, she thought. The fixed income traders at Concorde were always rushing off to Eurobond seminars given by New York investment bankers in the best Swiss and French hotels, always strategically close to three-star restaurants.

At first blush, Mather had struck her as standard-issue Wall Street. Attractive, probably a few years older than he looked — say in his middle forties. About six feet tall, maybe a shade less, with nice dark hair, neatly parted and cut on the short side, and brown eyes behind gold-framed eyeglasses. He was definitely on the thin side, but mercifully without that grayish, drawn look that meant jogging and health clubs and seltzer with all meals. His clothes were nicely cut: tweed jacket, a faintly checked shirt with what could have been a club tie, flannels, and those awful tasseled moccasins that American investment bankers favored. He had a pleasant voice, with occasional overtones of East Coast prep school, but he slid easily from French into English and back again. His French was neither labored nor affected. After she had observed him for ten minutes, Elizabeth decided he was a superior specimen of the genus *Investment banker Americanus*, with a good education that Wall Street hadn't completely worn away; although he didn't talk about tender offers and interest rates, she put him down as definitely Morgan Stanley or Goldman, Sachs.

Lunch was delicious, the Alsatian wine refreshing and spicy, and there was plenty of it. At least twice, Elizabeth thought she caught Mather looking at her with interest; well, looking at — as always seemed to be the case on first acquaintance — her bosom. In spite of herself, she started to flush faintly and drew the loose folds of her heavy sweater around her protectively. When she did so, she thought she caught him blushing in turn. He went back to digging at his truffle in pastry and began nervously to swap Wall Street gossip with Luc. His obvious abashment charmed her. She decided he was a very likable man.

After lunch, they drove over to Colmar. The late-afternoon light was just turning golden when they arrived at the Musée Unterlinden. They went directly to the Isenheim altarpiece. Elizabeth had seen it a half-dozen times, but it was still too strange and cruel and poignant not to be fresh even to her sophisticated eye. She stood back while Mather walked around it, examining the shutters, the wings, stopping to admire the bursting, blazing aureole of the Resurrection, finally coming back to stand beside her looking up at the central panel depicting the Crucifixion.

She wondered if Mather would like a little quick art history, a fast tour of the apocalyptic spirit in early sixteenth-century northern painting. No, she thought; something told her to keep still. In the background, Luc fidgeted. Museums bored him. He was probably already thinking about dinner.

She sneaked a sideways glance at Mather.

He was staring up at the torn and scourged figure of Christ, at the painful gaping night-frozen agony of the scene. Golgotha resembled the surface of the moon. Christ's agony was transformed into a frozen stalactite of pain and grief.

Mather was obviously unaware of any other presence around him. Somehow, Elizabeth sensed him experiencing the painting in a direct way she could not. It was as if he had physically entered Grünewald's fearsome tableau.

She looked again at Francis Mather and suddenly wanted to reach out and take his hand as if to comfort him. She realized that what he felt was beyond words, that there was something going on between him and the painting into which she dared not trespass. As he stood there and stared at the picture, she felt that he had left her and Luc and this museum. She found it hard to breathe, as if all the air had been pumped out of the moment.

Finally, he shook his head, as if to clear himself of the strong feelings that had gripped it, took a bright handkerchief from his jacket pocket, and wiped his eyes.

'Goodness,' he said, putting his glasses back on. He took a deep breath.

'You know,' said Luc, obviously immersed in his own sense of the moment, 'they do the best *noisettes de chevreuil* at Schillinger's. I think I'll have that tonight.'

Suddenly Elizabeth despised him. Unfeeling insensitive Luc! Stupid bloody trivial Luc! She felt diminished to be with him, embarrassed to be sharing his room, his bed.

Back at the hotel, Luc only made it worse. Mather was in the adjoining room and Luc, as if the proximity of his friend stimulated him, became ardent, insistent, uncontrollable, irresistible. He was — damn him! — ingenious and adept in his lovemaking. He could always do this to her, damn it, she thought, feeling the orgasm rising in her, feeling gross and vulgar to be doing this with Mather right next to them. The thick stucco walls, the fat oaken door, suddenly became as insubstantial as onionskin. Terrible delicious sensations she couldn't put off attacked her, came right up her legs, up her belly, demanding that she give them voice while Luc thrashed and slid and slopped inside her and grunted like an animal. Some small part of her mind held an image of Mather in the next room, reading, thinking long thoughts, long important thoughts; she saw him hearing the gutter sounds through the wall, saw him realizing that it was her making some of those sounds and hating for him to think that. Just at the end, just before her orgasm overcame her, she tried like hell to choke back the noises in her throat and prayed to sweet wish-granting God that maybe Mather had gone out for a walk, gone downstairs, gone anywhere but where he could hear her and Luc and what she heard herself saying . . .

At dinner, mercifully, Mather gave no sign of having been aware of anything. Perhaps the walls were as thick as they looked.

Luc continued to irritate her. He always liked to show off to his American friends and clients, but tonight he seemed worse than ever; he made an elaborate production of ordering, abused the waiters and the sommelier, sent back what she and Mather confirmed to each other by raised eyebrows was a perfectly good Riesling.

'What a terrible thing this business of Mallory retiring from CertBank,' Luc said. He waved violently for more wine. 'A great man, don't you think, Francis?'

Manning Mallory, thought Elizabeth. Funny to hear that name again.

'Not really,' Mather replied. Elizabeth thought she detected an edge under his mild tone.

'An absolute genius!' declared Luc. 'Without Mallory, banking would be *phmph*! *Tout phmph*!' He banged the table with his fork. A few droplets of wine splashed onto the table. 'Without Mallory, Mexico *phmph*! Argentina *phmph*! Everything *phmph*!'

Mather smiled.

'I didn't know you had such strong opinions, Luc. And I don't know that I agree with you,' he said. He was obviously trying to defuse the situation.

Luc waved an admonitory finger at him. Elizabeth felt mortified.

'The greatest banker ever, the greatest, my friend. No question! Without Mallory, banking would still be in the nineteenth century!' Luc refilled his glass.

'Where I'm not sure it doesn't belong,' said Mather genially. 'I must say, I can't deny what the man's accomplished, and

I certainly can't argue about his influence. He cracks the whip, and the rest of the bankers hop up on their stools and purr. But I do have to say, my dear friend, that it's my opinion — and its most unchristian of me, I admit — that twenty years from now, thirty, when the judgement of history is in, your Mr Mallory is going to be perceived as the fiscal equivalent of a war criminal. At least in terms of what he's meant to Western capitalism — or what he's done to it!'

Luc managed a crooked, condescending grin. '*C'est stupide, ça.*'

Mather leaned forward, his expression serious. Don't waste your time, Elizabeth thought; Luc's past trying to argue with. She wished there was some new topic she could gracefully introduce. She tried to pass a signal with her eyebrows.

'Look, dear friend,' said Mather. 'In my view, and I admit it's from a different perspective from yours, most everything Mallory's led banking into has been an unmitigated long-term disaster promoted in the name of short-term profits. Look at his great innovations: petrodollar recycling, which may have been the single dumbest idea any banker ever had; the institutionalization of corporate stock ownership — again an absolute disaster. Don't take what his PR puts out as gospel, Luc, because—'

Mather saw that his audience was far gone, so he pulled up short.

He looked over at Elizabeth and shrugged. Luc sat up with a start and called loudly for *eau de vie de poire Williams*.

'Sorry,' Mather said to Elizabeth. 'There are about three things in life that get my blood boiling, and Manning Mallory's one of them.'

'Don't give it a thought,' Elizabeth replied. She had very little opinion on the subject, although what Mather said certainly seemed to echo her own boss's apprehensions about the financial state of the world.

'I've always thought of banks as churches,' she said.

'And so, in their way, they can be,' replied Mather, smiling. 'But believe me, these days they're not.'

Should she bring up Uncle Waldo, she wondered? No, the

161

evening was difficult enough. Why did people have to get so excited about things like banking?

They returned to their hotel for coffee in the bar. Luc ordered another *poire* and fell asleep. Mather and Elizabeth talked about some of the other things they'd seen that day.

She felt that Mather was using his chitchat as a screen from behind which to observe her. She was doing the same thing, the way as a young girl she used to spy on her parents from behind the furniture. Mather really was very attractive. He didn't know much about art history, she guessed, but he appeared to love music and the opera, so he was no philistine. She wondered how he lived, what he did after and away from the office, whom he saw, whom he slept with.

Then her thoughts switched to Mallory. He couldn't be as evil as Mather implied he was. He was just a banker.

'*L'heure de sommeil est arrivée, mes enfants,*' Luc suddenly announced, and rose unsteadily.

The three of them made their way upstairs, Luc leaning heavily on Elizabeth. Outside their door, they said good night. Elizabeth felt Luc's hand slide from around her shoulders, pause with obscene obviousness on the side of her right breast, asserting possession, and descend to her haunch. She felt herself redden.

'Good night, Elizabeth,' Mather said, hand outstretched. Instinctively she presented her cheek to be kissed; he brushed it lightly with his lips. In the background, Luc mumbled something about touring the vineyards the next day.

'Good night, Francis,' Elizabeth said. Without quite realizing what she was doing, she reached out and squeezed his hand.

When she awoke the next morning, it was almost ten; a groan next to her, and a distinctive odor, told her that Luc was in the throes of a poisonous hangover and wouldn't come around until at least noon, when he would be able to force down a Kronenbourg and get going again.

She bathed, dressed, and went downstairs. The day was gray and the street slick with evidence of an overnight rain. There was a bit of frost in the air. It might even snow, she thought. Thank God they were flying back. The long train ride to Paris, with Luc in his condition, would have been a nightmare.

Just as she turned to go back inside, a car pulled into the courtyard and a hand emerged from the driver's window and waved to her.

'Elizabeth! Good morning!' Francis Mather's smiling face appeared.

'Goodness,' she said. 'Out so early, after all that *poire* last night? Poor Luc's in need of the last rites.'

'Well, then, maybe I *can* help,' said Mather. He got out of the car. Elizabeth felt her mouth drop open.

He was dressed in a black suit; around his neck was a clerical collar. A small gold cross hung at his throat.

My God, she thought, he's a priest!

'Am I really that frightening?' he said. 'I wish the devil thought so.'

Elizabeth simply didn't know what to say. She scrambled to recover her self-possession.

'Come on,' he said. 'Let's have coffee. You mean Luc didn't tell you about me? About his dear friend Francis who abandoned a Wall Street partnership to serve God?'

No, Luc hadn't, thought Elizabeth, damn his eyes, curse his scrawny French soul; may God visit him with boils and canker sores and a *geule de bois* as raw as horsemeat.

'No, I'm afraid he didn't,' she said.

'Well,' he said, 'permit me then to reintroduce myself: Francis Bangs Mather, DD, Rector of the Church of All Angels and All Souls, Two twenty-seven East Eighty-seventh Street, New York, New York 10028. Would you like to see my card? It's quite handsome. Engraved — from Tiffany's. A gift from one of my flock.'

'All Angels?' she asked. 'Is that Catholic?'

'Episcopal. Catholic churches don't have rectors. Besides, do I have the look of Rome about me, much as I admire my Catholic brothers in Christ? Ours is on the whole a somewhat simpler faith, although I will admit that, on demand, we can give good value in the incense and music department.'

Their coffee arrived. While he poured, she looked him over. Really quite elegant, she thought. The same tailor — probably

163

London, said her appraising eye — who had cut the jacket and trousers of the day before must also be responsible for this elegant flannel suit. His plain black shoes had the deep glow of St James's Street leather. The turnaround collar seemed to take years off him, she thought. It suddenly seemed important to know how old he was, so she asked.

'Forty-six,' he said. 'Just. Why?'

'No reason.' She felt compelled to say something clever. 'I assume, seeing you like this, that it's "Mather" as in Cotton Mather?' she added.

'Hardly. That Reverend Mather was more in the Jerry Falwell—Jimmy Swaggart line. My family's style is less aggressive — but no less devout, I hasten to add.'

'But you *did* have something to do with Wall Street? Luc did say that, didn't he? Or am I losing my mind?'

'You're not and I did. I was even a pretty big cheese down there once.'

Elizabeth had guessed right; it was Morgan Stanley.

'Actually, I still fool around a bit, at the edges; the firm let me keep a small interest in one of their limited partnerships. They bring me in now and then for a little spot consulting, strictly behind-the-scenes stuff — when they've run out of ideas.' He grinned. 'To tell the truth, I'm not so sure it's *my* help they're after, if you get my meaning.'

He lifted his gaze to the ceiling.

'Be that as it may, my bishop likes the idea of my staying in touch with the Street. He's very contemporary, my bishop! And I keep my hand in around the diocese, advising the episcopal office on investments, causing trouble with our hired money managers — that's one table I've really enjoyed turning — and giving inspirational speeches now and then; in general doing my best to see that Caesar doesn't get rendered everything. Actually, the reason I was in Basel was to do a seminar for a Swiss bank I used to do business with. On how to reconcile Christian ethics with sharp business practice. Sort of a road map through the eye of the needle. A dour town, Basel. Anyway, this morning I got up at the crack and drove over to Strasbourg and gave early communion at the Anglican church.'

'I don't suppose you want to tell me how or why you switched from Wall Street to God?'

The question just came out. Elizabeth felt embarrassed to be asking it. She felt as though she were nosing into the symptoms of someone who at first meeting immediately tells you of his terminal illness. Get hold of yourself, she thought. Religion isn't cancer.

'Unfortunately, we don't have a week,' Mather answered. 'Someday, if we do, I'll be able to tell you the whole story. I *can* give you the *Reader's Digest* condensed version. I come from an old church family, but I went to Wall Street.'

'Why?'

'Money, I suppose. I was curious about it. I grew up poorish among rich people. Anyway, it was fun for a while, and then I started to hate it and the sort of people the business began to attract, and then God came and got me. There I was on the Damascus road — Avenue of the Americas, actually — and he came and knocked me off my high horse. Just like Saul of Tarsus.'

Elizabeth reflexively thought of paintings of the Conversion of St Paul. There was the breathtaking Caravaggio in Rome, at Santa Maria del Popolo. And the Bruegel in Vienna at the Kunsthistorisches. She especially loved the Bruegel version, in which the saint's revelation was just one of a myriad of incidents along a busy highway. Had Mather's conversion been like that? she wondered. Had he been struck by the divine light while all around him New York foamed and roared and went on its noisy way?

Suddenly she found him utterly fascinating; she wanted to know everything about him.

'And who are you, Elizabeth?' she heard him ask. 'Who are you, what are you, and how did you get this way?'

She told him what she did. It sounded so vulgar, trafficking in art for money, especially works that had been originally made to celebrate the glory of the same God who had come to his man and seized his heart and soul.

She gave him a quick, edited version of Elizabeth, concentrating on the last fifteen years, the part of her life that

165

she considered suitable for public viewing. He listened intently. When she finished, he said, 'I'm not so sure what I make of this "art for investment" business.' She started to reply, but Mather held up a hand. 'I see something pale green wavering in the middle distance. Unless I am mistaken, it's your lover.'

Oh, please don't say that, she thought. Please don't think that. Luc and I are just something for each other for now — for yesterday. For lack of someone better.

Mather rose. 'Well, *bonjour, cher Luc*! Have a beer. You'll need it if you're to get back in racing condition.' He winked at Elizabeth. 'And, may I say, very impressive form it sounded to be on the evidence of yesterday afternoon.' Elizabeth felt herself turn scarlet.

They parted that evening. Mather was on his way to Geneva and then to New York. What a good time they'd had, they agreed. Must do it again. Promises were made to keep in touch.

On the way back to Paris, Elizabeth scolded Luc for playing games on her.

'Don't be silly,' Luc said. 'It could have been worse. He could be some Jesuit trying to convert us. People on Wall Street go crazy all the time, but not so crazy as Francis, I think. He was at the top. Mergers — very big! A million dollars a year, and that was ten years ago, when a million a year was real money. Then, *un vrai coup de feu*, he lost his wife and kids. You remember that plane crash in New Orleans; Pan Am, I think. A terrible thing. After that, what I hear, the money just didn't mean so much to him any more. But at least he's Church of England, so if he wants, he can have romance. He was always *très habile* with the ladies, was Francis.'

Randy with hangover, Luc reached over and slid his hand under Elizabeth's skirt, halfway up her thigh.

'*Et ce soir? Chez moi?*'

She took his hand away. She felt like cutting it off. 'No,' she said, 'not tonight.' She made no excuses. Luc looked hurt.

Not for a long while, *mon cher*, she thought. Very possibly not ever again.

CHAPTER FOURTEEN

PARIS
Monday, December 16th

In the end, the Foreign Ministry prevailed over the Intelligence directorates, and it was decided to give the Americans a little gift. The sinking of the Greenpeace ship had not gone down well in the United States. Relations between France and America were generally uneasy: the presidents of the two republics were hardly cut from the same cloth, and it took no sophisticated eye to detect a further fraying of the historic but always uneasy amity.

The Americans were reeling from one intelligence shock after another; anything that might bolster the CIA's stature would be gratefully received, even if it should turn out to be nothing more than a red herring.

And a red herring it would be. It wouldn't do to hand over the crown jewels. That was the mistake the British always made with the Americans — until they finally learned better. There were more holes in US secrecy than in a wedge of Emmenthal. Off the recent evidence, anything passed on to the CIA or NSA would be sold to Moscow, Beijing, Tel Aviv, or Damascus within months. One must understand this about the nature of treason in the States: where the traitors of other nations betrayed for love or ideology or hatred, the Americans seemed to do it strictly for money.

Accordingly, after much horsetrading between the Élysée Palace, the quai d'Orsay, and 'La Piscine,' the building behind the public swimming pool which housed the Direction Générale de Sécurité Extérieure, the DGSE, it was agreed to give the Americans this Menchikov thing the Sûreté had turned up, but to dress it like a Christmas goose with a few scraps from French intelligence's top table.

So the DGSE man went to see his opposite number at the US Embassy chancery.

'As you know,' he said by way of introducing his business, 'some years ago we penetrated Directorate T of the KGB, which is where they run their industrial and commercial espionage.'

'Jesus Christ,' the CIA man responded, 'I hope you guys haven't flipped for another KGB disinformation number.'

The Frenchman gave an inward shrug and smiled. He was used to this. Nowadays, the Americans saw the shadow of the bear, even on the sunniest morning.

'We don't believe so,' he said tactfully. 'It's something the Sûreté passed on in connection with a criminal investigation. But we have reasons to believe it connects with certain activities of Directorate T.'

The DGSE made more of the 'Directorate T penetration' than was perhaps warranted. In the two years since French intelligence had turned a clerk in the Directorate's file section, all that had been learned was that there *was* a section within the KGB which engaged in nonmilitary intelligence and trouble-making; as far as was known, however, its operations were in fact little different from the methods employed by Machines Bull or Thomson to extract trade secrets from disgruntled or venal employees of IBM or Fujitsu. Nevertheless, by tying in the fact that the concierge at the François Premier had been murdered, the DGSE story acquired a sheen of violence, which the Americans always liked.

The DGSE representative reached into his briefcase and took out a tape cassette and a thin clear plastic folder.

The American picked up the tape. 'Shall we go downstairs to the Red Room and have a listen?' he asked.

'It's not necessary. This isn't a Grade four-A Moscow telemetry intercept. It's just a tape from a little Sony.' From his briefcase he produced a portable tape player. It was a little bulky, a model three or four years old, and he saw a flicker of disparagement at the corner of the American's mouth.

'The original of this tape was recovered from the deceased concierge's safe at the Hotel François Premier, rue Bayard,' he recited patiently. 'It was apparently made by the concierge himself, one Wladimir Alphonse-Marie Coutet. Interestingly, Coutet's parents were Russian. Five days after the night on which we believe this tape was made, Coutet's corpse was fished out of the river.'

'Are the two connected?'

'We don't know. The Sûreté doubts it. It looks like some Belleville Arab put a knife into Coutet, probably a falling-out over narcotics.'

'The guy was a user?'

'No. More of a genteel supplier. We found evidence in the safe that he may have kept some of the *douce poudre blanche* on hand for special clients at the hotel. Service at the François Premier is extremely personal, my friend.'

'Everything from girls to goats, huh?'

'Essentially. Anyway, on the evening of November eighteenth, Coutet had elected to take the night shift. He always tried to arrange his hours around the sojourns of certain old and favored clients. Such was the case that evening. One Grigoriy Menchikov, a Deputy Soviet Minister of Arts, was in the hotel.'

'Menchikov? Does that ring a bell?'

'I can think of no particular reason why it should.' The DGSE agent opened the folder and took out a photograph and a dossier. It consisted of a single sheet of paper on which were typed no more than a dozen lines.

'Grigoriy Simonon Menchikov,' he read. 'Born 1900 in Tiflis. Trained as an economist. Member of the Economics Institute, Moscow. Delegate to Bretton Woods, 1944; Yalta, 1945. Obviously close to Stalin, and when Stalin died, 1953, Menchikov was moved to the arts, and away from the centers of influence. It was logical. Next—'

'Hey,' the American interrupted. 'You think you're talking to Joe Schmuck?' He got up and went across the room to a computer screen. The DGSE man shrugged and followed him. The Americans were absolutely in thrall to their computers. He watched as the American punched up some data and read from the screen.

'Menchikov, Grigoriy, etc. Born *blah blah blah*. Educated

169

blah blah blah. In London, 1935–1936, you guys don't show that; we sourced that from the Brits, it says here. Poet then. Hey, here: 1935 publishes something called 'Fire Visions' in something called *Criterion*; I bet that was bullshit! Ah, you're right. Switches to economics, because, see, 1938, Fellow of the Institute of Economics, Soviet Academy of Sciences. Let's see: Red Army 1940. Western Front against the Krauts. *Blah blah blah*. ADC to Zhukov; now, that's something! Anyway, wins medals *blah*. Ah! Bretton Woods, 1944, *blah blah blah*. No known connection Harry Dexter White, himself a suspected *blah blah blah*. Yalta, 1945. London, 1946 – for a funeral, Keynes's. Yeah – here, the guy was a cousin of Keynes's wife. OK, then let's see. Nothing until 1954, when he shows up here in Paris as an observer on some *Paris Herald* forum on "The Condition of Modern Poetry." Talk about bullshit! Wonder he didn't get the post-Stalin boot, end up in a gulag. What's next? OK: Deputy Arts Minister, ummm, *blah blah*. In charge of Franco-Russian arts exchange program, *blah blah*. Bolshoi Ballet *blah blah*. *Blah blah blah*. Durnstein Conference Medal, 1980, for services to world cultural understanding, *blah blah*. Honorary Colonel-General, Red Army. Member of this, member of that, *blah blah*. But no Politburo, no Central Committee, nothing big. Dies Paris, November eighteenth this year. So?'

'Our people at Études Sovietiques believe Menchikov may have been involved with clandestine economic operations against the West.'

They sat down again. The American said, 'So who needs "clandestine" when guys sell them computers, and the Krauts build their pipeline, and the Guineas build the tractor plant at Volgograd, and so on?'

'My friend,' said the Frenchman, 'why should you and I argue? My superiors think you might be interested in this tape. It has Menchikov's last words, which we find interesting.'

'So let's give a listen,' said the American. He sounded impatient, a man with larger fish to fry.

The DGSE agent inserted the cassette and switched on the player. The tape hissed; then there was an indistinct sound that suggested commotion — feet on marble floors, shuffling, faint shouts far back; next — more clearly, in a language that the American couldn't recognize, other than it sounded vaguely Russian, which he didn't speak anyway — a loud voice, crying out, punctuated with deep gasps, then more short phrases, more gasps, the voice desperate-sounding. Some of the words repeated. 'Let me in here!' An American voice. Then much confusion. Finally: 'Gone, I'm afraid. What was he talking about?' The American voice again. Then more talk. Another voice abruptly breaking in, a gruff commanding voice, in Russian, and the French voice replying, also in Russian, then back to English. Then the click of the recorder going off. Then silence.

The American looked at his watch. The tape had run approximately four minutes, although it seemed much longer. 'Most of that was Greek to me,' he said. 'I suppose your people have puzzled it out, though.' He nodded significantly toward the folder.

'Actually, it was a Georgian dialect the old man was speaking,' the DGSE man said. 'The American voice belonged to a doctor. His name's in there. The police questioned him briefly at the scene. A typical coronary attack. The French voice is the concierge, identified by the hotel manager.'

'Didn't I pick up another voice? Russian, maybe?'

'There is one, that's true. We're guessing it might be one of the bodyguards. That's what the young boy on duty at the door thinks. According to him, Menchikov had two with him. Interesting for a lowly Deputy Minister of Arts, don't you think? A lot of professional company for a small bureaucrat. Anyway, there it is, my friend. The transcript's in French. Your people will be wanting to make their own, anyway.'

The American saw his visitor out. He carried the tape and folder to his office. They could go out on the evening pouch to Langley.

He took the transcript out of the folder. The top sheet listed the dramatis personae. The dying man, Menchikov. Coutet, the concierge, now murdered. He didn't buy that business about the Reds icing the guy. It had to be a Belleville dope hit.

He read through the transcript. His French was OK, and this was pretty pidgin stuff. It was easy to read. Whoever had typed it up had arranged it like a script. He turned to the last page.

Lobby noise, shouts.

MENCH: Waldya (untranslatable), waldya (untranslatable), time to end . . . must end . . . must go, must go . . . maker of ropes . . . waldya . . . maker of ropes . . . over . . . over . . . must go . . . finish, waldya . . .

DOCTOR: (in English) Let me in here. (Pause) You've got to give us some room! Support his head, will you!

MENCH: (indistinguishable)

(Pounding by doctor)

MENCH: (indistinguishable) . . . *THEN*: Waldya . . . tell you . . . waldya . . . must go . . . is finish . . . maker of ropes . . . go now, waldya . . . (Dies)

DOCTOR: (in English) Gone, I'm afraid. What was he talking about?

COUTET: (in English) I don't know, I don't speak Russian.

MALE VOICE: (in Russian) What was he saying!

COUTET: (in Russian) It was a dialect. I don't know it. (In English again) I don't understand. I don't know. I don't speak . . .

Tape ends.

The American read it through again. Weird. What was all that shit about some guy making rope? Probably a work name of some kind. Langley would really go for that. Those Langley

172

guys went apeshit over work names. What the hell was a 'waldya'?

He sealed the tape and enclosures in an 'Eyes Only' envelope and took it down the hall to Dispatch. It would be at CIA Headquarters in Virginia in the morning. God was still looking out for him, he thought happily. He liked Paris, but Langley had threatened to pull him back, maybe send him to Managua, unless he turned up more product. And here it was. Wow, he thought; one minute your ass is grass, and the next the Frogs, who seldom did favors for anyone, drop this shit right in your lap. It sounded like chickenfeed to him, but these days the Company was so hot to get Congress off its ass, they'd pass it off as gold. Well, they could call it gold; they could call it chickenfeed; they could call it anything they wanted, just as long as they kept off his ass.

CHAPTER FIFTEEN

LONDON
Friday, December 20th

It had been, on the whole, a worthwhile day. Elizabeth spent the morning cruising the West End galleries. She'd seen a few good things: a Turner watercolor at Baskett & Day, nice but expensive, and a fine Stubbs drawing that she'd told them to reserve. Agnew's showed her a Watteau, for a price that would have fed Ethiopia, and Colnaghi had produced a dazzling pair of big Piazzettas. Great pictures — but she had to think of the market down the road. Monet, Manet, Renoir, Cézanne — you were home free. If you had the Parthenon for sale, you could count on the Getty or Berlin. But a million pounds for a pair of Piazzettas? Among the eighteenth-century Venetians, Canaletto or Guardi were no problem. Same for Bellotto. With Tiepolo, it started to get antsy. Tiepolo could outpaint the others six ways from Sunday, but his subjects didn't slide right down the way those views of Venice and Prague did. Still, these Piazzettas were beautiful. If it had been her money, she'd have written out a Concorde check on the spot.

The champagne she'd been given at lunch at Lefevre had made her a little giddy, but not too giddy to hold up Concorde's end when it came to negotiating the split between the money and the marketing if she and Lefevre and Thaw were going to be partners in buying a $2 million cache of Géricault drawings.

She emerged into Bruton Street after lunch well fed and satisfied with the terms of the deal. Their partnership would get its bait back quickly, thanks to a couple of Géricault fanatics the dealers had targeted in Barcelona and Lyon, and would still be left with half the drawings to dispose of gradually.

It was unseasonably warm. She was due in Curzon Street at four, so it simply wasn't worth rushing over to Knightsbridge to look at some carpets. Be prompt, John had told her. He was going to have to drive out to Heathrow to deliver some very expensive garden books to an American millionaire's panting Gulfstream.

With the weather this mild, she knew what to do with the next hour. She walked across Berkeley Square and up Mount Street, stopping at a newsagent to buy the latest *Tatler* and *Private Eye*, and went into St George's Gardens, the small green trapezoid nestled between South Audley, Mount, and South streets. It was a place she'd discovered when she'd first come to London years ago, a secret known to everyone, especially Americans, but still spoken of as a secret. It was just the place to while away the idle interval. She settled down on a bench marked with a small plate inscribed IN MEMORY OF MANY HAPPY HOURS/B.G./CLEVELAND, OHIO and started to read.

Fifteen minutes later, when she was well into a *Tatler* report on who was who in the Cotswolds, she sensed someone on the walk behind her, and a voice she now recognized said, 'Well, hello! Well met by sunlight, wouldn't you say?' and her heart leapt.

Francis Mather stood smiling down at her. My God, how well you look! she thought. 'Why, hello, Francis,' she said, trying to sound unruffled. Why was her breath stuck in her throat, her heart thumping, her legs jelly? 'What are you doing here?'

'Here? I was crossing through to my hotel. And you?'

'Just killing time. How've you been, Francis?'

'Busy.' She saw he was in uniform.

'Were you paying a diplomatic call down the way?' she asked, gesturing at the small Jesuit church which stood at the bottom of the little park. 'Making amends for Henry the Eighth?'

He smiled. 'Farm Street? As a matter of fact, I thought of it. Intellectually, I've got what it takes to be a Jesuit. But no taste for confession or celibacy.'

Was that a hint?

'How about a cup of coffee?' he asked.

175

'Fine,' she said. 'Fine. I've got an appointment nearby in about an hour.'

'And I have to be at Lambeth Palace at five to see the Archbishop of Canterbury,' he said. 'About his dollar investments. We can go to my hotel for a cuppa.'

They walked toward the Connaught. What kind of poor person can this man be, Elizabeth asked herself, to be staying at this hotel? Well, Luc had intimated that Mather had taken away a bundle when he left the Street. And he wasn't a monk; he didn't have to hand it *all* over to the church, did he? Idly, she wondered if he got his clerical collars at Turnbull & Asser.

Over coffee, she asked, 'Did you mean that about being a Jesuit? Could you really have?'

'Not really. But it's a pretty conceit, isn't it? Whispering in the Duke of Norfolk's ear; hearing Evelyn Waugh's confession. The odd essay in *The Times*. Keeping the ungodly on the defensive. The trouble is, it's a little too rigid. This business can be fun too, you know. The C of E suits me fine. Catholicism's a little too much like the gold standard: a fixed weight of piety translatable into a fixed exchange rate of grace. But it certainly worked for a long time. In a different world, however.'

'And could you stand the vow of poverty?' Elizabeth hoped she didn't sound impertinent.

'Actually,' he said, 'I did give most of what I had to All Angels when I was called there. But I can't tell a lie. I kept a bit aside. Enough to keep me in the odd suit and box seat at the Met. I like to be able to pay my own way, if it comes to that. And to have enough to give me a bit of a stake if I should ever feel an irresistible urge to get back in the game.'

'Wall Street? From what you said in Colmar, I got the impression that's not very likely.'

'It isn't. I love this work. It makes me feel like a human being.'

'And you're a widower?'

'Yes, for almost a dozen years. A plane crash. I guess that was one of the things that started me on the road to Damascus. After the usual false starts. But you don't want to hear about that.'

'Tell me.'

'Well, first I tried sleeping around, using the emotions of some very decent women as towels to dry my tears. That was no good. Then I tried analysis.'

'How'd that go?'

'So-so. I judge analysis to be about fifty percent cure, and fifty percent cauterization. I guess I needed one or the other, but not a combination. Then a friend suggested prayer. I gave it a shot, and it came naturally, and the rest is history. And you? Didn't Luc tell me you were an orphan?'

'I am. My father died of cancer after my mother went off with a man I wasn't crazy about — and then she and he and my half brother were killed in a fire. I somehow escaped. Everyone said it was a miracle.'

Was it planned by God so we could meet someday, Francis? she asked silently.

'And you like what *you're* doing?'

'I do. It isn't my money, and they aren't my possessions, but I see a lot of wonderful things and I like the game.'

'Games, games, games.' Mather sighed. 'The same the wide world over.'

'You didn't like your old game, I take it?'

'I didn't like what it became. For one thing, it got to be too easy. If you wanted something — another man's company, say, another man's lifework — you could borrow all the money it took, no matter who you were or what your credentials amounted to. The banks started lending to unfriendly takeovers. No amount too large, no deal beyond the pale. One of Manning Mallory's path-breaking innovations. That — I know this'll make me sound like a snob, damn it — made it just too easy intellectually. All you needed to become a worldclass financier was the chutzpah of a car salesman, the moral sensitivity of a stone crab, and a line of credit at CertBank. I thought I was better than that. I thought the business ought to be better than that. I don't suppose you ever read Grogan's column in the *Wall Street Journal*?'

'Never.'

'The house organ for the new capitalism and the paper

177

entrepreneurs. Read it sometime if you want to see truth turned on its head. The Russians don't do it any better. If you think the disinformation and propaganda coming out of the Kremlin are sophisticated, you ought to sample the Mallory-CertBank-Grogan variety.' Something caught his attention. He looked up, put on a hasty smile of recognition, and muttered, 'Darn!'

'Why, Francis Mather, fancy running into you!' called a cheerful voice from across the lounge. 'This *is* good luck! You can take me to Rosita Marlborough's tomorrow night.'

Elizabeth found herself being introduced to Mrs Leslie, a distinguished, relaxed woman of around sixty. She looked Elizabeth over carefully. Well, thought Elizabeth, when any of us has a treasure, we guard it jealously.

Mrs Leslie's husband had abandoned her in London in favor of a few days' shooting. She was at sixes and sevens.

Sadly, said Francis, he could not oblige about the Marlboroughs. He looked hopelessly at Elizabeth as the new arrival took a chair.

Elizabeth rose. 'I'm afraid I've got to run. It's been nice seeing you, Francis. And to meet you, Mrs Leslie.'

'I'll just see Elizabeth into a taxi,' Mather said, getting to his feet. She started to say, Oh, I'm going just a few blocks, but he put his hand under her elbow and, as he started her for the door, gave her arm a slight squeeze.

'May I say I certainly wouldn't mind taking you to dinner tomorrow night?' he said.

'You may. But I can't. Another time.' She started to mention New York in January, but decided to let it keep.

'Back to Paris?' he asked.

'No. I'm spending Christmas here. With a girl I knew from Sotheby's who had the extreme good taste to marry a property millionaire and the rare good luck to be happy with him — on very conventional terms. We're going down to the country after lunch.'

'How lucky. I wish you could be with us Christmas Eve. Our music's really quite good. Not St Thomas' standard yet, but coming on strong.'

'Someday, perhaps. I'd like very much to hear it.'

178

'Well, when you're next in New York, you have my card.' He stuck his hands in his pockets, hunched up his shoulders, and said apologetically, 'I suppose I should get back to Mrs Leslie. She's one of our patron saints at All Angels. Merry Christmas, Elizabeth.'

This time, when he kissed her cheek, Elizabeth could swear his lips brushed the corner of her mouth. Awkwardness? Hardly. Perhaps something was in the air.

She walked along South Audley Street. Evening darkness had set in. The elegant shops were gay and alight. London was a good Christmas city, she thought.

She had been tempted to make a date with Mather in New York. Why hadn't she? Well, she would keep her schedule loose. These new feelings needed to be examined closely, set down on a laboratory slide and inspected, cooled off and checked for color and consistency. At thirty-five, a girl had only so many cards left to play.

At Heywood Hill, John was pleased to see her. He complimented her on her appearance and said he hoped it had nothing to do with that ghastly Frenchman she'd brought round the last time. They got right down to business. John had uncovered a major botanical and gardening library in a private house outside Bristol. It was offered *en bloc*, which was why he thought of Elizabeth. And it was a treasure trove: there was a complete Redouté, including some of the original *Roses* water-colors; four Repton 'Red Books'; a mint *Temple of Flora* and many things he'd seen only at Chatsworth. It could all be hers for three and a half million pounds, with the exception of two items he would want to hold out for Mrs Mellon.

Elizabeth found herself interested. The money involved wasn't a great sum, but the rate of return could be exceptional. To new rich New York women, old flower books were instant passports to respectability. Price was no object.

As she thought it over, John suddenly looked up, gasped, and strode briskly over to where a handsome woman with astonishing blue hair was scrutinizing the flap copy of the latest Jeffrey Archer novel.

'Not for you, Your Grace,' Elizabeth heard him say. 'You

want something to *read* on Mustique, although this is quite satisfactory for putting over your face to keep the sun off.' He chose another book for the duchess and returned. 'It used to be I had to protect our fiction customers from going over their heads; nowadays it's just the other way round! Thank heavens for Anita Brookner and David Cornwell! Now, if I were you—'

She told him to go ahead and buy the books. As she prepared to leave, he produced a small, neatly wrapped parcel.

'And here are these very curious liturgical books you wanted. May I ask . . .?'

'No,' Elizabeth said, 'you may not.'

He showed her to the door. On the other side of Curzon Street, the lights over the passage to Shepherd's Market looked very festive. It was turning sharply colder, which could mean snow and would be lovely in the country. She wished John a merry Christmas.

'You know, Elizabeth,' he said, 'I must say you do look really bloody marvelous. Are you dead sure you're not in love?'

All she could say in reply, with a girlish coyness that embarrassed her, was 'Perhaps. Pray for me, will you?'

THE PAST

1970
and Afterward

Ropespinner

CHAPTER SIXTEEN

Mallory's assumption of the crown of state at CertCo in 1970 could not have been better timed.

Just turned forty-one, good-looking, articulate, charming, charismatic, he struck the foundering financial community as progress incarnate. Wall Street was at a crisis point. It needed a man like Mallory to get things moving again, a man with ideas, someone who could see beyond the horizon, show the way to the pot of gold at the end of the rainbow.

Washington was no help. Nixon was obviously a small-time grub, surrounded by charlatans and thieves. Vietnam was going badly, a small war fought to save a country no one cared about, and it was proving a horribly expensive way to keep idle black youths off the streets. The great sixties boom on Wall Street had petered out. For the first time since before the war, middle-class Americans were waking up in the middle of the night with money worries. Prices were rising, as they never had in international markets; the dollar was reeling.

The business cupboard was bare of heroes, of figures who radiated the kind of noble assurance that had gotten the previous decade off and running. It was as if the human race had shrunk.

At such a time, among such small and grasping people, Manning Mallory stood out. Men looked up to him; Wall Street idolized him. Almost overnight, he became the designated spokesman for American business, the man to whom the masses and the media turned for comment and wisdom and inspiration. Nine months after he succeeded Preston Chamberlain, a survey indicated that people almost automatically free-associated

'Manning Mallory' with 'banking.' He was, as *US News and World Report* put it, 'the epitome of the New Era in finance, attuned to change, oriented to new strategies and technologies which must alter, for all time, the face of the world's third oldest profession.' In a comparison that hearkened Waldo nostalgically back to London and Menchikov and their meeting after Keynes's funeral, a profile in *Fortune* solemnly opined, 'Just as the financial community hastened in time of crisis to the elder Morgan, to be advised that "prices would fluctuate," so today does it seek the insights and soothing confidence of the extraordinary head of the world's largest bank.'

Inevitably, there was talk of Mallory's going to Washington, but the minute such trial balloons were floated, he punctured them. His only politics, he declared, were those of the free market. He campaigned tirelessly for deregulation and decontrol in every sphere of economic life.

His very ubiquity was a tremendous asset for Ropespinner. An interview here, a speech there, only provoked a swell of demand for more interviews, more speeches. In the frenzy of publicity, the fact that he might be preaching arrant financial nonsense was overlooked. It was what people wanted; it smacked of fast and easy money to a financial sector that was finding the quick buck harder to come by; it sounded good.

Manning Mallory on *Meet the Press*: 'The time has come for an end to such constraints as Bretton Woods. World financial markets have shown they can handle any problem. Floating and flexible exchange rates are not only the wave of the future, they will prove to be the best thing that ever happened to economic man. The sooner we get off the gold standard, the better it'll be for everyone.'

Manning Mallory in *Dun's Business Review*: 'At CertBank, we think of ourselves as money salesmen. There is no limit to the forms and uses of credit that can be deployed. Many of these haven't even begun to be explored, and that's what bankers should be doing, and that's what CertBankers do. We're explorers. The "old-fashioned" banker who wastes his customer's time kicking the tires is soon going to lose that customer.'

Manning Mallory, speech to the National Association of Mortgage Bankers: 'The sooner banks are allowed to cross state lines, the better off you're going to be, and the better off your potential home buyer's going to be. The theory of the local bank with deep community roots was a nice idea in its time, but the efficiency and breadth of today's financial markets has made it as obsolete as the Model T.'

It was a dazzling view of the future, painted by Mallory in bright colors and meticulous detail. He and Waldo recognized that people were obliged to take the word of the first man to the summit as to what the view on the far side of the mountain looked like. Keeping CertBank ahead of other banks was something Mallory and Waldo worked relentlessly to achieve. Fortunately, Waldo was no longer obliged to lurk behind the curtain. Their partnership had — as Mallory put it with a sly grin — 'come out of the closet.' Indeed, *Institutional Investor* put them on its cover together when, in 1971, in memory of its tragically fallen late leader, CertCo established the Preston Chamberlain Professorship in Banking and Finance at the Harvard Business School, and Waldo fittingly became the first occupant of the new chair.

Waldo now came and went as he pleased at 41 Wall Street. He was formally appointed Special Consultant to the Chief Executive, and a small office was set up for him down the hall from Mallory, with a series of bright young MBAs assigned to run his errands. It was accepted that he was the accredited shaman-in-chief to the reigning potentate. And a good thing for banking in general, said the part of the world that attended to such things. The lights burned late on the twenty-eighth floor as the world's greatest banker and his mentor huddled and hatched the schemes and stratagems that kept CertBank out in front of a yelping pack of imitators and competitors.

Mallory himself seemed aflame with new energy. He had time and words for everything. There were no checks on him now, no need to look over his shoulder, except with satisfaction, at the panting hounds from Chemical Bank and First Pennsylvania and Security Pacific who dogged his steps and copied CertBank's every move.

Mallory admitted that knowing about Ropespinner had given a new point and dimension to his work.

'When I was at school,' he told Waldo, 'this guy Hillary came to speak. You know, the first guy up Everest. You remember what he said about it; he climbed it because it was there. Well, that's what this thing of ours is about. Before, what I supposed I wanted most — the point of the whole thing — was to get to sit at this particular desk, in this particular office. Now I'm here. After forty-eight hours the thrill wears off, and what's left? More deals? You see a dozen deals, you've seen them all. Money? How much money does a guy need? Your picture in the papers, your name in print? The first time it's a kick, but after that it's strictly blahsville. But now — with this thing of ours — I've got something real to shoot for.'

'And that is . . .?'

'Well, we're going to call it the outermost limits of plausible risk. The way I see it, we're no different from the guy who wants to climb Everest or descend the Mindanao Trench or go to the goddamn moon. When we had our little talk last year, the scales dropped off my eyes. I used to think that we "new age bankers" were heroes; what'd that asshole on the *Times* call us: "*conquistadores* of finance"?

'Then, when you confessed all, it started me to thinking: maybe we're *conquistadores* of ourselves. I mean, what the hell kind of a system is this where the line between being competitive and wrecking the whole goddamn shooting match is so faint you need a goddamn microscope to find it? Is there something basically rotten here?'

'And what have you concluded, Manning?'

'Nothing. The jury's still out. I'm not sure I'll have my answer until I know just exactly how far we can push it. Don't any of these guys chasing after us read the history books?'

Waldo smiled inwardly. He felt that Mallory was beginning to appreciate the intellectual niceties of Ropespinner.

'The way I see it working,' Mallory concluded, 'it's kind of like a top.'

'A top?'

'Yeah, spinning on a table. With what's going on everywhere you look, that top's going to spin faster and faster, faster and faster, till all it's going to take to send it careening off into space is the flick of a finger.'

'And you and I are—' Waldo began to say, but Mallory interrupted him.

'You follow me. You and I are that finger. Which is, I may say, dear Professor, a nice extension of your pet metaphor.'

'My pet metaphor?'

'Come on, Waldo, think.'

Waldo thought briefly, then smiled. 'Ah, yes,' he said. 'The invisible hand. And you and I are its fingers.'

187

The spring after the fire, Waldo set about rebuilding Quiddy. The building crew went to work with a vengeance, for it had been tacitly agreed that everyone was going to bust his hump to see that Mr Waldo's house was ready for Thanksgiving. He was beloved and admired, and up and down the coast his grit dominated the talk at hearth and counter. How bravely he'd borne his personal tragedy; the energy with which he had thrown himself back into life; how generous it had been of him to take the orphan of the fire into his own home, to nurse that 'sweet young Elizabeth' back to where she could cope with life; and how he'd fixed it up for her to go to Europe so as to get away from her troubles and start over.

Yep, it was agreed, it took quite a man even to think about rebuilding that house, what with all the ghosts there must be in it for him now, his brother and all. But wasn't it just like Mr Waldo to have kept the plans all these years, no mind that he was always so careful and all, even a bit of a fussbudget. And so Quiddy rose just exactly as it had been, right down to the last eccentricities, even the secret upstairs hideyhole, which old Felmer Lewis, Miss Martha's father, had built.

Almost a year to the day after its predecessor had burned down, Waldo reopened the house with a celebratory reception. The Quiddy community was right impressed when the big New York banker Mallory, whom people said was the closest thing to a son an old bachelor like Mr Waldo would ever have, personally came up from New York to join in the festivities; just flew right up in a big green helicopter that belonged to his bank, and darned if he didn't turn out to be a regular fellow, and so handsome and gracious too. Miss Elizabeth didn't come, of course; she was off in England to study, but Mr Waldo said even if she wasn't, he didn't think she'd have come anyway, because the memories were too awful for her, and when Mr Waldo said that, everyone understood, and there were some people even said they saw him weep a tiny tear.

And that night, when the last slightly tipsy Quiddyite had been carried off home by his wife, Waldo and Mallory sat by the fire and Waldo told Mallory how he had hit upon an idea that he was absolutely sure could guarantee a triumph for Ropespinner on a scale that was way beyond anything they'd ever dreamed.

They would begin, he said, by teaching the Arabs how to read.

Waldo got his inspiration when destiny, or so it seemed, contrived to place him in the path of the great concept he had begun to despair of finding. For all its successes, Ropespinner still needed 'the hedgehog idea,' the big, thrusting break-through. They had come a long way, but as Mallory said, 'It's been mostly barnacles so far, and it'll take a hell of a lot of those to sink the goddamn ship.' Now he had it.

Early that summer in 1971, he had accepted the invitation of a conglomerate to address its quarterly board meeting, in Venice. The invitation carried a handsome stipend and a week on the cuff at the Cipriani. With the house still unfinished, the money and the lodgings suited Waldo. In addition, he was curious about conglomerates. He had watched them rise in the sixties and bloom into a flower that richly pollinated the wallets of Wall Street; now the blossom was definitely beginning to fade.

The theory behind these companies — that a good numbers man could manage anything from a foundry to a ski resort — he regarded as entirely meretricious, although it was the theory he taught. Any reasonable man should see what Grigoriy's idol Bagehot had seen: that numbers were the end, not the means, of commerce. Nevertheless, he saw the con-glomerate idea as fodder for Ropespinner, and so he publicly

189

lauded the theory behind companies like ITT and Litton and LTV. To his students, he mouthed the buzzwords — 'synergy,' 'centralized control' — that had Wall Street marveling, and he added a neologism or two of his own to the jargon of self-deception. Conglomerates, he told his Money One sections, represented the finest flower of post-Sputnikian 'numeracy,' the great intellectual regearing that would regenerate the West. Young men and women who were inclined to believe that wealth equals character needed little urging to accept this gospel. Everyone knew you couldn't shoot down a Russian rocket with a Shakespeare sonnet or deliver regularly rising quarterly earnings per share by parsing Aristotle.

His students spoke of 'reducing everything to the numbers.' 'Reducing' indeed! he thought privately. Shrinking it until there was nothing left!

When he told Mallory about his upcoming Venice excursion, the banker laughed.

'I'd hurry if I were you. And take careful notes. You may be privileged to be in at the death rattle of the last dinosaur. Jesus, I wish I'd known about Ropespinner five years ago. We could've pumped about a hundred million more into conglomerate lending, even though your dear departed brother hated those companies. Said they were cooking the books.'

'And were they?'

'Does Escoffier make sense? Preston even got Abe Briloff to come over and give us a short course in conglomerate accounting, bring us up to speed on items like "deferred development" and "goodwill." ITT should've sold the movie rights to its annual report; greatest work of fiction I ever saw. Wish I'd known then what I know now.'

'I wouldn't worry about that, Manning. I suspect these conglomerates won't prove to be the last such opportunity.'

'Right you are. You know, I was over at Lehman for lunch the other day. The joke over the asparagus was: as much money as Lehman made helping Jim Ling put LTV together, the firm's going to make twice as much helping his creditors pull it apart. We all had a big laugh, ha, ha, ha. If I wasn't having such a good time doing what we're doing, I could kick your ass for talking me out of going to Wall Street!'

Mallory had just returned from a VIP tour of the Far East. He talked about it like a man who had seen God.

'You know, I don't see why your pal the Volga boatman needs us when he's got Henry Ford the Second and the UAW and those clowns at Chrysler working for him. The Japs are going to clean our clock ₊n the automobile game. Those stiffs in Detroit think the world ends at the Grosse Pointe city limits; they've been reading too much Casey Stengel.'

'Casey Stengel? I'm afraid I don't follow you.'

'Old Case said the Japs could never play baseball because they've got small hands. Detroit seems to think little yellow people with little yellow hands can't build something big and, quote, American, endquote, like a car. Are they in for a shock! I bought a Jap car for my kid. Little station wagon. It was cheap, runs like a clock, not too clunky and looks OK, and it gets about fifty miles to the gallon. You know what this old guy from Toyota said to me? He told me we Americans seem to think no one else in the world can do a damn thing. And he agreed with you about multinationals.'

This was one of Waldo's favorite subjects: how by setting up overseas in order to take advantage of cheap labor and get around local restrictions, American multinational corporations were bartering away the nation's long-term export capability.

'In return for a quick fix on the bottom line, we sell them competitive technology; we're exporting capital and know-how; we're eating into our export base,' Waldo told Mallory.

In a subsequent speech to the National Association of Manu-facturers, Mallory proclaimed the Ropespinner version: 'A Ford or a Zenith TV manufactured in Lille and shipped to Lagos is every bit as much "an export" as if it had been built in Indianapolis!' The high-powered audience, which — like the nation's President — enjoyed traveling and found domestic travails tiresome, had gone wild.

'And by the same logic, a dollar is a dollar is a dollar,' Mallory said. 'We're doing more business offshore than we are in New York. I need a chair and a whip to keep our foreign exchange traders in line, so how can anyone help it if some of these Eurodollars we're printing overseas start sneaking back into the domestic money supply and making poor Art Burns's head spin.' He grinned and nudged Waldo in the ribs. 'Maybe you should spend a few million lire at Harry's Bar, huh? Anything for the cause, right?

'You know,' he said thoughtfully as he showed Waldo to the door, 'that old Jap from Toyota said another thing that was funny. He said the only time we really ought to watch out is if the Arabs ever understand the power over us their oil gives them. What do you suppose he meant by that? Ah, well, the mysterious East, as they say. Have a good time in Venice.'

A fortnight later, as Waldo sat on the vaporetto and idly watched the palaces of Venice slide by, his mind exulted.

He had his 'hedgehog' idea at last. So excited was he that he had already sent off a five-page handwritten letter express Mail to 'Sr Dr Felipe Guzman' in Barcelona; it would take four or five days to get to Moscow, he guessed, and then a week for a reply. He doubted he could stand the wait.

Yes, Venice had been a total success, and not because of the $15,000 fee and the luxuries of the Cipriani, or the gondolas and motorboats on twenty-four hour call, or the chartered 727 standing by to take the directors and their wives and companions shopping and sightseeing in Rome and Florence, or the private yacht, provisioned by Harry's Bar, which took the party to Torcello and up the Brenta, or the amusing fact that the directors' conversation was more concerned with *risotto* than with the company's operations.

On the next-to-last night of his sojourn, Waldo found himself standing outside the Fenice theater during the first intermission of *Traviata* and chatting with one of the conglomerate's outside directors, a Spitsbergen tanker magnate who had been recruited to the company's board to give it an international flavor.

'I think you Americans may be in for a terrible shock,' the Norwegian remarked.

Waldo didn't respond immediately. In his experience, such remarks by foreigners were typically based on a sort of generalized anti-American envy and not on hard information.

After a suitable pause, he asked politely, 'In what sense?' The man probably had the gold standard in mind. There was no way it could last out the summer, the way the dollar was behaving.

'I spend a great deal of time in the Middle East,' said the Norwegian. 'I can tell you this: the Arabs are beginning to see how things really are.'

'I'm not sure I follow you.'

'Oil. You Americans live off cheap oil. Too cheap. So now you use so much you have to import — what, thirty percent of your requirements?'

'More than that, I think.'

'Whatever. It's a high percentage. Too high. Plus, in America, a gallon of oil sells for less than we sell a bottle of beer in Oslo. That's a gift to you from the Persian Gulf. The Arabs are beginning to understand that. Their primers are the profit statements of your great oil companies.'

For the remainder of the evening, while Alfredo agonized onstage and Violetta coughed herself to death, Waldo's concentration was elsewhere: oil.

Oil. Apart from money itself, the only world commodity.

The world was committed to oil because oil was so cheap. Oil powered not only the booming factories and freeways of the developed world but made possible the economic survival of backwater pottery yards; it powered not just the jetliners of Pan Am and Lufthansa but tinpot river steamers serving shantytowns. If you thought about it, the entire world order had come to be predicated on a commodity that sold for $3 a barrel FOB Kuwait or Houston or Tampico. A world commodity: and yet the swing supply, over 250 *billion* barrels, which cost virtually nothing to produce, was controlled by a handful of Arabs.

That night he couldn't sleep for puzzling out the political, cultural, and financial implications of the world oil market. If only . . .

The next morning he thought he had it. He sketched out his ideas and a number of Waldovian equations in a long letter to Menchikov. Anxious as he was to test his thinking on Mallory, he thought it best to hear what Grigoriy had to say first.

As he had hoped, Menchikov was completely enthusiastic. *Your idea is classic,* 'Prof. F. S. Mukerjee, BA, MA, DPhil (Oxon)' of the 'Bengal Academy of Applied Economic Philology' in Calcutta replied to Waldo's letter from Venice.

> *You have hit on a set of conditions unique in the recorded history of commerce. I agree with you that it is the political pathway that should be prepared and emphasized first. You may not be aware of this, but the bogus Metternich who whispers in Mr Nixon's ear about foreign affairs has also been busy in the Middle East filling the Shah's foolish head with dreams of glory. If my sources in Teheran are correct, I believe the point can be made by Washington that the Empire of Cyrus and Darius cannot be re-created with $3 a barrel petroleum. But at $20 a barrel . . .! Perhaps you and our persuasive banking friend should point this out in Foggy Bottom. And in Vienna also. Do not overlook OPEC, which is like a child that does not know its own strength.*

As for the economic outcome, Menchikov was sanguine.

> *Oil is like arterial blood. It nourishes every commercial organ, perfuses every financial tissue. It can therefore carry inflation, privation, and every conceivable form of economic infection to the tiniest hamlet and greatest city alike. A dramatic fiat increase in the OPEC price will unleash a fever of greed and retribution that will furnish us opportunities beyond anything you and I have imagined.*

Waldo ticked these off in his head. A traumatic boost in the price of oil would have to be funded at the printing press. The Federal Reserve's foot now weighed heavily on the money pedal and could only grow heavier still, what with an election year approaching. This would consolidate the economic rills and streamlets that Vietnam had created into a mighty torrent of inflation. America would export inflation in its money the way other countries haplessly exported fruit pests in crates of papayas.

To the wealthy, inflation was a serious hazard, but to the poor, it was lethal. Some sort of massive credit infusion would be required to get the nonindustrialized world through an oil shock. No debtor ever loved his creditors; few friendships ever survived a loan. Properly orchestrated, energy-enforced borrowing could be construed as a sort of reparations exacted by the haves upon the have-nots, a penalty inflicted upon them simply for being poor.

Best of all, the coin had two sides. Commodity bubbles — from tulips to salad oil — occurred when people were induced to believe that commodity prices no longer followed the law of supply and demand, when people no longer thought of commodities as commodities. This was the delusion that lured fools into the game, pushed up prices, and pushed up production costs in a mad bidding for a piece of the action. If oil prices rose, so would all energy costs, and so — in time — would the price of everything.

If history was any guide, inflationary forces would be set in motion which, in time, under the right conditions, could be pulled inside out into an equally calamitous deflation.

When Waldo told him what he had in mind, Mallory literally jumped to his feet with excitement. It was as if the idea already existed in a data base in the banker's mind and Waldo had merely pushed the button that brought it to the screen.

'Jesus, Waldo, say the bastards raise the price to ten bucks a barrel. Do you know what that means? Especially if they insist on being paid in dollars, as they always have. Overnight the money supply's got to damn near double. You can see what that means!'

'What about the Federal Reserve?'

'Fuck the Fed! We'll print the goddamn money ourselves, offshore. We'll print it in Hong Kong, or FOB Jiddah, or

London. The camel drivers are going to want Uncle Sam's patented green. No pesos, no zlotys, no Yap money. Oil trades in dollars; we'll finance it in offshore dollars. And if some of *our* money leaks back into the official figures, how can we help it? The Fed's ass will be in a sling anyway, because if the domestic price rises too, it's going to have to crank up the printing presses or watch the country go bust. Texas wildcatters are no different from the Sultan of Swat; they like to get paid too.'

Mallory looked closely at Waldo and smiled.

'Waldo, you once told me the point of this exercise was to induce the banking system to bust itself. Well, here's our big chance.'

'Tell me how you see it.'

'OK. Let's say the Oman of Umptysquat now sells oil to the King of Bongo Bongo. As long as oil's been at three bucks a barrel, Bongo Bongo's been able to come up with the ready cash. But now, suddenly, it's gone up — to ten bucks a barrel. Which Bongo Bongo hasn't got. Not in dollars. Now, Bongo Bongo's internal trade is denominated in bananas. But when King Bongo goes to the Oman and tries the old "How about if I pay you in bananas?" ploy, the Oman gives him a steely glare and says, no, we want no bananas today. No dollars, no oil. No oil, thinks King Bongo, means no hot water in the pot, and the local missionary's coming to dinner. It starts to look as if old King Bongo's going to end up in the pot himself. Now what he *should* do is call up the other Bongo Bongos and say, "Hey, guys, let's pull in our belts and sweat this guy out, and if nobody buys his oil for a while, and we all hang together, maybe the Oman'll get sensible and roll back the price to something we can afford." But the trouble with that idea is there's no money in it for middlemen, so *pouf!* just when they're wringing their hands, and beginning to talk about the possibility of the Oman extending terms and taking a chance on Bongo Bongo's credit, up pops the guy from CertBank's Bongo Bongo office.

' "Hey, fellas," he says, "no sweat! Tell you what we're gonna do. You, King Bongo, need a million bucks to pay the

Oman for his oil. We'll lend you the million, and you use it to pay the Oman. Now, Mr Oman, when the King forks over the million bucks, you place it on deposit with us, on demand at money market rates. I mean, everybody knows, your Omanship, that a dollar on deposit with the Cert's as good as the gold in Fort Knox.''

'So the Oman deposits the million bucks. Now, here's the good part, Waldo. The King's going to keep needing oil, which means he's going to keep needing dollars. So we take the original million and go back to King Bongo, and we tell him, ''Your majesty, why don't we lend you the million all over again, so you can build a banana processing plant to turn your bananas into health food, which you'll sell to American health-food nuts for many hundreds of millions and your pot will boil happily ever after!'' '

By now Mallory was fully caught up in his fantasy, his voice exhilarated, his words tumbling.

'And the King'll go for it, except he'll keep needing dollars to pay for oil — forget the banana plant! — and so around and around it'll go, and every time we ''recycle'' — good word, huh? — we'll hit him up for three points over the London rate plus fat loan fees that we can book as profit. Shit, Waldo, it'll be like one of those Gardena poker parlors.'

'Gardena poker parlors?'

'Yeah, those places in California where they play tablestakes poker and the house takes out a small piece of each hand — to pay for supplying the venue and the cards. If the game goes on long enough, the house ends up with all the money. It's called compound interest, and compound interest operates the same way in Bongo Bongo as it does in Gardena, California.'

True, true, thought Waldo.

'Now,' Mallory continued, 'there's no way that that merry old soul, King Bongo, can ever pay us, provided the price of oil stays up long enough for us to dig him a really deep hole.'

'What about the banana-processing plant?'

'That's the beautiful part.' Mallory smiled, obviously pleased with himself. 'King Bongo's no fool. He can count too. He'll personally cream off, say, twenty percent the first time around, then thirty, then fifty. We'll "recycle" the oil payments to Bongo Bongo, and he'll "recycle" them either to Zurich or to us in Grand Cayman. Now the bank's liable to both the Oman and King Bongo for their deposits, and all we've got on the other side of the ledger is a lot of Bongo Bongo IOUs that aren't worth shit. You might say it's a way of turning a debtor into a creditor. Just think for a second about some of these countries that are right now just breaking even importing oil at three bucks a barrel, someplace like Brazil with a big population and no oil of its own. Down the tubes. What do you think?'

'I think it's brilliant,' said Waldo, 'but I don't think you'd get away with it in a million years.'

'The hell we won't! Can't you see what this means to the banks. Furthermore, we're going to get hyperinflation thrown in as an optional extra. It's a lock!'

'You seem to be very certain, Manning.'

'I'll tell you what. I'll bet you five hundred shares of CertCo stock that if OPEC or the Shah will get the ball rolling, we can put a hundred billion of this kind of Bongo Bongo loans on the books of the big banks within five years. I think I'll start by calling on the president of the Shah of Iran Fan Club over at Chase Manhattan Plaza. You might drop down to Washington in the near future and have a little visit with your old Harvard colleague Henry the K. Point out to him that at ten bucks a barrel, Iran can buy a shitload of F-14s.'

He sounded as if it were a foregone conclusion, that one could tinker with the whole world's economic fate as casually as changing a light bulb. His extreme confidence concerned Waldo. Yet Mallory had never yet disappointed him, so why worry now?

The rest, of course, was history.

The initial shock of 1973, the second round of price increases and the embargo of a year later, and the final upheaval in the wake of the 1979 Iranian revolution, produced gross suffering and misery around the world and gross inconvenience to the American consumer. From the outset, proposals rang through

Capitol Hill and Whitehall and Tokyo that some international body, possibly an adjunct of the World Bank, should assume responsibility for coordinating and smoothing over the often terrifying financial disruptions that OPEC had wrought.

'That is one thing we cannot allow to happen,' said Mallory. 'This is clearly a job for the private sector,' he told a Senate Select Committee.

'Obviously only the banking system can handle this,' whispered Waldo in the ears of two muddled Presidents.

In the end, the prospect of profit carried the day. Rallying behind Mallory, the banks and financial middlemen mobilized in concert and beat back the dominions and powers who made so bold as to suggest that this was a task too important to be left to the 'free market' and who proposed instead that the energy crisis be handled by the IMF, or the Treasury Department, or a consortium of central banks.

The winning side fought under a banner that flaunted as its Excelsior! the phrase 'petrodollar recycling.'

Mallory had devised the slogan, but — for once — he was happy not to take credit for it.

'Once you've learned to swim in one-hundred-percent-pure bullshit, you never quite lose the knack,' he told Waldo. 'Doesn't ''petrodollar recycling'' sound great? It's pure crap, of course, but I thought it might play in Washington, so I tried it out at a meeting a few of us had the other day on how to deep-six a couple of senators on decontrol. I thought the guy from Citibank was going to shit in his pants trying to get back to Three Ninety-nine Park and earn a few brownie points with Walt, whose turn before the House was coming up the next day. And sho' 'nuff, there it was on the broad tape before lunch.'

'Petrodollar recycling' would be Ropespinner's most successful catchphrase. It sounded so rational, yet it fronted for a litany of outright folly committed in the name of profit. The private financial sector, fired up like zealots at the prospect of handling the torrential financial flows OPEC was generating, marshaled beneath the gonfalon of CertBank, took up the cry with one voice, and made it resound in every corner of the earth in which deals were made.

'Countries don't go broke,' Mallory reassured the world as the oil billions poured in one door and were sent out another, for handsome fees, to Mexico and Ghana and Brazil.

'Countries don't go broke,' chorused back the other big banks and Wall Street and the media.

'Pinch me, I'm dreaming,' said Mallory. 'You remember that old radio show *Can You Top This?* Well, this is the *Can You Top This?* of bullshit! Did you see that piece by Wriston in the *Journal*? Who writes that stuff for him?'

In 1979, Mallory returned from opening a CertBank office in Manila. When he and Waldo got together, the first thing he said was, 'You remember back in 1971, about Bongo Bongo and the banana plant?'

'You said it wouldn't get built, and I must say it doesn't seem to have been.'

'Well, so far we've taken in about three billion in deposits from private persons in Bongo Bongo and elsewhere. Did you see that piece of Grogan's the day before yesterday?'

Waldo had. In a *Wall Street Journal* editorial, Mallory's pet journalist had written, 'Petrodollar recycling has been a noble and inventive effort by market forces to ameliorate what might otherwise have been grievous financial dislocations throughout the world. The market has proved its character.'

'Well,' said Mallory, 'I can tell you that most of what we've loaned to the LDCs has been "financially dislocated" right back out again into the numbered accounts of the guys with the Porsche sunglasses and the Savile Row uniforms, just the way I told you it would. I'll bet petrodollar recycling has added a hundred percent to the price of Monte Carlo condominiums. My guy in Basel tells me Lausanne looks like downtown Ouagadougou. You remember our old London office, the one in Hays Mews with the butler? Well, we've built a replica on Grand Cayman so King Bongo or Mr Mobutu can feel like regular English lords when they come to visit their dough. We've got this new division called OPB — Overseas Private Banking. I put some of my slickest people in there. The amounts we're pulling out of Mexico would boggle your mind, and it looks like that's just starting. We hear some of our competition has taken on some very interesting new customers in Colombia and Bolivia. Dope money. A good whiff of corruption can only help when the time comes for us to pull the trigger. Which is something you must tell me about, by the way.'

'I shall — when the time comes.'

'That's extremely helpful of you.' Mallory snickered. 'Anyway, what with Iran down the tubes and a wimp in the White House, I think all we should do right now is hang on to our hats. The basic OPEC model's been great, and look how we've loaded it up with options — double-digit inflation, fifteen percent money, M-One totally out of control, a spot market in oil — and unless I miss my guess, we ain't seen nothing yet!'

As usual, he was right on the money.

201

The sheer velocity of financial activity and wealth creation that took place in OPEC's wake had no precedent in history.

The *size* of everything got so much larger. Waldo found his old frames of reference discombobulated, then obsolete. The Eurodollar market swelled from $150 billion to nearly *$2 trillion*. A reader who followed the tombstone notices that signaled major financings could not have helped but notice that what the sixties considered a big bond issue or syndicated loan would scarcely have paid the interest on its 1980s equivalent.

Volume produced a CertCo-led proliferation of new instruments and 'financial products': reshapings and reclothings of lending and borrowing packaged to take advantage of a now totally institutionalized market. First came listed options, then options on options, then futures on options on options. Along with money market funds that permitted the small depositor to move his money around as easily as an oil company treasurer.

New occasions teach new duties, the poet said, and these new financial products spawned new forms of parasites and purveyors: deposit brokers, risk arbitrageurs, discount brokerages. Along with all this nominally 'creative' activity, Waldo was delighted to discern a general ethical and intellectual deterioration within the financial community.

The face of Wall Street changed. Sometimes, in an old file, Waldo would come across a prospectus for a deal he remembered from the sixties and early seventies. He would trace his finger along the names that had made up the underwriting syndicate. By 1983, three-quarters of those firms no longer existed, either sunk without a trace in bankruptcy or swallowed up by the giant investment conglomerates that were emerging.

Disasters and near disasters became frequent; foreign exchange and securities scandals regularly convulsed the markets: 'scandal,' 'crisis,' 'collapse,' 'default' — once apocalyptic words — now regularly were found in the financial pages and discussed phlegmatically in private Wall Street dining rooms.

And there seemed no end to it.

'You know, Waldo,' Mallory announced one day, 'we've suckered over fifteen hundred banks into this "sovereign lending" racket. Fifteen hundred! Jesus H. Christ, can you believe it! But these out-of-town guys like to play international banker, and why not? — it isn't their dough! Our typical mullet's from some place in the heartland. Runs a bank with maybe a couple hundred million in assets, real chickenfeed. Now say we want to lighten up on our Zaire exposure. We've got these clowns called "country risk analysts" who give us the thumbs-up on whether Zaire's OK for now, or should we keep an eye on Venezuela. Have you ever heard such bullshit — like trying to read someone's mind with a ruler! Anyway, old Elmer from East Dipshit gets a call from one of my senior International guys. How'd the Second National of East Dipshit like to participate in the next round of Zaire Hydropower? Now all Elmer probably knows about Zaire is that "it's one of them nigger countries," as they like to say in East Dipshit, but he remembers how some guy from the First National of *West* Dipshit got his picture taken with Walt Wriston when Citi syndicated the Brazilian Power Authority loan — the proceeds of which kept half the hookers in Paris in caviar for six months.

'The fun's just beginning,' concluded Mallory. 'What did I tell you about letting credit run wild? It's the straw that sure as hell stirs the drink.'

Mallory was moving the Cert at a feverish pace. 'I want some of that Wall Street action for us,' he said. 'We want to put our own money on the line.

'You won't believe what's going on,' he told Waldo. 'I had lunch the other day with this kid who runs Bendix. He came in with his investment banker and his "strategist," one of those cute blonde MBA types dressed like a guy, with the little necktie and so on. He wants to make a run at Martin Marietta. He wouldn't know a missile if it flew straight up where the sun never shines. He wants the Cert to be his lead bank. We'll lend him the money, of course.'

'American industry is in the hands of a new generation,' Waldo observed.

'It sure as hell is,' said Mallory. 'My guys in our Southwest Banking Group tell me there's a chickenshit little bank called Penn Square down in Oklahoma City that's wholesaling loan participations a Brooklyn loan shark wouldn't touch. We've been invited in on the action. My people are tempted. You can guess why: "Because, sir, everyone else is doing it!" Best way in the world to go broke. Get in the game against your own better judgment just because the asshole down the block says he's going to play. Anyway, according to them, Continental Illinois is the big player in the Penn Square loan layoffs, well up into the ten digits, and Seattle First is right behind Continental, and − as you might expect − our little friends at Chase are practically peeing in their pants to be included.'

'And what will you do?'

'I think we'll give this one a pass. If we take too many hits, my image could tarnish. When they stop buying my act, we might as well pack it in.'

Mallory paused, then: 'You know what I think? I think OPEC's been a wave with no water in it. I think the price of oil is a hell of a lot more likely to go to $10 from here than to $100. I don't think the demand's there any more. When oil goes, watch out!'

Waldo agreed. In his mind, there were two kinds of inflation: demand-pulled and greed-driven, two fundamentally distinct reasons why the price of an economic unit − a BTU, an hour of labor, a can of soup − would rise without a commensurate increase in its intrinsic value. The OPEC fiat pricing had been greed-driven. Now that the industrial economies except Japan were stagnant, and the growth of the undeveloped world had been stopped in its tracks by its crushing indebtedness, the game was shuddering into a new, deflationary phase.

'My policy for the moment,' Mallory concluded, 'is therefore to be very nimble and not to push it too far. Sooner or later even the best of us lose the ability to hit the curve.'

Indeed, thought Waldo, it was almost athletic, the way Mallory managed to thrust the Cert into new areas of risk and then have the judgment and dexterity to withdraw or substantially cut back just before disaster claimed competitors panting blindly behind.

'Anyway, it isn't just energy lending that's gone bananas. I hear on the QT there's an outfit called Drysdale Something-or-other trading governments in the repo market that's going to hang the Chase out to dry. You know what finance and banking have become? Supersonic musical chairs!'

'What comes next?' Waldo asked.

'Hard to say. You and I are about five-sixths of the way home into turning the world into one giant arbitrage, and the possibilities for troublemaking are very interesting indeed. Last week I had an investment banker come in — what he wants from us amounts to a policy question, so I sat in at the request of our Wall Street Division. This guy brought his client with him. Chief Executive of—' Mallory named a consumer products company Waldo immediately recognized.

'Anyway, this investment banker specializes in "leveraged buyouts"; it's the new thing in Wall Street fashion. You can tell it's trendy, because none of the guys in it were anyone you ever heard of five years ago. Funny how ready credit makes geniuses out of people. As if a bank line adds fifty points to a guy's IQ. Anyway, this CEO's talking about doing an eight-hundred-million-dollar buyout of his public stockholders. Wants to borrow four hundred million from us, and he's got a bunch of pension funds that'll put up the rest. The actual equity investment amounts to maybe twenty-five million, but these days no bank gives a shit about a capitalization that's three percent equity and ninety-seven percent debt. I listened to their song-and-dance, then I asked to see their audited statement. Audited statement? These guys looked at me like

I was the village idiot. The management guy reaches into his briefcase and pulls out a single sheet of paper. Very confidential, he says with a big confidential smile. In other words, screw the audit; this is the real poop! We all give our best serious nod and put on our best serious faces and look at what he's got to show us. Which is sure as hell confidential, especially as far as his stockholders go: secret asset appraisals, cash flow figures, hidden depreciation reserves — the figures that the stockholders don't get to see. Plus a game plan that says in Year One he knows he can sell enough assets to pay down six hundred million dollars of debt, and the business he's got left should be worth the original eight hundred million, which works to a cool thirty-to-one return on the cash equity. I couldn't resist, so I asked him how come he didn't show these numbers to his present stockholders.'

'And what did he answer?'

'He put the paper back in his briefcase, winked, and offered us a ten-percent carried equity if we'd lead the bank portion with a two hundred million slice. Our interest wouldn't be in stock, of course. Glass-Steagall rules that out. It'd be what they call "an equity equivalent contingent participation." Who thinks up these labels down there?'

'And what did you say then?'

'I said exactly what anybody on the Street does now when a fellow offers him an envelope. I said, "Why, how thoughtful of you! Count us in, and thank you very much." When the great day of reckoning comes, it won't hurt for the stockholders of this great nation to understand the vital role we big banks have played in fucking them over.'

Mallory's face turned serious.

'You know, it really *is* sort of all falling into place. These LBO guys are recycling the stockholders' assets into their own bank accounts just the way our pal King Bongo's been doing. But, hell, that's only Step One. We've been backing this fellow Pickens. I doubt he can find oil in his crankcase, but we gave him a line of credit to buy oil stocks with, and between him and these money managers that would sell their own mothers below the bid price if it made their quarterly performance look good, the oil industry's going to be stood on its head when he's finished. And after that, watch out! When the Saudis take a look at some of these "restructured" balance sheets, they're going to need about ten seconds to figure out what pushing oil back down to ten bucks a barrel could do to a twenty-to-one debt to equity ratio at Texaco.'

Mallory's voice was full, exultant. Waldo wondered if any other American businessman in history had ever felt so flushed with triumph and possibility. It really made him quite exhausted just to listen.

CertCo and its siblings and offspring stood at the very heart of the credit vortex, engaging in commercial finance, financing securities brokerage and trading and mutual funds. CertBank was recognized as the lender supreme; the first place to which takeover artists and greenmailers and LBO peddlers came for cash and complicity was One CertCo City, and they seldom went away dissatisfied. There was no 'innovation' or new 'financial breakthrough' that CertBank didn't seem ready to endorse with its participation as a leader, its expertise as a packager and marketer, or by investing its depositors' or investment clients' capital. CertCo Investment Management held over a billion dollars in 'junk bonds' in its fiduciary accounts.

Debt had become a narcotic. If religion was the opiate of the masses, so was credit the opiate of capitalism.

'When I first came to the bank,' Mallory told Waldo over dinner in early 1980, 'your brother used to say: "If it's a good deal, we'll find a way to lend money on it." Well, it's taken over twenty-five years, but I've finally got it turned ass-backwards. Today, I've got our people thinking: "If we can find a way to lend money on it, it's a good deal!" That's going to be CertBank's motto for the rest of my watch. And, if I've guessed right, it'll be the marketing pitch of every other bank in America!'

The wheel whirled faster and faster, thanks to the unleashed power of the computer. It was estimated that while world trade had a total value of three trillion annually, the annual value of worldwide financial transactions came to twenty-five times that amount: a global paperstorm of seventy-five trillion!

Mallory was exuberant. He had plunged CertBank into the new technology. One CertCo City was a humming electronic hive.

'This is better than the sixties,' he said to Waldo. 'The marriage of information technology and speculation was made in heaven.'

It certainly seemed to be true. To Wall Street was reserved the true harvest of the Reagan boom. Nine of the ten most highly compensated executives in America worked on Wall Street. Banks like the Cert competed anxiously with investment houses for the services of prodigies — so anxiously that Mallory could boast that there were a half-dozen young people within the bank who were better paid than he.

'Bank' was hardly the word for what CertCo now was, Waldo thought. Banking was something shiny and modern now, scraped utterly clean of the encrustation of old cautions.

'You know a word nobody uses any more,' Mallory gleefully observed. '*Collateral.* Our new kids can't spell it, and the kids that are training them teach that it doesn't matter anyway. The only collateral we need is our capacity to find funds to lend.'

To hear Mallory talk, the people the press celebrated as being on the cutting edge were mere children, playing with dangerous toys.

'There's a new gimmick a couple of teenage space-scientist types we hired away from Salomon Brothers have come up with. They call it "program trading." So far we've peddled about thirty billion to other bank trust departments. Basically it correlates the S&P Stock Average and the futures market. The beauty part is: it's completely automatic. No human hands. Which means that every now and then the market gets the totally unexpected shit kicked out of it. Now we can do to the stock market what we've been doing to the foreign exchange markets for the last dozen years.'

So much had changed so rapidly, so many of the old safeguards dismantled by a financial community in which not a hundred people remembered 1929. No wonder older heads troubled. Bankruptcy, once a recourse of last resort, redolent of disgrace and failure, was now just another legal ploy, useful to avert a liability suit or abrogate a contract. America was awash in financial euphemism. 'Home equity loan' sounded ever so much more palatable than 'second mortgage,' palatable to the extent of seventy-five billion dollars already on the banking system's books. CHIPS — the New York Clearing House Interbank Payments System — was balancing the books on five hundred billion dollars of bank transfers daily, and the volume processed by its acronymic overseas offspring SWIFT (Society of Worldwide Interbank Financial Telecommunications) was hardly lagging. TIGRS and CATS prowled Wall Street.

So much velocity and volatility could only promote instability. But times were good; money was being made; to a nation to which an actor President could effectively speak of 'another American triumph' while standing beside a stack of Marine coffins, there was no such thing as bad news.

How well Ropespinner had done its work was brought home to Waldo when Mallory sent him a copy of his fellow Nobel laureate James Tobin's 1984 Hirsch lecture.

Mallory had marked the final paragraph with a series of exclamation points. Tobin's words were:

I confess to an uneasy Physiocratic suspicion, perhaps unbecoming in an academic, that we are throwing more and more of our resources, including the cream of our youth, into financial activities remote from the production of goods and services, into activities that generate high private rewards disproportionate to their social productivity. I suspect that the immense power of the computer is being harnessed to this 'paper economy' not to do the same transactions more economically, but to balloon the quantity and variety of financial exchanges. For this reason perhaps, high technology has so far yielded disappointing results in economy-wide productivity. I fear that, as Keynes saw even in his day, the advantages of the liquidity and negotiability of financial instruments come at the cost of facilitating nth-degree speculation which is short-sighted and inefficient.

Well put, thought Waldo. The greatest economist alive had roundly condemned a state of affairs brought about largely by Ropespinner's ingenuity, salesmanship and leadership. Could there be any higher praise? When they were this far ahead, wouldn't it be right to quit?

But that, he knew, was the last thing on Mallory's mind.

'Banking as we've known it is dead,' Mallory told the CertCo annual meeting. 'In five years, you won't recognize CertCo or CertBank. The wave of the future is merchant banking, investment banking, trading for our own account. Going head to head with Wall Street.'

Someone asked about the growing enthusiasm for a summit meeting to stabilize exchange rates. Wouldn't a decrease in the volatility of currency flows impact the bank's profits?

'It would,' Mallory said, 'if it came to pass, which it won't. The world banking system and Wall Street have hundreds of millions of dollars invested in a market system of exchange rates. We're not going to let that investment go by the board. "Volatility" is just a word the anti-marketers use to impugn a system that works splendidly.'

What about all this takeover and leveraged buyout lending? asked someone else. Was that a good thing?

'Absolutely. It keeps the managers on their toes. It's also about the only area where we see continued loan demand.'

After the meeting, he walked Waldo over to One CertCo City to see the new trading room under construction. To Waldo, it appeared to be about the size of a football field. When completed, Mallory boasted, it would provide space for four hundred traders making markets in everything from Treasury bond futures to Polish zlotys.

'This is the wave of the future,' he said exultantly. 'Trading. Leveraging paper! Hell, Waldo, in the new American economy, no one *builds* anything any more!'

CHAPTER NINETEEN

At the conclusion of the following academic year, Waldo Emerson Chamberlain gave up his teaching posts and his directorships and consultancies.

What a glorious career it had been! And what was its high point? asked the earnest economic columnist dispatched by the *New York Times*. Had it been the Nobel Prize, awarded late in his career for the work that led to the formulation of new regressions correlating population, employment, and money growth, the so-called 'Chamberlain Effect'? Was it the two generations of business leaders he'd trained, Manning Mallory above all, but also twenty-three other Fortune 500 chief executives? Was it his impact on the world of banking, his advocacy of a central international role for US banks?

All of these, he told the man from the *Times*. It *had* been quite a career. He was especially proud of the fact that in some small way he liked to think he had helped the US banking system — through the students he sent to it — to mold and dominate a truly global financial system.

Mallory had a more scathing take on the achievements of Waldo's progeny.

'Shock troops, that's what they are. You guys in the B-schools are disembarking forty thousand MBAs a year on the beachheads of capitalism. "Master of Business Administration," my ass! Today's MBAs are nothing but overdressed computer programmers. Tell me, Waldo; when I was at the B-School, was I an arrogant little know-nothing too?'

211

'I'll take the Fifth Amendment on that one, Manning.'

Waldo quit the academic stage heaped with tribute and laurels. CertCo established Waldo Chamberlain Fellowships for Applied Monetary Theory at Harvard and MIT. Lectureships and endowments in his honor were created by old corporate clients. Perhaps the most touching commemoration was the presentation to him, by his fellow CertCo directors, of a pretty little sloop, which he promptly named *The Prime Rate*.

More honors awaited overseas. The year after his retirement, he traveled to Europe, calling in at London, Paris, Frankfurt, Padua, and Stockholm. At each stop, more medals, plaques, scrolls and emoluments were pressed on him.

Finally, in April 1984, not far short of the forty-eighth anniversary of his first and only visit to Russia, Waldo descended from an SAS jet in Sheremetievo airport.

He was in Moscow ostensibly to address the Economics Institute of the Soviet Academy of Science. In his heart, he prayed he would see Menchikov again.

And yet he was prepared to be disappointed. Common sense told him that as long as Ropespinner was still in operation, it was unlikely that Grigoriy would want to risk any overt connection.

Still, at the back of the lecture hall and in the distance at a reception at the Academy, Waldo thought he caught a fleeting glimpse of Menchikov, but when he looked again there was no one.

With his sojourn drawing to a close, he began to despair. If not now, ever again? he thought.

On the last afternoon before he was due to depart, he was stretched out in his hotel room, trying to nap, when the door from the adjoining suite opened and closed quickly, and there was Grigoriy!

They embraced and looked each other over. Menchikov was a wizened old bear now, shrunken, bent, but still gallant. His spirits seemed undiminished. He caught Waldo's solicitous look and laughed.

'Oh, Waldya, don't be looking at me like I am a fossil.

Regardez!' He danced a wheezy Cossack step, banging his heel on the floor, his head thrown back, eyes fierce in his old face.

Then he sat down heavily on the edge of Waldo's bed, puffing.

'Now, let's be talking seriously.' He saw Waldo look anxiously about him. 'Not to be worrying about surveillance,' said Menchikov. 'Don't forget, in Moscow you are — as you say in your baseball — on the home team.'

For the next hour the two men talked like veteran campaigners swapping anecdotes, going over and over Ropespinner's triumphs. Waldo was thrilled to be able to convey personally his and Mallory's excitement at what they'd done, to give Ropespinner a living dimension he feared his dry letters might sometimes not have done.

Menchikov beamed appreciatively.

'Oh, I'm loving this "petrodollar recycling" so much, Waldya. Are you knowing George Champion who was head of Chase Bank? One thing he was always saying: Never, but never be lending overseas except to central banks. If I am lending to US, I will lend to Federal Reserve Bank, but never to US Government. How easily your country has thrown aside things it took old men such suffering to learn.'

Menchikov told Waldo about other things he'd had a hand in — about the Herstatt collapse, about Calvi and the Banco Ambrosiano, about the Nugan Hand scandal in Sydney; about an operation just getting under way: the looting of a London bullion firm called Johnson Matthey.

'Will be causing Bank of England much embarrassment, which in England is almost as bad thing as bankruptcy.'

Waldo asked him if he had been active in the United States. Menchikov roared.

'My God, Waldya, why? Sometimes I'm reading what this Wriston is saying, and I'm wondering, I'm saying maybe has Waldya got big ideas and is recruiting this man too? Sometimes I'm looking at editorial page of *Wall Street Journal* and thinking, Who is telling people to be writing such things? Trotsky?'

He rumbled with laughter.

'No, no, I'm leaving America in hands of you and Mallory. A few years ago, some idiot in Dzerzhinsky Square is thinking, Hey, bright idea, comrades! We'll be buying control of some little California banks — in what you're calling "Silicon Valley" — and this way we'll be learning secrets about US high technology. I'm saying, Why is KGB buying banks when is just as easy to buy secrets, but KGB likes things to be complicated, so they try to buy bank in Walnut Creek and, as usual with KGB, *pied d'éléphant*! Big stupid mess!'

'Which reminds me, Grigoriy,' Waldo asked. 'Who else here knows about Ropespinner! I know you have people at your beck and call in the States. I know you've been able to — well, *arrange* certain things.'

'Not to worry, Waldya,' said Menchikov disarmingly. 'Here only First Secretary and I know *whole* thing about Ropespinner. Only he and I know you and Mallory are Ropespinner. Has always been this way — since Stalin. I brief each new First Secretary. For other matters, when I'm needing to *arrange* something, I'm working with certain people in Dzerzhinsky Square. But no one is there at KGB who knows about Maine. That was long time ago. Now let's be talking of other things. It's a crazy world now. There's much I don't understand. I think your President would bomb Moscow tomorrow, and yet the Narodny Bank is overdrawn maybe two hundred million, three hundred million overnight on its settlements with your banks. America sells *us* grain on terms you don't give your own people for to buy houses or saving farm. You're cutting taxes with such a deficit! Crazy!'

Waldo said nothing. He shared Menchikov's puzzlement. America seemed to be turning economic rules upside down, and yet the country went from strength to strength — if the big money being made on Wall Street was in fact strength.

'Sometimes,' continued Menchikov, 'I am lighting a candle of thanks for having your President. He is better for Ropespinner than OPEC, even. He is telling America that it is 1945 again, when you are alone in victory and virtue and the whole world loves you. What would your President know of 1945, Waldya? He fought the war in a movie

214

studio. But I can tell you is not 1945, is more like 1929.'

'There are considerable dissimilarities between now and 1929,' said Waldo evenly.

'Are there? Were you there in 1929, other than as a boy?' Menchikov saw Waldo's face turn petulant. He reached out a placatory hand. 'Now, now, I'm not picking on you. But I'm telling because I was in New York in 1929, and I was then almost thirty, a grown man, a man who had fought in the streets of St Petersburg. All people talked about in 1929 was money. All people respected in 1929 was money. All people wanted from life in 1929 was money. Our New York KGB station tells me is same now. Waldya, it is as dangerous for men to think just with their wallets as just with their cocks. Can only end in trouble. Also, then was terrible people as big financial heroes: Livermore, Raskob, Durant. No different from now. Pigs and sharks on top then; pigs and sharks now. This Pickens, this Boesky, this Drexel Burnham — phooey!'

'I don't disagree entirely, Grigoriy. Yet people also have concern about the trade deficit, about the budget deficit, about the amount of debt that's being taken on everywhere one looks—'

'Concern? Phooey!' Menchikov interrupted. 'Should be terror, Waldya, terror! Has gone too far. Look at America and Japan. Tangled up like two drowning men. If one struggles, both sink more. Beyond help. And that's what I'm wanting to talk with you about.'

'America and Japan?'

'No, about how is time now to think about finishing with Ropespinner.'

'Now? But there's still so much that could be done.'

'Is there. From here is mostly dressing, no? I know you're not thinking much of Marx, but you know what he's saying: that when it's finished, capitalism resolves everything in life to exchange value, to price. That's happened. All that's left is a last big boom in the stock market, and that's coming.'

'How can you be so sure?'

'Waldya, think what you wrote me two years ago. The dirty secret of how the rich get so rich. Inflation in the cost of living is dead, but the money that was printed to pay for inflation

215

didn't disappear, so now there will be an inflation in paper, in stocks and bonds. The pressure is there. Then, what next? Just think of your Adam Smith: "overtrading, followed by discredit." '

Waldo nodded.

Menchikov looked at Waldo earnestly. 'Waldya, I'm old man now, very old. Eighty-four. As old as the century. How long can I have left? Some mornings, I awake and look in mirror and say, Grigoriy Simonov, you're having maybe five minutes more. Other mornings, I'm thinking, Ten years more, easy. I have a cousin in Tbilisi, he's a hundred and three. But to expect I'm getting to a hundred myself is not a good bet.'

Menchikov shifted closer to Waldo and let his arm drop heavily on his friend's shoulder.

'Waldya,' he said, 'Ropespinner is for your Grigoriy what St Petersburg was for Peter the Great. Is my monument. I want to see it finished, see it whole, not with towers almost topped out but finished, complete!'

'And how *does* it finish?' asked Waldo, thinking he knew the answer.

'It finishes when the world knows what we have done. When you and Mallory come here and we tell the world that Western capitalism has been toy for Moscow, that famous CertCo bank is black angel doing devil's work, that Brazil, Mexico, Argentina are just big swindle on poor peasants by Wall Street. That Holy Mother Russia has turned capitalism upside down. That white is black, and day is night!'

'And you think that will precipitate a crisis?'

'Of course. Do you think Mexico will pay if paying back US banks makes it accomplice of Soviet plot? If big bankers and financiers are so stupid and greedy to let themselves be moved like puppets, can people be having confidence in capitalism? No! There will be confusion, disbelief, and then repudiation – because everybody who's owing money welcomes excuse not to pay. And then chaos, panic. Like a great fire, and we shall sit here and watch it like a beautiful sunset in the Caucasus. You're knowing Guy Fawkes, how he's putting gunpowder in Parliament? Now is time for us to be putting match to our powder. What more can be done? Waldya, I am too old to wait for spontaneous combustion. The time has come to light the fuse.'

'Which means that Manning and I must flee to Moscow to tell the world about Ropespinner?'

'Exactly. People must be shown who to blame, who to hate, how and why has happened this way.'

Waldo returned Menchikov's smile. 'I always suspected, Grigoriy, that this was what you had in mind for a final curtain. I do have one problem, though.'

'Which is?'

'Manning. He's at the peak of his game. I doubt he'd be anxious to cut it off just now. You and I are old men, Grigoriy. Fine for us to see the fireworks and then retire as venerated members of the *Nomenklatura*, with special shopping privileges and dachas and Zil limousines. But Manning's still a relatively young—'

Menchikov cut Waldo off. 'Waldya, of course I'm knowing this. A man like Mallory must always have a challenge. The First Secretary and I have discussed it. There is always work for the greatest banker in the world.'

'Knowing Manning, I doubt he'd find much of a challenge in running the Moscow Narodny Bank or the Banque du Nord.'

'Of course not. But from the ashes of capitalism will rise a phoenix. The need to *conquer* capitalism will have disappeared, because American capitalism will have disappeared by itself. Now will come a true socialism, a socialism based on industry, not finance, just as Marx saw, a good socialism. And there will be a great role for Mallory in that.'

Menchikov paused, looked around the room, lowered his voice and winked conspiratorially.

'In the words of the First Secretary himself, ''Comrade Mallory will be the 'economic' First Secretary''!'

Waldo's immediate reaction was dubious. Then he thought, Perhaps not, perhaps this would intrigue Manning.

'It just might appeal to him, Grigoriy. But I still think we should allow a bit more time. At least another year or two.'

Menchikov looked momentarily chagrined. Then his expression cleared.

'Well, maybe I'm not so old. So — I give you a little more time. But not more than two years.'

Menchikov rose, steadying himself with one hand.

'Now, Waldya, you'll be standing up straight, please. I'm having something for you and Comrade Mallory.'

And with a properly formal kiss on each cheek, he pinned the Order of Lenin to Waldo's suit jacket. Then he put a second medal in his hand.

'Is for Mallory. The same. And now, I'm kissing you again, Waldya — technically as proxy for kissing Mallory, but also because I'm so happy seeing you again.'

With that, the two old men fell into each other's arms. Then, after a moment, without saying anything, they shook hands and Menchikov left.

CHAPTER TWENTY

It took almost a year, however, for Waldo to summon up the courage to tell Mallory that Ropespinner must at last be brought to its conclusion.

The opportunity finally arrived when the banker came up to Quiddy for a weekend in early October. He had just been through a tiring round of negotiations on the rescheduling of the Argentine loans; Mexico still remained on the agenda.

'I don't know why everyone's shitting their pants about the goddamn Third World,' he said amusedly. 'You have any idea how much we've got in domestic commitments off the books? Do you know what an NIF is, a Note Issuance Facility?'

'Vaguely,' answered Waldo, handing Mallory a drink.

'It's a kind of now-you-see-it-now-you-don't letter of credit. An NIF commits a bank to lend if no one else will. Add those in with standby letters of credit and interest rate swaps and a whole lot of other crap we and Wall Street find we can peddle for fat fees we can book into current profits without showing the contingent liability, and you're probably talking a trillion plus.' He grinned. 'I tell you, this thing just gets better. I'm kind of looking forward to the day we pull the plug and watch the whole shooting match disappear up its own asshole.'

Waldo sensed his chance.

'That's what I want to talk to you about, Manning. I have agreed with Grigoriy that this must be Ropespinner's last year.'

Mallory looked nonplused. Then he held up a hand. 'Now, whoa there, pardner. Why the hurry? I have got some unbelievably good ideas on the burner I haven't put into play yet.'

'Manning, we owe it to Grigoriy. He wants to see Ropespinner's triumph before he dies.'

'And what's the plan? I suppose you and I hit the road, do a Philby, shuffle off to Moscow to join the Volga boatman and Gorbachev on the Kremlin wall? And we all fiddle together while Wall Street burns, and then live happily ever after? Is that it?'

Mallory's bantering tone irritated Waldo. Recently he'd found himself wondering if Manning wasn't too confident, too cocksure and facetious. He hadn't liked it when Mallory showed up on Labor Day in a T-shirt that said *Supermole*. He hadn't thought it very discreet of Mallory to commission Mrs Arthurs to make him a sampler to mark the thirtieth anniversary of Ropespinner. Overconfidence could get even the brightest people into trouble.

'We won't discuss it again tonight,' he said. 'But I want you to sleep on it.'

That night, Mallory lay awake — adding it all up.

The old boy had a point, he decided. The real work *was* mostly done. The germs were deep in the system now, at work inside its vital organs. It was like AIDS. Abuse any system long enough and it would fall apart. Look at the banking system. Banks were supposed to be like churches, but here the Bank of Boston was caught washing money for the Mob; the Security Pacific had knifed Unocal, its client for decades, in the back during the Pickens bid; Citibank had tendered the Martin Marietta pension stock it held as fiduciary to Bill Agee. Old Giannini had built the Bank of America like a rock, and look at the shape it was in! The catalog of self-inflicted, Ropespinner-inspired disasters was endless.

There was just no way the LDCs could pay as things stood, which sooner or later meant back to the printing presses for the Fed. A sharp downward nudge on the economic needle, and a bunch of these leveraged buyouts were going to go bust. The smart money was secretly betting oil was on its way to $10 a barrel, which meant the Texas banks would have to kiss a few billion in oilpatch loans goodbye. Chevron would probably go down the tubes, maybe Phillips, and once the dominoes started, watch out! Hell, even credit card delinquencies were climbing. It was all in place. Time, indeed, to go.

The next morning, he suggested a sail. It was a fine, sparkling day with a hint of winter. Mallory could tell Waldo's mood was as autumnal as the morning. As they climbed down to the dock, he tried to divert him.

'You know how the *Times* has been all over us about CertCo City? I told Punch Sulzberger to call off that holier-than-thou architecture critic or no CertCo advertising for six months. Think he'll cave?'

'I suspect so,' said Waldo, taking a jib out of its sailbag. 'Times change, no pun intended.' They do indeed, he thought. Like banks, newspapers were also supposed to be something more than mere businesses: beacons to steer by, guardians of the public treasure. Well, now they were no different from any prisoners of their earning power, hostages to the price of their shares.

When they were well out on the water, gliding in the direction of the Quiddy light, Mallory looked at Waldo and said, 'I stared up at the ceiling most of last night. I think you and the Volga Boatman are right. This thing isn't going to fall apart all by its lonesome. It they'd left Regan at Treasury, I'd have said it would, but Baker's too smart. The system's tough as a turkey. It can take a lot of pounding. It might just keep staggering along, and then we'd have thirty years of our collective genius down the tubes with nothing to show for it. People need an excuse to panic. My only question is, What the hell am I going to do in Russia?'

Waldo told him what Menchikov had said.

Mallory reacted enthusiastically. 'Right on!' Building a bank was one thing, he thought, but building an entire economy, that was something else! It would be like going up against Chase or Citi, except a billion times bigger. The idea was enormously appealing.

'Count me in,' he said. 'I'm your boy. A year from next month we'll be sharing our Thanksgiving turkey with your old pal in Moscow. Barring unforeseen developments, of course. Don't forget to write it in your CertCo genuine leather 1986 datebook.'

They laughed together, then lapsed into silence.

Waldo brought the boat around smartly. The familiar prospect presented itself; the deep green smear of firs along the cliff, the ochre line of bluffs, the white angulation of the house.

Mallory watched the sharp morning sunlight glitter on the bay and wondered what it would be like in Russia. Cold. He'd have to get some heavy suits. From the pictures he'd seen of the Soviet leaders, there wasn't a decent tailor between Leningrad and Vladivostock. Hadn't that been Burgess's complaint? He was glad now he'd boned up on Philby and the rest of them. He wondered if Philby was still alive, what he was like.

Wasn't Philby a general? Well, they'd have to make him a general too.

Hell, he thought, compared to what he and Waldo had pulled off, Philby and those other guys were just chickenfeed. Of course, Ropespinner had been right out in the open, up front all the way. None of that spy novel shit: code pads, letter drops, microdots, safe houses.

He thought about the Russian economy. Plenty to work with there. The Russians had gold, oil, captive manpower. What they didn't have, they'd soon enough be able to buy for ten cents on the dollar, maybe less. Ropespinner would see to that.

It was going to be some show, so let it begin!

The notion made him laugh out loud, startling Waldo so that he missed his mooring and had to come around for a second pass.

THE PRESENT

January

CHAPTER TWENTY-ONE

NEW YORK
Sunday, January 12th

The dream always began the same way: Elizabeth found herself locked in a small room, a tiny chamber tight and airless as a coffin.

Then, somehow, two men got in there with her, always the same two men. Sometimes they were dressed in costumes, ordinary or fantastical; more often, like now, they were naked. Except the one advancing on her appeared to be clad in church robes, but why were his garments green with red tabs, like a soldier's uniform? The man's lower body was bare; his penis was enormous, and now there were hands everywhere, and three or four men, also naked, including Uncle Waldo and a man whose face she thought she recognized, if only he'd just turn a shade more toward her, but of course he wouldn't; and Peter was there too, but only for an instant, vanishing into a door she hadn't noticed just as she reached him. Was the scene in color or black-and-white? Or brown, the sepia of old photographs; yes that was it, it was brown! Ruddy brown like sunburn, and the sun was overhead and dropping through a brimstone sky, and there was a beach in the distance, but who was that with Uncle Waldo, or was it Peter's face on Uncle Waldo's body? Walking on a beach. Water below: wild, rushing water breaking upon the trees of a deep green forest, the beach now rocky, suddenly falling away as cliff face. Heat. Each tree now a column of flame. It was so confusing, she kept turning, encircled by pillars of fire that reached to the dull sky, and then she felt hands reaching for her, she heard voices, low, secret voices, as if in a dream within the dream, speaking to each other in a strange language, in words she didn't understand but thought she did. She tried to squirm away from hands that grasped her and propelled her toward a black window behind which were flames. She cried for help to Uncle Waldo, now naked again, but as she watched, horrified, his body blistered and then she felt other hands on her, felt them tear away her dress, felt fingers on her breast, icy hot fingers, burning like charcoal, pushing her toward the fire that was suddenly everywhere, as if the surface of the moon were burning with a freezing flame, and she looked around and one of the men pushing her was Peter, and another man, faceless except he really wasn't, was holding him, holding Peter — or was it Uncle Waldo, or some other man? Or maybe it was Peter after all; she heard herself screaming in terror and frustration — all these men holding each other by the penis, dancing around her in an obscene circle. She shut her eyes against the sight, but her eyes wouldn't close. Flames were everywhere now, but her feet were mired and she couldn't flee. She felt the heat, heard the strange mutterings in the dark, heard a roaring like a great wind. The fire was coming at her snakelike; it was at her ankles; she knew she was about to die . . .

The force of the dream pushed Elizabeth awake so abruptly that it was some time before she could figure out where she was.

She shivered under the covers. Outside she heard the hiss of tires on a wet street.

She looked around. The room was dark. Hotel, said her mind. She shook her head to clear it. A bureau and mirror, an armchair with a dressing gown thrown over it, a television set. Slowly it came into focus: a hotel room. A hint of dull morning light edged through the curtains. She turned her head on the pillow. A clock on the night table blinked 7:24. Her awareness skittered over these facts, seeking a purchase. New York, she thought, I am in New York. I am in the Carlyle Hotel.

All at once she was fully awake. She snapped on the bedside light and sat up. The cover slipped away and she hugged herself. Was it really that chilly — or was it the dream?

New York. Manic, ruinous, indispensable New York. A place that made her nerve ends simmer. Necessary to visit

226

professionally, but no place to live. She'd hated it when her mother left her father and brought her here to live with Peter in that large, gloomy apartment on Park Avenue, and she'd never liked it since. Chicago had been spacious and sunny; she'd loved Winnetka, loved New Trier High School, loved the openness of downtown and the lake. In New York, everyone was sealed up in an envelope of self-absorption. People were always talking about the 'energy' of the place, but to her it was just so much commotion and noise. A city of strangers without pasts.

Nevertheless, New York was the great coagulation of wealth and striving that nourished a booming art market. No point in complaining, she told herself. You come here; you do what you have to do; and as soon as you can you rush back to blessed, civilized Paris and breathe deeply.

This particular trip — except for Chicago — had been a waste of time. The main purpose of her journey was to look in on Sotheby's and Christie's semiannual Old Master sales, but the stuff was dregs and the estimates clearly reflected a frantic market rather than artistic quality or condition.

Her mind returned for an instant to her nightmare. Versions of the same dream had been haunting her sleep on and off for a month now, worrying her mind like a terrier. Elusive as smoke in the hand, the mélange of faces and images merely grazed the borders of recollection; she knew them and she didn't. She wished the dream would either resolve itself or take its troubling baggage of puzzles away.

She swung her legs out of bed. Damn, she thought, and why haven't I called Francis Mather?

She walked naked across the room and pulled the curtains apart. The sky over the park was murky. Far below, Madison Avenue looked deserted.

More than anything else she wanted to see Francis again; she'd certainly had all the time and opportunity in the world, and yet she'd done nothing. Damn! And why? She should have telephoned the day she got here, but she'd let the time go by, knowingly permitted her schedule to be eaten up by one small bit of wasted time after another, and finally it was too late; to call now would seem insulting. Stupid. Stupid! Stupid! Stupid!

I'll call him from Paris, she told herself. I'll pretend I never came.

Grow up, she told herself. Absently she looked herself over in the mirror.

Well, she *had* had to make that unplanned trip to Chicago. The Art Institute had been offered a fantastic Renaissance painting, an 'Allegory of Love' by Lotto, a mysterious and irresistible painting that could have hung without apology in the Uffizi. It was priced at $7 million, which was well beyond Chicago's purse of the moment, but the Art Institute's director had come up with the notion that Chicago and Concorde might buy the picture jointly, on a buy-sell first refusal arrangement that would ensure Concorde a good return on its money. It made sense, and Elizabeth was 90 percent along the way to doing the deal. Concorde's role would remain strictly anonymous. As Tony liked to say, 'We make money the old-fashioned way. We don't talk about it.'

Back went her thoughts to the subject of Reverend Francis B. Mather, DD. Indeed, her thoughts had been so thoroughly anchored there for the last three weeks — since their chance meeting in London — that on one occasion she'd caught herself doodling *Mrs the Reverend Francis B. Mather, DD*. Just like a schoolgirl scribbling in a textbook. Elizabeth Bennett Mather. Didn't sound bad, did it? Why hadn't she called him?

She hadn't called him, she knew, because she was scared. But of what? Of failure, of disappointment, of using up what she was convinced were scant remaining rations of unhedged feeling?

While she was drying her hair, she had an inspiration. She hurried into the bedroom and rummaged around for the newspapers of the day before; she knew she'd hung on to Saturday's *Times* because there was something she wanted to clip. She located the paper and riffled through the first section.

Here it was: RELIGIOUS SERVICES. She skimmed the Protestant Episcopal listings. Ah! 'Church of All Angels and All Souls. The Rector will offer communion at eleven o'clock.'

It took her a good deal of trial and error, but finally she

put together what she thought was a reasonable go-to-meeting outfit. Sunday communion was not the place for Armani. Then she went downstairs to the hotel dining room. She dawdled through the papers, but her mind refused to concentrate. To her surprise, she could hardly get her breakfast down. Time seemed to move at half speed.

When she finally went outside at ten thirty, it was nippy and damp and chilly. The streets were quiet; the city was closed up like a clam. She walked up Madison. This far north, the standardized Milan-Paris-London cosmopolitanism of midtown began to peter out; it began to feel like a neighborhood, to have some of the same quality she loved so much about Paris.

All Angels's neighborhood, however, struck her as definitely on a downward drift, shabby, unswept, not yet caressed by the intrusive fingers of gentrification. The red stone bulk of the church anchored a row of deteriorating townhouses between Third and Second avenues. She judged All Angels to have been built toward the end of the nineteenth century. It was plain, solid and tough. It had seen a lot and it would be there at the end.

People were drifting in. She found a seat at the far end of a pew about halfway back in the church; she was half hidden from the pulpit by a column.

It had been a very long time, she thought, since she had been to church. Funerals and the pretentious bourgeois country weddings to which Luc dragged her didn't count. She looked around. All Angels wasn't packed, but it was full enough. Like the neighborhood, the congregation was a trifle frayed, although here and there a sable coat gave off a whiff of important money.

The service was elegant and moving. She was impressed by the dignity and commitment with which Francis handled himself. She became aware that she hadn't really taken any of this seriously; all too carelessly she had assumed that his vocation was something he did with his free time, when he wasn't having a martini at his club or being fitted for a suit or discussing Eurodollars with Basel bankers. The realization made her feel like a jackass and a lightweight. What was she doing here?

She found his sermon amazing. It was eloquent and fierce, and that impressed her. But what stopped her cold was that in her wildest imaginings she could never have conceived that she would hear, in a middle-class Upper East Side church, before a congregation like this, what amounted to a crusade preached against a bank! He gets this from his Abolitionist forebears, she thought.

The sermon was based on Matthew 21:12–13: 'And Jesus entered the temple of God and drove out all who sold and bought in the temple, and he overturned the tables of the money-changers and the seats of those who sold pigeons. He said to them, "It is written, 'My house shall be called a house of prayer'; but you make it a den of robbers." '

As he read the text, Elizabeth reflexively thought of paintings of Christ and the Money-changers. There were the versions by El Greco in Washington and in London, along with a disputed version in the Fogg she remembered from her student days. The Fogg, she thought. Cambridge. Cambridge and Uncle Waldo; Uncle Waldo – and Manning Mallory, against whose very bank Francis Mather was preaching! El Greco-Fogg-Cambridge – Uncle Waldo – Manning Mallory. Odd, small world.

'We must think of this city, this whole wild world beyond the walls of this church, as God's temple as well,' Francis preached.

He didn't fulminate; he didn't thunder or harangue, yet as she listened, Elizabeth felt she was hearing the trumpet of righteousness.

'The city is a place where men are brought together and have need of each other and of the love of God to sustain themselves. And yet I fear that this larger house of God, of which this church is but one tiny chamber, has become a nest of money-changers, a den of robbers.

'On Friday last, one of the towering institutions of this city, an institution which has sucked from our streets wealth for itself and it stockholders and fame and power for its chief executive, announced that it would no longer cash public assistance checks, welfare checks. It would cease to do so because, according to the chief executive of CertBank himself,

230

there is no profit in it! The business is inconvenient, Mr Mallory says; it has no prospect of earning a return for his bank, he says, a bank whose profits last fiscal quarter were in excess of two hundred million dollars, whose profits last quarter represented an increase of nearly thirty percent, at a time when hundreds of thousands of people in this city alone can find no work, no place to live, can earn no money.

'Twenty years ago, this same bank, and this same banker, for exactly the same stated reasons of profit, decreed that entire areas of this city, poor areas, humble areas, were beyond the credit pale and the inhabitants of those districts were exiled from creditworthiness. That foul practice was called redlining. It is still in effect. Mr Manning Mallory and his Certified Guaranty National Bank, his CertCo and his CertCo Commercial Finance Company and his CertCo Realty Credit Corporation, can make hundreds of millions available to the leeches of Wall Street, to arbitrageurs and greenmailers and takeover artists and speculators of every kind; Mr Manning Mallory and his great bank can make hundreds of millions of dollars available to the real estate barons who have robbed the neighborhoods of this city of every vestige of light and spaciousness; Mr Manning Mallory and his great bank can organize a four-hundred million-dollar loan to the Soviet Union, which is sworn to efface from the earth the name of the very God we come to this house to worship. For such men, Mr Manning Mallory and his great bank will do all these things, but for a Puerto Rican laborer trying to finance a *bodega*, or a black man a truck, or a community a day-care center, it is impossible to borrow a small sum!'

Francis paused. His eyes swept the church; instinctively Elizabeth bowed her head, not wanting him to see her. She couldn't explain it, but she felt like an eavesdropper.

Francis began to speak again.

'I know what I have to say may go down badly with some of you. There will be those among you who own shares of CertCo. Those who in one way or another are obligated to this bank, or other banks, or possibly to Mr Mallory personally. To you I say, Know that it is in God's work that we are joined.

231

'I also say this. Christianity and capitalism, faith and money, ethics and speculation, despite what some people would have you believe, are not mutually exclusive. To be sure, they do not exist easily together, but we cannot take that to mean they are totally incompatible, locked in an unendurable, eternal conflict. A man can epitomize Christian virtue — be moral, just, honest, charitable, and devout — and yet be a success in business, provided he tempers the urge to acquire wealth with a leaven of concern for the general good and a sense of obligation to those who invariably must live with the consequences of his success. Wealth is a fine thing to possess, but wealth is not wisdom, not character, not license to abandon all Christian principle. We must be caring of each other or we shall perish separately, broken up into tiny striving cells of selfishness.

'It was not money Christ scourged and sought to drive out of the temple. It was the meanness of spirit of the money-changers, the bird sellers. It was the worship of money — of profit — for its own sake.

'God trusts us to do His will. He gave us His only Son that we might be given a fresh start. We owe some mite of our own toward giving the less fortunate a decent start — if it can be done at no real cost to ourselves.

'It is with this sense of Christian duty, therefore, that I want to ask you to join with me in applying pressure to CertBank, and to Mr Mallory, to reconsider its position. This church has had long-standing connections with the bank. Some of you may maintain, or be able to influence, substantial accounts or relationships that CertBank values highly. All this may have some effect.

'But to make our position plain, I should like to invite you to join me a week from tomorrow, on the twentieth, in marching in protest outside the bank's main office at One CertCo City.'

A murmur rippled through the congregation, part dismay, part approbation, part surprise. I don't believe it, Elizabeth thought. She looked up at Francis Mather and saw him now as the man her romantic imagination had so many times prefigured: the very parfit gentle Christian knight, Donatello's 'St George' brought to life, who would take up her cause, do battle with

232

the dragons and nightmares that haunted her.

When the service was over, she lined up to greet him. When he saw her, his eyes widened; he smiled and hurried the line along.

'Hello, Francis.'

He looked her over. 'I ought to be very cross with you. I've waited all week for you to call.'

'I barely got here when I had to rush off to Chicago and I've had to cut the trip short,' she fibbed.

'Well, no harm done now that you're here. How about dinner tonight?'

She saw his face fall as her own expression gave her answer.

There was absolutely no way she could. The firm's biggest client was arriving in Paris tomorrow afternoon for the annual review of his account. Tony had ordered all hands to be available: no ifs, ands, or buts.

'I'm leaving for France in about six hours,' she added helplessly. 'I have to.'

'Darn!' he said. 'Is this always to be our destiny?'

'It seems to me that destiny's your department,' she said.

He twinkled. 'Well, look,' he said, 'I just can't let you get away like this. *I'm* stuck for lunch, and I have my Career Counseling Group at six. What about tea? Where are you staying?'

'The Carlyle. But let's not go there. It's deadly dreary, and it's full of art dealers and English merchant bankers.'

'The lowest of the low. Why don't you come here?'

'Here? In the church?'

'No, you dope. My office. Four o'clock? Just go around to the side and ring where it says RECTOR.'

At four o'clock to the minute, Elizabeth presented herself at the All Angels rectory office. She wondered whether she should have worn something sexier — with nothing underneath, the way the heroines of shopgirl best-sellers did. To give herself as much time as possible, she had dressed for the flight: loose flannel trousers, an oversized cardigan and a Brooks Brothers shirt she'd filched from Luc, old espadrilles. She had arranged for a limousine to pick her up outside All Angels at six.

'Welcome,' he said. He had changed out of uniform and was dressed about as she was.

She looked around. So this is where God's work gets done, she thought. This was where he worked and prayed and saw people who needed help in the worst way. Comfortable and warm and fairly frayed. Piles of books and papers. The inevitable computer. On a low bookcase, a photograph of a dark-haired woman with two children.

His dead family, she supposed. Do I remind you of her, Francis? Is that what the attraction is? She made herself look away from the picture.

He showed her to an old leather armchair. 'Is this where you live?' she asked.

'No, I have an apartment off Lexington that goes with the living. Small world; it's the apartment I was born in. My father was the rector here too, back before the war. I suppose that's why the vestry intrigued with the Bishop to get me here. You'd better believe I'm happy they did. In the normal course of things, I'd probably be in Kalamazoo.'

'Tell me about the church.'

'Architecturally or sociologically?'

'The latter, I suppose. The congregation looked very *vieux* New York.'

'You noticed that stunned look, eh? Well, they are. Life hasn't turned out the way they were brought up to believe it would. Yes, we're a classic WASP parish. Not as fancy as St Thomas' or as rich as St James'.

'My flock,' continued Francis, 'are really a bunch of nice genteel people clinging for survival to a very thin ledge of moral and behavioral superiority. They are appalled by what's become of this city and how the new ruling class behaves. They were educated with the wrong values. Places like this are about all the sanctuary they've got left — along with a few clubs, although those are going fast too, from what I hear. In their eyes, the barbarian has pierced the gates.'

'And is their Rome yours?'

'Well, a bit, frankly. I don't want to sound like a snob, but it does seem to me that people used to do things differently,

234

to handle themselves differently. This new lot's pretty brash. I'm sure you see it in your business. One can only hope they'll settle down. My flock was taught the wrong lessons about money. Not to talk about it. Not to know, because every debt was in a way personal; that if you borrow money, you're supposed to pay it back, which I personally doubt is high on the list of future intentions of the junk bond crowd.'

Junk bonds? She remembered Tony's little oration on the subject. 'The man I work for sold us out of junk bonds back in November.'

'Then he's got egg on his face. Anyway, I'm just opposed to hocking companies up to the point where ninety percent of the management's attention is focused on taking care of the debt. But we're living in a brave new world. Washington's running the country for the benefit of Wall Street and Wall Street's become a gigantic video game dominated by twenty-five-year-olds.'

'Are you really going to picket CertBank?' Elizabeth said.

'You bet we are! Wait until you see my blue-haired Valkyries in action. I wish you could be there.'

'I will be, if only in spirit.'

'So my message this morning got through? Good for you. More tea?'

I'm not sure, she thought. No, make that: I don't know whether *it* did, Francis, but *you* did.

As he poured, she glanced at the tea service. Her appraising eye went right to work. English, she thought. Early Georgian. Not Lamerie or Storrs, but not bad. Worth about fifteen thousand. His, she wondered, or the parish's?

Back to business: 'You spoke of Mallory as if he were really some sort of devil. When you disagreed with Luc in Colmar, I thought you were just pulling his leg.'

'How is Luc?'

'I don't know. Well, all right — I suppose. We've sort of drifted apart. You weren't teasing, were you?'

He suddenly looked very serious. 'I meant what I said to Luc, Elizabeth. I think people like Mallory have put our whole way of life at risk. In terms of the long-term economic interests

235

of this democracy, I think what Wall Street and the banks are up to is akin to sabotage.'

'Isn't that a little extreme?' Elizabeth tried for a light tone.

'We shall see. Perhaps not. Perhaps I'm just as much an anachronism as some of my older fogies. Miniver Cheevy with his collar backward. It's the young people who worry me so. I just can't help thinking that it must mean something awful when the fair flower of this nation's future takes the Boeskys and Icahns as its idols of choice. Sometimes it makes me so angry I have to take a walk around the block to cool down. Here, look at this.'

He crossed the room and took a manila folder from a table.

'This is a collection I've made of inane pronouncements from our great financiers. Many about banking, many from Mr Mallory himself. He's the *capo di capi*, drum major, chief propagandist, Pied Piper. He's got the rest of them saying and doing even stupider things just trying to keep up with him.'

He put the folder aside.

'He's too smart, too glib, to get caught himself. And it hasn't hurt to have a Nobel Prize winner coaching from the sidelines.'

Uncle Waldo. Should she tell him about her connection? No — at least not now.

'I keep thinking I'll write a book,' Mather continued. 'A great fat exposé of what these people have done. I have a great title: "Paper Termites." Good, huh? Take the average reader point by point through the so-called great changes wrought by the Mallorys of this world and show that, despite a very handsome immediate profit to the promoters, all done in the name of progress, they've actually put our system in peril of its life.'

'What sort of great changes?'

'Oh, I'm sure you know as well as I do. Petrodollar recycling was probably the worst. CertBank pioneered that game. Financial futures. Programed trading. Junk bonds. The list goes on and on. I suppose it all comes down to making a change in the pathology of credit. It doesn't matter whether you're talking about a billion-dollar leveraged buyout or a secretary overdrawn on her VISA line. Anyway, that's enough

236

about me and my gripes. What about you? Why are you always running away from me?'

'It seems to me we're both guilty there.'

'I take your point. Will you be coming back soon?'

'Not until March, if I can help it. I hate New York.' She paused. 'Present company excepted.'

'Not till March?' He looked crestfallen.

Oh, please, can we stop making small talk? she suddenly thought fiercely. Do you want me, Francis? Will you say so? Can I have some of that commitment for myself? Why don't you just come over here and kiss me? You can take me now, all of me, right here, on consecrated ground.

But she made herself sit straight and still, despite the sudden excitation. She subjugated her passion with small talk, exchanging likes and dislikes, mildly arguing the theory and morality of art investment, fencing with him and feeling him out.

Then, too soon, it was time to go.

Francis rose to show her out. 'Do you ever get away on your own?' she heard herself ask.

'Now and then. Actually, some of my flock are taking me to Vienna at the end of the month. A birthday present for number forty-seven. Do you know Vienna?'

'I do. And I love it.'

As he helped her into her coat, she began to hatch a scheme.

Outside it had begun to drizzle. The dull wet gleam of railings and lampposts gave a romantic look to the battered street.

'Nice without the people, isn't it?' he said. 'Not much of a night for flying, though. I'll pray for you.'

Do that, Francis, she thought; do that. She saw her car approaching down the street.

He stood back and looked at her. Let my memory drink you in too, she thought, and then without thinking moved over and kissed him quickly, and then hurried into the car as it slid up, leaving Francis on the pavement. Had the night sky been lit up by the fire in her cheeks?

237

CHAPTER TWENTY-TWO

NEW YORK
Wednesday, January 15th

The notices on the bulletin board were emphatic. It was
forbidden to display papers or briefcases in the dining room
or other public rooms of the Gorse Club; house accounts were
to be paid only from personal funds of the members - corporate
checks would be returned. Reading these notices made the
visitor from the National Security Agency chuckle. They were
obviously intended to sustain the pretense that what transpired
within the handsome McKim, Mead and White building was
strictly old shooting chums and golfing pals eating breakfast
and lunch, swapping comradely anecdotes over the driest
martinis this side of the Sahara, or having the odd meeting
to organize a testimonial dinner, an outing to Yankee Stadium,
a golf or bridge tournament. Purely social.

The fact was, he knew, the Club was the refuge where the
aging Grand Wizards and Kleagles of the Fortune 500 withdrew to rage and plot against the changing of the times. The
place fairly reeked of *ancien régime*. He could hardly imagine
one of the new tycoons being invited to sit down to the Gorse's
famous chicken hash.

Other papers tacked to the bulletin board noted the recent
deaths of two members, names which in their day had been
familiar to anyone remotely familiar with the Armerican legal
industrial-financial establishment; there was an announcement
of the annual spring golf outing and a list of committees.

More crucial information — he knew — was on discreeter
display elsewhere: the names of those men fortunate enough to
have passed the scrutiny of the Membership Committee and to
be poised on the cusp of election, and another equally brief list

of those unhappy few who, thanks to adversity or forgetfulness, were posted for nonpayment of dues or house charges. The club bulletin board was a nice paradigm of American business: the upward and timely passing the downward and obsolete.

Although he doubted that his name would ever be added to the membership roll, the man from the NSA was extremely pleased to be here, pleased that the club had been chosen as a regular venue for the semiannual meetings of the Special Advisory Committee on Economic Countermeasures and Security. They had been gathering here for almost five years now, which made him feel almost like a member. He acknowledged the hall porter and strode briskly up the broad stone staircase, nodding to the members he passed on his way to the private dining room.

As he expected, none of the committee had yet arrived. The room was in its usual spic-and-span order. Fresh coffee was steaming in a samovar on a sideboard. Fresh pads and newly sharpened pencils were at each place. Unopened bottles of Poland Water and heavy crystal goblets had been set out. The leather backs of the eight chairs at the table gleamed. After the meeting, an excellent lunch would be served. Pheasant, he hoped - perhaps with a noble representative of the private stock of burgundies maintained by one of his committee members.

A first-rate lunch was a fair exchange, he thought. They fed him pheasant and he fed them chickenfeed. These meetings and this committee were a complete waste, as far as he was concerned, a useless idea that had become a useless habit. Allen Dulles had started the group in the late 1950s as a way to maintain connections to Wall Street and industry. Over time, only one potentially good idea had come out of the committee, the effort to build up a subversive "rentier" class within the Soviet Union, and that had gone nowhere. Certain members of the committee had permitted the CIA and the USIA to channel funds through their private charitable foundations. That had been damn useful, especially in the colleges during Vietnam. The Carter bluenoses had shut the activity down, but this Administration, which understood you had to play hardball with the other side, was fortunately putting the activity back on stream.

Anyway, reflected the man from the Agency, the committee did have its attractions for him personally. Like the food. The club chef was famous. None of that nouvelle cuisine here, no quarter millimeters of undercooked veal swimming in two teaspoonsful of purplish-brown sauce garnished with varnished vegetables the size of a thumbnail. And the cellar: at the last meeting a '47 Haut-Brion had been served. Best of all, however, were the acquaintances he had made in the three years he'd been briefing the committee; he was pretty certain that when he got ready to leave Washington, one of these guys would help him land a fat job in the private sector. Maybe not on the Bill Simon–Kissinger–Stockman scale, but something lucrative enough for most men's purposes.

All in all, he felt, it was a fair trade. Six or seven hours of his time for two yearly briefings. The big shots got to play James Bond. It was real low-level stuff he fed them, carefully sifted by Langley, by his own outfit, and by the Pentagon; classification-wise, it was marked 'confidential', or about as secret as the evening news. Riskless stuff which made these big hitters feel like they were 'inside,' and 'inside' was what made the cash register sing at election time.

By eleven thirty, the committee was settled around the table. After thanking them for attending, the man from the Agency opened the proceedings.

'Well, gentlemen, today I'd like to do a little brainstorming.' He was careful not to appear officious or unctuous. 'I want to talk about commercial and industrial espionage and subversion. Although, I must caution you, there's also the possibility that what I have to lay before you may be just so much Russian disinformation.'

He looked around the table, confirming that he had their attention.

'Our French friends at DGSE, that's the Frog CIA, think they've come up with something, and frankly the Agency thinks it's worth spending a little time on. Does the name Menchikov mean anything to any of you?'

There was a moment's silence. Then a voice from the end of the table said, 'Wasn't there a Russian ambassador of that name? Back around Ike's time?'

'JFK, I think, sir,' said the NSA man. 'This one's no relation. Our Grigoriy Menchikov was actually born Grigor Chavadze in 1900 in Tbilisi, then called Tiflis, in what is now Soviet Georgia. He died two months ago. He was a Colonel General in the Red Army right after the war, but he ended his days as a low level Assistant Deputy Minister of Culture. An old-line Stalinist; he was lucky not to have ended up in Siberia.

'What intrigues us,' he said, after reviewing the known facts of Menchikov's life, 'is that the guy was at one time high up in Soviet economic affairs. He was one of Stalin's economic advisers at Yalta; Averell Harriman remembers him clearly. Before that, he was at Bretton Woods in 'forty-four possibly to make contact with Harry Dexter White.'

'That was never proven about White,' creaked a voice from the table. The man from Washington looked up. The speaker was the oldest member of the committee, over eighty, and he liked to parade his recall — to the exasperation of all. In 1984 he'd written checks totalling $200,000 to various Republican campaign organizations because he thought the incumbent President was Calvin Coolidge, and so he was indulged.

'Yes, sir,' said the NSA man deferentially. 'I just mention it. Now, before that, and this is interesting, Menchikov was in London, in the Bloomsbury set. According to our information, he was a poet who was very close to John Maynard Keynes, the economist. Now that is suspicious. I don't know if you gentlemen are aware of this, but there are two scholars at the American Enterprise Institute who are close to proving conclusively that Keynes himself was recruited as a Bolshevik agent as early as 1923. The AEI is *very* interested in the material I'm going to show you. They believe that Menchikov may have been Keynes's resident controller even back then.'

'That is absolute poppycock,' said a voice from the end of the table. 'Keynes hated communism.'

The man from the Agency looked up. It was that smart-ass professor from Georgetown. If he doesn't watch those opinions, the Agency man thought, he'll be lucky to get a job at Podunk State.

'Mine not to reason why, Professor,' he said placatingly. 'I think the evidence of what Keynesianism has done to the economies of the West is on the record. It is interesting to note that, according to British counterintelligence, Menchikov traveled to London in 'forty-six to attend Keynes's funeral.'

'So did half the world,' said the professor. 'He could just have been a friend.'

'I doubt the "just friend" theory, Professor.' The Agency man beamed pruriently. 'Our man Menchikov was strictly one for the ladies, and we all know about Mr Keynes's sexual preferences. The AEI people think he might even have turned Keynes by blackmailing him. The homosexual angle was very big in the UK in the thirties.'

'How did Menchikov die?' asked someone else. 'Anything suspicious there'

'No, sir. He died of a heart attack in the lobby of a swanky Paris hotel, the Francois Premier; maybe you know it? Menchikov was a regular at the hotel and something of a big liver.'

The NSA representative picked up the pile of red-plastic embossed folders in front of him and distributed them around the table.

'This is a transcript of a tape of Menchikov's last words.'

'Tape?' asked one of the committee members.

'Yes, sir. Apparently the hotel concierge, who was half Russian himself and a buddy of Menchikov's, was kind of an electronics nut. When Menchikov went down in the hotel lobby, he hustled out there with his tape recorder and got down the last words.'

'Amazing,' said someone.

'Anyway,' continued the man from Washington, 'the next thing that happened was that the body of the concierge was found in the Seine. He had, however, placed the tape in the hotel safe.' This made it exciting, he thought.

'Let me get this straight,' he was asked. 'Following Menchikov's death, the concierge was murdered?'

'Yes, sir. The French police think it was narcotics-related. The concierge apparently wasn't above taking care of certain of his show business clients' needs in that department. What does interest us is that Menchikov had a couple of Russian hard cases keeping an eye on him — in a friendly way, mind you — which seems pretty unusual for a guy whose thing was supposedly limited to booking the Bolshoi Ballet. That's what made French Intelligence sit up and take notice. Do you gentlemen know about "Directorate T"?'

No one did.

'Well, Directorate T is the KGB department having to do with industrial espionage and stuff like that. Think of it as the black-hat equivalent of Economic and Commercial Affairs at Langley. Everything from stealing computer secrets to blighting the Turkish coffee crop. Now there is absolutely no proof of this, but the French seem to think that the Directorate's also into troublemaking in the financial markets. The power behind the Credit Suisse scandal in Chiasso and this Johnson Matthey bullion scam in London.'

'And what does Washington think?' asked the man directly opposite. He sounded sarcastic.

The NSA man put on his toughest cold warrior voice. 'Frankly, Mr Mallory, we think it's bullshit. More Red Menace *disinformetszya*.'

'Really?'

'Yes, sir. First, this Directorate T thing is a unit the French seem to have a handle on. Second, nobody — but nobody! — knows anything about this Menchikov. We've run his name by all of our defectors; Golitsin, Shevchenko, even Yurchenko before he went back. Zero. We got M15 to check him out with Gordievsky. Zip. We think it's a fairy tale the Frogs have concocted to get back in good with us.'

He opened his copy of the transcript.

'The first column,' he explained, 'is what Menchikov actually said. It's Georgian.'

'Actually, this dialect is called Mkhedruli,' said the George-town professor.

'Mkhedruli?'

243

'Yes,' said the professor. 'It means "secular writing." Who made this transcript?'

'The CIA, from the tape the DGSE gave them. Now, to continue, if I may, the second column is this Mkhe-whatever put into our alphabet, and the third is *our* house translation. We have pretty good in-house Georgian people ourselves.' He nailed the offending professor with a significant glance.

'Now, what's got the French stirred up is right down here at the bottom of page one. Where he starts talking about "Ropemaker"—'

'Actually.' said the Georgetown professor, 'I read it as "Ropespinner." '

'I'll concede that, Professor.' Might as well go along, he thought. Just to keep things moving. 'Anyway, Paris reads it as a reference to Lenin's remark about capitalism hanging itself—'

'Actually, selling communism the rope.'

'As you will, Professor,' the NSA man said testily. 'I think we all get the point. What the French think this means is that Menchikov was in fact more than he appeared and was running some kind of swindle or economic destabilization program.'

'Such as Chiasso or JMB and the others you mentioned?'

'Just so, Mr Mallory.' The man from Washington chuckled, working to establish a bonhomous men-of-the-world-together cordiality with the only member of the committee he considered to be really an A-1 Superstar Big Hitter.

'The way we and Langley see it, sir, the French have over-reacted to this.'

'So your people think it really is just disinformation?'

'Yes, sir.'

'Do you people in Foggy Bottom think *everything*'s disinformation these days?' The professor again.

'No, sir, we do not.' His voice was firm, but the man from Washington wasn't so sure. This Yurchenko thing had been a real kick in the butt.

For the next desultory half-hour, the committee tossed various ideas around. It could have something to do with oil, said one. Now that the oil companies had hocked themselves to the teeth running away from Boone Pickens, maybe the Saudis and the Reds were going to flood the spot market with cheap oil and put Texaco, Phillips, and Chevron down the tubes. Hell, maybe Pickens himself was a goddamn Red agent! (Laughter.)

Maybe this Menchikov was running Iacocca, said someone. Guy talks a big free-enterprise game, but when push comes to shove he goddamn near nationalizes Chrysler! Hey, Manning, said another, teasing, what about you guys in the banks? What about the Third World, the less-developed-country loans? When you had the US banks as friends, someone else said, who needed the Russians as enemies? Everyone laughed, Mallory the loudest. How about South Africa? said someone. Maybe the Red Knave was playing the Jack of Spades. More laughter. What about the foreign exchange markets? The jolly mood became infectious; the suggestions became farfetched, then silly, the way such discussions always went among overgrown boys when no quick and easy answers were forthcoming. Perhaps Menchikov had been pulling the strings at Penn Square Bank? Maybe Moscow was manipulating the bond market, the dollar, the deficit? Ho-ho-ho. Soon it was time for cocktails.

'Not for me, I'm sorry to say,' Manning Mallory said as the committee rose to regroup at the portable bar that had been wheeled in. 'I'm afraid I've got to hurry off.' He picked up the transcript. 'Mind if I keep this?' he asked the man from Washington. 'My secretary will kill me if I don't keep my committee file up.'

'No problem, sir, although I wouldn't put it out over the bank wire.'

The two men laughed, peer to peer. Mallory departed. Over lunch, the Georgetown professor continued to irritate.

'You know,' he said, 'I think the translators have got it wrong.'

'Really?' said the man from Washington. He wasn't interested. Not with pheasant and wild rice before him.

'Yes. See here? The man keeps saying "Waldya, Waldya." '

'So?'

'Well, actually, the concierge's given name — according to

the list — was Wladimir, and the diminutive of that is "Wolodya," or possibly "Wlady," a variant I've sometimes seen. But not "Waldya." '

'Does it matter?' The NSA man held back from sounding contentious. Mend fences, he thought. 'Actually,' he went on, 'it's probably just a typo.' He returned to his bird and the excellent '79 Clos Vougeot the club wine steward had chosen to accompany it.

CHAPTER TWENTY-THREE

VIENNA
Friday, January 31st

Francis's letter had made Elizabeth's mind up for her and brought her halfway across Europe in search of him. She had to admit the letter wasn't much as an overture to passion. She'd read it, thought about it, read it again, and thought about it again. Well, as Tony said, 'Don't ever count on someone else to close your deals for you.' She thought she knew her feelings and what she wanted. So she'd come to Vienna to close.

The photograph in the clipping he'd sent had clinched it. There was Francis in charge of a small parade of elderly and determined men and women. He was looking directly into the camera and vigorously brandishing a homemade placard. He looked about eighteen, and nothing like a church dignitary.

The accompanying article was headed CERTBANK PICKETED BY CHURCH GROUP. The subheadings were 'Social Insensitivity Charged' and 'Bishop Silent on Silk Stocking Protest.'

After giving the bare facts, the *Times* report allotted plenty of space to the bank's response:

Chairman and Chief Executive Manning Mallory stated that the bank's function was above all to earn a profit for its stockholders. While he sympathized with the needs of welfare recipients, the bank's internal analysis indicated that the business would be marginally unprofitable, with no offsetting deposit growth or productive future customer relationships.

'Charity should be a private function,' Mallory said. 'I deplore the continued attempt, by Catholic bishops, Episcopal clergymen, or whoever, to morally blackmail this or any business institution, and to attempt to interfere with the workings of a free market that has brought this nation a prosperity and freedom unmatched elsewhere on earth.'

Lord, thought Elizabeth, if you wanted your bank to be hated by poor people, or anyone with the slightest conscience, for that matter, you couldn't write a more effective script. Was this the tone in which the Bourbon aristocracy handled its public relations in 1789?

She tried to remember the few times she'd met Mallory with Uncle Waldo. Had he been this tough and coldhearted? All she could remember was a rather good-looking but unsexy man, who seemed quite distant.

Francis's note read:

See! How do you like my genteel legions? We didn't exactly come down on Mallory like the wolf on the fold, but it made us all feel better. These days, God needs all the help we can give him.

The letter went on to talk of his forthcoming trip to Vienna.

I really am excited. My Three Graces are bearing me off to Wien on the 28th for a week of opera and Wiener schnitzel. Must our next time together really be as far away as March? It was wonderful seeing you. XXX. F.

Abelard and Romeo and Keats probably did better than *XXX*, she thought, but *XXX* wasn't to be sniffed at, especially from a man of the cloth. *XXX*: it was like a brand on her heart. She came to a decision, called the parish office in New York the morning of the twenty-ninth, ascertained what she needed to know, and got Concorde's travel agent to book the earliest Friday flight to Vienna and a room at the Bristol Hotel.

It was a little before ten o'clock by the time she got to the Bristol. The concierge told her that Pastor Mather's group had gone off a bit earlier with their driver. To the Wienerwald, he thought, even though it wasn't such a good day. He looked Elizabeth over. His long experience told him that this handsome, well-dressed woman before him was in love like a schoolgirl and anxious not to show it. Very handsome indeed, she was. The American pastor was a lucky man.

'From the Wienerwald they go to Schönbrunn, and after, I have made a reservation at one thirty at the restaurant in the Palais Schwarzenberg. I would be happy to make a reservation for Fraulein Bennett.'

'I don't wish to impose . . .' Stop explaining, she told herself. She was nervous. Should she have come? Classic feminist doctrine would have said no. Women didn't chase men. What did it matter? She wasn't a feminist of any kind and this was what she wanted. "Yes, please — a table for one.'

'Exactly,' said the concierge. 'I will book a table. Strategically situated, of course. The captain at the Schwarzenberg is a good friend.'

Elizabeth's heart lightened. She nodded happily to her newfound co-conspirator. Surely his complicity was a favourable omen. Or had he expected her? It was almost as if he had. Was Francis that sure of her? Had he left word that she might turn up? Should she go back to Paris?

Don't be an ass! This is what you want, she told herself. What did it matter? Either way, any way, it was good news, wasn't it?

She went upstairs and hung up her clothes. It had been a while since she'd been to Vienna; the last time had been to compare two Dürer watercolors offered to Concorde with 'The Great Piece of Turf' in the Albertina. She went to the window and looked across the Kärntner-ring at the opera house. Opera. The word filled her with dread. She was as lost in classical music as Francis was in fifteenth-century painting. Would they invite her? If they did, she'd surely make a complete ass of herself. Damn! She should have found out what was being performed, bought some recordings, bought a plot book! Why had she come?

She decided to walk off her anxieties in the Kunsthistorisches

Museum. It was an unpleasant day, the gray air sweaty with mist and drizzle, but anything was preferable to stallwalking in her hotel room.

In the museum, she went right to the Brueghel gallery. She stayed there a half hour, drifting from painting to painting, not particularly concentrating, simply letting her unfocused mind take in the overall effect of Brueghel's extraordinary vision. There was a rough, cruel edge to the world depicted in these paintings that reminded her of Grünewald, which made her think of Francis. She went across the room to look at 'The Conversion of St Paul.' Yes, she thought, that's how it must have been when Francis heard the call: a small incident hardly noted by the bustling world's traffic.

She wandered from gallery to gallery, seeking out old friends from earlier visits: the incomparable Correggios, the Parmagianino, the Giorgione, the two great Dürers, the Vermeer 'Artist and Model,' possibly the greatest painting in the world.

When the sequence of pictures began to blur, she went back outside and ended up wandering around the Belvedere with over an hour to go. In no mood for more great galleries and noble staircases, she walked around the perimeter of Hildebrandt's majestic palaces; fidgeted on a bench; wished she'd brought a book. It began to drizzle again, driving her at last into the Palais Schwarzenberg fifteen minutes earlier than she'd planned. Damn! She'd orchestrated the whole scene in her head so carefully. She took refuge in the ladies' room and renewed her makeup. She liked what the looking glass told her: You look as fresh and rosy as a debutante. It was the first time she could recall construing her dark looks as rosy. 'You are absolutely falling to pieces, you cow,' she muttered to the mirror.

On the half-hour exactly, she presented herself at the dining terrace, glassed in against winter. The captain showed her to a discreet corner table. It was one away from a table set for four with a reservation slip sticking out of a glass. The rest of the room was full, and she couldn't see Francis anywhere. She couldn't remember whether she'd decided it would be better to enter and find him there and feign surprise, or to be there when he came in and give him a smile that would declare, This is an accident that isn't! Well, the die was cast.

She gulped down a glass of Velliner. God, she thought, am I crazy! The Austrians put antifreeze in their wine. I'm probably poisoned. That would be typical Elizabeth luck. Here I am, close at last to the man I think I want to be with, or at least try, and the goddamn Viennese have probably poisoned me. Should I have stayed in Paris? God, I wish I'd never met him. What a fool I've made of myself!

At a quarter to two, her heart leapt out of her mouth and her palms went damp. She saw Francis shepherd three distinguished looking women into the dining room: the Mrs Leslie to whom she'd been introduced in London and two other well-turned-out women of around the same age. Old New York, thought Elizabeth.

He didn't see her at first. She watched the captain skillfully maneuver the new arrivals so that Francis took the seat facing her. Thank the Lord for the sodality of concierges, she thought, and made a quick note to press a few hundred schillings on the captain just as she saw Francis catch sight of her.

He didn't quite do a movie double take but close to it. Then he broke out into a smile that told her that she'd done exactly the right thing to come. Her heart sang, and she put everything she had into the smile she gave him back. This is no surprise, she made her face say, and no miracle — I am really here — and I am here for you.

She watched him say something to his ladies, something obviously flattering, because they nodded first and then turned as one to look at her, smiling too, and a nice little wave of recognition came from Mrs Leslie, which made her feel good even though she was acutely aware of the appraising and evaluating behind those cheerful, welcoming expressions.

Francis got up and came toward her. He leaned down and kissed her and whispered, 'Bless you!' Then he straightened up and in a more formal way asked her if she would like to join them.

Of course she would. There was a brief shuffle while a fifth place was set, and the ladies shifted, and a chair was brought.

Francis introduced Elizabeth, managing to convey the impression that their acquaintance went back to his Wall Street life. The other two women were called Mrs Gaile and Mrs Lynde and were every bit as friendly as Mrs Leslie. They looked the way she hoped to look when she got to sixty or seventy; their faces were living proof that life couldn't lick character, no matter what it threw at you. Francis's Old New York, indeed: the sort of women around whom had once been built a matriarchy that was civil, discreet, and as tough as it was gracious.

It was clear that they doted on Francis. They also seemed glad that she had turned up. Mrs Leslie made no bones about it.

'I'm so happy we found each other,' she said. 'Three days with old bags like us is plenty for Francis. It's nice for him to be with someone his own age. Not that any one of us wouldn't go off with him in a minute if he wiggled a finger, although I rather hate to imagine what the congregation would say, let alone the Bishop! I hope you'll join us at the opera tonight. There'll be no problem about the tickets. That concierge at the Bristol could part the Red Sea if you asked him. They're doing *Traviata*: Ashley Putnam's the Violetta. Do you know her? So pretty and sings like an angel. And some new Italian everyone says is frightfully good. We were at Schönbrunn this morning. So many rooms! I thought my feet were going to fall off with the cold.'

They came out after lunch to find it was raining quite hard. The ladies wanted a nap. It had been tiring, and lunch had involved more wine than usual.

'How about another coffee?' Francis asked. They were back at the Bristol, in the small bar off the lobby. The Three Graces had departed upstairs to rendezvous with Morpheus. It had been agreed to convene in the lobby at seven for a glass of champagne; a reservation had been made after the opera at the Drei Husaren. Elizabeth insisted that supper be her treat.

She sat with Francis in the inner lobby. Coffee came. Conversation proved difficult, jerky, like an old automobile sputtering down a street.

'A penny for your thoughts,' she said after one silent interval that seemed painfully long.

'Logistics,' he said.

'Logistics?'

He looked at her. His eyes are gray she thought. Storm gray: the sky before thunder. Why didn't I notice them before? She looked into his eyes. I want to drown in them, she said to herself, knowing she'd read that line somewhere, wondering where.

'Logistics?' she repeated. He's put on a little weight, she thought. It became him. There was a touch of a second chin she hadn't noticed. Hadn't she observed anything? And she was supposed to make her living with her eyes!

By way of answer he reached out and put his hand on hers. A thousand volts went right through her, as if lightning had struck her. The vibrations had started at lunch. No, they hadn't; they'd started back in Colmar, on a Sunday morning that seemed a thousand years ago.

Oh, Francis, she thought, you know, I know.

'Let me go up first,' she said. 'We're all on the same floor, aren't we? That's what you mean by logistics, isn't it?'

His hand drifted up and smoothed her cheek, touched her hair. 'Something like that.'

'Whatever you want. Only, please, quickly. I feel like I'm about to break in half.'

'I'll come to you.'

'Four-oh-six.'

'I know. Now go ahead. I'll be there in ten minutes. I just have to change.'

Change, for God's sake, change!

'Change?'

'Out of this. We don't want to shock the chambermaids if they see me leaving your room, do we?'

He pointed to his collar.

Francis was in uniform.

She waited for him upstairs in a panic. A human heart couldn't beat like this without breaking apart, could it? She didn't know what to do. Should she take her clothes off, get into bed, put on a dressing gown?

She turned to the window. The day was gathering up into

253

gloom. She looked at her watch. Almost four. How much time could they have? Stop it, she said to herself, you're thinking like a whore.

The door sighed behind her. She didn't turn, not for a second, so that when she did he was right there and she was in his arms.

Their first true embrace, their first real kiss, and the kisses after that should be invested, they knew, with a rare wonder, and so they each tried to put a special delicacy into this initiation, as if they were entrusted with something fragile, incomparably fragile and rare; strange and delicate — even dangerous — to clutch too tightly or to be the least bit rough with. They proceeded carefully, sometimes as if in slow motion, but not — it seemed to her — because they wished to prolong sensations or to attenuate their feelings, but for fear of bruising, of chipping, of leaving the tiniest scar or stain on the perfect patina of what was happening to them.

He undressed her. When he unhooked her brassiere and slid it off, she heard his breath catch at the sight of her breasts, so she reached out and drew his head to her bosom, as she had so desperately wanted to in New York and forever before that, wanting the gesture to mean, Don't worry, my love, it can't be helped; it's the way God made me.

When he began to make love to her, his rough ardor was surprising. Well, she thought, what did you expect; a parson among the teacups?

Don't be too knowing, she told herself, as she began to respond, we don't have to show all our tricks, she thought, kissing him, feeling his tongue in her mouth, and thinking that whatever they did couldn't come within a galaxy of what she felt in her head and soul. Let him do what he wants, but don't *you* be a whore. Let him show you what he wants. And she opened herself to him, and felt him slide down and begin to kiss her, and when he reversed himself, she took him happily into her mouth, feeling it all building up inside him; not wanting to proceed too quickly, but wanting it any way he wanted it nevertheless. Then he moved on top of her and kissed her mouth, saying something, and she reached down, and he was like stone, as if all his feeling had been gathered frozen

254

in this burning stalactite she held; he began to tremble, so she guided him into her, feeling him go in easily, helping him start a rhythm that made the frictions begin to work for her too, so she let him take over, and just let herself slip away into pure sensation, drawn down, like drowning, into the vortex of excitement that was spreading concentrically from where they were joined together. She felt the familiar tingle starting in her legs, felt her skin flush, felt him withdraw until just the tip of him lingered within, felt him do that again, and again, slide and pause, slide and pause, and after that she was pretty much busy with what was going on with her own nerve ends, and she heard something she could have sworn was her voice, and just as she did, he did, he eased on top of her, and she knew he was coming and then she was too. He made no groans or grunts, but a sound more like a sigh, and inside her she thought she felt him flowing, and then the whole world clenched, and clenched, and clenched a last time.

When he slid off her and lay beside her, and her breathing slowed and her vision cleared, all she seemed to be able to think was, Thank you, God; thank you for lending me this man of yours. I know he's yours, but just let me keep this small part of him you can't possibly use, won't you? She didn't have the slightest idea where these notions were coming from. Were these the voices heard by saints in ecstasy; was this what Bernini saw in St Theresa's transport?

She felt Francis prop himself up on one elbow. He pushed the hair away from her face.

'That was like the first time ever,' he said. 'Sweet. Now I know why God made me an Episcopal priest and not a Catholic one.' There was a chuckle in the phrase.

Why oh why oh why, thought Elizabeth, must all men always try to put a light touch on these moments after first lovemaking? Why not just tell me what you think? That you love me, or you love my body, my pussy or my bosom or the sound of my voice, but please don't make it sound that now you've gotten your rocks off maybe you'd like to go back to your own room, maybe to call New York and talk to the girl you're engaged to that I don't know about, or the one you've also told you love. I've been through those, Francis. Don't tell me lies, priest or no priest. But she knew she was wrong to doubt him. She knew he was hers for as long as she wanted.

'What brought you here?' he asked. 'Did you come for me?'

'Of course I did. Don't you see that? All you and I ever do is catch planes that take us away from each other. Remember Colmar? Did you know it then – I think I did! Remember London, and three weeks ago in New York? Well, I got tired of that. I thought I'd better catch one plane that brought us together.'

'Thank the Lord you did. And now, can we stay together?'

'If you want. I do. It'll take some working out. I hate New York.'

'It'll work out, my darling. It must. I have a feeling it's God's will.'

They made love again that afternoon, and again that night. They were right for each other. Beyond lay complications and arrangements to be meditated, negotiated, compromised. But those seemed manageable. They would work it out; they were both old enough to realize how much they really had. They were in the sublime no-man's-land of middle age, free from that desperate fixation on time that unhinges the extremities of adulthood.

He left her bed before dawn on Monday. She had to take an early flight to Paris. We'll talk, they whispered, as if the world beyond the door of her room were straining to know their secrets. We'll talk, make plans, get our act together.

After he left, she drifted off. An old dream returned. It seemed to go on for hours, complex, shifting, frightening, a kaleidoscope of faces and fire, but when she awoke, her clock told her it had only been fifteen minutes since Francis had tiptoed away. But now something was different. The familiar faces from the dream had not been sucked back into her subconcious. They were lodged in her awareness, and she knew why and how she had known them.

THE PRESENT

February

CHAPTER TWENTY-FOUR

NEW YORK
Wednesday, February 12th

As if he had sensed the call coming in over the line, Francis reached for the telephone as it began to ring.

I'm too old for this silliness, he thought, smiling. And yet I love every minute of it. He didn't say hello. 'Ridiculous,' he said. 'This is ridiculous.' His voice softened. 'But I love it. I love you. I miss you.'

'As much as you did ten minutes ago? What are you doing now?' Elizabeth said.

He put on his sternest now-see-here-young-woman voice. 'The same thing I was doing when you called the last time. And the time before that. And the four times before that! I am composing a sermon on First Timothy, chapter four, verse eight. A mild rebuke to the joggers and health-club addicts in the flock.'

'What does that mean?'

'First Timothy four:eight says: "For while bodily training is of some value, godliness is of value in every way, as it holds promise for the present life and also for the life to come." A good thing Paul didn't live to see the Walkman and the jogging shoe. Anyway, I expect to be able to live off his first letter to Timothy for most of Lent. It's loaded with good things for this harrowing age.'

'Such as?'

'Well, I could preach ten sermons on, and I quote: "the law is not laid down for the just but for the lawless and disobedient." We've quite a few lawyers in the flock, although mostly of the old-fashioned, bond-indenture variety. And then there's "No longer drink only water, but use a little wine for the sake of your stomach." And of course, let us not forget

"For the love of money is the root of all evils," and so on.'

'Where was Timothy living when Paul wrote to him, on Fifth Avenue?'

'In spirit, you might say. In Ephesus, in point of fact. How's Toronto?'

'Not much different from the way it was when *you* called *me* ten minutes ago. Very nice, actually.'

'And the Degas monochromes?'

'Mono*types*, my blessed love. I can see there are aspects of art history in which you're going to need my guidance. Do you really love me? If you do, when I come back, will you let me take you to the Met? The museum, not the opera. I loved being with you last weekend.'

'I did too, my angel.'

'Francis.' She made her voice sound tiny. 'Does the congregation know about you and me? Have your Three Graces blabbed all over town? Is it too scandalous, the way we're carrying on? I felt as if I was lit up like a neon sign in church last Sunday. Tony thinks I'm crazy: flying to New York for a weekend.'

'My dowagers are foursquare behind us. All the world loves lovers, don't you know?'

'Is that also from St Paul?'

'Could have been − in one of his rare sunny moments. I hope even though I'm not as great a convert, that I'm not as gloomy a one. Tell me more about Degas.'

She had flown to Toronto to look at a trove of twenty rare monotypes a local art scout had turned out, five of which didn't seem to be in the books, but she was certain the Degas gurus would bless them. So she'd left a nice offer on the table, a very nice offer. Right now Degas was better than IBM, at least works like this were: big, dramatic, sexy, with a great auction track record. She thought she'd get them if the deal could be made quickly, the heirs were anxious to sell and get moving in Calgary real estate. Now she was off with the lark to Shannon to huddle with the Knight of Glin, Christie's Irish representative. He had the inside track on the contents of a great Anglo-Irish Georgian house, and she was tempted to make a pre-emptive bid for the entire lot.

Elizabeth knew the minds of the style dictators; in the same way that Concorde's people kept in touch with investment firms around the world, she kept an ear to the ground in London, Paris, and New York, stayed in touch with the people who serviced the big rich who were her market of last resort: the interior designers and life-style purveyors and *Architectural Digest* editors. Irish Georgian definitely still had some life left to it. England had been bought bare of country furniture, but the chic American decorators still needed similar stuff to jam into Fifth Avenue and River Oaks drawing rooms and South-ampton and Santa Barbara cottages like corn down the throats of Strasbourg geese. And here were forty rooms of 'not bad furniture; some of it actually rather good, considering who these people were,' according to the Knight. The fad should hold for another two years, which meant a nice profit.

'Francis,' she asked, 'do you miss me?'

'Indeed I do. And in ways most unchurchly. I *do* miss you in every way, my darling. But you're wearing me out. It's too much for a man my age.'

And indeed he did miss her — missed her, loved her, ached for her. Francis felt himself in the grip of an emotional force and certitude he had never before known. Possessed, he found himself trying to remember if the urges and needs that had conveyed him to God had been this powerful. In the next thought, he wondered if his passion for Elizabeth was a dilution, by distraction, of the purpose and commitment that only months earlier had seemed unchallengeable, all-consuming. It was like being thrust into one of those Graham Greene novels about tormented priests.

Tinged with guilt, too, was the self-admission that his feeling for Elizabeth had leveled his memory of past emotions with the force and efficiency of a bomb. His dead wife, his little boys: until Elizabeth, they'd haunted him waking and dreaming. Now they seemed laid to rest.

'Francis,' Elizabeth said, 'I feel like I'm sixteen years old.'

'I would hope that at sixteen you weren't doing some of the things you're teaching me.'

'Stop that! Don't be a dirty middle-aged man.'

'It's extremely difficult when you're around. I need to catch my breath. When do you finally get back to Paris? What about the weekend?'

'Thursday night. We have a big meeting at the firm Friday afternoon. The weekend's out: I've got to be there first thing Monday morning. Ward Landrigan's flying over from New York. The estate of a recently deceased Rothschild mistress is disgorging some major stones.'

'Do bejeweled mistresses still exist?'

'They're all but extinct. Rich men don't have backstreet ladies and *cinque à sept* trysts any more. They prefer the embrace of their bonds and stocks.' Across five hundred miles he heard her breathe deeply. 'Francis . . . ?'

'Yes, my darling?'

'Francis, I love you so much! God, I really do! Francis, do you thank God for bringing us together?'

'I do — hourly, minutely, secondly. You can too, you know. He's always available. You don't have to get your girl to call his girl and set up a lunch.'

It must be tough for her, he thought, to be in love with a priest. How must she think of God? Did the shadow of God fall across the course of her feelings like a tree across a path? Did she imagine him in the room with them, looking on disapprovingly in the bedroom when they made love, when they touched each other, staring down at their rapture — censorious, sanctimonious, jealous?

'What are you doing now?' he asked.

'Right this moment? Just lying here. Thinking of you. Dirty thoughts. Oh, Francis, I want you so badly it makes me squeak!'

He visualized her, thought of her narrow, intelligent face, her fine swinging gait, the way she dressed, the way she bent over him; thought of her figure, her hair, her mouth wide in passion, pursed in reflection; thought of each detail of her and silently sent up thanks to god for sending her his way.

'Look,' he said, 'now you're making me have unseemly thoughts too, and I've got to get this sermon put together.'

'You don't have to preach until Sunday.'

'That may be, but my time is not entirely my own. The

Bishop's sending me to huddle with His Eminence the Cardinal tomorrow. Our brethren in Christ in the Church of Rome aren't sure which way they should jump in a certain takeover offer. All told, the Vatican holds almost five million shares of Allied Interchem; Drexel Burnham is playing hardball with the Cardinal, and my Bishop feels we men of the cloth should hang together in these atheistic times.

'Then the Winter Church Fair kicks off Friday, and the politics of *that* makes what went on at Lehman Brothers look like Camp Sunshine. Finally, the old firm asked if I could drop in. They're having trouble piecing out a financing and seem to feel that a dose of the famous Francis Mather creative juices may be just the tonic. I was always pretty handy with a tricked-up convertible preferred stock, you know.'

'Don't go back to Wall Street, Francis.'

'Don't worry. This is just a one-shotter. If I come up with the answer they need, it'll pay for a new kitchen for the parish house. We're feeding double the number of people off the streets we did a year ago, and it shows no sign of slowing down.'

'What about using some of it to buy some new vestments? You looked awfully cute Sunday, but a little more glitz wouldn't hurt. I thought your dalmatic, or whatever it is, looked definitely ratty.'

'My alb, darling. Anyway, angel, this is All Angels, not St James'. Now, I have to go. I love you. Bless you, my sweetest.'

'Don't forget to pray for me. Good night, my love.' She blew him a kiss and hung up.

He tried to return to his sermon, but the thoughts he needed wouldn't come. He pushed his chair back and stared at the ceiling; maybe inspiration would come to him like the angel annunciate in the painting Elizabeth had taken him to see the previous Saturday at the Frick Collection. It had been a perfect fleeting lovers' weekend. Up and down Manhattan they'd coursed: SoHo, Columbus Avenue, every nook and niche. Sunday, when the last parishioner had been seen off, he'd changed into mufti, and they'd headed for the Village. Going down Fifth Avenue, she'd spotted something.

'There's my New York,' she said, pointing. 'That's what I hate about this place.'

Their cab had halted for a light at Sixty-fifth Street, outside Temple Emanu-El. In front of the Fifth Avenue entrance, a wedding party was gathering: young, sleek, well off, optimistic, a bright world before them at Goldman, Sachs, or Physicians and Surgeons, or Price Waterhouse. Down the side street, not twenty yards away from the glossy celebrants, trailed a ragged line of men and women, some sunk beyond hope, others — to judge from their clothes and posture — only recently pushed over the margin.

'That's New York,' he said.

Elizabeth sighed. How he loved her for that sigh! The light changed, the cab pulled away; before them the great Fifth Avenue skyscrapers sparkled in the frosted sunlight.

She was perfect for him, he thought. She didn't keep after him to explain himself or his change of life. She took him as she found him. She didn't ask about his dead wife and children. Above all, she didn't press him on his reasons for leaving Wall Street.

He was so tired of that question. It was asked in a dozen ways, but always with the same subtext of disbelief. How could anyone in his right mind walk away from all that money? Don't you know, Francis, how much people on the Street are making these days?

Well, he did know, and he didn't much care, especially if he counted what he saw as the cost to character. Success in today's Street took a certain kind of moral opacity and brashness he was pleased to think he simply couldn't find in himself.

Not that he didn't think he had a gift for the game. Francis was passionate about talent. It was, he believed, the one fair way God discriminated. But gift or no, his personality was all wrong for the way it was played now. And to say that could only sound pompous, condescending, sour grapes. Still, people always came back to the money: how could you . . .? Maybe he quit because he cared.

Francis had been brought up to venerate capitalism. What

264

he saw happening now seemed like sacrilege — a wanton disregard for everything he had been taught to believe. The future of millions placed in jeopardy so that a few hundred venal sharks could go clad in silk. And yet, at such a time, what could a man like him do? Pray, for one thing. And speak out.

He had no doubt of the courage of his convictions. When he looked into his mirror, he fancied he saw a good man armored in understandings beyond the compass of the new breed of Wall Street titan. He was a decent man, upholding and continuing a decency that had run through generations, through the nation's whole history, like an unbreakable shining thread. He saw a man charged with an almost genetic responsibility for lengthening that thread and, by implication, the life of that nation.

He came from a long line of prudent and concerned men, decent, humane, worshipful men, perhaps not saints but not animals either: preachers, bankers, lawyers, surgeons. Men who saw no contest between 'principle' and 'principal'; the man of character took the former ten times out of ten. Eight generations of Mathers stretched back to the cold Massachusetts shoreline and the Bay Colony. Generations who had heard John Winthrop preach; who had fought the King and the Confederacy and the Kaiser and Hitler, believing themselves to be fighting God's fight, for God's idea of freedom. Mathers were raised to believe that God had ordained capitalism as his way, which was why communism hated the name of God as passionately as it hated the name of Rockefeller, but Mathers believed that capitalism could be fair, generous, productive, good-hearted. It could be Christian. In the Mather view of things, a man was entitled — at the least — to a chance at the lowest rung, to a hand up, and to whatever fruits his talent and capacity and effort could produce, but not to walk all over the rights and lives of others.

Finally, there was the fact that — as a man and as a priest — he was committed to peace. Wall Street had become so combative — its activities and culture phrased in the language of war.

That it was that way Francis attributed to Mallory and his emulators. It worried him terribly. This was a difficult time

265

in history; this was a complicated, troubled world, needing its best wits and its best instincts about it, and yet its answers and direction were being provided by false prophets. It like praying for salvation and being sent Antichrist. Some of his more morbid ecclesiastical colleagues said God was testing the West. Perhaps, thought Francis gloomily; if so, the West, and America in particular, did not appear to be making passing grades.

Still, as much out of habit as anything, he stayed in touch, kept his lines open to the Street. It helped when he needed an extra thousand dollars for the parish soup kitchen. He read the *Wall Street Journal* every morning, although sometimes – reading its editorials – he gasped with incredulity. He maintained subscriptions to *Forbes*, to *Business Week*, to *Institutional Investor* and *Corporate Control Alert*.

The more he read, the more convinced he was that the nation's economic birthright was being leveraged away. No matter how many millions or billions were supposed to be made in the process, the bottom line was pottage.

At the root of the trouble, as he saw it, were the banks. Without the complicity of the banks, Wall Street's mischief would be impossible. They were the necromancers charged with measuring out the magic potion of credit; they were supposed to be the last redoubt of economic probity.

But thanks to Mallory and his imitators, the banks had pulled up a chair at the speculative table. He had often wondered how it would all have turned out if Mallory hadn't been there to pipe his seductive tunes from the matchless podium of CertBank. Mallory dominated the world of high finance as possibly no man since Morgan.

Francis sometimes found himself so enraged by what Mallory got away with, or seemed to be able to persuade others to do, that he found himself literally trembling with anger so strong he didn't seem able to pray it away. He found himself wishing there was a way to destroy the man, which made something Elizabeth had told him very interesting.

They had awakened in the middle of the night and made love and afterward lain and talked, the way lovers do in the early

266

going, when all is fresh and novel. She had told him about her childhood and early life, about growing up near Chicago and then in New York after her mother had married — 'run off with' — Peter Chamberlain. She had reminisced about Waldo Chamberlain, who was nice to her, and of his house in Maine and the Thanksgivings there, and finally, about the fire.

Francis wasn't pleased to hear her speak so warmly of Waldo Chamberlain, her 'Uncle Waldo.' Francis had taken Chamberlain's Money One at the Business School, and while one had to be impressed by the man's intelligence and scholarship, all that hail fellow 'Uncle Waldo' stuff struck him as specious. The guy had been a cold fish, a neuter with nothing between his legs or beating in his chest. All pulp, no juice. Besides, everyone knew that Waldo Chamberlain was Mallory's mentor, guru, and closest adviser, which in Francis's mind was terminal guilt by association.

According to Elizabeth, she hadn't much liked Peter Chamberlain. He was fresh with her, sly and too intimate, too physical; she was sure he would have taken her to bed if he could have. Everything he said seemed to incorporate a dirty double entendre. Francis half-listened to this; his interest picked up when Elizabeth related how Peter hated Waldo and said terrible things about him behind his back, calling him a 'dirty old faggot.' Peter also had no love for Manning Mallory, Elizabeth told Francis; it was almost as if Peter had been jealous of Manning Mallory's relationship with Uncle Waldo, and — through Waldo — with Peter's own father.

As Elizabeth told it, Peter had been after her on the day before the fire, the Friday after Thanksgiving, 1970.

She had been downstairs working on a term paper. The rest of the house had gone off on a picnic, except for Peter, who'd had to stay behind for a phone call. He'd come up behind her and sneered at her in the awful way of his that made her feel he could see right through her clothes.

'Hey, Liz,' he said. 'Want to get in on Uncle Wally's dirty little secret?' He'd gestured at the ceiling. 'C'mon.' Lord, how she hated being called Liz!

Climbing the stairs. Peter told her how, as a boy, he'd caught

Uncle Wally sneaking around upstairs. He led Elizabeth down the hall, paused, looked around with theatrical alertness, and then reached into a bookshelf and worked some kind of latch. A brief shove from Peter, and the bookshelf had slid aside, revealing a tiny, closet-sized office fitted into a space between the bookshelves and the outer wall. It contained, barely, a small desk, an office chair, and a file cabinet with a pile of books on it.

'Welcome to Uncle Wally's little lair,' Peter had said triumphantly. 'C'mon.' He had barely made way for Elizabeth to squeeze past into the secret room, making sure her breasts rubbed against him as she went by.

'Here,' Peter had said, opening a drawer in the desk.

Elizabeth remembered that on the desk was a photograph of Waldo Chamberlain, Preston Chamberlain, and Manning Mallory in the cockpit of a boat.

'Look at this,' Peter said; he took a photo out of the desk drawer.

The picture had obviously been taken many years earlier.

'It was quite something,' Elizabeth told Francis. Outside a car's horn squawked in the night. 'It was Uncle Waldo, all right. In his early twenties, I'd guess. He had all his hair then. And he was totally naked. There was another man in the picture. He was also naked. And they were — well, holding on to each other.'

'Did you know the other man?' asked Francis.

'No. Not then, at least. I do now. He's in my dream too. He's called Menchikov.'

She explained to Francis about having seen the photo in *Match*, the photograph of a dead Russian whose face had rung a bell. It was the same man who was in the photograph with Uncle Waldo.

'And that was that?' Francis asked.

'Almost. Peter put the photo back. He swore me to secrecy, and of course Uncle Waldo would have just died if he'd known I'd seen that picture. Peter closed up the office. On the way back downstairs, he tried to kiss me. Then he said something else. Funny, I'd forgotten.'

'What was it?'

'He said Uncle Waldo was holding in a big secret about the bank that must be killing him.'

'Did he tell you what the secret was?'

'I didn't want to ask. I knew Peter's game. He probably thought he could trade me the secret for a kiss or a feel. His own stepdaughter, imagine! Anyhow, all he specifically said was something to the effect that ''Uncle Wally's Mr Mallory'' was in for ''the surprise of his life.'' '

'He mentioned Mallory in particular? As if he was part of the secret?'

'He did. Then the phone rang and he went to take his call. By the time he got off, the picnickers were back.'

'And . . . ?'

'And that was that. That night Uncle Waldo got a phone call from St Louis. One of his companies was having an emergency board meeting. So early Saturday morning off he went, and that night Quiddy burned down.'

'And everyone was killed?'

'Everyone. Except me, naturally. But don't ask me about it. I don't remember a thing, although now and then it seems that there were voices, strange men's voices. One minute I was asleep; the next I was crawling around on the lawn with a broken ankle and bleeding like a pig from glass cuts — except that in my delirium I'd put a towel over my face, so at least it wasn't cut — and the house had burned down and all of them were dead. And I alone escaped to tell thee.'

'You and Uncle Waldo.'

'Well, he wasn't there, was he? Anyway, aren't you supposed to say, ''Praise be to heaven''?'

'I do.' Francis had leaned over and kissed her. 'Praise be to God. How lucky for me.'

'Well,' Elizabeth said sleepily, 'Uncle Waldo always used to say that luck was the residue of design.'

'He cribbed that one from Branch Rickey,'' said Francis just as he too drifted off. 'And you're too young to know who Branch Rickey was.'

On Monday Elizabeth had flown off to Toronto. Francis had

been unable to get what she'd told him out of his head. Now he looked at the ceiling, tapping his pen nervously on the desk top. The sermon wouldn't come. It was swallowed up by the workings of his imagination. If a line ran from a Russian diplomat to Waldo Chamberlain, might it extend to Manning Mallory and might it mean something sinister?

He dismissed the thought. Russians, Waldo Chamberlain, Mallory. Don't be ridiculous, he told himself, and returned to his sermon.

CHAPTER TWENTY-FIVE

CAMBRIDGE, MASS.
Thursday, February 13th

Waldo's lip trembled. Very carefully, he set the embossed scarlet folder down on the table; his hand was shaking so badly he spilled Mallory's coffee.

A waiter bustled over, mopped up the spill, and refilled Mallory's cup.

The banker looked quickly around The Faculty Club lounge. 'For God's sake, Waldo,' he hissed, 'get hold of yourself!'

I should never have shown it to him, he thought. The old boy looks as though he's going to pee in his pants.

'When did you say you got this?' asked Waldo. His voice sounded very unsteady.

'Last month. At that security oversight committee that Don Regan asked me to sit in on. I've told you about it. We meet twice a year at the Gorse to Scratch our chins and think up new economic dirty tricks to play on our friends in Moscow, or try to guess what they're up to. This was the January luncheon special. I could hardly keep a straight face when they passed it out. I thought you'd get a kick out of it too.'

He leaned over to poke Waldo, but when he saw the strained expression on the older man's face, he drew back.

'No, look,' he said seriously, 'there's nothing to get your ass in an uproar about. Actually, I think it's a gas. All these big shots sitting around trying to figure out how to undermine the Reds by implanting the seeds of capitalism in the USSR. The very guys who brought us socialized banking at Continental Illinois, socialized automotive at Chrysler, socialized aerospace at Lockheed.'

'I don't like it, Manning. They may be on to us.'

'Look, cool it!' Mallory tried not to sound sharp, but it was hard. 'On to us for *what*! You're acting like we're a couple of Red spies with a neutron bomb checked in the cloakroom and our pockets stuffed with plans for Star Wars. What have we done, anyway? Is it our fault if a bunch of jerks take our good ideas and push them too far? Hell, it's not the Cert that's got half its capital down the toilet in South America, like Citibank! Not us that's got three times its equity committed off its balance sheet, like Bankers Trust. Or going bust in the oil patch! Hell, I'm just the piano player in the whorehouse. When all hell breaks loose, it's the rats they'll go after, not us!'

'It still bothers me.'

'Look,' Mallory said patiently, 'there nothing — *zero*! to tie us to Menchikov. I wish I'd never shown you the goddamn file. I just had this bright idea you'd like a gander at your old chums last words, because I know how close you two were. If I'd thought for a minute you'd react like this—'

'I'm very, very upset by this, Manning. It's not Grigoriy's death that bothers me. I appreciate your thoughtfulness. It's what he actually said that I find disturbing.'

'You mean about ending it?'

'Precisely. He and I discussed this very matter in Moscow, as you know. And you and I agreed—'

'*We* agreed on next Thanksgiving as getaway day, if you recall.'

Mallory paused for a moment. He drummed his fingers on the table.

'Look,' he continued, 'if I get your drift, you want to cut and run right now, or yesterday, if that's possible. Well, it isn't. Waldo, nobody wants to see our Turkey Day fireworks go off more than I do. And I agree that this end's getting played out. Frankly, I'm getting bored. It's become too damn easy. Back when we started, we had to sweat blood, you and I, to put some of this shit over. Now it's a cinch. Sure, there's no time like the present to get Moscow cranked up, but what are we talking about?' Mallory ticked the remaining months off on his fingers. 'Nine months? Nothing!'

'I don't care, Manning. I think Grigoriy was trying to tell

us something. Maybe the French *were* on to him. Didn't you say that Washington had been told by French intelligence about a secret Russian economic subversion unit? Something within the KGB? Perhaps that's what Grigoriy worked out of.'

'You mean this so-called "Directorate T"? Forget it; it's strictly a red herring, according to my little mouse inside the CIA. Besides, what about that card your pal sent from the Crazy Horse in Paris? Postmarked — what? — two days before he corked off? Did that sound like he was worried? Was there anything to get the wind up over? I can answer that for you: nothing! You told me yourself the old boy sounded in top form: eating and drinking and looking at tits like there was no tomorrow. I promise you, Waldo, neither Paris nor Washington knows shit about anything. All the CIA thinks about is Nicaragua. So let's just stay with our original plan. Besides, as I said before, what have we done that's illegal, that isn't — in fact — official Administration policy!'

'What about the fire, the people who died?' It was more of a murmur than a statement. 'What about Preston and Peter?'

'What about them! I don't know anything about them; hell, I wasn't even in the country, if you remember. That was strictly your ball game. And it was fifteen years ago, for Christ's sake! Shit, Ropespinner's never even rigged an OTC stock! We just lead; it's the other guys who go too far.'

He paused as a stranger approached their table. Waldo introduced him as a former colleague on the Business School faculty. He shook Mallory's hand ethusiastically.

'I just wanted to say how much easier and more gratifying you've made it for people like me to teach banking, Mr Mallory. Twenty years ago I had to beg in the street for students. This year, for the first time, more people signed up to interview CertBank than McKinsey and Company.'

'Well, isn't that wonderful!' Mallory put on the engaging, sincere face that over three decades had conned the world's wise men into taking their fiscal lives in their hands. 'You keep up the good work, and I'll tell you: I'm not going to be satisfied until more Baker Scholars interview the Cert than Goldman, Sachs!'

The other man went away.

'See?' said Mallory. 'See how we stand? As long as we stay cool, what can possibly happen? You think some guy's going to go up to Volcker and say, "Paul, we've got these two guys cold who've spent the last thirty years cutting the world's financial nuts off"!'

Chamberlain shook his head. He looked shriveled and rheumy. 'That's still not the point. I'm worried!'

'About what! That someone's picked up on us? Look, I'm telling you, it's cool! Stop blubbering. You'll get upset and lose your lunch.'

He grinned — the same confident expression that had time after time soothed the tumultuous anxieties of markets and their men.

'Hey,' he said, 'do you want a laugh? Guess what. You know how many offers I've had for my autobiography since I announced I was leaving the bank next year? Ten! Everyone in seven figures! I could be another Iacocca!"

Waldo remained glum.

Mallory leaned forward and hissed, 'For God's sake, Waldo, you're talking like the goddamn FBI's on our tails, waiting for you or me to drop an envelope in a trash can in Harvard Square for Gorbachev to pick up. C'mon — this isn't something out of Robert Ludlum.'

It sure as hell wasn't, he thought. This was real life and not merely some Navy enlisted man peddling a trash bag full of Trident printouts for a few thousand bucks.

All I want is to work it a little bit longer, thought Mallory. Let everyone get in a little deeper. The heat was on the banks to step up to the LDC plate one more time. Push takeover lending and corporate 'restructuring' that last extra yard. The stock market was boiling. People tended to spend Their paper profits before taking them, started to think 'rich.' People began to forget that stock booms came and went but what they owed didn't.

Right now, fast easy money was like a fever in the nation's brain. The collapse in commodity prices meant that the less developed countries were subsidizing the rich nations to the tune of $65 billion a year — $65 *billion*! — and still their feet were being held to the fire by the banks and the IMF. Now people said OPEC was falling apart. He saw it differently; it looked to him as if the Saudis were establishing a powerful common interest with Texas and Oklahoma. Those chickens would sooner or later come home, which was something he and Waldo would have to be sure to point out at their Moscow press conference.

The man on the street really hated banks now. Real interest rates were still high, and bank profits were higher, while steelworkers and roughnecks were going broke or delivering pizza. Installment debt was still priced at eight over prime. Places like the Citi worked the small depositor's float for two or three weeks while bouncing his checks all over the neighborhood. When Ropespinner's great day of revelation came, thought Mallory, when people saw how the banks had been tools of the Evil Empire their debtors' animus would find a focus: banks would be overrun by mobs, bankers lynched in the streets, mutilated like medieval usurers.

All he needed was enough time to dress up the poisoned cake with a little tasty icing.

Still, he felt, that's all it was: icing. With the old man shitting in his pants, it probably wouldn't hurt to get the show on the road.

'Look,' he said, 'I'll make a deal with you. Let's split the difference. I'm willing to go out this summer. How about July Fourth? How's that sound?'

What a great trick, he thought. Give Independence Day some real fireworks. Light up the sky and see the goddamn sky fall in!

'Look,' he told Waldo, 'if you start getting your shit together now, July Fourth'll seem like no time at all.'

Waldo looked dubious, but finally he nodded. July Fourth it would be.

CHAPTER TWENTY-SIX

QUIDDY POINT
Saturday, February 15th

By the time it began to get dark, Elizabeth had driven to within a half hour of Quiddy. She had forgotten how savage and bleak this country could seem. The evergreen forests in winter had a menace that summer dispossessed. She shivered. Her dominant memories had been of a cheery house, full of family and warm fires; she had put the rest out of mind — until recently. Now she noticed how the woods impinged on the road, full of dark mysteries.

Uncle Waldo had sounded so pleased to hear from her. When she told him that business would be taking her to Boston and she was just dying to see him again, his high, scratchy voice had immediately proffered an invitation to Quiddy for a long weekend. Ordinarily she would have demurred, but as it happened Francis was off on Saturday morning on a retreat for All Angels's Alcoholics Anonymous chapter. Now or never, she thought. Francis wouldn't let her alone about the damn photograph, and she herself was curious to see it again. Of course, it could turn out to be a wild-goose chase.'

In any case, it would be fun to be reunited with Uncle Waldo. And to see the house again. He'd assured her it would be just exactly as she'd known it. He hoped she could overcome her sad and terrible memories.

She was sure she could, she told him confidently.

Her original plan had been to go up to Maine on Friday from Boston, where she had a couple of meetings, but at day's end she felt pangs of longing and desire, so she telephoned Waldo at his Cambridge office and said she'd have to arrive on

Saturday instead. By eight she was reunited with Francis back in New York.

Which made it one whole week they'd been able to be together. Bliss — except for his damn questions!

She'd hardly caught her breath when Francis started in. She had gone straight from the airport to his apartment, wanting nothing more than his company and his embrace. What *he* had in mind, it turned out, were not kisses and embraces but questions. And then more questions. She should have been alerted when he called her in Paris to get a *Match* tearsheet with Menchikov's picture. He even brought it to the restaurant, and now he examined it closely, scarcely tasting his roast peppers, scarcely looking at her.

Right through dinner at Elio's, while his Veal Cutlet Capricciosa grew cold, he'd peppered her with questions. He seemed obsessed with the time around the fire. What exactly had Peter said about 'a surprise'? Did it sound like a surprise for Uncle Waldo or Manning Mallory, or both of them? Was she sure it was St Louis that Waldo had flown off to! Had anyone else said anything interesting that weekend? What about Preston Chamberlain? Did she remember anything about the fire, anything at all? She'd just woken up, alive on the lawn, with no idea how she'd gotten there? Was that how it was?

That was how it was. Under his questioning she raked and dredged her memory, but she was certain there was no more there beyond what she had told him.

'Francis, my love,' she'd finally said, 'if this swordfish was grilled as thoroughly as you've grilled me, it would be charred to a cinder.'

'They do as it is,' he said smiling. 'Now, tell me again what Peter said . . .'

Love could not always be courtship. At least that's what she's been told by others, never really having gone farther than the early stages herself. But for twenty-three and a half hours a day she still saw him with the eyes of first passion: indecently boyish for his age, intelligent, committed, yet wise and principled — and how attractive he seemed, and how lovably cute, leading the congregation in 'From Greenland's

Icy Mountains.' And yet how profoundly serious he was, too, preaching and praying; committed in a way that no other man she had ever known had been, bound to values and standards that she couldn't quite grasp, something larger and better than the world in which she trafficked.

And yet, he had this obsession with banks and Wall Street!

She couldn't help wondering about it. Was it purely intellectual, or had he been done dirt in some deal? His rage seemed larger than that. Wall Street wasn't, on its merits, worth so much emotion. She knew Wall Street as well as most. Concorde, Tony, herself: they *were* Wall Street. Well, she decided, it would just have to make itself known in the natural course of things. In the meantime, she would play along with this fixation of his on the Chamberlains and the Quiddy fire and Uncle Waldo and Manning Mallory. She was his beloved, his helpmate; it was the least she could do.

It was during his sermon the next morning that the idea came to her. He was preaching Luke 8:32−33, the parable of the Gadarene Swine. 'Then the demons came out of the man and entered the swine, and the herd rushed down the steep bank into the lake and were drowned,'

He developed this into an excoriation of financial speculation and program trading and finished with an impassioned attack on takeover lending. Always finance, she thought. Her mind began to wander.

I'll get him the photograph of Uncle Waldo and Menchikov, she thought suddenly. That'll be my contribution to this discussion.

She wasn't quite sure exactly how she would bring it off. Not to worry, my dear, she told herself while from the pulpit her beloved lit into index funds; you're on a roll. The same luck that was now working for her in every other part of her life would work for her in this. She wasn't quite sure why she was doing it. Simply as a tribute to the man she loved, she supposed. What else? What would he do with the photograph if she got it; what use could it be to him? But she wanted to show she was with him right down the line, and what better way than this?

So here she was, driving through the twilight on roads that no longer looked familiar, on a mission for her man.

Minutes later, she crested a hill and suddenly saw with reawakened memory the little valley sliding down to the shoreside blinking lights of the town and the dark void beyond that was bay and ocean. Just at that moment, her spine went cold with the realisation that she'd let her feelings choke off her common sense, that what she had come to find could not possibly be here, that she had traveled all this way on a fool's errand, that the photograph could not possibly exist. It must have perished in the fire.

CHAPTER TWENTY-SEVEN

QUIDDY POINT
Sunday, February 23rd

By the time she'd finished her second glass of wine at Saturday dinner, Elizabeth decided that, fool's errand or not, it had been a good idea to come back to Quiddy. Uncle Waldo was as solicitous and charming as ever, although she was surprised how old he had become. Little was left of the impudent if aging cherub he'd been the last time she'd seen him. Still, he had enough of the old sparkle left to belie the grave image of the 'great man' that stared at her from the photographs on the living room tables. He seemed — just as he told her — to have put the house back together exactly as it had been. It not only looked the way she recalled, it felt the same: a cheery, sprawling place with nooks to sneak away to, flooded with the best of the light in any season and graced with the spectacular sweeping panorama of the bay.

She and Uncle Waldo had dined together alone; the meal had been left on the stove by Mrs Arthurs, still on the job after all this time

'Thank goodness I didn't have to rebuild *her*,' Uncle Waldo had said, chuckling. 'The house was one thing. She's quite another. An amazing woman, Mrs Arthurs. She made me that sampler in the drawing room when I went to Stockholm for the Nobel ceremony. And you should see the cummerbund she embroidered for my seventieth birthday. I make quite a dashing figure at the Yacht Club on the Fourth of July. Yes, she's a real Renaissance woman, my Mrs Arthurs. Just as, may I say, you've turned out to be, my dear.'

There was real affection and pride in his voice. It made Elizabeth feel guilty to think that she had come here with the intention of snooping on this old man. She felt bad that she hadn't come back to see him before this. To have let so many years slip by with only a couple of dozen postcards to mark the passage and the changes.

She slept like a baby that night, windows open to the raw air off the bay, waking with first light to a Sunday that was bright and brilliant. She went downstairs and made herself coffee. At nine Mrs Arthurs came in with the Boston and Portland papers. Elizabeth carried them into the living room, plunked them on a couch, and went out on the porch. It really was a perfect Maine winter day, the air biting just above the bone. She could barely hear the breeze in the pines nearest the house; below her a small sailboat barely swayed on the splintery lights of the waves.

'Pretty little thing, isn't she?' said Uncle Waldo behind her. 'The bank gave her to me when I retired from the board. I christened her *The Prime Rate*.'

He looked out at the flagpole.

'Very bearable,' he said. 'Less than three knots of wind, I'd guess. We might sail her over to Quiddy after lunch for the *Times* if the weather holds. She goes very well in light air.'

But the weather didn't hold. By late morning the wind had freshened and a line of clouds had blown up from seaward. The little sailboat now bobbed vigorously at her mooring buoy. Elizabeth lazed in the drawing room. Music came from an elaborate stereo system housed in a mahogany rack; set in to the lid was a brass plaque on which was engraved *To Waldo Emerson Chamberlain in appreciation of service 1957–1979 as Special Adviser to the Federal Reserve Bank of Boston.*

Uncle Waldo had gone upstairs to work on some papers. He reappeared just after noon and asked if Elizabeth would like to drive with him to Quiddy.

'If we could sail over, I'd insist, my dear, but as it is, you look so comfortable, I'll quite understand if you don't. I shouldn't be more than forty minutes.'

Elizabeth heard the front door shut, then the car engine start. Without thinking, she got up and went quickly to a window and watched as the car turned down the driveway and disappeared among the trees.

She acted entirely without thinking, she later told Francis. Perhaps it was only that she wanted to see if he *had* rebuilt Quiddy just exactly as it had been. She waited for five minutes, making certain he was gone, then ran up the stairs. As she did so, her imagination and memory joined forces to carry her back to that afternoon long past. She imagined Peter just ahead of her, saw him exaggerating the sly movements of a sneak and a snoop, heard him chuckling; saw him pause at the bookcase at the end of the hall, put his finger to his lips, gesture at the bookcase. Saw him pull out three books at the end of the third shelf from the top and place them sideways on top of their neighbors. Saw Peter reach into the space . . .

And found herself gripping a round knob. She twisted it first one way, then the other, and heard something unlatch within the wall. She seized the edge of the bookcase where it extended from the wall and pushed, just the way she remembered Peter did. It slid aside.

It was just exactly as it had been, just as she remembered it. A small desk: metal instead of wood. A chair. A cheap metal file cabinet with two drawers. She moved into the windowless room gingerly, as if squeezing past the memory of Peter Chamberlain; she could almost feel him still standing there, expectant, waiting to feel her rub against him.

The place looked as if it hadn't been used for a while. There was a thin film of dust on the modest furniture. On one wall, a yellowing newspaper clipping was tacked. She examined it. It meant nothing; the date on top had been half torn; all she could see was '1977.'

She got the desk drawer open by hooking a forefinger under the handle so as not to disturb the dust. Elizabeth the superspy. She giggled. Nothing: a few paper clips, a pencil stub, a scratch pad three quarters used, lint, a bottle of cement hard as a rock, half a dozen dead ballpoints.

The top drawer of the file cabinet was empty. The second held a few files. She spread them as carefully as she could. Most of them seemed to date from around 1971 and 1972, or soon after the house had been rebuilt. She was replacing them when she saw something pushed to the back of the drawer. She pulled it out.

It was a framed photograph. As she looked at it, she could almost hear Peter's heavy breathing behind her. It was the same picture, all right: an old photograph, now turning slightly brown at the edges, inserted into a cheap black frame. A photograph of two men — naked men, squinting in what was, from the quality of the light, a high summer sun. Two young naked men, white teeth grinning out of tanned faces, their arms thrown carelessly over each other's shoulders and each reaching across in front with his other hand to grasp the other's obviously erect penis. One man was Uncle Waldo, a young Uncle Waldo. The other was the man whose face had come to haunt her, the man from *Match*, the Russian named Menchikov.

She heard her own heavy breathing. The once-welcoming house now seemed to creak ominously. She strained to hear, but there was nothing but the wind outside. She looked at the photograph again. There was writing across the bottom, in white ink. She looked at it closely. The characters themselves were Russian and meant nothing to her. The ink they were scripted in stood up from the paper and was cracked like old oil paint. It was obviously the original.

Without thinking, she shoved the photograph under her arm and gently pushed the file drawer shut. As she did, she noticed that the file cabinet was set out a bit from the wall; instinctively she looked behind it. Something was there. She put down the photograph and lifted up the roll of cloth hidden behind the file cabinet.

It was a sampler, similar in size and stitching to the one downstairs. About a foot and a half square, very closely and artistically worked. Elizabeth studied it carefully, committing it to memory.

Along the top were the dates '1955 — 1985' worked in silver and red thread. Running down either side were a number of closely spaced figures and inscriptions, each about two inches high: an Arab, an oil derrick, EURO$, the letters CD to which minuscule wings were attached, a Mexican (Elizabeth assumed) in a sombrero, an African chief, a tiny two-pillared building with FED meticulously worked on its portico lying toppled on its side, a hypodermic needle marked DEBT.

In the center bottom, an old-fashioned spinning wheel had been stitched, bestrode by two Grandma Moses figures, little men, one of them obviously Uncle Waldo, bald with tiny white side curls.

From the wheel, a skein unspooled in a dashing curve into the very center of the sampler, where it looped into an obvious hangman's noose within which were the initials G.S.M., W.E.C., M.M.

W.E.C. and M.M.: Uncle Waldo and Manning Mallory, obviously. G.S.M.? Could that be Menchikov?

In the lower right-hand corner, Elizabeth found the initials M.A. and the date ''85'. Mary Arthurs, she thought. Quiddy's answer to Isabella d'Este.

She stared at the sampler for a full minute, committing it to memory the same way she filed away a Rembrandt drawing or a Sevres garniture. Then she slipped it back behind the file cabinet.

It was an instant's work to slide the bookcase back, relatch it, replace the books that concealed the knob, and trot down the hall to her bedroom, where she hid the photograph in her suitcase. Taking a pad from her briefcase, she quickly penciled a sketch from memory of the sampler she'd just seen. Her excitement pummeled her like the ocean; she felt momentarily witless.

When Uncle Waldo returned, fifteen minutes later, she had pulled herself together. Behind her smile and the jolly small talk she managed to make during lunch, she couldn't get the photograph out of her mind.

And the sampler. What did it mean? Where did Mallory fit into all of this? Obviously there was some connection between all three: Menchikov, Uncle Waldo, and Mallory. Why a hangman's noose?

Francis could probably sort it out. But if he did, would it send him off on another tear? She wished she'd never mentioned Peter Chamberlain and his 'secret'.

284

After lunch, she kissed Uncle Waldo goodbye and promised not to let this much grass grow before she saw him again. Perhaps this summer, she said. It occurred to her that she hadn't so much as mentioned Francis to Uncle Waldo. Odd, she thought. Had some internal security system cut in without her even being aware of it?

Uncle Waldo insisted on carrying her suitcase to the car. She felt as if the photograph inside it were radioactive; how could he not see the suspicious glow, sense the dangerous crackle?

'Well, my dear,' he said, 'I do hope you'll return to Quiddy this summer.' He sounded oddly wistful. 'Perhaps for July Fourth, when I show off Mrs Arthurs's cummerbund.'

CHAPTER TWENTY-EIGHT

HOBE SOUND, FLORIDA AND NEW YORK CITY
Thursday, February 27th

As a schoolboy, Francis Mather had been bored to tears by *Les Misérables*. Now, driving back down the Florida Turnpike, he began to appreciate Javert's obsessive pursuit of Jean Valjean. The quest itself became the thing; the objective became secondary. Men set out for India and found America, but Inca gold made them just as happy as the spices of Malabar.

There was something else he couldn't get out of his mind, something one of his theology professors at the seminary had remarked.

'Man-made disasters differ from acts of God in that they are usually the results either of accident, or stupidity, or malignity.'

Accident. Stupidity. Malignity. Ascending stages in the attribution of causes; angles of vision for looking into the origin of events.

Take as a given that the banking system has been put at risk, he reflected. Was that accidental? Hardly. Stupid? Possibly. Nothing disarmed prudence like greed. But look at the facts, at history. There was more than greed at work here. There was intelligence, innovation, brilliance. There was the inventive, brilliant team of Mallory and Chamberlain, creating a great innovative banking institution every competitor was willing to go to the limit to emulate, to compete with.

Stupid, then? Not necessarily. Mallory and Waldo Chamberlain were careful, brilliant men who knew what they were doing.

And that left malignity. But if so, why? None of the usual motives seemed to apply. Was this some kind of a swindle, on a gigantic scale; was it just for money? That didn't feel right. Perhaps some kind of generalized revenge on the system, on people? That made more sense. It could also be the most gigantic piece of sheer mischief ever conceived. The game *ad absurdum*. That made more sense — but not enough.

He went back over what he knew.

From what Elizabeth had told him of the photograph, it seemed clear that Waldo Chamberlain had been involved in a homosexual affair with Menchikov sometime in the past. Had Waldo Chamberlain been blackmailed by the Soviets? If so, for what, to what end? To hand over secrets? What secrets could Waldo Chamberlain possess? He made a note to find out if Waldo had ever had a security clearance. Had he ever served on the board of a defense contractor? Could it be something like that?

The Russian angle bore looking into. Other avenues looked more immediately promising.

To begin with: Mallory. CertBank's own public-relations department was only too happy to supply the Reverend Mather with a copy of the bank's official biography of its peerless leader. Francis read it carefully, learning nothing, but he had a long memory and he vaguely remembered that, at just about the time he himself started to make his own name on Wall Street, Mallory had been involved in a highly publicized two-horse derby at the Cert. The years 1970 − 71 had been a watershed time for the changing of the guard at the big banks.

So Francis went to the New York Society Library and immersed himself in microfilms of the newspapers of the time and in back issues of *Business Week* and *American Banker*. Sure enough, in the late sixties, Mallory had a serious competitor for the succession at the bank, but the guy had been disabled in 1969 by one of those teapot foreign exchange scandals just strong enough to break a reputation and a career. The ground had briefly trembled, the sun had stood momentarily still, CertCo shares had taken a two-day walloping, and then Manning Mallory was free of any rival within the bank.

Next, the fire. Even if he gave in to his darkest suspicions, Francis thought, what could have been the point of the fire? Sure, it put Mallory in Preston Chamberlain's office, but

287

only two or three years ahead of schedule. Why the rush?

Maybe it wasn't a question of time. Maybe it was something tangible. Maybe it was Peter Chamberlain. Just suppose, Francis speculated, that Peter Chamberlain's big secret had been that Mallory wasn't going to get the job after all. It could be something like that, the way Elizabeth remembered it. Just suppose that Peter Chamberlain knew — from his father — that Mallory was going to be passed over.

And then — take the next logical step.

Francis remembered reading somewhere that all secrets are twofold: there is the secret itself, and then there is the fact that it is secret. Elizabeth had assumed Peter to be exhilarated simply because he knew the secret. But what if there was more? What if Peter himself was part of the secret?

Was that possible?

Peter Chamberlain was no dummy, Francis reflected. For understandable reasons, Elizabeth had taken him too lightly, but Peter had made it on his own, right to the top of the Chase. He was a proven, certified banking heavyweight. If it wasn't to be Mallory at the Cert, who would it have been? One of the runners-up elsewhere? Not likely.

The idea of Peter Chamberlain supplanting Mallory made sense. Wasn't Preston Chamberlain the archetypal dynast? So Francis had gone back to Seventy-ninth Street and reread the microfilmed accounts of the fire and the Chamberlain obituaries.

The fire had been page-one news; why didn't he remember it more vividly? Then it came back to him that he'd spent a good part of that month in Japan vainly hustling investment banking business; by the time he'd returned to New York the tragedy had lots its immediacy. He flicked the microfilm and reread Peter Chamberlain's obituary. Elizabeth described him as a lecherous jackass, and maybe he had been — around her — but he had also been a Senior Executive Vice-President and Director of the Chase, a director of half a dozen well-known corporations, and a trustee and board member of the right schools, clubs, charities.

Francis let his suspicions run. But how . . .?'

Waldo Chamberlain. The name lit up in his mind like neon.

Waldo Chamberlain had known the secret.

And Waldo Chamberlain had been fortuitously called away on the very morning of a fire which otherwise would surely have claimed him as a victim.

Francis shut off the microfilm reader and went across to the members' reading room, which was pleasantly empty this early in the day, and took a chair by one of the high windows overlooking the street. Go back, Francis, he said to himself. Take it slowly, point by point. Two accidents, miracles as far as Mallory's concerned. Why was no one suspicious?

Because whoever would have thought of it that way, that's why, he told himself. Because who on Wall Street could for a moment have credenced such a thing? Where was the motive, where was the money? The motive wasn't lacking; it was just that what he suspected was utterly beyond the interest or comprehension of the financial community, and so suspicion would never have been raised.

To commit five murders to become CEO of a bank? Why? Think again. Personal ambition? Possibly. Had there been some scheme afoot to loot CertBank? It made no sense. If some kind of massive pecuniary shenanigans were the object, the last place you would want to try to fiddle would be a big, influential, highly scrutinized, politically sensitive bank like the Cert. You'd want a bank in the sticks, possibly, some place out of the spotlight. A place like Chattanooga or Midland. And if thievery was the object, the last place to start was with a bank's CEO. The right man for that kind of job would work in the room where they counted the money and securities, or in a teller's cage, or lower down on the lending ladder.

He got up to go, still trying to pull it together. Absently, he looked down at a table on which a number of papers and magazines had been spread out. A headline caught his eye and he picked the paper up. 'THE KGB IN OUR MIDST' was printed boldly on the first page of the Review section of the *Sunday Times* of London. It was an advertisement for a new book on spying, and it listed, as a come-on, a dozen overt ways for the KGB to attain control of Britain — 'Encourage activists like the Greens to organize strikes . . . Propagate the view through special groups, like the Alliance, that Government policies are wrong ... Use normal channels to move weapons into the country' — the usual litany of how to poison a democracy from within through legitimate channels.

Francis looked at the advertisement again. Suppose, he thought, for names like 'the Alliance' or 'the Greens,' one substituted 'CertBank' or 'the thrifts' or 'Drexel Burnham.' Did a weapon have to be an atom bomb or a grenade launcher, and did it have to be smuggled in? Suppose the weapon was on the ground already, already assembled, merely needing to be armed and aimed? If the fiscal system was the target, say, couldn't the weapons be easy credit, junk bonds, petrodollars, anything that encouraged and facilitated institutional destabilization and reckless speculation?

He examined the advertisement more closely. The book it touted seemed to be yet another in the endless recapitulations of the Burgess-Maclean-Blunt-Philby affair, claiming to expose yet another 'Fifth Man,' 'Sixth Man,' 'Seventh Man.' Funny, he thought, the great English traitors always seemed to come from Oxford and Cambridge; in this country they're lowlifes selling secrets for small change.

Blunt, Philby. England in the 1930s. Cambridge. Something rang a bell.

Of course. He remembered reading that Blunt had recruited an American, Michael Straight. And Straight had written a book, Francis recalled.

His watch told him he was due shortly at a meeting of the Ladies' Parish League. He ran into the stacks and found Straight's book and checked it out.

That night, he got home late. He had been to the opera and supper afterward at the home of an important parishioner, and he was slightly muddled by the excellent Bordeaux his host had poured in obscene quantities.

He settled down with Straight's *After Long Silence*. He skipped to the account of Straight's years at Cambridge. The influence of Keynes on Straight, evenings at the 'Keynes Club.'

Keynes? Was that another link? Keynes's two great American

290

disciples were James Tobin at Yale and Waldo Chamberlain! He read on, through Straight's account of evenings at the Keynes Club. Odd, no mention of Chamberlain, although the economist's canned biographies all stressed that he had studied with the master at Cambridge in 1935 and 1936.

Finally he came to what he knew he was looking for. It was Straight's account of his recruitment by Blunt.

'Some of your friends,' said [Anthony Blunt], 'have other ideas for you.'

'Other ideas?'

'Your father worked on Wall Street. He was a partner in J. P. Morgan. With those connections, with your training as an economist, you could make a brilliant future for yourself in international banking . . . Our friends have instructed me to tell you that is what you must do.'

'What I must do? What friends have instructed you to tell me?'

'Our friends in the International. The Communist International . . . My instructions are to inform you of your assignment . . .'

'My assignment? What assignment?'

'To work on Wall Street. To provide appraisals, economic appraisals, of Wall Street's plans to dominate the world economy . . .'

Francis shut the book. Was it possible, he wondered, that the same scene, with different actors, might have been replicated a year or so earlier, also in Cambridge; and then — years after that again, in a different Cambridge?

Two days later Francis traded on an old favor and spent an afternoon in the Merrill Lynch research library. He had worked out what he needed to know — if it could be found — and how best to go about finding it. That was as far as he allowed himself to think ahead. If the puzzle fitted together, and if the picture it produced was as extraordinary as he conceived it might be, he would then have to figure out what to do next. And that was so daunting, he found himself wishing his guess would come to nought.

He started with the 1969 and 1970 volumes of *Who's Who*. He read through Waldo Chamberlain's entry twice, making a list of the economist's board memberships at that time. Then he read it again for confirmation of another point. Sure enough: 'Graduate Study, Cambridge University, 1935–36.' The years that the Russians were trolling for future spies among the exquisite, dissolute, idealistic young men who made up the 'Cambridge Apostles.'

Francis returned to his main line of inquiry. According to the 1969 and 1970 *Directory of Directors* and *Poor's Register*, Waldo Chamberlain had numbered among his boards during those years the Mission Chemical Corporation of St Louis. Francis now pulled the annual reports of Mission Chemical; they only went forward as far as 1982, when (a note in the file report) Mission had been merged into Conoco. Mission's last report as an independent public corporation listed an M. S. Timmons, presumably the name partner of Mission's local law firm, as on the board in 1982.

A helpful research librarian punched up the additional data Francis wanted. Elizabeth had said that Waldo Chamberlain had flown off to St Louis on short notice, that there had been some kind of an emergency or special occasion at the company involving management, but Merrill Lynch's vast data base failed to show any special activity in MCH shares for the five days on either side of Thanksgiving 1970, and the only news item from the same period reported merely that the company had followed Dow Chemical in posting a tenth-of-a-cent-per-pound price increase for certain grades of polyvinylchloride. This was hardly sufficient reason, Francis knew from experience, for a $500 million corporation to summon its prominent board from around the country on short notice over a holiday weekend.

Francis now went to the *Martindale-Hubbell Law Directory* and ascertained that the St Louis firm of Timmons and Oakey was now known as Timmons, Muller and Muller. An M. S. Timmons was still listed as a name partner.

He now turned his attention to the 1969 and 1970 annual reports of Certified Guaranty National Bank. The later report was prefaced with a black-framed color photograph of the late Preston Chamberlain, followed by a handsome, personally heartfelt eulogy over the signature of Manning Mallory, the late Mr Chamberlain's successor. Francis read this with some amusement; his close attention was reserved for the listing of board committees at the end of the 1969 annual.

Just as he had expected, in order to prosecute its members' responsibilities most efficiently, the CertCo board had been sub-divided into a number of committees — Executive, Personnel, Compensation, Audit, and so on — consisting exclusively of outside directors, with Preston Chamberlain an ex officio member of all and Chairman of the Executive Committee. Francis concentrated on the Compensation and Executive committees; he assumed it would have been to either of these groups that Preston Chamberlain would have been obliged to communicate a decision to bypass Manning Mallory. Waldo Chamberlain did not sit on the Compensation Committee, and Elizabeth had very firmly asserted that Waldo Chamberlain knew the secret. Assuming it was passed to Waldo as other than a brotherly confidence, he would have most likely heard it through the CertCo Executive Committee, the appropriate forum for news of this magnitude. Francis had done some reading up on Preston Chamberlain; he was certain that, in something like this, the older brother would have been an absolute stickler for form.

With his short list of names and affiliations, he left Merrill Lynch and headed uptown to the Public Library. A fast check of *New York Times* obituaries eliminated two names, leaving two others unaccounted for: a Boston attorney and the president of a Cleveland machinery company. He went back to his rector's office and got on the telephone. His first call established that the Boston attorney had passed away in 1984. The Cleveland executive, however, was still alive; he had retired in 1979 and now lived in Florida in a hyper-WASP resort where Francis had once preached.

His next call was to St Louis. He asked for Mr Timmons,

was put through to a secretary, identified himself as the Rector of All Angels calling from New York on a confidential parish matter, and was connected with a voice that sounded much younger than he expected.

The confusion was soon cleared up. This was Mr *Merlon* S. Timmons: it had been his late father, Mr *Marvin* S. Timmons who had been a director of Mission Chemical.

'We still do a good bit of their work, though,' said the younger Timmons, 'mostly local stuff — United Way, some OSHA and employee benefit. All they have left here now is a laboratory out near St Charles. Conoco was bought out by Du Pont, you know, and they closed down the big plant in East St Louis right afterward. Put fifteen hundred people out of work, but Du Pont had all those interest bills to pay. It didn't help around here. Anyway, that's our sad story. How can I help you, Reverend?'

Francis spun out his carefully concocted fib. Two of his elderly parishioners, he told Timmons, were in a dispute of the sort only very old people got into. As usual, it involved a small sum of money a long time back; at issue was whether Mission Chemical had split its stock in December 1970 or January 1971. One old man was asserting his cousin had stolen the extra shares out of a family trust.

'I used to be on Wall Street,' Francis told Timmons, 'and so I volunteered to try to get things squared away. I couldn't see any point in litigation, not for this kind of money. I can't find any record of a stock split back then, but one of my old gentlemen swears that there was a special meeting of the board to authorize it. I believe these people were related to one of the directors back then.'

Francis gave the name of a former Mission director he had ascertained to be safely dead.

Timmons said he'd try to help. Two hours later he called back.

'I'm afraid to disappoint you, Reverend, but we've talked to Wilmington and they checked the records. In 1970 and 1971, the only board meetings Mission held were its regular quarterlies: April, July, October, and January. The second Tuesday of each month.'

'What about board committees?' Francis asked.

'I can answer that. My old man was on the Mission board for thirty years. They didn't have any. The guy that ran Mission didn't like committees. As a matter of fact, he didn't like boards.'

Francis thanked him and hung up.

So Uncle Waldo had lied. Now to make certain of his motive. It took Francis a day to set up the appointment he wanted; on Wednesday he caught the noon flight to West Palm Beach, rented a car, and drove north to Hobe Sound.

The highway seemed to spin on endlessly. Francis, bored, turned off the air conditioning and cranked down the window of his rented car. Even in winter, the Florida air had a damp weight to it.

He fingered open the top two buttons of his shirt. His clerical collar lay on the seat beside him. He had thought it desirable to appear in Hobe Sound in uniform. Hobe was that kind of place. They didn't fancy their clergymen in golf shirts.

It hadn't been difficult to arrange to see the retired Cleveland executive, although protocol required that Francis go through the rector of the little church on Jupiter Island, de facto chaplain to the wealthy retirement community which the racier folk downcoast in Palm Beach dubbed 'God's Waiting Room.' In fact, Francis rather liked Hobe. He had preached there twice since his ordination and as a child had come there with his parents as guests of old Cape Cod friends.

The retired machinery magnate had been most welcoming. Francis's cover story was that he was writing a history of All Angels since the Depression, which would center on its more important parishioners, of which Preston Chamberlain had certainly been one.

'He was our chief usher,' Francis said, 'back before my time. When Jay Mortimer was still rector, before he was called to St Henry's in Southampton.'

'Never knew that,' said the man from Cleveland. 'Wouldn't have thought Pres Chamberlain to be much of a churchman. He was a great friend of mine, though. Knew him thirty years — right up to the day he died in that fire. Tough as nails, Pres.'

'I gather he had a real soft spot for his son,' said Francis, seizing the opportunity.

'Petey? Absolutely! Funny you should know that. Most people thought Pres never got off Petey's back. All that business about exiling him to the Chase. That was just Pres seeing the boy got a loose enough lead to prove himself. Which he surely damn well did. Just ask George Champion!'

'I gather the son was very bright?'

'Petey? Smart as a whip. Too much so, sometimes; there were times when I thought he was a bit of a smart aleck. I know his father did, especially around the ladies, but the bottom line was that Petey had the right stuff.'

Francis decided to take the chance and ask the question on which his whole theory hung. 'I gather that's why Mr Chamberlain wanted to bring Peter in to run the Certified Bank?'

The old man smiled and shook his head. 'Well, I'll be damned,' he said. 'Funny you mention that. You know, I haven't thought of it in years. That's the damn trouble with life, Father. After a while, you just forget, you're so busy moving ahead. Companies don't have memories, only portraits of dead men in the boardroom.'

Francis nursed the old man's reminiscences along. Hell, yes, there had been a meeting of the CertCo Executive Committee just a week or so before Pres and Petey got burned up.

'Never forget it. There was a real pier-sixer between Pres and his brother, Wally. You know who he is, Father: Waldo Chamberlain, the big economist?'

'I know who he is. So Preston and Waldo Chamberlain were present. Yourself. Anyone else?'

'Let's see: there was Pres, his brother, me, and Rob Archer from Hale and Dunn in Boston. Nice fellow, Archer — he dropped dead of a heart attack right on the first tee at Gulfstream. I think that was it. There were only seven of us on the Committee — Pres didn't like too many talking — and I seem to remember Jim Moran from Flintkote and Miller from Amalgamated Stores were both in Europe. They're dead now, too. Mallory was off somewhere. Yes, just the four: Pres, me, Archer — and Wally, of course.'

'Did you know Waldo Chamberlain well?'

'Not really. Funny you should ask, though. Saw him at the bank's alumni day last fall. Not a whole lot of laughs, little brother Wally. Pretty smart fellow, though in all my years at the machine company I must have hired fifty of those Business School graduates that Wally taught and never did get one who was worth a damn . . . Anyway, back to your question. Yes, Pres called a meeting, and right off the bat he announced he was bringing Petey over from Chase to run the bank.'

'The bank or the holding company? CertCo or CertBank?'

'Both. Pres Chamberlain did damn few things by halves, I can tell you.'

'And what was the reaction of the committee?'

'Well, frankly, some of us weren't so sure Pres was doing the right thing. We had Manning Mallory on board, you know.'

'Who runs the bank now?'

'That's him. He was a real winner, a comer from Day One. Knew the bank inside out. Had a lot of time in the outfit, and smart as a whip, too, he was!'

'Did you like Mallory? Was he popular with the board?'

'Like him? No, I can't say I liked him, but I sure as hell respected him. The man had brains and drive, Father — in spades! Anyway, it was Pres's store and this was what he wanted. Petey was sure as hell qualified too, though, and who is to say he wouldn't've been as good for the bank as Mallory's been? Anyway, in those days, when it came to boards, it was ''I'll scratch your back and you scratch mine.'' Probably still is. I went along with Pres and so did the others. I know I sure as hell would've resented it if my outside directors had butted in at Midwest Machine and tried to tell me what to do. Yes, we all went along, but I can tell you Wally was mad as a snake at Pres.'

Francis thought the pounding in his mind must be drowning the smooth distant rumble of the ocean.

'Did he object out loud?'

'Object! I thought he was going to shit his pants! I could understand that. Mallory was Wally's boy. Hell, he found him, recruited him, trained him from a pup. Wally coached him on the QT: do this, say that. I think Pres resented it, but it was good for business, so what the hell. Mallory got the credit, but half the stunts were Wally's idea. Damn foolishness, if you ask me. Lend billions to a bunch of South Americans and watch our own steel industry go bust! How are we going to fight a war without a steel industry? If you ask me, we've made as much mischief for ourselves around the world with all these loans as anything the Soviets have done.'

Francis nodded sympathetically.

'Anyway,' the old man continued, 'there was no discussion. Pres told Wally to shut up and swore us all to secrecy. He still needed to work it out with Champion and David Rockefeller. Never got the chance.'

'And did anyone else know? What about Mallory?'

'Not unless Wally told him. Hell, I don't think Petey even knew. Pres was that kind of guy. He swore us all to secrecy. Anyway, turned out to be academic, didn't it?'

'A sad occurrence.' Francis put on his most parsonly voice, wanting to sound like an unctuous vicar in an old Ealing comedy. 'And, one assumes, after the fire, it was time to close ranks behind Mallory.'

'Exactly so. These things happen, and there's nothing to do but carry on. It might have been different if Pres had gone down with a heart attack, or if Petey'd been alive, but that's not worth thinking about. The institution's got to go on; that's what business is, institutions, not people. This wasn't the first tragedy like this or the last. TexasGulf lost a bunch of their top people a few years back. Plane crash. We were lucky at CertCo; we had Mallory right there, ready and raring to take over. He had it all: brains, training, connections — hell, Wall Street ate out of the man's hand, still does! I guess he just wasn't Pres's sort when you got right down to it. I loved Pres like a brother, but, Lord, he could be a terrible snob!'

The old man's eyes narrowed. He'd realized he'd been talking quite a lot.

'You're not going to let some of this out, are you, Father? Some of these people are still around. No point in hurting any feelings.'

'Heavens, no.'

In fact, Francis wasn't sure what he was going to do. He managed to sit still for another half-hour with the old man, absorbing his views on paper entrepreneurialism, Nicaragua, and the Japanese, then pleaded a plane to catch and left.

Signs for West Palm Beach began to appear by the side of the highway. In a way, thought Francis, I wish I could stay down here. Go to sleep and wake up and have all this turn out to be a bad dream. Now I have to face the consequences of what I think I know.

And what might those be? Had he stumbled on some great and sinister design right out of a spy novel? Would they come after him? Who might 'they' be?'

He would say nothing about any of this to Elizabeth, he decided. Better she think him caught up in a childish fixation with Mallory, the way some people hated Roosevelt or the incumbent President.

He could not escape the feeling that he might be entering a danger zone. As he guided the car onto the off ramp toward the airport, he prayed long and intensely to God to see him through whatever was to come.

The usual winter travel delays saw to it that Francis didn't get back to his apartment until after midnight. He was tired and he had a Community House ecumenical breakfast at eight the next morning, as his secretary's voice reminded him on his answering machine; then lunch at the Downtown Association with the wardens of the vestry. There was another beep, and here was Elizabeth, speaking very rapidly:

'Darling I just got home from London. It's Saturday night here; call me in the morning. Where are you? I love you desperately and all sorts of other things I can't possible say over a consecrated answering machine. Did you get your present? I can't think why I did it, but there it is. I love you. 'Bye, my love.'

Present? Francis was having trouble keeping his thoughts organized. On the interminable trip north he'd gone over the ground again and again, even to the point of writing the different names down on a sheet of paper and drawing lines between them, just the way they'd done a million years ago at the B-school: 'Decision Trees'.

He had all the pieces, or most of them, but they didn't cohere. The fire. The circumstantial evidence of Waldo Chamberlain's hasty departure on a faked excuse. But what did that have to mean, after all? Waldo could have white-lied about being called away for a hundred reasons. He could have been keeping an assignation with a sailor in a Portland motel. Yet Waldo knew about Preston Chamberlain's plan to install Peter at the Cert.

But to kill four, five, six people? It made no sense. There must be more to it than that, much more at stake.

He kept coming back to the Russian; it was a speculation he couldn't suppress. He thought again about Michael Straight.

Present? He looked across the room. His housekeeper had stacked his mail on the living room desk, but there didn't seem to be any parcel there. Well, he thought, crossing the room, let's take this thing all the way out, let's be Alice in James Bond land. Let's say Mallory's a Russian recruit and they've gone through all this to put him on top of the Cert, sparing only Elizabeth because Uncle Waldo the Spymaster had taken a fancy to her. This is crazy, he thought.

He thought about this while he riffled through his mail. Present? What had she meant?

There was the usual garbage mail of circulars and claims on his credulity and bank account. Then, at the bottom, tucked between two magazines, was a Federal Express envelope. Origin: Boston. The sender had been E. Bennett, Ritz-Carlton Hotel.

'Francis tore it open. It contained three pieces of paper. The first was a note in Elizabeth's hand:

*Here are two souvenirs from Uncle Waldo's secret room
at Quiddy. I am sure the photograph is the original P.C.
showed me in 1970. Does the fact that it's still intact
mean what I think it does? The other is a sketch of a
sampler I found behind a cabinet. Now you can go back
to thinking about us. I love you.*

He looked at the photograph.

'Jesus,' he said softly, and in the next breath apologized
to the Divinity for his profanity.

He put the photograph down on the desk. As he started to
study her pencil sketch, he found himself thinking, Damn it,
Elizabeth's gotten herself into this now.

The sketch was very rough. There was a date and a series
of small figures embroidered on each vertical edge. In the
center was some kind of elaborate rebus: a large spinning
wheel straddled by two stick figures. The thread spooling from
the spinning wheel ended in a hangman's noose, in the loop
of which were three sets of initials. Two he recognized at once.
The third he could guess at. Elizabeth had circled W.C. and
M.M. and drawn arrowed lines from them to the stick figures
manning the wheel.

'Oh, my God,' he breathed. Like an illusionist's trick, it
had all come together, impossible to believe, impossible to
deny. And impossible to know how to deal with.

THE PRESENT

March

CHAPTER TWENTY-NINE

WASHINGTON
Friday, March 7th

'Now let me just get this straight, Reverend. People been saying for years that these big banks couldn't have screwed things up worse if they'd been trying, and you're telling me that's exactly what's been going on?'

Francis nodded.

'You are alleging that what we've been told was the genius of capitalism at work was actually the genius of Moscow at work, call it "economic sabotage"?'

Francis nodded again.

'Which means, Reverend, that you are accusing two of the most splendid ornaments of our free enterprise system of being — what? — Soviet financial moles?'

Francis nodded a third time. He supposed he was making a complete fool of himself to the black man behind the desk. He knew what he had just finished reciting must sound incredible.

'It makes too much sense, Mr Forbush,' he said with conviction. 'All the pieces fit.' Pretty circumstantially, he thought, watching his listener carefully.

Phillips E. Forbush was built on the squat, sloping lines of an artillery shell, two-hundred-odd coal-colored pounds compacted on a frame an inch or two under six feet. His hair was grizzled, but Francis judged him to be several years younger than himself. Forbush's voice struck Francis as improbable. It was completely at odds with the man's physical appearance: high, almost reedy. Above all, it wasn't black.

'You know, Reverend,' Forbush said, 'there are a lot of people who'd say right off the bat, "Man, you crazy!" '

'I know.'

Forbush's tone was mildly skeptical, however, and he had sat right through Francis's recitation, all two hours of it. He had asked fewer than half a dozen questions during that time, but the thrust of these told Francis that Forbush got his drift.

He looked around. They were sitting in Forbush's office in the Rayburn Office Building. It was not a 'good' office, situated as it was on a low floor with no view at all. Not surprising: the Washington lawyer who had directed Francis to Phillips E. Forbush had implied that the man was lucky to be in a cage.

The office was fitted out with low-ranking steel furniture. On the walls were framed certificates: a West Point degree and commission dated 1969, a law degree from Howard, an MBA from Georgetown.

Francis took the books in Forbush's office bookcase as an earnest of a sympathetic point of view. They were virtually identical to those in Francis's study and were not books found on the shelves of the fat and sanguine: Martin Mayer's *The Bankers* and *The Money Bazaars*; works on the debt crisis by Makin, Delamaide, Lever and Huhne; Kindleberger's *Manias, Panics, and Crashes;* Galbraith's *The Great Crash*; the Nader report on Citibank; popular works on banking and Wall Street by John Brooks and Anthony Sampson and Penny Lernoux; Kaletsky's *The Costs of Default*; and a few well-worn older volumes whose titles he couldn't make out.

A sympathetic bookshelf was one thing; but even if Forbush bought his story, was there anything that could be done?

Or should be done? Here Francis faced a conflict between conscience and desire, a question with which he had wrestled through several uneasy days and sleepless nights.

Why do anything? Didn't Wall Street deserve the hell it had brought on itself? If it was simply to be determined by his own personal satisfaction, let the greedy bastards go down in flames. The problem was, if the Chamberlain-Mallory scheme succeeded, a lot of people would be hurt who didn't deserve to be, and a system whose wonderful promise was worth a million times the scum it spawned would be gravely, possibly fatally damaged. Its successor would be an atheistic or totalitarian alternative that was much, much worse. For a priest, there could be no choice. Francis was God's soldier; he wore God's uniform. This, ultimately, was God's fight; the enemy was God's sworn enemy, the godless Soviet, so fight that enemy he must, even though he might find himself saving the bacon for men he despised, who would be undeservedly spared the pain and punishment they otherwise merited.

Looking around the modest office, he wondered what Forbush would think of 'God's fight.'

All he'd told his friend at the big takeover law firm was that he needed someone in Washington to consult about 'finding out some SEC-type things on the QT.' Someone with access; someone straight.

That might not be so easy. His lawyer friend had laughed; made a fellow long for the good old ethical days of Harding and Fall.

Try, Francis told him. He had a big due bill out on this law firm; he'd thrown them a number of good pieces of legal business during his Morgan Stanley years. Forty-eight hours later, his friend called back with the name of Phillips E. Forbush, special assistant to an obscure investigative unit attached to the House Banking Committee.

'This guy,' said Francis's source, 'is so fucking straight it's gonna finish him off.' Forbush was a West Pointer who'd served in Vietnam. 'Came out with a chestful of medals and every GI grudge you ever heard of,' Francis's source put it. 'He's a black sheep in every sense of the word.'

After mustering out in 1973, Francis's source told him, Forbush had taken law and business degrees at Howard University and Georgetown while supporting himself clerking at the SEC. The director of enforcement, Stanley Sporkin, had taken a fancy to him and recruited him for the Enforcement Division.

'Having this guy working for Sporkin was like throwing gasoline on a fire, Francis,' his source said. 'He went after 'em all. Insider trading, Ten-B (five), Sixteen-B, you name it! Totally out of control, as if the goddamn system were something sacred and he was personally charged by the Big Fellow upstairs to keep it on the up-and-up.

'Anyway, when Sporkin went over to Langley as general counsel for the CIA, he took Forbush with him. It was not a great success, and Forbush was out of there within a year. Since then, he's been bouncing around. Worked over in the Comptroller's office for a while, until he tried to get the entire board of the First Pennsy indicted for gross fiduciary negligence. He troubleshot for the Fed for a while, until he got crossways there; apparently Forbush wanted to let Bache go down the tubes when the Hunts went loco in the silver market. Then the FDIC, where it was more of the same; he was opposed to using federal deposit insurance to bail out Continental Illinois's bondholders, and so once again it was over and out for P. E. Forbush. He doesn't get the picture about subsidized laissez faire; thank God he wasn't anywhere near Chrysler!

'Then somehow he hooks up with the Fed again — they say Volcker kind of likes the guy — but this time he goes too far. He tries to hang the big New York arbs and greenmailers on the margin and short-swing profit rules. They reached for the phone, and that finished him at the Fed. Now he's marking time on a dipshit subcommittee that's prowling around the edges of farm lending.

'Strictly a go-nowhere do-nothing job,' said Francis's source, 'but Christ! — sorry, Francis — you can't keep the guy down! He seems to be freelancing, from what I hear over at Skadden, Arps. You know that big food-company LBO the Cert and a bunch of Chicago banks are financing; Drexel's coming up with the junk money? The deal's been going smooth as silk, the stockholders sullen but not mutinous, and there's I-can't-tell-you how many millions in carried interest and fees for the insiders and the management, when out of the blue this fucking Forbush pops up in court in Wilmington all on his lonesome, *as a hundred-share stockholder*, if you can believe it, asking for an injunction on the grounds of "misappropriation of corporate information"! Ever heard anything like that?'

'He probably has a point,' Francis commented.

'Now, padre,' his source said with obvious sarcasm, 'don't be naive; you and I both know that no management we've ever met would possibly consider taking advantage of its stock-holders, not even if said management stood to earn, say, a twenty-million-dollar piece of the action off the top, plus whatever cut of the investment banking fees they could nego-tiate under the table. Anyway, it's a total waste of Forbush's time and money. The Delaware court's gonna do what it always does: let the deal go through and then get the guilty parties to sign a consent decree promising not to do it again. Anyway, you want an honest man inside the Beltway, you go see Phil Forbush.'

And so Francis had come to Washington to try out his far-fetched story and suspicions on a man who was a pariah and probably of no official use even if he bought Francis's theory lock, stock, and barrel.

He had walked Forbush through it right from the beginning, interweaving his own slanted capsule history of thirty years of American banking and finance with what he had been able to reconstruct or guess at about the Mallory-Chamberlain collaboration. He was candid about the blanks. Menchikov was still an enigma, for example. He took Forbush forward from the creation of the negotiable CD in 1962 and its consequences, through the effects of 'spread banking,' through all the tricks and contrivances that had passed into general acceptance. Look at it from my angle, he argued. Every one of these great Mallory-Chamberlain innovations could just as easily have been deliberately engineered to wreck the system.

He retraced Mallory's career for Forbush, highlighting the man's luck at crucial turns. He quoted from Michael Straight's autobiography. Then he produced his hard evidence: the photo of the young Waldo Chamberlain with the young Menchikov; Elizabeths sketch of the sampler; the circumstances surrounding Waldo Chamberlain's fortuitous absence from Quiddy the night of the fire; what he'd learned in Florida about Preston Chamberlain's intention to pass over Mallory in favor of his son, Peter.

309

Forbush had studied the photography closely. Then, with a grin, he'd passed it back to Francis.

'Man equipped like that Russian boy could pass for a blood. Anyway, Reverend, I take it your point is: How suspicious that this precious memento of a summer sucking cock beside the Black Sea survived the fire!'

'Exactly. It survived the fire because it wasn't there. It wasn't there because Waldo Chamberlain knew there was going to *be* a fire, and so he took his precious photo away with him on a phony errand.'

Now, having had his say, thrice Francis had been queried by Forbush and thrice Francis had nodded.

The black man steepled his fingers and looked calmly at Francis. 'So,' he said, 'take it from the top: It's the thirties, and Moscow's seen what Wall Street can do if you let it run wild. One more time, they figure, and democratic capitalism's through for good. The trick is to get to 1929 all over again.

'But Wall Street's in the doldrums and in disgrace, so there's no way - not right then. But Moscow thinks long-term. Why not get a few moles burrowing in the banking system as well as the Foreign Office and the State Department? They sign up Blunt, Philby, Burgess; Bill Haydon at M16; they go after Straight, maybe Hiss. And let's say this Menchikov's a talent-spotter, assigned to hang around Keynes's circle, because that's where the bright Econ boys are.

'He runs across old Waldo and seduces him. The guy's perfect for what they want. He's smart; he's a potential fag; he's got a brother who's a big deal on Wall Street. So Menchikov shows Waldo some tricks he'd never dreamed of and takes a few eight-by-ten glossies just in case he needs a backup someday.

'Anyway, the war comes, which makes Wall Street and Moscow friends again, and Menchikov somehow hooks up with Waldo and signs him up to do talent-spotting for Uncle Ivan at the B-School, plus his brother is running a bank, which is manna from heaven. He recruits Mallory and away we go! That about it?'

'That's about it.'

310

'I have a couple of questions. Hell, I've got a hundred but these'll do. Mallory. What's his motive?'

Francis couldn't answer that. He'd run through all the likely possibilities - money, power, prestige, politics. None quite fit. 'The best I can come up with is: he's obsessed with the game; he likes moving the pieces.'

'Maybe so,' said Forbush, but he sounded dubious. 'I guess we'll just have to ponder that point, if indeed it matters at this late date. Now, my second question: How about lunch?'

'Sure, if you have the time.'

'Reverend, my time is your time. I find your tale, however improbable it may seem at first blush, intriguing — to say the least. Certainly it's the most interesting thing to come my way in several moons. Around here I am 'the canker in the fragrant rose,' as the Bard says, so my phone seldom rings and my appointment calendar resembles the surface of the moon.

'Besides,' added Forbush, 'today's "white envelope" day for my committee. The first week of the month the PACs come calling. Lunch at Sans Souci or Mel Krupin's for the chairman and the key committee members. Couple of martinis, lots of good fellowship, and, along with the coffee, a few thou in a plain white envelope to help with the high cost of maintaining the democratic process. Come on.'

They went to a fish joint a few minutes' walk from the Hill. Forbush ordered two beers, oyster stew, and crab cakes; Francis followed suit.

Over lunch, Forbush talked about himself. He was from Detroit. His father was a professional man, an accountant at Ford Rouge.

'They put him in an office overlooking the assembly line. All glassed in, so the big shots from Grosse Pointe and Dearborn could point him out to visitors as a living example of democracy in action. He wanted to be one too. Daddy loved the establishment. Guess what the 'E' in my name stands for?'

'I wouldn't dare.'

'Exeter. Phillips Exeter Forbush, that's me, Reverend.'

'Call me Francis.'

'Maybe when I know you better. How about "Rev" for

the time being — just to keep you comfortable?'

'As you will.'

'Anyway, I never got to Exeter. Or made Princeton either. But I did get an appointment to the Point. Where'd you go to school, Rev?'

'Harvard.'

'Ah, Harvard, fair Harvard. You know, Rev, we *lost* more guys in 'Nam out of my one class at the Point than even *served* out of fair Harvard during the whole war. I always thought that was kind of chickenshit of the Crimson.'

There was nothing for Francis to say.

'Don't look so guilty, Rev, you ain't the only one. Take our fearless President, the Freedom Fighter. Strikes me like he's got an A-Number-One case of the Freuds for sitting out the big war in Culver City. Won his medals on the dance floor of the Mocambo. Thinks blood's just a kind of thinned-out ketchup they use in Hollywood. Let me tell you, Rev, it isn't. You'd hate to put what I've seen on your French Fries.'

Forbush had flown helicopters in Vietnam. He'd been wounded. Had, as he put it, 'come within a couple of yards of getting my name on the sad Black Wall down on the Mall.' Francis felt shamed; the man was talking about places that to him had been abstract, distant television names: Hue, Bien Hoa, Da Nang.

Then Forbush spoke of 'life after 'Nam.' About getting his graduate degrees and working for Sporkin. About the CIA.

After that, it had been one Washington agency after another. He didn't seem to fit. It was, said Forbush, getting harder to keep his illusions intact.

'But it can't go on forever,' he remarked as they walked back to the Hill through a graying afternoon. 'Either things are going to change or it's the walls of Jericho. I hate to think what it's going to be like after 1988, when this President's gone and the country wakes up and finds out the last eight years were just a dream. We may find out we've been dead all this time without knowing it. And you know what the coroner's verdict is gonna be? Terminal brain damage from self-inflicted injuries.'

Back in his office, Forbush asked Francis, 'From Morgan Stanley to Union Theological. Must have been a real trip, huh, Rev?'

'It was a change.'

'Well, I want you to know you've sung your sad song to friendly ears. The Street'll make any thinking man sick.'

'I was — well, alienated.'

'And so you might be. Funny how money can change a man. All these names you read in the paper, the arbs, the takeover guys? Take away their credit lines and what have you got?'

'My guess is, not much,' said Francis. 'The paper entrepreneur has given way to the blip entrepreneur. Computers let him strike much faster, which makes him much deadlier.'

'What I don't understand,' said Forbush, 'is how much do these guys want? How many millions does a person *need*? How many deals do you have to do? I suppose after a while it's just like any other compulsion, no different from drinking or screwing or golf; you can't help yourself. Like the shark, you got to keep swimming or you die. But, Lord, Rev, after a while, the next drink, the next piece of ass has got to look pretty much like the one before, wouldn't you think? Then it's just something you do because you can't think of anything else.'

'It seems that way to me.'

'Anyway, Rev, I think you may be on to something. You know what Martin Mayer says?'

'I'm not sure. I've read most of his stuff.'

'He says, and I quote: "If the central banks cannot influence efficiently what happens in the market for the one commodity created by government itself, the theory of liberal democracy is in some trouble." '

'I couldn't agree more,' said Francis.

'Then, Rev, take a guess how much they've got off the balance sheet.'

'I think I remember reading something like two hundred billion dollars.'

'Try quadrupling that! And then add the interest rate swaps, and the oral understandings that the accountants don't make

313

the banks count but the courts will — just ask Texaco — and a whole lot of other off balance-sheet stuff that nobody seems to understand, and what do you get?'

'I don't know. Five hundred billion?'

'The best guess I've heard is a *trillion* five, but nobody knows. Not Volcker, not Congress, no one! Not even the banks!

'I worked my ass off in this town for nine years, Rev, doing my little bit to try to keep the game on the up-and-up. Then I got kicked out of the main stream in 1981, along with some other people, because it was felt that folks like me would get in the way of the brave new world of supply-side laissez-faire that was going to bail this country out. 'Bailout' was the right word: Lockheed, Chrysler, Continental Illinois. Now Mallory's talked the Fed into going on the Mexican paper. The funny thing is, if you look at the figures, the lender of last resort's broke hisself!'

He pulled open his desk drawer and took out a messy folder.

'Rev, I am a magpie just like you; I clip everything that tells me I'm right.' He grinned sheepishly as he fumbled through the papers. 'Ah, listen to this. Galbraith wrote it in the *Times* last year. Maybe you saw it. I'll just read you the good part.' He took out a pair of metal-framed eyeglasses. 'Marx, in his innocent and now obsolete way, thought it would be the workers who would force the pace of socialism. He must, from wherever he now resides, have little hope for help from . . . American working-class Marxists. And he must be looking with surprise at the way, in our time, it is the bankers and the big industrialists who lead the march, carry his flag.'

He nodded with relish. 'How about that?' He picked up another slip of paper.

'Here's another good one: 'The most mischievous doctrine ever broached in the monetary or banking world . . . is that it is the proper function of the central bank to keep money available at all times to supply the demands of bankers who have rendered their own assests unavailable.'

'I like that,' Francis remarked. 'Who said it?'

'Some English cat back in the 1800s. Makes me think of Continental Illinois. The FDIC was set up to protect the *bank's* depositors, you know, not to make the Stockholders of the holding company whole.'

Forbush slid the file back in the drawer, replaced his glasses in his breast pocket, and looked at Francis. The smile was gone. 'Rev, I'm gonna do what I can to run this down. I guarantee no results.'

'I can certainly understand that.'

'What I'm trying to figure out: how does it work?'

'Work?'

'Yeah. What's the bottom line? Does it just run on until the whole deal collapses on its own, like the one-hoss shay?'

The line from the Holmes parlor poem came back to Francis: *All at once and nothing first, just as bubbles when they burst.*

'Or,' Forbush continued, 'is there a trigger point? I kind of think there must be. No matter what these finance sons-abitches try to do to it, this is a goddamn tough system we've got here. I don't see a scam like this running on hope alone. The timing's too vague. If there was any logic to life, the patient would have expired long before this. So − first − I have to find out what I can, from the few people in this town who both know what's going on and will still talk to me, although I do have to say there's a fair amount of closet rectitude left inside the Beltway. Then − second − we got to scratch our heads and figure out how and when and what.'

Francis agreed with Forbush's notion. He too thought there would have to be a specific incident to trigger the final crisis.

'You're gonna have something specific − a reserve city bank failure, maybe, or a mass default, or the Japs taking a walk on the treasury market. Something that'll cause a real collapse in confidence. In markets like these, if that happens, everyone'll try to hit the silk at once and no one'll get out the door. If the world finds out that laissez-faire's been turned inside out, and by the Red Menace no less, that'd do very nicely. Hell, nobody'd wait to take the time to figure out what it means, or if it in fact means anything, and that sort of reaction's what causes panics.'

He paused, as if something had intruded on his line of thought.

315

'Didn't you say your lady friend went out through a window in that fire?'

'As far as she knows.'

'That definitely smells like KGB. Dzerzhinsky Square's very into defenestration, and very skillful at it too. If I find something, I'll let you know. In the meantime, you might just pray, because if you're right, this could make 1929 look like Bingo night at the church social.'

CHAPTER THIRTY

CORAL BEACH, BERMUDA
Saturday, March 15th

In the hot island sun, thoughts of Mallory and Chamberlain and Forbush, of Soviet plots, conspiracy, and murder, seemed part of another planet.

They had really been lucky with the weather. Even in mid-March, Bermuda could be unreliable. Barbados would have been a sure thing, but Barbados was too far out of the way to manage. He could only steal two days, and even for that he felt twinges of guilt, because it meant postponing the Sunday school's trip to St John the Devine.

Well, Angela Bowman, the assistant rector, was going to preach on Sunday, and just as well; it was time for the All Angels flock to get used to seeing a woman priest at the altar and in the pulpit. The ordination of women had been a shock to many of his parishioners, old-fashioned men and women who'd cut off their old schools and colleges just for admitting the opposite sex, but nostalgia could be given its head for only so long.

Did the parish think that all Elizabeth had to do was crook a finger and he'd hop on the next flight to wherever? Did it make him look like a lightweight, unserious about his calling? He was glad to be here, but — damn it! — would she ever stop moving? This time she was off to Caracas to look at some pre-Columbian gold. Bermuda had been the most agreeable convenient place to rendezvous.

Turning his head, he looked at the bikinied form lying next to him on the sand, absolutely still, hands folded primly over her middle, a faint smile on her lips. Behind them the easy swish of the ocean was interrupted now and then by a child shouting. They'd been lucky to get a room at the Coral Beach, but somehow Elizabeth had managed, just the way in his own Wall Street time he'd managed to conjure up 'impossible' hotel suites and theatre tickets.

Did they really know each other? he mused. Theirs had been a romance of glancing blows.

Yes, they belonged together. He wanted her, he needed her by him; she felt the same way, that it was the right thing, yet the withdrawal pains could be severe. God's work wasn't the same as that of Morgan Stanley or Concorde Advisors. Not a business of billions. God's work was a business of small people and their troubles. Centuries ago it had been different, a stained-glass affair of resplendently armored bishops and martyrs proclaiming crusades and toppling kings and sultans in the name of God and the Mother Church. Today, God's work was left to be done outside the tinted windows of twenty-foot Cadillacs, the same limousines that had once swished Francis himself down Park Avenue to breakfast at the Regency.

Elizabeth shifted beside him, bringing a hand up to her forehead. 'This beats working, doesn't it?' she said.

'It sure does.' He stretched his arms out in the sand, catching up two handfuls, crunching the grains in his hand as if to buff his skin.

'You're sure you don't feel guilty?'

'About Sunday? Don't be silly. It's good for them to get used to Angela.'

'I wouldn't think it very difficult. She's quite attractive.' He let that go by. Angela Bowden was very attractive. There had been once or twice when he . . .

He shut off the thought. 'Besides,' he said, 'the lesson for the fourth Sunday in Lent hardly shows me at my best.'

'Francis.' Elizabeth changed the subject. 'What does that sampler of Uncle Waldo's mean?'

He rolled over and looked at her. He didn't want her involved in this.

'I don't know. An inside joke, I guess. A celebration of the Chamberlain-Mallory partnership. The free market triumphing over the devils of regulation and restraint.'

''Hmmm,' she said and rolled back to face the baking light of the sun.

Francis hoped he didn't sound it, but he was worried. He was beyond his depth. It was up to Forbush. If the black man came up empty or lost interest, that would be that. Events would have to take their course. He would be just another fellow who'd cried 'Wolf!' at the wind in the trees.

Here, under the sun, it was possible for these concerns to be absorbed in his feelings for Elizabeth. It was the right time of life for him to be in love. He was past the first, worst stages of learning to love. Past the anxieties of possession, the sexual jealousy, the inclination to drill for one's own emotional oil in the psyche of another.

He didn't push his values on Elizabeth. Neither of them used the other; that was what was so good about it. He loved her wholly, without restraint or shame, as he found her — and not as an extension of himself. That she led a rich, busy life out there on her own didn't bother him beyond the scheduling of problems. The two of them would take life one step at a time, just as they had from the beginning of their affair, and it would work out.

His musings were interrupted by a hand snaking across the sand. A finger trailed along the edge of his bathing suit; he felt a fingernail trace its way up, around, and down the rapidly thickening shape beneath the fabric.

'If you keep that up,' he said, feeling suddenly strangled for breath, 'something embarrassing is going to happen. And on a public beach.'

Elizabeth levered herself onto an elbow. For an instant she let her hand remain where it was, then took it away and pushed her sunglasses up.

How beautiful you are, he thought.

She looked frankly at the outward signs of his excitement. 'There is undoubtedly something going on there. How embarrassing I can't say. But I've had enough sun. Shall we repair to our room for independent verification?'

'Only if you come to early communion with me tomorrow.'

She took his hand. 'Francis, my darling love, I will go with you to communion as long as there are communions to go to. Whither thou goest, I will go. Thy people will be my people.'

Her words corroborated what she knew in her heart to be true. As far as she was concerned, all that was left was the arranging. The hard part. And the easiest.

Later that afternoon, he asked her to marry him and she said yes.

Before that, however, she asked him again about Mallory and Chamberlain. 'I have to know, don't you see, darling? Because it's obviously so important to you.'

She did have to know. This man had changed her life, her way of seeing things. She was no longer entirely comfortable with what she did. This business of buying and selling works of art, to which she'd been able to accommodate herself with so little thought, now seemed sullied, a betrayal of sorts. He was in touch with something else that went on in life – call it God, call it truth – and it was starting to get to her. Buying and selling, getting and spending: it suddenly seemed so – well, limited! She found herself looking at people differently, stripping them of their wealth and whatever qualities or perquisites the wealth bought or brought, saying to herself, 'Now what would this man or this woman be like without the money?'

Not that she had ever been taken in by wealth. But after a long time working with the rich, one came to accept wealth as an integral aspect of personality, to be reckoned up along with this or that man's voice or manners or behaviour.

Now Francis was changing that, showing her that money was strictly an add-on, no more a part of character than Victorian varnish was part of a trecento painting.

She repeated her questions about Waldo and the sampler. 'I don't know what to make of it,' he said. He sounded impatient. It was obvious he didn't want to discuss it.

'I promise I won't say anything to anyone,' she said, trying to persuade him to open up. Why not? Everything Francis had ever said about Mallory she'd heard a hundred times at the office from Tony, even though Francis's version seemed to intimate downright evil.

'That's not the point,' said Francis.

'Uncle Waldo and Mallory, they've been up to something naughty, haven't they?'

Francis rolled over on his side and looked at her. Without thinking, she reached up and brushed a lock of hair back on his forehead.

'Let's not talk about it,' he said. 'Please. This is a beautiful day and you are a beautiful woman and I love and adore you.'

More than you adore God? she asked silently.

'And it's too nice a day to talk about the likes of Manning Mallory,' he concluded.

Well, she thought, he just doesn't want me to know, and so be it. She wasn't going to let him off scot-free, though.

'Francis, do you hate Mallory personally or on principle? I can't figure it out.'

'Both.'

'I told Tony what you said about Mallory in your sermon. Tony said you sound like every other guy who missed the market.'

The measured tone in which he replied told her the barb had caught fast.

'Look, Elizabeth. I am as conservative and capitalist as anyone, but my true belief is being tested. I am sick and tired of being called a bad sport because I don't happen to like the way things are right now. I grew up in better times than these, or so I think. I prefer the eagle to the golden calf as a national emblem. I think we're in deep trouble, that we have been fed a dog's dinner — by the President, by the Mallorys and the Wristons and the Simons, by all the people who raise up the market as the one true faith — and I think we're going to find that our puppy chow's been poisoned. Do you know about an economist named Joseph Schumpeter?

'I don't think so.'

'Well, Schumpeter said that the essence of capitalism is change. Decay and regeneration and alteration. Old industries die, new ones arise. A cycle: obsolescence, change, creation, obsolescence, change, and so on. He called the process "creative destruction." I accept the idea; it's in the nature of

321

things. But the operative word is *creative*! And despite what people like the *Wall Street Journal* say, I do not think Schumpeter would so describe what's going on today: this slimy, insanely leveraged takeover game played by sleazy people trading in inside information! It looks suicidal to me. I call it "*destructive* destruction!" Force-fed into the system by the Manning Mallorys and their money salesmen. I was brought up to believe that if you were lucky enough or smart enough to get your hands on a lot of money, one of the luxuries you could afford was a conscience. It seems I was wrong. I hate that, Elizabeth! Which is why I like to think God decided Wall Street was not what he had in mind for me, and so he called me to his work elsewhere. Now can we please change the subject? Please! It depresses me to have to talk about this subject and these people.'

'I'm sorry,' she said and smiled at him.

I *am* sorry, she thought; you are a lovely, decent man, and it is wicked of me to push you like this, but I must get all the way inside you, don't you see? She did have some idea what he was talking about when he talked about new people. There were new people comming into Concorde, men and women who demonstrably increased the place's noise level; Tony said they were also doing wonders for the profits in the place, trading 'financial futures.' It did sound like a game; the enormous sums in which her new colleagues at Concorde so casually dealt might just as well have been colored pebbles. The largest amount she'd ever paid for anything in the Treasure portfolio, $15 million for the Raphael predella from Merrimoles house, 'The Miracles of St Christopher and St Nicholas,' wouldn't even have financed the ante in the new people's game.

Yes, yes, you are a lovely, decent man, she thought. And we will have a lovely, decent life together, and if we make a quick start on it, we can even have lovely, decent children, despite me being a tired old bag whose shinbone aches when it rains.

She moved over to him.

'I love you,' she said. She kissed him and reached for him,

322

as he reached for her, touching her breasts, letting his hand drift between her legs. She wanted to press against him so that they would become one single body, one single being.

Their lips moved over each other, tasting some sweet, some salt. The air seemed thick with the musky waft of lovemaking.

Then he put his mouth to her ear and whispered the question.

'Oh, yes,' she whispered back. 'Oh yes yes yes.' She canted up and he entered her from behind, pushing himself into her a hair's fraction at a time, smooth and wet; he reached around to stroke her breast, she reaching back to grasp him gently. Yes yes yes. They shifted, he mounted her, slid along and slowly into her, kissing and being kissed, delicious with sweat, feeling as if he were a fine wire with an unendurable flame burning at its tip, felt her gathering under him—

Then, with a sharp, inconsiderate sound that burst apart the damp, cocooned stillness in which they moved, the telephone rang.

Elizabeth sighed and picked it up. A voice said he was Mr Forbush in the Bishop's office in New York. She handed the phone to Francis with an irritated, quizzical look.

'Yes?' said Francis impatiently, breathing hard.

'Sorry to bother you, Rev, but I think you better get your ass back up here pronto!'

323

CHAPTER THIRTY-ONE

WASHINGTON
Tuesday, March 18th

'You were kinda out of breath when I called, Rev,' Forbush said, deadpan. 'Must have just come back from a jog, I guess.'

You're testing me, thought Francis. Tastelessness wasn't Forbush's style. He's sending me a message: respect is breeding familiarity.

'Sounds nice, Bermuda,' Forbush continued.

'We were lucky with the weather,' Francis said.

Forbush nodded. 'Well, good for you,' he said. 'I guess it's been lonely for you since your wife died. Sounds like a nice lady who picked up my call.'

'Actually, I guess you'd have to call her my fiancée. Since Saturday night.'

'Well, congratulations! That's nice, Rev, that's real nice. You two going to live at your place on Eighty-fourth Street. The parish apartment? Born there, weren't you? Nice place, I hear. Three bedrooms, three baths. Room for kids.'

Francis got the message: I have looked you up, Francis Bangs Mather: I have done my research. I know where you've been and how it was for you. I know who you've slept with and what your bank balance is. I don't just know your address and Social Security number; I know what the label on your underwear reads.

'I don't know,' he answered. 'I think we'll just take one thing at a time.'

Forbush smiled. 'Rev,' he said, 'that's the only way. As your sainted Professor Chamberlain likes to say, first things first. I've been skimming his stuff, all his books and articles and speeches. Amazing how a man can prescribe cyanide and make it sound like sarsaparilla.'

He removed his hands from where they rested on his stomach, tilted himself forward, and relocated his clasped hands to the desk top.

'Rev,' he said, 'you came here and told me what you knew and what you guessed. I told you I would find out what I could. I have looked into Mr Grigoriy Simonon Menchikov — né Chavadze, as it turns out — and I believe we have ignition, as the flyboys say.'

'He *was* some kind of KGB official?'

'That I can't say for absolute certain. But he has led a full and interesting life. I have to tell you, I've been downright impressed by how many places his name pops up.'

'The CIA, I assume.'

'Them among others. I did glean a few straws at Langley, which I then asked the Schweizer Finanzpolizei about. I had a nice chat with French External Security, the DGSE. They dropped this Menchikov in Langley's lap, but it went nowhere. I also talked to the Brits, and the Crown Police from Hong Kong, and Rome and Caracas. I've run up a hell of a phone bill.'

'And . . .?'

'Well, what I got back from all my calls was just bits and pieces. Little flashes of Mr M's petticoat here and there around the world. It turns out Bern thinks the Russians were involved in the Chiasso swindle, which wasn't so different in modus operandi from the scam that cooked the goose of Mallory's only remaining rival at CertBank back in 'sixty-nine. A guy named Laurence. Left CertBank in disgrace; he works for E. F. Hutton now. Anyway, the Italians think maybe Moscow was running Sindona and Calvi and the Ambrosiano. MI5's got a theory that the KGB may have gotten its hooks into Lloyd's. But the French are the key, because they actually penetrated the section of Dzerzhinsky Square that runs the industrial and technological scams. They passed their stuff on to us, but they might just as well have been whistling Dixie, because somebody's told the President and Bill Casey that Mitterand socialism's the same thing as Marxism-Leninism. Result: anything we got from Paris was read as just more

Bolshie lies and disinformation. Including the 'Farewell' product the DGSE has been handing Washington. It went straight to the dead file. When the French realized this, they stopped passing us the good stuff and started feeding Langley chickenfeed. Or what they thought was chickenfeed. Like the Menchikov file.'

He held up a red plastic folder in which some kind of official seal was embossed.

Francis reached for it, but Forbush drew it back.

'Just a sec, Rev. As you will appreciate, this is *not* chickenfeed. Not to you and me. Because you and I have the other half of the torn dollar bill, so to speak.'

He held up Elizabeth's sketch of the sampler in his other hand. Then he gave Francis the scarlet folder.

'I got this from the National Security Agency. They think it's so low-level they'd sell it to *Playboy* if they could. I think you will interpret it differently. It's a transcript of Menchikov's last words. To make a long story short, he had a heart attack in Paris, and lo and behold the concierge had a little Sony right there. Now enjoy, Rev, enjoy.'

Francis felt Forbush's eyes on him as he read. When he finished, he looked up.

'Rosespinner?'

'Elementary, my dear Rev. And I think you can guess who "Waldya" might be.'

Francis nodded.

'Anyway,' Forbush continued, 'after I read this, I went way, way back. Guess what? Menchikov was in London 'thirty-five and -six. He was at Bretton Woods in 'forty-four, and in London again in 'forty-six — for Keynes's memorial service. And guess who else was present and accounted for on all such occasions? And of course, our genial friend was in Moscow himself about a year before Menchikov died. They could have met then, but there's no record of it. Why should there be? Who'd suspect Uncle Waldo? And everyone knows economists don't know diddleysquat about the real world, let alone function in it.'

'So where do we go from here?'

'That depends. You see, you and I are only part of the total world population who know both about this folder and that sketch. The other part being none other than Mr Mallory and his good friend and counsel Comrade Waldo. Waldya. It turns out that Mr Mallory sits on a blue-ribbon security panel to which this exact same document was distributed back in January.'

'What does that mean for our side?' Francis asked.

'I'm not quite sure,' said Forbush, 'but it's got to be an advantage. They don't know that we know what they don't know anyone knows. Anyone outside of Moscow. Anyhow, the thing is, you were dead right in the way you worked it out.'

He picked up a book. 'Listen to this: "In the absence of any previous experience and traditions, the New York banking houses plunged with reckless enthusiasm into international lending . . . Loans were granted to provinces whose very existence was unknown until their names appeared on the prospectus." Guess what particular year that refers to?'

'Nineteen eighty or 'eighty-one?'

'Try 1925. Suppose the Soviet objective was to get the Western banks to do it all over again?'

'I can suppose. Where do we go from here?'

'I think I know — provided I'm right about the bottom line on Ropespinner. Let me try something on you.' Forbush was dead serious.

'Start with your idea that Mallory is playing it like a game. But if it's a game, what's the point? What's the point of any game, Rev?'

'To win?'

'Exactly. But what's the point of winning unless people *know* you've won? There has to be a scoreboard. That's why all the guys on the Street have press agents now: so the rest of us can know what big deals and sharp guys they are. There's no such thing as a famous anonymous winner.'

'I'm not sure I follow you.'

'You will. Because it all fits. Let me ask you this, Rev. Suppose we all woke up one fine morning to be told that the biggest, most admired, most quoted, most *everything* banker

327

in the world had been a Russian agent for thirty years and that our entire financial system had been systematically manipulated by him to destroy itself. Think he'd get his picture on the front page of the *Times*?'

'If there was a *Times* left to put it on.'

'And it doesn't take much imagination to see what would happen then, does it?'

No it didn't, Francis thought. The lid of a financial Pandora's box would be blown open. Anyone in the world would have a license to repudiate. The Mexicans, Argentina, the Third World. The farmers and the oil patch. Anybody who owed a dime and either couldn't or didn't want to pay. Out would fly every anticapitalist, anti-American thought ever conceived or voiced. Every 'conspiracy' dog would have his day. The banks and exchanges would have to close. Capital flows would freeze as if King Winter had waved his wand, but that wouldn't matter, because paper capital would be worthless. The computer screens in the banks and trading rooms would fall dark. Nuclear winter, financial style. And then would come witch hunts, and social eruption — and violence.

'I can imagine,' he told Forbush.

'I bet you can. It ain't pretty, is it?' Forbush said. 'Can't you hear Castro and Quaddafi on the subject? Castro's been calling for ''repudiation'' for a couple of years now, and even without his help the lid's just barely on as it is. There's eight hundred billion in LDC debt out there, and I don't think they're exactly head over heels in love with Uncle Sam. The B of A's probably busted, at least technically. We know what the footings of the New York banks look like if you net out the shit. And how about all that foreign dough locked up in those lovely treasury bonds and notes? The Japs alone are in a dollar trap that probably comes to fifty billion.'

He laughed. 'Not that it wouldn't be kind of fun to see what the Street would look like with the Dow at zero.'

He held up a book that was studded with paper markers. 'You know this? Kindleberger, *Manias, Panics, and Crashes*?'

'It's been a while since I read it.'

'Well, it's kind of a bible with me. I preach it around here like I bet you preach St Paul. I hope your congregation pays better attention than mine. Anyway, listen to this: "A boom is fed by an expansion of bank credit which enlarges the total money supply. Banks typically can expand money, whether by the issue of bank notes . . . or by lending in the form of additions to bank deposits. Bank credit is, or at least has been, notoriously unstable." '

No argument there, thought Francis.

Forbush traced his forefinger down the page. 'Kindleberger based a lot of this on the work of a guy named Minsky, who teaches in St Louis but who was at MIT once, I think. I almost went down there to try out your theory on him. You know, now that I think about it, Chamberlain would've known all those guys at MIT: Kindleberger, Modigliani – hell, maybe even Minsky.

'Anyway, what Kindleberger and Minsky say is that to make a crash you first have to make a credit boom. And then, listen to this: "At a late stage, speculation tends to detach itself from really valuable objects and turn to delusive ones. A larger and larger group of people seeks to become rich without a real understanding of the processes involved. Not surprisingly, swindlers and catchpenny schemes flourish." Just like Ohio thrifts, huh, Rev?'

Forbush flipped ahead in the book.

'Now we come to the crisis point, "Revulsion," revulsion against commodities, paper, and so on, You can try to fix this by trying to buy your way out – like Richard Whitney on the Exchange floor in 'twenty-nine – or you can shut the banks and markets down for a while, or a last-resort lender can come in. Or you can have war – but not with the bombs we got now. What we're talking about is bigger than any of those things. The important thing is that everybody's got to know about it, so they can all head for the door at once. Here's how Kindleberger puts it:

' "What matters . . . is the revelation of the swindle, fraud, or defalcation . . . The making known of malfeasance, whether by the arrest or surrender of the miscreant, or by . . . confession, flight, or suicide, is important as a signal that the euphoria has been overdone . . . The curtain rises on revulsion, and perhaps discredit." '

Forbush closed the book.

'Talk about the domino theory! In the 'twenty-nine bust-up, the lender of the last resort lacked the guts. Today he lacks the money, especially now that the Japs have been sucked in by Uncle Greenback to the tune of about fifty big ones. All that debt riding hell-bent for devaluation. When the shit hits, the supplier will be blamed, not the user. It's the American way.'

'I can envision the consequences,' Francis said. 'What I'm having trouble with is what we can do about it.'

'I'm getting to that,' Forbush said, smiling. 'Let's assume that I'm right, that Mallory and Chamberlain are going to do a Burgess-Maclean-Philby and hit the high road for Moscow, to tell the world what they've been up to for thirty years. As a matter of fact, I'll lay you twenty-to-one on it, I'm so sure. And the great day can't be too far off.'

'Why do you think that?'

'Because I'm a quick study, and in a matter of days I've become the world's greatest expert on the private life of Mr Manning Mallory. Know what his weakness is?'

'I didn't think he had one.'

'Come on, Rev, that's no fun. I was hoping you'd guess something like he goes for small Asian boys. That's very big right now in certain New York conservative circles. Anyway, Mr Mallory's weakness is suits.'

'Suits?'

'Clothes. He's a regular Beau Brummel. While you were off having fun in the sun, I went up to the Big Apple and visited Mr Mallory's tailor. Posed as an agent of the New York State Tax Bureau looking for sales-tax cheats. Scared the shit out of the guy. He fell all over himself to show me his order and delivery books. They were so clean he has to be skimming. Anyway, guess what? A month ago, Mallory ordered some new suits. Guess how many?'

'I can't.'

'How about a dozen? One dozen. At eighteen hundred

330

dollars a copy. To be delivered no later than the end of June. What do you make of that!'

'Suppose he just needed some new suits?'

'Guess again. This is one of these fancy tailors who pins swatches to the client's record. The cloth Mallory chose would stop a bullet. The kind of suits you need in Lapland. Nothing like he's ever ordered before. I said to myself, ah-hah! Then guess what? I did a little more checking up on Waldo Chamberlain. He's a notorious cheapskate, you know. The kind of guy who'll nickel-and-dime his own mother. And I find he's already booked a one-way flight to Zurich on July first. Apex, which saves him about two hundred bucks.

'Now as I learned during my brief career with cloak and dagger, this is what the pros call "exfiltration." Chamberlain will fly to Zurich, go for a stroll beside the Zurichsee, and that's the last we'll see of him until "Good Morning, Moscow." Mallory probably flies the Concorde to Paris, checks into the Ritz, checks out with his dozen suits a couple of days later on his way to someplace else, and — *zap!* — gone but not forgotten, because the next thing we know, there he is on the TV, with Comrade Gorbachev doing the David Hartman bit, and the fan is full of bodily wastes.'

'So what are you going to do? Go to the SEC, the FBI?'

'Rev, in this town, with this Administration? Don't be a meathead. What's the charge? Corrupting the morals of capitalism? First-degree inducement? Possession of debt with intent to use it in the commission of a crash? Now don't look so chagrined. We've got one big thing going for us.'

'Which is?'

'As financiers, these guys are real pros, but as secret agents they're amateurs. Maybe we can take advantage of that. The first thing we have to do is get them off their game plan and onto ours, move them from their timetable onto Forbush-Mather Local Time.'

'And how do you propose to do that?' Francis felt himself sinking out of his depth.

'What we got to do, Rev, is spook the tiger. Make him come to us, show himself. We got to tether a goat in the clearing and see if the big cat's nostrils twitch.'

'And how will you do that?'

Forbush grinned. He reached across the desk and shook Francis's hand. As the black fingers took his own, Francis was struck by how supple they were; they looked as if they could render a Scarlatti sonata or crush a larynx with equal ease.

Forbush shook his hand with exaggerated enthusiasm. 'Well,' he said, 'all I can say in answer to that is, I'm right pleased to make your acquaintance, Reverend Goat.'

Then the smile went away.

'Rev, it's a very long shot and one we have to play entirely by ear. See if they react, and what they do, if anything, and how they do it. If they're smart, they'll just stay at home, as my defensive coach at the Point used to say. Keep to plan A because that freezes us in place. My bet is they won't, because they're so close to home free they can smell it, and that's when amateurs panic and do dumb things if something suddenly goes wrong. But keep one thing in mind.'

'What?'

'Don't for a second' — Forbush was utterly serious now — 'lose sight of the fact that even though these two cats may be debutantes at the spy scam, they probably have some guys backing them up who aren't!'

CHAPTER THIRTY-TWO

QUIDDY POINT
Friday, March 21st

Well, aren't we right crotchety this evening, thought Mrs
Arthurs, bustling about the kitchen. As always on a Friday
night, she had stayed late to cook and serve Waldo Chamberlain's dinner.

Seeing as he was so out of sorts, there was no point in adding
to his botheration by telling him about her visitor of the
morning. Maybe tomorrow — if his mood got better. It
wouldn't do to get him any more riled up than he was, not
at his age.

As concerned her caller, Mrs Arthurs' view of the world
held that there were two kinds of people: Quiddy Pointers and
others. Us and them. So, even though the young fellow was
plausible and engaging and seemed to have his facts down pat,
she hadn't told him anything and she wasn't going to, at least
not unless she got the go-ahead from Mr Chamberlain — which
she didn't think was very likely, him being as private a person
as he was.

Mrs Arthurs had accurately judged her employer's frame of
mind. Waldo was very upset. He hoped his agitation didn't
show, but he had been left confused and vexed and fearful
by his recent visitor.

He should not have consented to see the fellow, but now
it was too late. And how could he have known? The man
sounded plausible on the telephone. 'Keynes, Marxism, and
Christianity' was a perfectly reasonable subject for a book,
and the fellow *was* an Episcopal priest, for heaven's sake, and
he *was* a Business School graduate. Waldo hadn't remembered

the name, but why should he? For forty years, two hundred new faces a term had passed through Money One. You only remembered the great ones: the Mallorys, the Kelleys, the Andersons, men who went on to amount to something. Men who made names for themselves in the business world, who gave their names to famous cases or endowed a chair or lectureship.

Furthermore, wasn't it the responsibility of a sage, which was what the world considered Waldo to be, to keep his door open to all seekers after truth and wisdom?

He was sure he hadn't given himself away, hadn't shown his visitor the scantest hint of his inner tumult when, at the end of an hour that had grown to seem like a lifetime, he finally saw the man out. He'd barely been able to control the quaver in his voice when he'd then telephoned Alumni Records. Yes, indeed, Professor Chamberlain, the fresh young voice had replied to his query, there had indeed been a Francis Mather in the Class of '63.

Then the voice on the phone took on a tone of mild wonderment. It seemed that Mather was no longer at Morgan Stanley; he had been ordained as an Episcopal priest ten years earlier and was currently the rector of a church in New York City. The young woman gave the address. According to the alumni records, Mather was a widower. No other relatives were recorded.

The name of the church and its address were exactly as engraved on the card his visitor had left with Waldo, the card Waldo had turned over and over in his hands in the back of the Quiddy taxi, which came to Cambridge every Friday after lunch to fetch him.

The Reverend Francis Bangs Mather, DD
Rector, Church of All Angels and All Souls
227 EAST EIGHTY-SEVENTH STREET
NEW YORK, N.Y. 10028
212-281-1616

All, apparently, on the up-and-up. And to top it off, All Saints had been Preston's church, which this fellow hadn't mentioned, possibly hadn't known.

But damn it, how had the fellow known about Grigoriy? The conversation had started innocently enough. Reverend Mather, good New England stock from the look of him, had outlined a conventional view of Keynes as a nonconformist Christian and had nattered on about how the Keynesian fear of the social evils of unemployment was obviously rooted in a deeply Christian worldview. Fine, thought Waldo, just so. Keynes had been the most humane and generous-souled of men, which Waldo had been only too happy to confirm from personal experience. Nor, though it now started to get a little far-fetched, had Waldo found anything to get upset about in the fellow's subsequent contention that, by extension, the Keynesian scheme of macroeconomic manipulation resembled certain Marxist doctrines. Any man who examined capitalism, no matter from what sector of the ideological compass he came from, would have to fasten on certain of its self-contradictory aspects. It was in the nature of the beast.

But then the fellow has started in with some wild-eyed theory of perverse economic manipulation, something he called 'crypto-Keynesian subversion,' and out of the blue he'd brought up Grigoriy's name. Did Waldo know that until recently there had been a man in the Kremlin who had been, like Waldo, a friend of Keynes, a man named Menchikov who — until his recent death — was rumored to have been experimenting on certain Western economies the way vivisectionists did on animals?

Waldo was sure he hadn't seemed to overreact. He inquired mildly how in the world the Reverend Mather, by all appearances an intelligent man, had come by such an incredible idea? Mather said it was something he'd been told by a highly sourced French journalist he'd sat next to on an airplane. It seemed an idea worth following up. There could be a bestseller here, didn't Professor Chamberlain agree? He'd already done some fieldwork. He hinted ominously of dark findings, of spies and stratagems.

Waldo's first reaction after his visitor departed was: Poppy-cock! Then he found himself wondering whether this so-called Mather might be some sort of secret agent or FBI man. No, no, no, he thought. Manning was keeping his finger on the pulse of Washington. After all, Manning was consulted by the CIA and NSA on economic warfare against the Soviets. Hadn't he declared that the thing about Grigoriy was a 'dead file'? Maybe the French *were* up to something Manning hadn't learned about. All the allies seemed to spy on each other as much as they spied on the Russians. Was this 'Reverend' a French agent? Had Paris pierced the veil and tumbled to Rope-spinner? Hadn't the NSA file come from French intelligence?

No, Waldo concluded, Reverend Mather was probably just another conspiracy addict. But even if he'd happened on Grigoriy's name completely by chance — and Waldo didn't see how — he could still be a threat if he continued his investigations too far. That was the one contingency no one could plan for: another man's blind luck.

Then, out of the blue, Mather asked him if he'd by chance met this Grigoriy Menchikov in England in the thirties. Had their paths perhaps crossed at Keynes's?

'If they did,' said Waldo, 'I certainly don't recall it.' He'd kept his voice as level as he could. 'You can't imagine how many people came and went in Gordon Square or King's or Tilton back then. It was a regular international levee.'

He laughed as disarmingly as he could. When he at last got rid of Mather, however, he expelled his tension with a sigh that seemed to shake the apartment.

Ah, well, there were only three months to go. Until Mather's appearance, it had seemed like no time at all. Everything was in order. He had his ticket to Zurich. He was converting his US holdings piecemeal into Swiss francs. And now this!

'Would you like to come in to table, Mr Chamberlain?' It was Mrs Arthurs.

The excellent meal helped soothe his agitation. He found his mind turning to plans for his last meals in this house. Lobster, certainly. Mrs Arthurs could contrive to get him some of those small 'chicken' lobsters, scarcely larger than crawfish, that the locals took illegally from the bay. A real shore dinner: lobster, steamer clams, fresh corn. Steak, too. The meat was said to be awful in Russia. There were those good thick steaks from Locke-Ober in the freezer. And, of course, he'd have to have turkey at least once. For the Quiddy Thanksgivings that would never again take place.

'Would you be wanting anything else?' Mrs Arthurs asked, after he'd polished off the last crumb of Apple Brown Betty. His concern about the intrusive Reverend Mather was starting to recede.

Mrs Arthurs brought him coffee in the drawing room. She had a good fire going; outside it was a howling night.

'Well,' he said, 'thank you very much, Mrs Arthurs; that was delicious. You can go now. Why not come in on the late side tomorrow? Just to set out the dinner things. I'll drive into Quiddy for the papers myself. I can use the exercise.' He chuckled; she giggled. It was an old private joke between them.

'Yes, sir,' she said. She judged her employer's mood to have improved sufficiently. No time like the present, she told herself. 'Um, sir . . . ?'

'Yes?'

'Um, I thought . . . well, something happened I thought you'd best be knowing about. A man came to see me yesterday. Over to the house. Nice-looking and well spoken. He wanted to know all sorts of things. Said he was writing a book. Said it was going to be a real blockbuster — that's the word he used. He wanted to know all sorts of things about you and the house and the fire what killed poor Mr Preston and all them, and how it was you weren't killed, or Miss Elizabeth neither. Terrible how folks won't leave a tragedy like that alone, but these days it seems everybody's snooping into everybody else's life so as to make a book. Well, naturally I didn't tell him anything, even though he did seem to know a whole lot about you and Mr Preston and Mr Peter and Mr Mallory and such.'

Waldo's stomach began to churn.

'Mr Mallory?'

'Yes, sir. That was real strange. Do you remember, sir,

337

that sampler I stitched up for you a few years back? The one Mr Mallory gave you that you used to keep up in the bedroom?'

'Yes, Mrs Arthurs?' Waldo felt faint.

'I must say, I was right proud of the sampler. I couldn't do that work now; my eyes aren't what they once were, I'd have to say.'

'Tell me about what this man wanted to know about the sampler, Mrs Arthurs.'

'Well, sir, this fellow knew all about it. He even showed me a drawing of it. I can't say that it was the exact same drawing Mr Mallory gave me to sew it from — matter of fact, I'm sure it wasn't because I remember giving that drawing back to Mr Mallory, just like he said to, when I finished. Maybe I was confused because this drawing the man showed me was on a sheet of paper from Mr Mallory's bank: you know, the Certified down in New York City. Had it in a kind of red plastic folder, very official looking, with a stamp and all. Anyway, I recognized the bank paper from when Mr Mallory helped me set up a little savings account there. For my old age. Such a gentleman, Mr Mallory!'

'And what did you tell this man about the sampler?' Keep calm, he thought; deep breath — in and out, in and out.

'Oh, nothing, sir. As far as he knows, I never heard of or saw any such thing. Of course, if you want me to call him up and—'

'No, Mrs Arthurs, you did fine not saying anything. We should not place our trust in strangers. Who was he anyway? Some kind of journalist? Perhaps a federal agent: I believe my security clearance is up for renewal. That must be it.'

'I don't think so, sir. Well, that's the funny part. He was dressed up like any nice businessman. Perhaps a stockbrocker, like Mr Geary over across the bluff, that's what he seemed to me. Nice tweed jacket and all. But you know what, sir, he wasn't any of them things. He was—'

A priest, thought Waldo. Say it.

'A preacher,' said Mrs Arthurs. 'A so-help-me-goodness regular Episcopal preacher! I was fit to be tied. Here, he left me his card.' She fished in her skirt pocket and produced a visiting card that she handed to Waldo.

He didn't have to read it. He knew what was engraved on it. He handed it back, hoping his hand wasn't shaking.

'Well,' he said, 'that's all very interesting. I can't say the name means anything to me. Ah, well, I mustn't be keeping you from your good husband any longer. I'll see you in the morning. Don't worry if you come in late. I'm just by myself this weekend.'

For an hour after his housekeeper left, Waldo Chamberlain's mind whirled in phase with the heavings of his stomach. What could it mean? Who was this intruder who had suddenly appeared on his doorstep? Was this Mather sent as a premonition, like the man in black who came to call on Mozart? What did he represent? Whom did he represent? Waldo suddenly knew fear.

He tried to tell himself again that it was only three more months to July, but now that seemed like an eternity. He would never survive it; his heart would give out.

Grigoriy had known something. Yes, that must be it! That tape had been a warning. He should not have listened to Mallory. Mallory's self-confidence was going to be the death of both of them.

Mather would be back, with more questions, wouldn't he? Waldo was sure of it.

What to do, what to do?'

He should call Mallory. No, he said. Mallory never appreciated his apprehensions, never heeded his admonitions. Manning suffered from hubris, the sin of overweening pride. Manning would just wave his concerns off airily, would tell him to keep calm, to stick with the plan. Manning believed his intelligence and articulateness made him invulnerable.

Still, he *should* call Mallory, consult him. He got up and went across the room to the telephone.

And at that moment, with his hand poised over the instrument in a last gesture of reflective hesitation, Waldo Chamberlain's intellect and courage deserted him. Perhaps it was age giving way to the cumulative strain. It had gotten to be like keeping an even keel in thrashing seas; finally the arms and eyes grew weary, let go of the rudder.

It was time to flee. The conclusion was like a scream in his mind. This Mather was an omen. Fly, fly, wailed a voice inside his brain, Fly, fly!

Oh, if he could only talk frankly to Mallory about his fears! But he couldn't. Funny, he thought, not even after thirty years together in this great clandestine undertaking.

Well, he had to do something. Instinct suggested that this Mather was working on his own, so he could be dealt with. But quickly — and then: fly, fly!

He paced back and forth in front of the dying fire, making up his mind, bringing himself to the point of resolve. He decided what to do.

He went upstairs and got the current emergency number from the desk in the study off his bedroom. It had been over fifteen years since he'd needed it. Yet every three months, a card still arrived bearing the emblem E-Z TYPEWRITER SALES AND SERVICE, with an address and phone number. Every three months for fifteen years: sixty-one cards since he'd made the last such call. He knew the postmark rotation by heart: Birmingham, Hartford, Tacoma, Baltimore, Cincinnati, and Fort Worth.

That was the thing he admired about Grigoriy and his people. They took the long view. Like the British. If it had been the CIA or some other agency of this instant-results-crazed country, his call for help would go unanswered; his account would have been closed for inactivity.

He dialed the Tacoma number, spoke briefly, and hung up. Fifteen minutes later, the phone rang. The new caller was confident and reassuring. Waldo explained his concerns. Not to worry, the caller said. If there was a problem, it would be dealt with. The thing was to be judicious and careful, to remain calm. Yes, of course the caller agreed with the professor that an immediate alteration in the departure schedule plans might be prudent. The situation would have to be looked into. In the meantime, the professor should be relaxed. Yes, it would be best not to inform Mr Mallory until final arrangements were made.

The professor should not worry, please. A trip could be planned on very short notice. Not to worry, not to worry.

The next morning, the phone rang again. He could lay his mind at rest about this Reverend Mather. Their own sources had checked him out. He was nothing more than he claimed to be, a nosy priest. If he became a further nuisance, however, it would be no difficulty to neutralize him. . . . Of course, if Professor Dr Chamberlain insisted, action could be taken . . .

CHAPTER THIRTY-THREE

NEW YORK
Palm Sunday, March 30th

Francis Mather removed his embroidered chasuble and stole and placed them carefully on the shelf in the vestry cabinet. He shrugged out of his alb, hung it up, and blessed the vestments. Slipping into his suit jacket, he went out into the church.

The congregation had long since dispersed to other pleasures. It was a bright, unseasonably warm Palm Sunday, notably so, since Easter fell so early this year, and Francis had observed how restless the younger worshipers had been during the service, obviously anxious to escape outdoors after a disagreeable, flu-filled winter.

He walked down the center aisle, admiring the flowers the Ladies' Committee had badgered out of the very smart and expensive society florist over on Lexington. He looked around the church admiringly. Good, solid old brownstone New York, he thought; it had had its day and might again. Who could tell? He prayed that it was not God's design for New York life to be lived according to Donald Trump.

At the head of the aisle, he turned to face the altar, genuflected, and whispered a brief prayer. Rising, he reflected how well dressed the altar and nave were, splendid still with the lilies that later in the afternoon would be carried by the sexton to Sloan-Kettering cancer patients. Even the second-rate Victorian stained glass – depicting the arisen Christ in glory – looked quite beautiful on a day like this.

Pomp and splendor were very much a part of worship, he thought; perhaps he should jazz up the service even more: go in for the incense and incantation they did so well downtown at St Mary the Virgin. All Saints was a last bastion of a self-effacing upper-middle-class New York. A social order on its way out, its furs grown a little ratty, its patina cracking like the carefully tended surfaces of its old Brooks Brothers shoes.

It was very warm out. The air carried a premature whiff of summer. Along the street, people were out on their stoops.

He went down the church steps, nodded hello to the knot of neighborhood troublemakers lounging in front of the Chinese takeout across the street, and headed east, bound for Park Avenue and lunch at the Leslies' apartment.

He tried to remember to keep alert. Forbush had laid down only three or four rules. Watch out crossing the street; walk in the middle of the sidewalk; above all, don't leave yourself alone with strangers.

'You're safer in the Russian Consulate — provided you stay away from the window — than alone in your apartment with some guy you've never seen who shows up and says he's there to fix the heat. Keep clear of construction sites. Things have a way of dropping on people. Otherwise just live the way you New York people always do — finger on the trigger.'

It was hard to take seriously, even though — as Forbush said — bad things seemed to have a way of happening to people who'd gotten in Chamberlain and Mallory's way.

I have the true courage of ignorance and disbelief, he admitted to himself. I'm in an operational vacuum and I don't really think stuff like this happens in the real world. It was nice to hear Forbush say 'I'm gonna cover your ass, Rev, like snow on the Rockies,' but cover it against what? None of it seemed real.

It pained him to recognize the fact, but it was plain to him that he had no more idea of fear than he did of hunger. The closest he could come to imagining fear was as a sort of extended, intensified anxiety, an escalation to some horrible degree of the apprehensions that had sometimes gripped him in sports and love and business. His memories of those feelings were sharp, but how pale and tame they must be compared to the real thing, to what men felt in battle, to what Forbush must have known in Vietnam. The only time he'd felt his bowels turn to water had been the consequence of a bad bit of fish in a Positano seaside hotel. He rather expected he would never know the genuine article, at least not until he looked up and found Death in the next chair, and even then his faith braced him, assured him that God would hold his hand and see him safely to the other side.

Certainly on this sunny morning it was hard to think about ambition or danger or fear, or about anything other than how young and fresh the world seemed. Palm Sunday was a happy occasion at All Saints, by tradition a time for families to gather and worship, so that the congregation this morning had been dotted with young people and children, family clusters gathering around grandparents. While preaching, he had noticed quite a few known but infrequently seen faces, men and women one or two decades younger than himself, many of whom had been christened at All Saints, who had attended Sunday school there, been confirmed and married there, and never came afterward, except to weddings and funerals. He made a mental note to get out a pastoral letter to them to try to bring them back within the wings of the church.

He'd given a good performance this morning, he thought; the congregation had prayed as if with one voice, and he thought they'd belted out 'All Glory, Laud, and Honor' with uncommon gusto. At least in this little corner of New York, God seemed to be holding his own with Mammon.

As he strolled down Park Avenue, he reviewed the week to come. It was crazy! In spite of all his resolve, Elizabeth had cajoled him onto a plane again. He was to leave Monday night, meet her in Munich, and drive up to Salzburg. Through powerful connections, a room had been found for them at the swank Goldener Hirsch Hotel and two tickets to hear Karajan conduct the St Matthew Passion. Then they would fly to Paris; he would spend the night with her and take the Concorde back on Friday morning, which would get him to New York in plenty of time to perform the evening service on Good Friday. The trip was Elizabeth's treat. Sort of an engagement present, she said. It was frantic, as they both admitted, but what was

344

love if not to find a way, and, besides, how much longer would Karajan be around?

Forbush had OK'd the trip.

'Might keep you out of harm's way,' he'd said.

Harm. A word from another life. From the movies. From a game that wasn't life. Harm, danger, fear. Words with about the immediacy of 'Park Place' and 'Boardwalk.' Even Forbush was playing the game, making an obvious joke of asking Francis for his next of kin — 'just in case you get run over' — and winking naughtily when Francis named Elizabeth.

It looked as if they were right and they were wrong. Forbush had expected Mallory and Chamberlain to panic, had dragged Francis under their noses like a fox's brush before hounds, and they hadn't. Nothing had happened, which added to Francis's increasing feeling that this was all a dream. He himself had volunteered to take it a step further and pay the same sort of call on Mallory that he had on Chamberlain, but Forbush had vetoed the idea.

'In this game, about the worst thing you can do, Rev, is overegg the pudding, push too far, too hard. Do that — and like as not, it'll just send them to ground.'

Well, he couldn't make himself worry. There was just too much going on for him. As he entered the lobby of the Leslies' apartment building, he told himself, Even though I be up against the Devil himself, I have many rods and staffs to comfort me.

When Francis went back outside a little after three, he was surprised to see that the fair day had flown and a dull cover of clouds had blown up from the west.

It had been a very pleasant lunch. Possibly emboldened by the heavy Burgundy that Stoddard Leslie had produced with some ceremony, Francis had told his hosts of his plans to marry again. The Leslies were delighted. As Francis and his bride-to-be had no family, they declared, it went without saying that they would give the reception. Of course he would be married at All Saints; was it possible, Mrs Leslie mused, for a priest to marry himself? Around again went the decanter of Corton.

345

After lunch, he and his host had fitfully chatted and dozed in the library, halfheartedly watching a basketball game. Finally, when it was clear to Francis that his host's head had become too heavy by half, Francis said his thanks and goodbyes. He had some paperwork in the parish office that he wanted to clear up.

He stood on the corner of Park Avenue and Seventy-fifth Street waiting for the light to change. There weren't many people around; the schools were out and it was warm enough to have sent people to the country for the weekend. He looked around. Across the avenue, a young couple embraced. Not far away, a delivery boy lounged against his bicycle, smoking. Behind him Francis could hear a ball being desultorily bounced against a wall. An old black man with a pushcart full of raggedy luggage shambled toward the park.

His mind was on Salzburg, so he didn't really take much notice of a small man being towed up Park Avenue by a large rambunctious Alsatian. Otherwise, the collision might have been avoided. In any case, as the little man prepared to mount the curb where Francis waited, something, an automobile horn perhaps, spooked the dog, which abruptly bolted, pulling his owner violently up onto the sidewalk and into Francis. Fighting for balance, the little man swung up his free arm against the strain on the leash, and the tip of his umbrella struck Francis sharply on the thigh.

'My God,' he exclaimed. 'Sorry! Oh, God!' The recognition that Francis was a priest seemed to shock the little man into a state of mumbling confusion. 'So sorry, Father, so sorry . . .'

'Don't worry,' said Francis. 'It's no problem.' The Alsatian was tugging fiercely against his lead, threatening to pull the little man off his feet.

'So sorry, really . . .'

'Don't worry, I assure you. It was nothing. An accident. Really. No harm's done.'

Francis patted the man consolingly on the shoulder. The light was green, so he started across Park Avenue. On the far corner he paused to turn around; the little man was still being dragged uptown; even across the wide avenue his futile curses could be dimly heard. That dog wants his dinner pretty badly, Francis thought.

He turned north on Lexington. His thoughts returned to the glorious week to come.

Then, crossing the avenue at Eighty-fifth Street, his heart suddenly seemed to turn over in his chest and he felt a suffocating rush that closed down his breathing and set his legs tingling. The world went fuzzy. Involuntarily, he put a hand on a nearby mailbox to steady himself, shook his head, and went on his way.

Now his head felt light; the exact sensation — prickly, swollen — wasn't anything he could remember having experienced before. He felt his eyes seem to start to swell. His lungs were pushing hard for breath. Mechanically he put one foot before the other, not wanting to draw attention to himself. Food poisoning, he thought, but that was as far as his brain would take the idea. There was an unfamiliar electricity loose in his mind, burning out the circuitry.

Please God, just get me to the church, he said. I'll be all right if I get to the church. Something was awfully wrong; something awful was wrong. Please God.

He had to gulp for air. Oh God, don't let me collapse in the street to be stared at by strangers. Every New Yorker's nightmare. Please, God, not right here. Just another hundred yards. His legs felt stiff as stilts; his eyes were about to pop out of his head.

Down the block he could see the steps of the church. Sanctuary, he thought. Oh, God, God, God, let me get there. Eighty-seventh Street looked deserted. The church seemed miles distant.

One foot — now the next. He made it down the block. At the church, however, his legs went entirely to sleep, and he sat down heavily on the lowermost step, then felt himself slide over, as if his spine had turned to water.

The world was going red, orange; the world was burning up. Oh God God God, he said silently, don't let me die. Was he starting to cry? He tried to remember his prayers.

On the fringe of what little awareness he had left, the clunk of a car door sounded. Excited voices. Footsteps quickly on the pavement. Now a shadow loomed between him and the crimson film that was all that was left of the world.

'Shit, shit, shit!' a strange, high voice he knew. 'Goddamn fucking fucking goddamn *shit*!'

Forbush. Doesn't matter, thought Francis. Too late, too late. Dying.

He felt arms around him. His whole body had gone numb; the rest of him was off to dead dreamland, except for this tiny corner of his mind that was telling him he was going to die. Right here. Right now. Oh God, someone said in a voice that might have been his. Please don't. Please. Why do You do this to me? Oh God, please.

The commotion around him was slipping away. The cradle was warm now. He was too tired to say Oh God, any longer. The crimson of life grew deeper; it darkened as he watched it, darkening to black. He was outside himself now, and he made no sound, no prayer, and as he hovered in the twilit air and watched himself die, he felt God at his shoulder, watching with him, and His company was no comfort at all.

HOLY WEEK

CHAPTER THIRTY-FOUR

COLUMBIA, MD
Tuesday, April 1st

One eye open.

Yellow sky. Bright cheery yellow.

He was flying through a bright yellow sky.

Overhead, there was fantasy: Walt Disney characters flying with him. Dumbo, Bambi, Goofy, Mickey and Minnie. Was heaven made by Disney?

This wasn't the Holy City for which the seminary had prepared him. Had there been a mistake in God's paperwork?

Angels were staring at him.

Child angels. Little brown angels, two solemn little brown faces framed in tight curls resplendent with bright ribbons.

Hey, Francis, his mind told him, move your leg.

It moved.

Hey, Francis, his mind told him; open both your eyes.

But they're open, he told his mind.

So move your head. Look around. What do you see?

He moved his head, looked around. They were indeed there, those big Disney figures, but now he saw that they were oversized cartoon decals affixed to a bright yellow wall. His hand grasped something, a soft frilly something. Bedcover. Bedroom. His mind was working at quarter speed; thoughts lumbered to its surface like long-submerged swamp logs. He felt sleep returning.

'Well, hello, Rev,' said a familiar voice just as he went under again. 'Welcome back to life.'

When he next awoke, the little brown angels were still there, small serious sentinels overwatching his sleep. A childhood prayer popped into his mind: Matthew, Mark, Luke, and John/ Guard the bed that I lie on.

'Hello,' he said, surprised at how strong his voice sounded.

'Well, Rev, how you doing?' Forbush loomed dark and reassuring above the two little heads. 'Better? Try moving your arms and legs.'

Francis complied. His limbs felt like nerveless sausages connected by mere accident. Yet the more he tried to wiggle, the more sensation seemed to return.

'Good work,' said Forbush. 'Another twenty-four hours and you'll be back in the starting rotation.'

'Where am I?' His voice had come closer.

'Columbia, Maryland, *Du côté de chez* Forbush and family. That's 12334 Mornington Circle Drive, Sussex Estates. A hotbed of integrated upwardly mobile middle-class values and second mortgages a mere forty minutes from our nation's capital. Have you been formally introduced to my daughters? This is Traysha and this is DaNeese. Say hello to Reverend Mather, girls.'

The two little heads bobbed in curtsey.

Forbush bent closer.

'Don't you worry, Reverend,' he said with a big smile, 'it wasn't even close. Let me say you do a great death scene, but I'm afraid you didn't get the Thomas à Becket part in this particular revival. Of course, the guys in the funny fur hats don't know that. They think you're in dress rehearsal - set to open in heaven in about a week, if you're not there already.'

All he could think of was Elizabeth. He knew there were other questions he should be asking.

'Elizabeth?' he croaked. 'What day is it?' Something about Salzburg bothered his mind.

'Later,' said Forbush. 'Now just lie still.' A large black hand holding a small syringe appeared at the edge of Francis's vision. Then he felt just the faintest sting of the splendid butterfly that now appeared and bore him away to more darkness.

The third time he awoke, it was just before noon. Forbush informed him that Rip Van Winkle had only been out for three hours.

Francis felt whole. He could articulate his larynx and his limbs. He tested his voice with a couple of verses of 'Onward, Christian Soldiers.' He stood up and tried to walk, and found he was no worse than shaky.

When he came out of the shower, the same clothes he remembered wearing to Palm Sunday lunch were laid out on the bed, newly clean and pressed. As he dressed, he looked around the bedroom, greeting the decal characters like old friends: Hello, Dumbo; hello, Bambi; hello, Mickey and Minnie.

Forbush's voice boomed from what he assumed was somewhere downstairs. 'Time for your Wheaties, Rev!' Francis tracked the voice to a pleasant sunny kitchen. Forbush was sitting at the table, the *Wall Street Journal* spread out in front of him. A handsome woman was busy at the stove; Forbush introduced her as his wife, Myra. From the kitchen window, Francis could see his 'angels' playing on a jungle gym. Over the stove a clock said 12:35.

Oh, it was good to be alive! But Francis's euphoria lasted only through his greedy breakfast. Then reality, complication, truth, and their minions burst in simultaneously on a dozen fronts of his awareness, each clamoring for instant attention.

He didn't know whether to start with gratitude or questions. As he attempted to get his thoughts in some sort of order, Forbush rose from the kitchen table and gestured Francis to follow him.

They went into a small study. One wall was covered by a bookcase filled with a miscellany of lawbooks, finance texts, thrillers, and a Time-Life series on Vietnam. Francis wondered if Forbush was in one of those volumes. An old wooden desk stood against a narrow end wall; its surface held a jumble of papers and objects.

Francis felt he had to say something meaningful. 'I can't tell you—'

Forbush held up a hand.

'Rev, you don't have to say it. What I can see in your face is plenty good enough for me. We good guys gotta stick together. I'll cover your ass, you cover mine.'

353

He grinned and pushed an easy chair at Francis.

'You might as well have a seat. Save your strength while you can. Besides, I don't want you to fall over and hurt yourself when I tell you what's been going on.'

Francis did as he was told. Forbush went over to the desk and picked something up, a small glass laboratory dish. He held it out toward Francis and shook it. Something tiny rattled. Forbush handed him a pocket magnifier; in the bottom of the dish he could barely make out the gleam of a tiny metal ball the size of a pinhead.

'That is the micro-BB that stung you,' Forbush said. He put the dish down on the edge of Francis's chair, went back to the desk, and picked up a sheet of paper. 'And this is what poisoned you.'

Francis took the paper, a page torn from a back issue of the *National Geographic*; it showed a close-up photograph of a singularly hideous toad.

'*Bufo marinus*,' said Forbush. 'The voodoo toad of Haiti. All the rage this year with professional assassins. A totally contemporary poison, suited to the with-it-life-style favored these days by your trendier cloak-and-dagger guys and gals. Strictly organic, of course. The active ingredient's called tetrodoxin. Sounds like a soap commercial, doesn't it: "Try Bufo, with tetrodoxin. It'll kill you." '

Forbush chuckled.

'Actually, most of the time, that's just what it will do. Or it'll turn you into a permanent zucchini or a lifetime extra in a Boris Karloff movie; sometimes it only knocks you out for about a year. Unless you know what to do.'

'The umbrella tip, right?'

'Right. What'd I tell you about the other side, Rev? If an idea works once for 'em, they beat it to death. Ever since the Bulgarians iced Markov in London a few years back, it's been right out of *I Spy*! "Aha! The old poisoned umbrella ploy!" Mercifully for you, they don't seem to get the picture that it doesn't go down like it used to. Hell, they tried it a couple of years ago not ten miles from where we're sitting: tried to off a cat named Korczak in a Food Fair over near Arlington, and he hardly blinked! Dirty tricks is no different from hemlines. This year it's toads, next year who knows? The KGB's got their Haitians; we've got ours; I don't doubt that the French and Brits and Mossad have got theirs. Me, I think it's too damn complicated. As I see it, if you want to blow away some dude, tape a kilo of C-Four to his engine block or hose him down with an AK-47.'

'And the man with his dog?'

'Long gone. Just a bindle stiff they flew in specially for this job. We let him go in the interest of keeping up appearances. Personally, if I don't get an Oscar for my own performance on the church step, I'm gonna be deeply disappointed in the Academy. My only worry is that the bad guys got a good look at me; they had a watcher in a car down the block. Which means by now they may have made me as ex-Agency, although I doubt it; all I did at Langley was smile and say 'Yassuh, boss!' and dance de jiggetty-jig for the visiting firemen. I think I came across as a helpful, distraught passerby.'

Forbush shook his head and sighed. Francis started to speak, but the other man raised his hand.

'Rev, I got to level with you. I hope you'll forgive me. I had to use you, see. It wasn't moving along right; what I think happened was the local hoods quieted old Waldo down. We had to really scare the shit out of 'em. Get the pros worried that if they let it ride, their two amateurs might get scared enough to do something dumb, like spill the beans to Uncle Sam or the *New York Times*.'

'Wouldn't that do the same thing as defecting?'

'I don't think so. I think the fly-to-Russia angle's the key to the big bang. Anyway, as neither of the things I was looking for had happened, I had to implement Plan B.'

'Plan B?'

'Kind of a fallback, Rev. I got the name of the guy that runs the NSA committee that Mallory's on, and I put on my best white voice, and called him, and said I was you and that I have very sensitive information concerning the activities of Grigoriy Menchikov.'

'And . . .?'

'And I gave him just enough hints so he couldn't just put me down as a fringe loony; I came over plausible enough for him to do what I needed.'

'Needed?'

'Yeah. To call a meeting of his blue-ribbon committee to hear me out. I kind of hinted that was the best approach, given the extraordinary nature of my material. It was right up his alley. A good excuse to let the big shots do their George Smiley imitations, while he gets to cozy up to them, plus another big lunch at the Gorse. Think they've ever seen a black man at the Gorse?'

'And what did he do?' asked Francis.

'You ever see any Washington guy not fall all over himself for a chance to spend an hour with the million-dollar-a-year men? He called a meeting. Eleven A.M., next Tuesday. I'm afraid by doing that I may have forced their hand vis-à-vis you, Rev, and for that I'm just going to have to beg your forgiveness.'

'Well, it seems no permanent harm's been done. I gather you kept me under surveillance?'

Forbush nodded.

'Which means, I assume,' Francis said, 'that you've gotten Washington involved?'

'Well,' said Forbush, looking sheepish, 'let's just for the moment say yes and no and leave it right there. You're right about the surveillance, but that was off the books. I didn't want to use a bunch of Agency footpads who are in the mug file at the Soviet Mission on Sixty-seventh Street. Instead, I used a private agency out of Boston I got to know when I was working for Stan Sporkin. Told 'em you were under suspicion of embezzling church funds. I'm getting real good at my "nice colored Mr Forbush from the archdiocese" role. Anyway, just so you won't feel slighted, we had a cool dozen working the tail. The big thing, the bottom line, is that it seems to have worked. Our birds are getting ready to take wing.'

'How do you know that?'

'After this long in the business, I've kind of developed

a nose for Mickey Mouse. Something's up. The Moscow Narodny Bank has started running up its short position in the clearances market. They should be over thirty billion by now. Gold's up fifty bucks since Monday. The buying's all over the place, but the word on the street is that most of it's coming from Ost-West Handelsbank, which is Ivan's Frankfurt outlet.'

'Why would the Russians by buying gold?'

'Rev, it never fails. When there's something going down in the money game, there's always some inside money looking to cream off an extra nickel. Nine times out of ten that's what blows a deal.'

'I know what you mean,' said Francis, 'but isn't that all pretty circumstantial?'

Forbush smiled.

'Remember I told you about Mr Mallory ordering a dozen tundra-weight suits?'

'I do'

'Well, after I found that out, I had a bug put on his tailor's phone. Just in case.

'And guess what? Right after I got confirmation from NSA about the committee meeting, Mr Mallory himself called up. Those dozen new suits have absolutely positively gotta be ready — no ifs or buts — no later than the morning of Friday, April third. That's the day after tomorrow, Rev. That's when I knew it was for real. Then Chamberlain canceled his June thirtieth ticket to Zurich. Cost him a hundred bucks to cancel, which must have killed the old tightwad. So there we are. Maybe I should have clued you in, but I figured, as long as we had you covered, let nature take its course.'

Francis didn't know what to say. It was too late to be afraid, and the information that he had been put in harm's way deliberately didn't seem to hit him as hard as he might have expected. He shrugged.

'Any questions?' asked Forbush.

'What's next?'

'We wait. Their move.'

And then Francis suddenly remembered what he should be doing, where he should be, and he got mad.

'For God's sake, Forbush,' he exclaimed angrily. 'Sit? Sit! Do you know where I am supposed to be? Salzburg.'

With Elizabeth. What about Elizabeth?

'And Miss Bennett, for heaven's sake?'

And the church? It was almost Easter!

'And my parish. I just can't sit here, Forbush, and play games. It's Easter! Don't you understand that, man?'

It was Forbush's turn to shrug. 'You just got to stay cool, Rev. Only for a few days. I have to tell you I'm afraid your lady's not doing really great right now. She loves you a whole bunch and she's pretty broke up.'

'What in God's name does she think has happened to me? Does she think I'm dead?'

Forbush smiled. 'Hey, Rev, we wouldn't push it that far. But you have to understand. The folks who love you — and it seems there's a mess of them — believe you've had a severe stroke, a cerebral hemorrhage; our cover neurologist at Columbia-Presbyterian publicly puts your chance of survival at one in eight. I'm afraid that's what we had to tell Miss Bennett. She does not know you are sitting here drinking Myra Forbush's excellent coffee in a medium-grade row house in a Washington exurb. She thinks you are in Harkness Pavilion in intensive care — no visitors, twenty-four-hour nurses, the works! If she or anyone comes asking after you, they are referred to a Dr Garvey, and that excellent doctor puts them off and fills me in. I'll say this, Rev, your ears would be burning, if you knew how much those folks in your church love you. They're keeping a regular vigil. Round-the-clock prayers, candles, the works!'

'Are you an animal?' Francis asked coldly. 'Do you think you can just routinely do this to people?'

' "Routinely" hardly seems the right word, does it, Rev?' Forbush was obviously being patient. 'Anyway, come next week, maybe earlier, you're gonna stage a recovery that'll make Lazarus look like chopped liver. Your lady'll keep till then, don't you worry. I've spoken to her twice. She's got character; she's quality folks. I told her to stay put in Paris until we get a better prognosis. I believe she will.'

Francis got up. 'Do you mind if I excuse myself for a few minutes. I'd like to pray.' He felt awful. He had thrown a heavy deceitful cloak of grief on a lot of innocent people who cared about him.

Forbush spread his hands palms up. 'Rev, you do what you have to do. But just keep it between you and God. No phone calls. I reckon he'll watch out for your flock while you're pulling this duty; after all, it's his business we're on, isn't it?'

When he came back downstairs, Francis felt better. He had prayed for help and reason, and God had vouchsafed what he asked for. Elizabeth must feel awful: lonely, afraid, deserted by fate. Yet Forbush was right; it had to be this way. The alternative was unconscionable, and if Elizabeth's temporary grief and pain, however sharp, was the cost of forestalling it, then she must bear it and he must bear the knowledge of it. There must be a light somewhere at the end of this endless tunnel; in his prayers, God had given him a glimpse of it, had signaled him that they would come through.

'Well,' said Forbush when he reappeared, 'how about a little TV? While you were out cold, Mr Mallory was up and going about the nation's business. I made a tape of the news. He and the President deep-sixed the Congress and pushed through repeal of Glass-Steagall in two days. I thought you'd get a kick out of it.'

Francis watched as the image came alive on the television screen. Familiar faces in the East Room of the White House. The President and First Lady, he beaming and ruddy; she oddly sour and tired. The leaders of the Senate and the House of Representatives. The Secretary of the Treasury. And Manning Mallory. When the President signed the bill, the first symbolic pen went to Mallory. Mallory grinned. Surprisingly, as Mallory took the pen from the President, the First Lady, standing next to the banker, shot him an expression of almost violent distaste, or so it struck Francis. Probably jealous of him, he thought, just the way she's supposed to be envious of the White House Chief of Staff.

'Not bad, eh?' said Forbush. 'This week he gets a pen from the President. Unless I miss my guess, next Monday or Tuesday the Soviet Premier is probably going to lay the Order of Lenin on him. A busy time, even for a great man like Manning Mallory, wouldn't you say?'

From the TV screen the President gave a homiletic speech about economic freedom and the dangers of regulation. He spoke warmly about Manning Mallory's role as the private sector's premier representative in bringing the Congress around to a proper perception of the dangers of laws like Glass-Steagall to the market economy.

'This administration is really something, isn't it?' Forbush commented. 'You know what I hear they call Harlem in the White House mess? Nigger-agua! And you and I are probably gonna save their collective ass!'

'If you feel that way about them,' Francis said, 'why not just let this thing play itself out?'

'Rev, if I had my druthers, I'd be working to save a different President, but I got no choice. I got one Purple Heart, one Distinguished Flying Cross, one country, one President. I got one future — me and my people. Like it or not, the way it happens to be just now, this country's the last best chance. I got to do what I can. Otherwise America's gonna be flat gone before we black folks ever catch up to it.'

He smiled.

'You know, I've been watching you trying to figure out what it must be like to be black. You'll never know, and I'm not quite sure I could ever make you know, even a high-class overeducated nigger like me. I can tell you what it's like to be white, though, because I know. I've been white myself, at least on the telephone. I can be white just as long as nobody gets a look at me. Not that I think black or white's going to matter if Mallory pulls it off. Maybe not even if he doesn't. I personally think our kids are gonna get the licking *we* deserve either way, because we don't give a shit about the schools and poor folks and the deficit, not while the Dow's headed toward nineteen hundred and the President tells us that everything is just great. Now, how about a little TV? I got some great tapes. All the good Bogarts. Or Alec Guinness in *Tinker, Tailor*. Nothing like a good spy thriller. There's no point in fussing, Rev; you and I just got to sit here till that phone rings.'

CHAPTER THIRTY-FIVE

COLUMBIA, MD
Good Friday, April 4th

On the TV screen Jimmy Stewart was wisecracking his way through *Philadelphia Story*. This must be what exile is like, Francis thought. He had watched at least a dozen movies since Wednesday.

He could hear Forbush on the telephone in the kitchen. They were alone in the house. Myra Forbush had taken the two girls down to Richmond for a long weekend at her parents' house. Something was in the air; something was about to happen. He could feel it.

For one thing, the phone had come alive. It had started ringing early, while Francis was still asleep, and had continued to ring intermittently through the morning. Something was definitely up.

He tried to turn his attention back to the movie but found himself worrying about Elizabeth and the damage this must be doing to her feelings. Damage he'd caused. Would it have been better if he'd never started asking the questions that had brought him here? And was she safe? What about the photograph? Would Waldo Chamberlain have discovered it was missing? He tried to remember how much Elizabeth knew, how much she might be able to infer. No, it was all too incredible, he thought. She was out of harm's way. Dear God, he prayed silently, make it so; do for me just this one thing.

Damn it, he thought, of course he was right to have taken up the trail and followed it. Forbush was right. The alternative was unthinkable. What the current crop of swine in Washington and Wall Street were doing wouldn't go on forever; this new breed was no more than a temporary aberration, a cold sore on the face of an otherwise good system. All systems were about the same, anyway. In the Soviet Union, the brass ring was plucked by the agile bureaucrat. In America, the blue riband was claimed by the wise guy with the fast mouth and a friend at CertBank.

Ah, well, in time the constitution or the actuarial tables would eliminate this President and disenfranchise the hardline capitalism he fronted for. These years would be seen as just another passage in the unending cycle: from noble to base and back to noble again, from communal and collegial to selfish and solipsistic and return. Sooner or later, the nation would find itself tired of the money binge and set about repairing the damage. Nothing was terminal.

Except this. If Mallory and Chamberlain pulled it off, not even a Washington or an FDR, not even a Lincoln, could hold things together.

The kitchen phone rang again. He heard Forbush pick it up. Then he heard it slammed down and, an instant later, Forbush appeared in the doorway. He sounded elated, a man of action at last summoned to his true vocation.

'Time to drop your cock and grab your socks, Rev. Away we go!'

Francis seized his jacket and followed Forbush out the door.

As they drove south at the speed limit, Forbush explained.

'Our friends are cutting and running, thank God. I was afraid when they tried to snuff you, it was so they could sit tight and stick to schedule. But either they hit the panic button, or they figured there was more than just you on their scent. So they've moved up X-Day.'

A sign declared that it was ten miles to Andrews Air Force Base.

'What is their plan now, do you think?' asked Francis.

'I thought they'd probably go out commercial anyway. But nothing's turned up on the reservation computer, and a big shot like Mallory wouldn't fly standby if it was the last flight to heaven. So, I said, how about surface transportation? Maybe they drive to Canada or Mexico, but that means Customs and

Immigration. More likely, they just go through one of life's little normal routines and vanish. Get up from the dinner table to take a leak and do a Judge Crater. But how and where? Then I said to myself, Hey, Phillips E. Forbush, what about Quiddy Point, Maine?'

'Chamberlain's house? How?'

'Elementary, my dear Rev. It's secluded, it's habitual, and it's accessible by plane or boat. So I ticked off the possibilities. Seaplane? No. Ocean's too undependable this time of year, plus I figure they'll want to be leaving at night. Boat? I don't like it: rough seas again, and the old man's pretty fragile. The Reds'll want him in good fettle to publicly wipe his ass with the Freedom Medal the President gave him last year. Which leaves only one likely means of transportation.'

'Helicopter?'

'Hey, you're picking this up pretty quickly. Which brings me to the next question. How? Uncle Ivan can't exactly come and get them in one of his own. The Coast Guard might object. Which rules out a round trip originating from a ship offshore.'

'So it has to start onshore somewhere?'

Forbush grinned.

'Rev, you are getting to be a downright whiz at this shit. But where? The Soviet missions in this country don't maintain a fleet of choppers of their own, so they have to rent one, fly it out to sea, drop off the passengers, and then jettison it overboard. Then I ask myself: who's gonna fly the fucker? Some know-nothing charter pilot who they then have to figure out what to do with? I don't see it. This is an important operation. Nothing can be allowed to go wrong; so it's gotta be one of their own people on the joystick. And what do you think? Lo and behold, who flew in early this week but a new low level attaché to the Soviet UN Mission. When I ran him through the computer at Langley, he turns out to be a colonel in the Red air force.'

'Knowing your omniscience,' Francis said, 'the man's undoubtedly a qualified helicopter pilot.'

'Right on, Rev!' Forbush laughed. 'Now there ain't but about a dozen Hertzes for helicopters within five hundred miles of Quiddy Point. One of them's in Hartford, and guess who's reserved a Jet Ranger at Bradley Field at four o'clock this afternoon? Don't say; I can see by your face you've guessed.

'Now comes the clincher: that last call I got was to tell me that the chief KGB resident on Sixty-seventh Street seems suddenly to have decided about an hour ago to take a drive in the country, namely north on the Merritt Parkway, straight north for Hartford, golden-domed capital of the Nutmeg State and site of Bradley Field. Looks like he's been asked to do some aerial babysitting.'

A sign pointed to the turnoff for Andrews Air Force Base.

'Could you stop the car for a minute?' asked Francis.

'Sure.' Forbush pulled over into the emergency lane. He turned off the ignition. When he turned to look at Francis, the sun reflecting off the dark mirrored lenses of his aviator glasses made him look surreal, threatening.

'Look,' Francis said, 'I just want to have some idea what's going on. You seem to have people covering every inch of territory between here and Maine. Nobody picks up the phone but you're listening in. Is it safe to assume that you — we — are no longer working off the books as you put it? And if that's the case, who's footing the bill? And, for that matter, where are we going?'

Forbush took off his glasses. He looked out the window for an instant, compressing his lips in an expression of faint chagrin, and turned back to Francis.

'I'm going to make this quick, Rev. I have to get to Andrews. I have contracted to do a job of work on a tight schedule. Contracted! More than that I cannot explain right now. You can come along if you want; that was our deal. I promised you I'd see that you would be in on the end if you wanted. You said you wanted, but if you don't, you can get out of the car when we get to Andrews, and I'll see that someone takes you to a safe place. You have to stay on ice until this is over.'

Forbush pulled back on the road. 'Now, I got to be on my way. You want to come, you come. Any questions you want to ask, they'll be answered, but later. What's your pleasure?'

Francis said nothing. He said nothing when Forbush passed through the armed and armored gate to the airbase, showing the sentry a pair of passes and nodding at Francis. He said nothing when a jeep pulled up beside them, signaled them to follow, and led them for what seemed like an eternity to a Learjet parked on a remote taxiway.

Nor did he say anything on the flight north to Bangor. He said nothing because he had nothing to say and because he wanted to be there at the end, wanted to be where he guessed they were going. It was beyond his control now; it reminded him of a time, swimming in the ocean, when he had been borne a hundred yards out to sea by a perverse tidal rip. He hadn't panicked; he'd just ridden it out until it exhausted itself and then swam easily back to shore. It was the same way now. He was in God's hands, surfing along on whatever destiny the Lord intended for him. God knew what He was doing. Trust him, Francis.

From the Bangor airport, they were driven north for about forty-five minutes to what appeared to be a corporate fishing camp. Francis thought he recognized some of the country from his one visit this far north. Had it been only three weeks ago that he'd called on Waldo Chamberlain's housekeeper? Quiddy couldn't have been too far from here; he guessed the coast to be perhaps thirty miles east as the crow flies.

The main house and cottages of the camp were closed. Francis and Forbush were shown into a one-room hut containing soft drink and coffee machines. Probably where the guides wait, thought Francis.

Forbush left Francis to his own thoughts. From time to time, the phone rang. Progress reports, Francis guessed.

At five fifteen, the phone rang again. As Forbush talked, Francis looked out the window. It was still daylight. The camp was situated on a small lake surrounded by high pine forests. It was very peaceful. He noticed that a concrete helipad had been set into the lawn that ran down to the lakeside. All on the stockholders' money, he thought.

Behind him, Forbush chuckled.

'You might like to know that Manning Mallory flew into

Bangor in a CertCo Gulfstream just twenty minutes after we did. I call that going out in style. His limousine has just pulled into Mr Chamberlain's driveway. He's come up to spend the Easter weekend with his old chum. No one thinks it's peculiar that he's got six suitcases with him. In his world, nobody ever asks how come. Tell me, Rev, do you want to hear what's what? Are you over the sulks?'

I am, thought Francis. I got myself here. Nobody kidnapped me.

'Sorry,' he said. 'You have to understand, Forbush. This is just — well, beyond me, most of it.'

'Hell,' said Forbush, 'you think I don't understand? But stop making yourself sound so naive. These guys built this scam over thirty years; they have goddamn near busted the world, and they may still do that if we get unlucky or they're cleverer than I think. Funny, when you look at it now, how easy it was for them. Everybody just kind of rolled over and wagged his tail. People do that when you show 'em the color of a whole lot of money.

'We all got taken in. Look at me. I hate these sonsabitches on Wall Street, and even my first reaction to your theory was, uh-uh, here's another guy wants to tell me that Jack Kennedy was assassinated by the League of Zion. You unwound Ropespinner, Rev. You and nobody else but you. You could see how it worked. Maybe 'cause you aren't in the business any more, maybe 'cause you got lucky. Does it matter?'

Francis shook his head.

'Anyway, let me fill you in. One, Mallory's arrived with more luggage than the Duke of Windsor to spend a quiet Easter with his old chum Waldo Emerson Chamberlain. Two, a Soviet trawler that's been shadowing the Canadian Navy on exercises off Newfoundland broke off yesterday morning and hightailed it south. Busted its butt to do it, but two hours ago it settled down a hundred fifty miles north-northeast of Quiddy Point. International waters, but well within helicopter range. Three, our friends from Sixty-seventh Street picked up their hired Jet Ranger at Bradley right on schedule and were airborne twenty minutes ago; our "eye in the sky" people tell me they'll probably arrive at Comrade Waldo's between seven twenty and seven thirty, the way the wind is blowing. Quiddy's about twenty minutes' flying time from right here, and I'm planning to be there no later than seven ten.'

Francis started to ask what was going to happen between 7:10 and 7:20, thought better of it, and instead said, 'I'm going to repeat a question I asked earlier. Today, I have breezed with you into a top-secret air force base. I have been flown to Bangor in a presidential jet and then driven to what can only be a Fortune 500 company's fishing camp. Whenever you pick up the phone, it's either the Strategic Air Command or the Department of Naval Operations. I'm surprised the White House hasn't telephoned. There appears to be nothing going on in the Atlantic Northeast that you don't have under surveillance. You are an undoubted man of parts, but this is a very elaborate, complex, *expensive* operation you have got going!'

'As the man said, you ain't seen nothin' yet.'

'Nevertheless, I—'

'You want to know who's backing our play?'

Forbush leaned forward on the edge of the daybed. He smacked his lips and tapped a heavy foot on the floor. The clock on the wall behind him read 5:57.

'Let's say it's someone who's close to the President, a keeper of the flame, you might say, who understands that posterity is kindest when you take good care of the present. This person was very upset with what I had to say, so this person asked what I needed to make sure Ropespinner didn't happen; what I needed in order to — well, straighten things out. To keep America safe for capitalism and immortality secure for our beloved leader.'

For no good reason, Francis recalled the videotape of the White House signing ceremony.

'Can she really swing all this?' he asked.

'She?' said Forbush, smiling. 'I didn't say anything about "she." ' He began to study a map, chuckling.

Nearly an hour later, the aircraft came out of the west, with a deafening roar and a downdraft that threatened to sweep the aluminium canoes on the wharf into the lake. It settled on the helipad, the blades ceased to chop at the air, and the world was returned to silence. Francis went to the window and looked out. In the waning light, the helicopter, black and bristling, looked like a horrific mutant insect in a science-fiction film. It was much bigger than he expected.

From the door of the hut, Forbush had been following the progress of the incoming aircraft. As the engine noise died away, he seemed to hug himself against the cool of the evening. He turned back into the room.

'OK, Rev,' he said, 'show time!'

They walked outside to the aircraft.

'All yours, Major,' its young pilot said, saluting Forbush. A flight sergeant handed over life vests and helmets.

'All systems go?'' asked Forbush.

'Armed and fueled, sir.' Another brisk salute.

'I'll have her back to you in an hour, Lieutenant,' Forbush said.

'Roger, sir.'

Francis looked at his watch: 6:35.

Forbush helped him get buckled up and plugged in.

'From here on out, Rev,' said Forbush, 'we don't talk. We must assume we aren't the only ones with big ears out there tonight. Besides, I'm going to be right busy. These things are a bitch to fly all by your lonesome.' He began to work the knobs, gauges, and levers. The blades started to turn in swooping, awkward slices.

By Francis's watch they had been airborne for twenty-one minutes. It was 7:06. Five minutes from whatever.

It was absolutely black beneath them. He had no sense of altitude or bearing. Now and then he thought he saw a light off to the left, but he couldn't be sure.

Forbush was completely preoccupied. He seemed to be navigating by a digital display projected on the inside of his plastic helmet-visor. The noise inside the cabin was over-powering. The helicopter had seemed large from outside, but the interior was suffocatingly cramped.

Suddenly, Forbush threw the aircraft into a tight leftward

bank. After ten seconds, he leveled out and just as suddenly turned on the helicopter's spotlight.

Water. They were over water. The aircraft was swaying slightly. It must be a windy night, thought Francis.

He looked around him. Darkness. Nothing. Below, he could see the ripples and wavelets on the water in photographic detail. They couldn't be more than ten or fifteen feet up, he thought.

Then he saw it: a small light in the distance, slightly to the north. Forbush corrected the helicopter's course; the light now grew larger with each second. Francis felt the helicopter descend slightly. The detail below grew even more distinct.

The light toward which they were making held steady, and Francis realized what it was: Waldo Chamberlain's house on the cliff.

Now they seemed to be going faster, sweeping in over the sea. The spotlight flashed over a small sailboat, a plank wharf, the white wash where the bay broke on the foot of the bluffs.

They passed over a flagpole and then over the house itself. Forbush braked the helicopter; it seemed to stop dead in the air, then swiveled on its axis to face the house and settled gently on the lawn about thirty yards from the front portico.

Francis found breathing difficult. Beside him, Forbush sat robot still, expectant, his face concealed behind his mask. The helicopter spotlight had been turned full on the house.

Then the front door opened.

At this point, time changed for Francis. Not into slow motion, but as if each second, each fragment of time, was a separate slide, projected rapidly and jerkily: appear, focus, pause, change.

The first to emerge was Manning Mallory, a suitcase in each hand. Smiling, squinting into the light. Then Chamberlain. Taller. Older. Briefcases held against his chest. They walked uncertainly toward the helicopter, bending over out of instinctive fear of the rotor blades. Francis watched, breathless. Mallory. Chamberlain. Mallory putting down one suitcase to shield his eyes against the glare of the spotlight.

370

Chamberlain still coming forward. *Click-click*. Next slide, please. *Click-click*.

Did Forbush move? Did he push a button, actuate a lever? Francis could never remember.

What he could remember, what he would never forget, was what happened next.

From the guts of the winged monster in which they had flown to this place there suddenly bellied a dragon's breath, a greasy, billowing, thrusting cloud of flame, a vile, fiery wind, oily and searing, driving toward the house with a life of its own.

It swallowed up the two men in the driveway. As Francis watched, it seemed they turned into negatives of themselves; pale flesh became black, dark-clothed limbs became white bone, white ash. He thought he heard a scream even above the enormous noise of the helicopter. Then the men were engulfed as the fire swept on and the house itself began to burn.

He scarcely heard the engines roar as they lifted off. He was numb with horror, hardly able to take in the house blazing and the small, lazy flames dancing on the charred loglike bodies in the driveway.

Minutes later, he was barely able to acknowledge Forbush, who tapped him on the shoulder and jerked a thumb seaward, toward a distant blinking light making its way northward through the night to a rendezvous now past keeping.

It was as if his mind and not his eyes had been seared blind by the flames. All he could think of was Revelations: 'fire and smoke and sulphur issued from their mouths.' He began to pray — for forgetfulness, for forgiveness — angry with God for having taken him into the very innards of hell but thankful beyond measure that He had at least brought him out again.

CHAPTER THIRTY-SIX

NEW YORK
Holy Saturday, April 5th

Now that she found herself in New York, Elizabeth was at a loss as to why she'd come at all. She wasn't allowed to see Francis; worse, the headlines in the newspaper eliminated any silly thoughts she might have had of revenge.

Well, she told herself, there must be something she could do! She'd wept herself dry; back in Paris her throat was strained from sobbing and cursing; she'd paced the nap of the carpet smooth.

This wasn't supposed to happen to modern women. Modern women were tough, businesslike, took life as it came. Weeping and howling happened only in novels written for shopgirls. No one 'dissolved' in tears any more.

Well, dissolve is just what she'd done. Dissolved, melted, lost her inner structure, her emotional cartilage.

People were always telling her they remembered exactly what they were doing when they heard the news of Jack Kennedy's assassination. As if it was sort of a touchstone, a defining fact of the American psyche. She herself recalled where she had been: in the cafeteria at New Trier High School, getting ready for cheerleading practice.

And when she'd heard the news about Francis? Would that forever be such a memory?

She'd been at home, packing. Listening to a silly, soppy phonograph record he'd sent her from New York.

This will be the last trip I'll make him take, she'd been thinking. Salzburg is special, but if I keep this up, I'll wear the poor thing out, and I want him for the rest of our lives. She remembered wondering how long that might be. Francis was forty-seven. At least thirty years.

Where had Francis ever found this dopey record? Anne Ziegler and Webster Booth were two English singers unknown to her, and now she'd always remember those names. Singers and songs from the thirties. Francis was always talking about the thirties as if he'd been there, as if he'd lived right through the Depression, and yet he'd been born in 1939. He was one of those people for whom history was so real that he could stroll into the past as easily as into an adjoining room. Sometimes it made him seem awfully old-fashioned, but it was always charming.

'If I only held the key to your heart,' the man was singing when the phone rang. She could hear that sweet confiding tenor as if he were singing still.

'I'd will you to the key to mine . . .'

And then the phone rang. She would always remember the exact time: 11:13 PM on her watch: 23:13 European Standard Time; 22:13 GMT. In New York, 5:13 PM Eastern Standard Time. To distract herself, she would try to make a game of it, to calculate what time it was in Aden, in Tucson, in Kuala Lumpur.

Yes, 5:13 EST, and the voice on the other end asking if that was Miss Bennett and when she said yes, the voice saying this is Phillips Forbush, from the Bishop's office.

Forbush? Forbush again? The man who'd managed to interrupt their love-making in Bermuda, with what Francis said was news of the parish house having been vandalized? Francis had told her Forbush was some kind of social worker.

Was Forbush her Person from Porlock in perpetuity, always to call and destroy the moment? Irritated, she only half listened at first, but then — What was this man saying? What was he talking about? He was talking about Francis; about a stroke, about possible brain damage, about hospitals, critical lists, one chance in eight, ten, a hundred! My God, he was talking about *Francis*!

After that it was dim. Awareness disappeared in a terrible screech.

Was it her? No, she hadn't screamed. Not right away, at

373

least. She had started to shake; she was pretty sure of that.

She must have then called Luc, because he appeared not much later, but by then her world was reduced to spasms of rage and anguish and self-pity, was blurred by convulsive sobs. How pitiful she must have been! How embarrassing!

The kindness of people had been considerable. Tony came and took charge. A doctor showed up with his needles and produced an interval of blankness. Someone was found to stay with her, a kindly woman who obviously enjoyed midwiving the misery of others and talked about her own son *'mort dans la guerre'* until Elizabeth felt herself about to scream. Her colleagues from Concorde trooped in and out. Even Mrs Leslie called from New York and wept together with her by satellite.

By the end of the week, her little tragedy was essentially played out. She lost her hold on her friends' emotions. Other concerns reclaimed their interest; the stream of visitors trickled out. Life hadn't ceased outside her window and they were obliged to rejoin it, as she knew she herself must.

Tony offered her his house in the Dordogne. Luc beseeched her to accompany him and his fiancée Marie-Georges to her family's château near Grasse. She was invited to attend the private evening mass at Sainte-Clotilde; the Faubourg Saint-Germain could make no more magnanimous gesture. Other offers to console herself on shipboard or on private islands or vineyards came from friends, from colleagues and clients.

She declined them all. She preferred to walk the streets, to talk to herself. Do not go to New York, everyone told her. It is hopeless; you cannot see him, it is hopeless. They spoke with such fatalism that she herself began to believe that Francis's death must be only a matter of time.

She began to blame God. She'd never trusted him. He'd led Francis down the garden path. She stared into her mirror, shocked at what she didn't see, stricken not to find the face of a grief-ravaged hag, a Donatello Magdalene, staring back at her; I've looked worse than this in my time, she thought, and blamed herself that this somehow meant she was disloyal. Wasn't she at least entitled to the full fruits of her anguish? Is this what you do to your servants, she hissed at the air in general; do you deprive them of the last little mite of pain that might at last make them feel whole?

By Friday afternoon the urge to go to New York was irresistible. She booked a flight and wheedled a room out of the Carlyle. Saturday morning she had Alexandre cut her hair; she caught the afternoon flight to JFK.

And now she sat on the edge of the bed, watching the evening news go on for the fifteenth time about the tragic fire that had taken the lives of two of the most distinguished figures ever to grace the world of America business and economics.

She had seen the headline in the *Post* when she disembarked at JFK Saturday evening. In the taxi to Manhattan she'd pored over the story. It was a virtual repeat of the fire that had taken her own family. A kerosene space heater had apparently exploded in the drawing room. According to the local police, the effect had been like napalm. Mallory and Uncle Waldo had been consumed by the flames. The house had burned to the ground.

The Carlyle found copies of the late Saturday *Times* for her. She turned to the obituaries. Nothing. The fire had occurred too late for the final edition. She would have to wait until Sunday.

She didn't mourn them. In her mind's eye she summoned up the house, Uncle Waldo's kind face, Mallory. In the background the newscaster was going on about telegrams of condolence pouring in to the Cert and to Harvard and MIT. The President and his wife would attend a joint memorial service. What empty lives to have lived, she thought, to have only a bank and two business schools and this shallow President as your principal mourners.

She felt no grief for Uncle Waldo. It wasn't just that her capacity for sorrow had been exhausted in Francis. She knew somehow that what had happened to Francis was mixed up with Uncle Waldo and Mallory, with that picture of Uncle Waldo and Menchikov, and with that sampler in the office. They had killed Francis.

Now it seemed God had made retribution for her. She remembered from her high-school religion courses that there was a fierce side of God. It had been he who'd dealt with Uncle Waldo and Mallory; she hoped he had made it painful and excruciating for them. He wasn't the God Francis talked about, but he was more Elizabeth's type. She hoped that Uncle Waldo and Mallory had screamed as the fire ate into them, and that God had heard them and laughed.

Propped on the bureau was the engraving she'd bought in Paris and planned to give to Francis. It was a funny sixteenth-century thing, after Brueghel: a weird and Boschian phantas-magoria titled 'The Flight of the Money Bags.' Francis would have loved it. The thought made her start weeping. And you thought you were through with tears, she swore at her mirror: you stupid, lonely cow!

She looked at herself again. 'You have got to cut this out,' she told the reflection. She needed to get some air, lose herself. She grabbed her coat and purse and left the hotel. It was dark out. Muggy for this time of year, she thought.

She started walking.

Walk, walk, walk, she thought. Just walk. Walk all your troubles away.

Without being aware of it, she turned into Eighty-seventh Street and drew up sharply when she found herself at the steps of All Angels. People were going up the steps. Some sort of evening service, she decided, and without thinking she entered the church.

From the table near the entry, she took a printed Order of Service. 'The Great Vigil of Easter,' it read. Someone handed her a candle.

Inside, the church was dark, and it was difficult to make anyone out. The pews seemed to be full. She found a place near the back. She prayed; the entire church seemed to vibrate with devotion.

Behind her she sensed movement and turned. A small fire had been kindled in a bowl on a stand. She saw a deacon taking a burning brand from it and light a great candle. Beside him stood a tall, fierce-looking old man arrayed in cope and mitre — the Bishop himself, she guessed.

'Dear friends in Christ: On this most holy night, in which

376

our Lord Jesus passed over from death to life, the church invites her members, dispersed throughout the world, to gather in vigil and prayer. For this is the Passover of the Lord, in which, by hearing his Word and celebrating his sacraments, we share in his victory over death.'

I am praying for you, Francis, she breathed, and looked around to see if her neighbors had heard her. Please pray for him too, she wanted to say. Somehow she thought they were.

Now the deacon began a slow procession through the church, bearing the paschal candle, pausing at each pew to let the worshipers dip their tapers in the flame. By the time he reached the altar and placed the paschal candle in its stand and launched into the Exulset — 'Rejoice now, heavenly hosts and choirs of angels' — the church was ablaze with flickering points of light.

It was a moving service. How Francis would have wished to be here! It was obvious that the Bishop's presence was a deeply felt personal gesture to Francis's stricken congregation. And yet the word of God would go on, 'the Morning Star who knows no setting . . . who lives and reigns for ever and ever.' It was amazing, thought Elizabeth, how easily prayer came and how much it did for her bursting heart.

CHAPTER THIRTY-SEVEN

NEW YORK
Easter Sunday, April 6th

The next morning, Elizabeth was back at All Angels.

'Not with old leaven, neither with the leaven of malice and wickedness,' read the young woman priest.

'But with the unleavened bread of sincerity and truth,' returned the congregation.

Elizabeth was surprised at the strength of her response. Had anyone in the congregation noticed? No, they were preoccupied with following the words from the altar.

'Christ being raised from the dead dieth no more.'

'Death hath no more dominion over him.' Elizabeth lowered her voice. Up the aisle she could see Mrs Leslie and her husband.

'Likewise reckon ye also yourselves to be dead indeed unto sin.'

Elizabeth turned her eyes to the minister.

'But alive unto God through Jesus Christ our Lord,' she murmured. This must be Angela, she thought, Francis's assistant. A nice-looking woman. Very handsome. Were you ever tempted by her, Francis? she thought; did she ever turn you on? Perhaps if she thought about her lover this way, the jagged hurt would abate.

There was a shuffle and rustle as prayerbooks were put down and hymnals taken up, and then the choir launched into 'Christ the Lord Is Risen Today.' How beautiful the church looks, Elizabeth thought. Suddenly she felt like crying. How Francis would have loved to see it! Oh, I miss you so, my love, she said silently, unable to go on singing.

She hurried away after the service. One of Francis's

dowagers would surely spot her and make a fuss, and that was the last thing she needed. So the instant the priests had passed by and the last notes of the Recessional had sounded, she made for the side door.

The day was overcast and cold; it felt like rain. She walked briskly up Eighty-seventh Street toward Lexington Avenue. She was glad she had gone to church; the service had braced her, and she had been touched by the vigor with which the All Angels congregation had plunged into a special prayer for Francis.

She would go and see him now, she decided, and doctors be damned! She'd already called the hospital five times. Dr Garvey had been sympathetic but firm. Absolutely no visitors, the doctor said. Maybe by the end of the week. There was no reliable prognosis as yet.

Well, thought Elizabeth, we'll see! If she went up to Columbia-Presbyterian and found the intensive-care ward and made enough of a fuss, surely they'd have to let her see him.

She heard footsteps hurrying up behind her.

'Miss Bennett?' said a voice she thought she recognized.

She turned to find a stocky black man smiling at her. She looked him over. Gray suit that didn't quite fit; heavy cordovans. Sincerity written all over him.

'Yes,' she said. 'I'm Elizabeth Bennett.' She looked him over. 'I guess you must be Mr Forbush. From the Bishop's office?'

'Yes, ma'am,' the man said. 'I recognized you in church, and—'

'Come now, Mr Forbush,' Elizabeth interrupted, 'you must have some new bad news for me, you always seem to have bad news for me; you—'

She stopped herself. What is the matter with me? she thought. Francis would kill me if he heard me talking like this!

'I'm sorry, Mr Forbush,' she said. 'You must understand—'

Forbush shook his head. He rolled the brim of a stiff brown fedora nervously in fingers that seemed oddly slender and sensitive.

'Well,' he said, 'when I recognized you, Miss Bennett, the

Reverend having shown me your picture and talked so much about you and all, I thought I should speak to you. It's Dr Mather's apartment, you see. I have his keys and I thought maybe you'd like to have something to keep by you, a picture or something, till the Reverend pulls through.'

Elizabeth shook her head. 'No, I don't really—'

'I know the Reverend would be mighty pleased if you did,' said Forbush. He practically tugged his forelock.

Well, why not? she found herself thinking. At the very least, there was no point hurting the feelings of this nice man. It wouldn't take any time at all; Francis's apartment was only a couple of blocks away. And yes, she thought, I would like to see it again, which she told Forbush.

On the short walk over, he left her alone with her thoughts. She guessed he assumed she'd need to steel herself before visiting a place in which she'd known such happiness, and perhaps he was right.

The place was dark and musty.

'Shall I open the curtains?' he asked.

'No, that's all right,' she said. She looked around. The living room had been straightened up. It looked oddly, unfamiliarly bare.

'Where are his books and pictures, his personal things?' she asked.

'I put them back in the bedroom,' Forbush said. He gave an open-palmed shrug. 'I don't know why, really. Just seemed like the thing to do. Here, I'll show you.' He started for the hall which led to Francis's bedroom.

'Don't bother,' she said, 'I can find it. Would you mind leaving me alone in there for a few minutes?' She felt as if she were about to enter a sanctuary she wanted Forbush to have nothing to do with. Was this, then, the end for her and Francis and everything that they could have been? Done and finished. Over. Permanently, forever, for all time?'

'Here, let me fix it so you can see,' he said, flicking on the hall light.

She had barely started toward the bedroom when she heard the switch click behind her and the lights went out. As she paused in the dark, a terrible instinctive fear sliced her spine. She gasped in fright and had started to cry out when she thought she heard a chuckle and Forbush's voice say, 'Make the Rev happy,' and the sound of the front door closing. The shriek died in her throat. As it did, she heard another click and saw a band of light appear at the end of the hall, a narrow strip under the door to Francis's bedroom.

For an instant she stared at it. Then her heart knew before her head what it must mean, and she hastened toward it with a small cry of joy. And as she did, the band of light seemed to widen, spreading and spreading until it filled the whole wide world with its warmth and brightness.

AFTERWORD

This book is intended as a cautionary entertainment. Readers wishing to look further into banking history and financial crisis, past and present, may find profit in consulting the books in Phillips Forbush's bookcase.

We seem to ignore history, although the evidence seems clear that we do so at our peril. A book like Gouge's *Paper Money* suggests, from the distance of a century and a half, that there is little new under the sun in the way of financial folly. How comforting to sense that as hard as we have worked to undo ourselves and our special advantages as a nation and as an economic system, we somehow have always gotten by.

So far.

M.M.T.
Bridgehampton, 1986

**THREE MORE GREAT
THRILLERS FOR YOUR
READING PLEASURE . . .**

THE CHINA CARD

by John Ehrlichman

With this startlingly authentic novel John Ehrlichman steps into the front rank of the masters of espionage fiction. At the heart of *The China Card* is the possibility that the Chinese Communists have planted a 'mole' deep within the Nixon administration, within the White House itself. In the hands of an author who *was* one of Richard Nixon's closest advisers, the premise takes on a chilling plausibility that places the President's China 'initiative' in a shocking new perspective.

The China Card is a novel of stunning force in which the reader becomes engaged in the dramatic power plays of history itself.

£3.95

The White House

FALL, 1974

'We did some very good things, Henry. I wonder if any-one will remember them.'

'Of course they will, Mr. President. Within a historical perspective you will be seen as a strong President who brought the nation through difficult times.'

'I wonder; people seem to recall only the worst about a President. Look at what they did to Wilson. Won't the historians dump me in with Harding and Grant? Do you think they will?'

'How can they, sir? There is SALT and China and an honorable end to the Viet Nam war. Achievements like that will not be overlooked.'

'Perhaps you're right, Henry. China is the big one that can't be taken away from us, isn't it? We did that, didn't we? From now on the world is changed because the American President holds the China card in his hand. They have to give us credit for that, don't they, Henry?'

Henry Kissinger nodded slowly. It was idle, Kissinger reflected, to be concerned with history's ultimate judg-ment at the moment when the White House was about to collapse around their heads. 'To a great extent history will be what we make it, Mr. President,' Kissinger replied. 'You will write. I will write. Our colleagues will write. We can do much to direct the historians' vision.'

'That's true, isn't it?' the President said. 'We must be very certain that our friends are encouraged to be among the first to write. What can we do about the others, though? What can we do about Thompson?'

'Not much, Mr. President, beyond what we have done. Thompson is gone. Wherever he is, he fears the Chinese, I am sure. I doubt that he will write a book.'

'Good. It's people like Thompson who could badly confuse historians about the way we opened up China.'

'Yes, Mr. President, he could,' Henry Kissinger agreed. 'He could indeed. But I think the risk is small.'

LOST

by Gary Devon

One of the most riveting and tension-filled novels of recent years, *Lost* is the story of Sherman, a deranged and evil boy who will stop at nothing to gain possession of his abducted younger sister Mamie. Accompanied by a vicious, wolflike hound known as The Chinaman, Sherman follows a trail from state to state across the frozen wastes of the eastern American seaboard after the worst blizzard in two decades. Fleeing before him is the woman, Leona, a 35-year-old spinster who has befriended Mamie and two other small and love-starved children, and who will protect them unto death.

Lost is a novel of unbridled menace and breathtaking tension that will engage and terrify you from the first page.

£2.95

Only the sound of his footsteps and the soft padding of the Chinaman's paws broke the night silence. Sherman did not hesitate or look back, striking deftly through the dark countryside. 'Goddam her,' he muttered under his breath; 'goddam her to hell,' the words like a chant, marking his stride. The pills held his pain to a low humming at the back of his brain.

They kept to the high ground parallel to the Scranton road. When the dog wandered down too close to the ditches, Sherman called him and made him come back. Otherwise he let the Chinaman roam. Very little traffic moved on the highway this late at night; for long periods it stood completely empty. Yet he wanted to be sure that their departure wasn't noticed by anyone. He spoke to the dog sparingly and used his pencil flashlight only when he had to – when the darkness of wild bushes blocked his path or the dog slipped into a gully that opened in the ground like a trap.

Moving quickly, they crossed pastures and fences and woods. As soon as the sun came up, Sherman opened his shirt and removed the papers and pictures he'd taken from the Mattingly house. The snapshots, blown up to frame size, had faded to a bronzy orange. The two women, the one he'd just hit and the one who'd taken Mamie, were in both the photographs. He immediately folded them, scored them with his thumbnail, and tore them in two. Then he tore the two halves showing the Mattingly woman into little chunks and threw them to the wind like confetti. In the two half-photos he kept, the woman looked younger than she did in real life. His teeth began to ache from the angry set of his jaw. From his billfold, he removed the print of Mamie's school picture that he'd torn from a newspaper, folded it with the two pictures of the woman, and returned all three, in his billfold, to his pocket.

Methodically he flipped through the sheaf of papers – most of it yesterday's mail, he guessed. All the envelopes had been opened. He separated them quickly, sorting out the circulars and bills and holding the two envelopes addressed to Leona Hillenbrandt in his teeth. The stack of useless material he tore into small pieces and let them dribble and flutter from his hands as he walked. Of the two remaining pieces, one was a letter on good-smelling paper from Cornelia Dunham, Ridgefarm Road, Brandenburg Station, Kentucky. But the other letter, from the Citizens National Bank of Scranton, held his attention and he placed the Kentucky letter inside his shirt.

Sherman tore the bank envelope apart. He paid little attention to the actual writing as he repeatedly formed the woman's name with his lips: Leona Hillenbrandt. Scranton. That had to be where she was taking Mamie. Nothing else made sense. He folded the letter with the envelope and tore them to pieces. The little wad of money he'd found wedged under the Mattingly woman's vase – the three thousand-dollar bills wrapped in a five-dollar bill – remained untouched in his jeans pocket.

It was still very early in the morning when he saw a country gas station far below and wondered if it was safe yet to hitchhike, if he was far enough away from Graylie. He was crossing an area of hills, and had wandered higher from the road than he meant to. While he looked down, two cars moved like minnows onto the asphalt drive, headed in opposite directions. He wanted to be riding in a car. He called the dog and started down the steep embankment.

He counted four cars parked on the grounds, none of them police cars – nothing that looked suspicious. As he and the dog crossed the highway through the morning fog, he saw a clump of road signs. In black letters, one said: SCRANTON 72 MI. The idea of seventy-two miles stretched deep in his imagination and, with it, the minutes ticking away and Mamie slipping farther out of his reach. He pulled a piece of clothesline rope from his hip pocket, tied it to the Chinaman's collar, and they jogged through a display of chalk figures strung out on the ground – reindeer and donkeys pulling carts, and birdbaths – and slipped between the parked cars.

Fog hung in scraps over the road, but the traffic was fairly brisk. As they moved into the shadow of the gas station, a car came in headed north toward Graylie. The attendant ambled from the garage, pumped the gas, and went back to work, frowning at Sherman and the Chinaman as he passed. A lull settled over the station. For several minutes nothing moved on the road.

Come on, Sherman thought, his anxiety mounting. He sat down on the concrete curbing, then stood up and scuffed back and forth.

Two cars came in and stopped on either side of the gas pumps. While the attendant handled the car pointed north, Sherman tapped the passenger window of the one going south, a maroon car. The driver leaned across the seat and rolled the window down a few inches. Sherman asked for a ride to Scranton. The man seemed to consider it, lowered his head as if to decide. 'I need a lift for him, too,' Sherman said. 'He's with me,' and nodded toward the Chinaman. Without answering, the man cranked the window up and turned to stare at the road.

Before the attendant had finished with the maroon car, an old blue coupe had pulled in behind it. Sherman tapped the window glass, and again he thought he might be getting somewhere until he pointed to the big grisly dog; then the driver said, 'Sorry,' and went on studying the map spread on the steering wheel. The car radio was turned low, but the emphatic voice could still be heard: '*Graylie police continue to investigate last night's assault and battery of a local woman, Emma Mattingly, of 210 Columbia Avenue. Mrs. Mattingly has been listed in critical condition. . . .*'

Sherman heard only that much as he withdrew from the side of the car, concentrating on the man reading the map. Fright ran through him like quicksilver. She's still alive, he thought. If she could describe him, it would only be a matter of time before the cops figured out who he was and what he had done – not only what he'd done last night, but all the other nights and other things, the paperboy who'd taken his place, the fire. I should of finished her, he thought; I should of.

Even after the coupe had left, he went on glancing about, alert and cautious. He saw no immediate threat, except the attendant was coming toward them in his blackened coveralls, wiping his hands on a greasy rag. 'You can't hang out here,' the man said. 'You'd better just run along.' The Chinaman clambered to his feet and started to growl, his hackles rising.

'We're tryin' to catch a ride,' Sherman said, pulling the dog's collar, telling the Chinaman to shut up.

'You better catch it someplace else. I want you to clear out of here.' He went inside the garage.

Sherman slowly brushed the seat of his pants. Another car came in headed the wrong way, and the frowning attendant glared at them as he adjusted the pump handle. He had the hood up when a white pickup rolled in, going in the right direction. The driver's window was down, his elbow resting out in the chill November air. Sherman started talking to the man in earnest, telling him he had to get to Scranton because his sister was there and he had to take the dog, and could they ride in the back of the pickup, when the attendant came around the front of the truck. 'If you don't head down that road right now and stop bothering my customers, I'm going to go inside and call the county sheriff.'

Sherman opened his mouth to speak.

'No buts,' the attendant said. 'Either you go down that road right now or I call the cops. Take your pick.'

Tugging at the dog's rope, Sherman tore from the pickup window and marched past the attendant. Angry tears stood in his eyes. He knew when the cards were stacked against him, knew when to keep his mouth shut. He jerked the dog to him, moved down the drive, crossed the highway, and slipped into the ditch so he could let the Chinaman loose. His good hand was curled tight on the blackjack in his pocket. He wanted to take it and beat that sonofabitch to death. He hadn't gone very far when he heard a horn honk and saw the white pickup truck swerve to the side of the road above the ditch. It's about goddammed time, he thought.

He squatted down in a corner of the truck bed, pulling the dog in beside him, and the irregular houses and foot-hills and pockets of trees wheeled alongside the truck and sank away in an ever-deepening V.

CROWS' PARLIAMENT

by Jack Curtis

Simon Guerney plies a lonely trade. He specializes in the rescue of kidnap victims; his unrecognized skills the last resort of the rich and desperate.

At first the disappearance of David Paschini seems a straightforward abduction case and Guerney joins the boy's mother in New York to play out the usual waiting game. Once there he begins to sense inconsistencies in the pattern of events – but it is not until the unknown kidnappers demand that he travel to London that Guerney realizes the game has turned and that suddenly he is the prey not the hunter . . .

Strikingly original in its combination of power politics, the growing menace of kidnapping and the disturbing but very real world of ESP, *Crows' Parliament* will take its place amongst such classics of the genre as *Rogue Male* and *The Third Man*.

£2.95

Like a shadow moving on a shadow, Guerney went down the slope towards the hut, his body slung in a crouch, arms loose. Not for a moment did he take his eyes off the door and the window next to it. Twenty yards away he stopped and listened. At first there was nothing to hear. Then there came a breathy drawn-out *Aaaaaaah*, then another, then another, rhythmic and monotonous, the sound a mother makes to soothe a fretful child. Guerney circled to the window, waited motionless for another full minute, then edged his body up to the frame and looked in.

The woman was belly up across the table, her buttocks on the edge, her legs trailing down to the floor. She was wearing only a blouse that was torn down the seam on one side, exposing most of one breast. There was a fading bruise on one side of her face, and her nose looked a little out of true. She was staring at the ceiling, offering no expression; tears were trickling from the corner of the eye that was visible to Guerney, running into her hair and blackening a lock by her temple, but she made no sound of sobbing and no movement.

One man was standing close to the window with his back to Guerney. Another was close to the woman. He was holding a rifle in one hand, gripping the stock; the tip of the barrel was probing between her legs. Like a child prodding a small animal with a stick, he gave the gun a little push, laughing, then turned his wrist. The woman's legs jumped, and she turned her head to one side; her hand, on the rough wood of the table, fluttered as if calibrating the pain. The shepherd laughed again, looking over to where the boy was standing. Behind the boy was a third man, his hand fastened in the child's hair, painfully tight, as if he had dragged his captive to his feet that way and maintained the grip. He was forcing the boy to look, shaking the blond head every now and then by its hair to keep him attentive, to remind him to keep his eyes open.

The noise Guerney had heard was coming from the boy. He stared at his mother fixedly and made the cooing pained sound over and over without closing his mouth. His nose was running, but he made no effort to clean himself. His hands stayed where they were, convulsively kneading the flesh on his stomach.

Guerney moved back from the window and unfastened two of the buttons on his shirt. Beneath it, he was wearing shoulder-holster strapping that supported a long-barrelled handgun. He edged up to the window again.

The second man had put down the rifle. He was standing in front of the woman and untying the cord that supported his pants. As they dropped, he shuffled forward a pace and caught the woman at the back of her knees with bent forearms and hoisted her thighs so that her shins were trapped by his shoulders when he leaned forward. He yelled as he pushed into her; then he gripped her upper arms, stretched his neck so that he was looking over her, beyond her, at the far wall, and began to pump.

Guerney let five seconds pass, then moved to the door. He judged the place where the wood stuck, hit it left-handed and stepped inside. His first shot took the woman's assailant in the side of the neck. The man's body convulsed massively, then went rigid; he neither moved nor collapsed; still bowed over the woman, still supporting himself on her arms, he opened and closed his mouth reflexively.

Guerney went past him. The shepherd holding the boy had time to thrust his captive away, but no more. Guerney fired twice, hitting his target high in the chest. He turned again, dropped to the floor, rolled once, took the third man's half-raised rifle to one side with his left hand and brought the gun under his chin so that a line of blood was drawn where the skin grazed. The kidnapper let his rifle drop. Four seconds had passed since Guerney had come into the room.

As if she were removing a mote from her eye, the woman eased out from under the dead man – bracing herself, turning her lower torso as she pulled back; then, when she was free, she raised a foot and kicked him to one side. He went over like a sack of wheat. Before she went to the boy, she pulled on the skirt that was lying on the floor, and looked for a moment at the streaks of blood on it. Then she picked the boy up, pulled his face into her shoulder and went out of the door.

Guerney hadn't taken his eyes off the man he was holding at gunpoint. When the woman was clear, he turned the barrel so that the sight drew a little more blood, then took the man by the upper lip, painfully, and led him into the open. The woman was waiting, still holding her son. Guerney looked at the shepherd – holding the expressionless stare that was fixed on him – but spoke to the woman. 'Montez jusqu'au sommet de l'arête et attendez-moi lá-bas.'

She nodded, but transferred her gaze to the shepherd. Carefully, she set the child down, turning him away to face into the night. Then she walked over and spat, carefully, into the man's face. She continued to look at him but seemed to expect no reaction. Hawking slightly to summon more spittle, she put her face close to his, paused, and spat again. The second time, the man flinched from the venom.

Guerney raised his free hand as if to ward her off. 'Dépêchez-vous,' he snapped, 'nous sommes pressés.'

She stood still, as if there were something else she had to do, then nodded again, picked the boy up, and made for the top of the ridge as she had been bidden. A few minutes later, Guerney joined her. He took the boy in his arms and turned to the woman once before leading off across the high plateau.

It was late the next morning before the dead men were found. A couple of islanders passed the place and were drawn to the hut by the sight of a body in the ravine. This corpse, in particular, puzzled them and they paused to look at it again after they had entered the hut and found the other bodies there.

The man had been shot, cleanly, through the back of the head, but his body had not been left to lie. It was lashed by the ankles to one of the ravine's stunted trees. It hung utterly still, seeming to curl stiffly in the heat, as if some flexion had been trapped by death. It was a ragged dishevelled thing; head down, it appeared awkward and in some way obscenely undignified. It had the abused look of the crows and weasels that English gamekeepers hang from a gallows-branch.

A SELECTED LIST OF FINE TITLES AVAILABLE FROM CORGI BOOKS

THE PRICES SHOWN BELOW WERE CORRECT AT THE TIME OF GOING TO PRESS. HOWEVER TRANSWORLD PUBLISHERS RESERVE THE RIGHT TO SHOW NEW RETAIL PRICES ON COVERS WHICH MAY DIFFER FROM THOSE PREVIOUSLY ADVERTISED IN THE TEXT OR ELSEWHERE.

☐ 13139 3	THE CHINA CARD	*John D. Ehrlichman*	£3.95
☐ 13081 8	CROWS' PARLIAMENT	*Jack Curtis*	£2.95
☐ 13061 3	LOST	*Gary Devon*	£2.95

All Corgi/Bantam Books are available at your bookshop or newsagent, or can be ordered from the following address:

Corgi/Bantam Books,
Cash Sales Department,
P.O. Box 11, Falmouth, Cornwall TR10 9EN

Please send a cheque or postal order (no currency) and allow 60p for postage and packing for the first book plus 25p for the second book and 15p for each additional book ordered up to a maximum charge of £1.90 in UK.

B.F.P.O. customers please allow 60p for the first book, 25p for the second book plus 15p per copy for the next 7 books, thereafter 9p per book.

Overseas customers, including Eire, please allow £1.25 for postage and packing for the first book, 75p for the second book, and 28p for each subsequent title ordered.